IN THE *LIGHT* OF DARK MATTERS

NOLAN JACKS

Unbound International Publising, LLC

NOLAN JACKS

Printed in the United States of America

ISBN 978-1-7346821-0-6

DEDICATION:

This book is dedicated to:

"Stephen Weber"

I met Steve in 1975. Fresh out of college, he and I had just started working at an Electric Utility in Denver as Electrical Engineers. Steve and I became the best of friends, Steve was the Best Man at my wedding, and we stayed friends until his death in 2007, from a decease which doctors never where able to exactly diagnose. Steve was always a good influence on me, but in April of 2020 I discovered that he may still be influencing me, which I will explain further at the end of this novel.

FACT SHEET:

All descriptions of historical events in this novel are based on extensive research and are intended to be close representations of those actual events.

All references, in this novel, to the bible and other religious documents are actual quotations.

All psychology, and shamanistic references, in this novel, are based on actual reported studies.

All references to mystics and psychic phenomenon, except for those out of body experiences described by the fictional characters in the novel, are based on actual reported studies.

Most importantly, all the math, physics and other scientific theories and studies described in the novel, except for those proposed by the fictional characters, are based on actual studies and actual facts, both current and historic. I would challenge you to fact check any of the references in this novel. What you may find, will fascinate you.

Finally, though the shadowy organization described in the novel is fiction, it is believed that organizations of this nature do exist, and things that often seem very improbable, may not be as random as you might think, and things that you may have thought were your fault, may not be your fault at all.

Contents

NOLAN JACKS

PROLOGUE

April 19th, 2007

"Steve died!" Rufus says, walking into his office, his eyes wet and red from grief.

Rufus' secretary Paula, quickly responds, her eyes welling up just from seeing Rufus' face. "You mean Dr. Weber?"

Rufus confirms, while nodding his head and slumping his shoulders.

"Oh, Rufus I'm sorry. I know you were close to him. But his abdominal cancer was very bad, and he had been in a lot of pain for quite a long time." Paula wraps her arms around Rufus waist. Rufus at six foot three, and two hundred a thirty pounds, was a giant compared to Paula's petite frame, but she squeezes him as tightly as she can and whispers, "We can only hope that now he can rest in peace."

"Yes, I'm grateful that he is no longer in pain. But he was such a great physicist and such a good friend. You know, he was just starting to make some progress in proving my theories on the *entanglement* of 'photons' and 'gravitons', and now there is no one exploring my theories at CERN in Switzerland."

"You know Paula," Rufus continues, now thinking further about Steve's death, "I have always been suspicious of Steve's illness."

"Yes, I know" Paula now returning to her desk as she responds, wiping the tears from her eyes, "I just completed the research you asked me to do. I think you'll find it very interesting. By the way, what prompted you to have me look into this?"

"You know, I met Steve in college, and we immediately became the best of friends, partly because we were both Jewish, but mostly because we were both so much into math and science. We made quite the pair. You know, me a large black man and him a much smaller white guy, we often drew attention."

"But Steve was in excellent health back then, and he always took good care of himself. He didn't smoke cigarettes, we were both in great physical shape, and after he became sick, he had told me that he had no family history of cancer."

"And then, just recently I read that Enrico Fermi had died of stomach cancer, and that is why I became curious about how other physicist had died. What did you find?"

Paula smiled as she responded, "I did a search of physicist associated with quantum theory, just as you had asked, and I came up with up with 12 names of physicist, famous for their work in that area. Here's the list:"

"Max Planck, Niels Bohr, Louis de Broglie, Max Born, Paul Dirac, Werner Heisenberg, Wolfgang Pauli, Erwin Schrödinger, Richard Feynman. Enrico Fermi, Robert Oppenheimer, and of course Albert Einstein."

Rufus was nodding his head, as he was familiar with all of these names.

Paula went on, "Amazingly, of these 12 men, 7 died of abdominal or related problems, including various forms of cancers. That's 58%." Paula now looking at Rufus to see if he was a surprised as she was, continued, "Here are the details on these seven men."

"Julius Robert Oppenheimer was an American theoretical physicist. who worked on the theory of electrons and positrons, and developed the Oppenheimer–Phillips process in nuclear fusion, and the first prediction of quantum tunneling, a major development in the field of Quantum mechanics. He Died February 18, 1967, in Princeton, New Jersey, of cancer of the larynx. He was 63."

"Richard Phillips Feynman, was an American theoretical physicist, known for his work in the 'path integral' formulation of quantum mechanics, and the theory of quantum electrodynamics. He died February 15, 1988, Los Angeles, California, of abdominal cancer. He was 69 years old."

"Werner Karl Heisenberg was a German theoretical physicist. He was awarded the Nobel Prize in Physics in 1932 for the creation of quantum mechanics. He died February 1, 1976, in Munich, Germany, of Kidney cancer. He was 75."

"Wolfgang Ernst Pauli was an Austrian theoretical physicist and one of the pioneers of quantum physics. He won the Nobel Prize in Physics in 1945 for the discovery of the Exclusion Principle, which was named the 'Pauli Exclusion Principle' and states that, in an atom or molecule, no two electrons can have the same four electronic quantum numbers. In 1958 Pauli was awarded the Max Planck Medal for extraordinary achievements in theoretical physics, and in that same year, he fell ill with pancreatic cancer and died."

"Erwin Schroedinger, was a Nobel Prize-winning Austrian-Irish physicist who developed a number of fundamental results in quantum theory, he also made several attempts to construct a 'unified field' theory. He died January 4, 1961, Vienna, Austria of tuberculosis."

Paula now looking up momentarily from the sheet of paper she held in her hand, saying. "And, as you mentioned," Now returning to her paper, "Enrico Fermi who was an Italian physicist and the creator of the world's first nuclear reactor. He was awarded the 1938 Nobel Prize in Physics for his work on induced radioactivity by neutron bombardment and for the discovery of transuranium elements. He also made significant contributions to the development of quantum theory and particle physics. He died November 28, 1954, Chicago, IL of stomach cancer."

"And finally," Paula briefly looking up at Rufus again before returning to the page, "Albert Einstein who developed the theory of relativity, received the 1921 Nobel Prize in Physics for his services to theoretical physics, and especially for his discovery of the law of the photoelectric effect, a pivotal step in the development of quantum theory. He died *April 18*, 1955 from an abdominal aortic aneurysm."

"Wow!" Rufus exclaimed, "That seems more than coincidental. It makes me wonder if some of these other physicists, that you mentioned, had some similar problems but recovered or, if they had one of these illnesses but it was not considered the cause of their death. Would you do a little more research and see if you can find anything."

"Sure," Paula says, "I will let you know what I find."

"Paula this really has me concerned. You know that Steve had received several death threats, but he always blew them off as idle threats from wackos, ---- but now I'm not so sure."

"Oh! Rufus." Paula exclaimed "We just received this in the mail, yesterday." Paula reaches into her desk drawer and pulls out a white letter sized envelope. It had already been opened, as Paula had been instructed to open all of Rufus' mail. Now with a look of fright on her face she continues. "I stopped reading after the first sentence."

Rufus takes the envelop from Paula and pulls out the single sheet of paper that is enclosed. The letter is written in all caps:

RUFUS MIDDLEMAN YOU WILL SOON DIE!!!

YOU MUST CEASE YOUR UN-GODLY PURSUIT OF THEORIES THAT ARE BLASPHIMOUS AND LEAD THE CHILDREN OF GOD ASTRAY, OR FACE THE CONCEQUENCES FROM THE THOUSAND POINTS OF LIGHT THAT ARE WATCHING YOU.

"Rufus," Paula cries out. "that scares me to death. What are you going to do?"

Rufus crumples up the piece of paper and throws it into a nearby trash can. "Paula, from now on I want you to open only mail that is from a known source. Give any other mail directly to me un-opened."

IN ANOTHER PART of Denver, the Reverend CyrIS Steel is preparing his sermon for his upcoming Sunday service. A sermon which he would use to build on his theories that tied recent advancements in the fields of physics, to religion. CyrIS had been inspired to pursue these theories based on an ancient scroll he

discovered in the wall of the old church in which he had begun his ministry, back in 1970.

As usual his desk was covered with magazines and a variety of articles on the most recent works in the fields of not only physics, but also psychology, mysticism and of course religion.

Along with the magazines and articles there were piles of mail. Most of the mail, not counting the junk mail and bills, were letters from various religious leaders and his followers, wishing to discuss or argue about his theories and these relationships he had been preaching.

However, today one particular envelope catches CyrIS' eye. It is a plain white envelope addressed to him, with no return address.

CyrIS opens the unusual looking envelop and extracts the single sheet of white paper, and reads the words written in all caps.

CYRIS STEEL YOU WILL SOON DIE!!!

YOU MUST CEASE YOUR UN-GODLY PURSUIT OF THEORIES THAT ARE BLASPHIMOUS AND LEAD THE CHILDREN OF GOD ASTRAY, OR FACE THE CONCEQUENCES FROM THE THOUSAND POINTS OF LIGHT THAT ARE WATCHING YOU.

CyrIS was used to letters and phone calls of this nature. Over the past few years, since he began preaching his theories of the relationship between the universe, scientific discoveries, and religion, he had received several threats. He mostly ignored these threats. He thought that *logically* these threats were coming from malcontents, and that they were nothing to really be concerned about.

But this one is different, because he had heard of an organization that often referenced a "thousand points of light", that were following through on their threats.

At that moment, CyrIS' wife enters his office. CyrIS immediately puts the letter in one of his desk drawers. There was a lot going on in their lives right now and he did not believe she needed anything else to worry about.

CHAPTER 1 – A MAN OF STEEL

April 16th, 1967
Geoffrey Hazelton, age 17- Logic

Geoffrey Hazelton sits in the last row of the First Pentecostal Church of Durham; his head is bobbing, and his eyes struggle to remain open. Geoffrey's broad shoulders and muscular legs are packed into the thick cotton pants and the starched white shirt that his mother always made him wear to church. His legs perspired as he shifted in his seat to find comfort where there was none. *God, I am so bored.* He rotates his head from side to side. *There's not even a single good-looking girl nearby to look at.*

Even though the back row of the church made it easier for him to nod off, it was far from perfect. Whiffs of cigarette smoke, carried by the slight breeze moving slowly through the opened front door of the church, assaulted his nose, and was mysteriously pushing on him.

That's strange.

Geoff turned and looked out the front door. The usual old geezers who came to church every Sunday, but never actually came into the church, were puffing away on the church's front porch, doing their fair share to support the economy of North Carolina, but Geoff could see nothing out of the ordinary.

Tobacco bred life into the local economy, but not everyone worked in the tobacco industry. Geoff's father Herald worked in a nearby quarry plant, and Geoff's mother, June, stayed at home with their nine children. June, born a Southern Baptist, discovered the Christian Fundamentalist church, which taught that the only true way to heaven was by following the scriptures to the letter, especially the Old Testament.

Every day, Geoffrey listened to his mother read the Bible and explain the passages to him and to his siblings as she read. Geoff really didn't pay much attention, instead he would dream of the day he could fly away from this miserable small-town life.

Geoff was born in Durham but had always felt, that he was somehow meant for greater things. None the less, here he sat listening to this sermon that could put a "coke" addict to sleep.

It's only logical, someday I'll be a pilot or a rocket scientist or maybe an astrophysicist, I'll figure it all out by then.

Geoffrey had an insatiable love of *logic* and strength, and as such he loved reading 'Superman' comics. He often envisioned himself leaping tall buildings with a single bound, flying faster than a speeding bullet, or even better, flying as fast as the speed of light. He wanted to be *a man of steel*, and a scientist like Albert Einstein. All in all, he wanted to understand everything.

But how could he learn about the world, when his parents wouldn't even let him listen to 'rock and roll' on the radio. The accepted genre in Geoff's house was Country Western...period.

Shit! I am so tired of Country Western.

But that was not the worst of it. Most of the time, they listened to some evangelist preacher, quoting the bible and droning on and on about how everyone was a sinner, and this same dark theme dominated all the sermons on the radio. We're all headed for hell if we don't pledge our souls and money, to *The Church of your money is now ours to keep.*

As far as Geoff's parents were concerned, a sure path to hell was watching television. According to Geoff's mother, television was the work of the devil. There was no 'TV' in the Hazelton house, however, Geoff had a friend, old Bob Stangley, and sometimes after school, Geoff would stop by Bob's house and they would listen to 'rock and roll' on Bob's 45 rpm record player or watch some TV. It didn't seem like a sin to Geoff.

There was this new show on called Star Trek that really grabbed Geoff's attention. It was great, and it was all educational as far as he was concerned. Geoffrey loved shows about science and TV was okay, but what Geoff really liked to do, was to go to the movies. Sometimes, he and Bob would sneak down to the local movie theater and watch whatever was playing, but what Geoff especially liked was science fiction, but he didn't like the kind of science fiction that was about unrealistic monsters or aliens. He

liked the science fiction that made him think, the kind that made him think about what was possible in the future, and the kind that made him think about the vastness of the universe and what was out there.

Geoff was drawn to math, science, and reading but he hated studying, and as such, even though his IQ was high he was only able to muster fair grades.

Not a great start to becoming an astrophysicist.

Realistically, the only thing Geoff was good at, was reciting passages from the bible. He read the bible some, but that's not where this knowledge came from. Even now, he could hear the high-pitched whine of some radio preacher reciting words from the bible, and or course he heard his father, and especially his mother, quoting it on a daily basis.

Geoff's mother often warned him, holding the bible in her left hand and pointing her right index finger straight at his forehead like a pistol. "If you do not learn the bible son, you are destined to spend eternity in hell."

This dark warning was - at least in part - Geoff's motivation to partly pay attention to what they were saying, but in truth, the bible didn't make any sense to him.

The book just isn't logical. Some of these bible stories are ridiculous, I know the stories are supposed to teach me some sort of moral, but most of them are just plain stupid. And it certainly doesn't help me understand the universe.

In any case, Geoff knew the bible through and through, and it was the only thing that saved him from being constantly whipped by his mother, because Geoff's mother was not one who believed in sparing the rod. But most importantly it sometimes kept him from being bludgeoned by his father. Geoff's father thought that the only way to beat some sense into a young man, was to beat the hell out of him.

This was all motivational for Geoff, and so he learned how to use his biblical knowledge to his advantage. Sometimes he would quote passages from the 'Old Testament' to his mother and father; just to get out of some punishment he was due.

"How could a young man so full of the devil, have such an incredible understanding of the Bible?" he had heard his mystified mother whisper to his father.

When Geoff was old enough, he got a driver's license. You had to be able to drive a truck, to work at the quarry, and Geoff's father was all for that. Even though Geoff and his dad both wanted him to get a license, they had different ideas about how that license would be used.

Working at the quarry, was about as appealing to Geoffrey as hearing another hell-fire-and-damnation sermon. Yet, he really wanted a license so he could get a car, and he wanted a car so he could get girls. So, he obliged his dad and when he turned sixteen, he began working at the quarry. Eventually, he saved up enough money to buy his own car. It was an old blue 62' Chevy Impala 'Super Sport' Convertible, with a 327 cubic inch engine, a standard three-speed transmission, and a gear shift on the steering column, *three on the tree*. His heart would race as fast as that engine at the mere thought of that car.

Geoff's parents hoped that he would, meet a nice girl settle down and get married. But Geoff didn't want a girlfriend, he just wanted to get laid, and get laid he did. Geoff turned female heads without effort and his naturally fit body only added to the attention of strangers. Geoff took it all in stride, but one time a female friend told him that he was a constant topic in the girl's locker room.

"Me?" he said. "Are you sure?"

"Yes you," his female friend laughed. "I guess they can't get enough of that smile and your witty charm. We girls are suckers for that."

"Wow," he said. "I never knew."

"You should have. It's not like you are ever hurting for dates. And let's not mention that sporty convertible."

"Oh, well ok, so it's the car." Geoff smiled.

"It helps, but there's more to it I'm sure. Believe it or not, I heard some of them say that they even liked to hear you quote the bible."

This had made him pause in thought. He had recently discovered that if he talked about the bible before sex, it discouraged his potential partners from actually having it. He began using it sparingly and now he was happy that he did.

He did, however, find that he could quote passages from the bible after sex, which seemed to help justify the act and sometimes made the girls feel less guilty about the 'sin' they had just committed.

He would look deep into their eyes, lower the tone of his voice and recite a verse from the Bible.

"Seeing ye have purified your souls in obeying the truth through the Spirit unto unfeigned *love* of the brethren, see that ye *love one another* with a pure heart fervently: Peter, chapter 1 verse 22." He would then explain that one must stay pure of heart. For as long as one is pure of heart and intention, then there can be no basis for sin.

The chase, as well as the capture…or rather the conquests, were always enjoyed by Geoff, but girls and cars were just a way to pass time.

What I really want is to be a scientist. But there is just no way, my parents can't afford college, and my grades are definitely not good enough to get a scholarship.

Once again this was just daydreaming. In all reality, Geoff felt stuck. Stuck in this backwoods town, and right now stuck in the back of this old church, staring up at the high ceilings and trying to keep his eyes open, but then he felt it again.

The preacher was imploring sinners to come to the front of the church and accept Jesus as their savior. The preacher was also urging them to confess their sins to the congregation. But this was not some passion fueled moment, this happened every Sunday. Geoff thought about how his dad had said, that it was just a bunch of hypocrites, sinning all week long and then repenting on Sunday.

Geoff once asked his dad what a hypocrite was, and his dad, responding in his usual abrupt manner, said; "You can read… go to the library and look it up."

So, Geoff did just that.

Hypocrite: *a person who indulges in hypocrisy.*
Hypocrisy: *the practice of claiming to have moral standards or beliefs to which one's own behavior does not conform; pretense.*

Are all these people hypocrites? Geoff thought.

Geoff usually paid no attention to the *goings-on* in the front of the church. But this time, that strange breeze of fresh air, that was coming in from the open front door and pushing away the smell of cigarettes, was now continuing to push on Geoffrey. It was a force he had never felt before but seemed irresistible, and just like that, he stood up and headed for the front of the church.

There were already five people in front of Geoff, moving towards the front, and they all slowly proceeded forward, as the congregation of about one hundred farmers and town's people sang Amazing Grace.

The old church was small with rough wooden benches and white plaster board walls. In the front of the church was a raised platform with a pulpit on it. This allowed the preacher to stand slightly above his congregation and preach down them. The church was lit-up from sunshine pouring through a small clear glass window, which was high above and behind the pulpit. This *light* seemed to be leading the way for the group of people now approaching the front of the church.

First in line was Jake Handcock. He lived in town with his wife Nora and three kids. Next in line there was nineteen-year-old Billy Prescott, who lived with his parent's just two farms over from Geoff's place. And then there was old lady Jenkins.

I think old lady Jenkins goes up there every week. Probably confessing to some old obscure sin, just to have something to do...she's too old to have any really juicy sins.

But what interest Geoff the most was the last person in line. It was Selma Potoski, and she was right in front of Geoff.

Hey, what do you know about that?

Selma was a middle-aged polish lady. Her mousy brown hair barely touched her bare shoulders just above the flowered sundress she was wearing. She and her husband leased the old Weaver farm about four miles west of town.

Selma was walking on crutches because her foot was in a cast. She broke her ankle, supposedly falling off their front porch, but there were rumors that she was actually pushed off the porch by old man Potoski.

As they slowly continue forward and Geoff listens to the alternating 'thud' and 'thump' of the crutches and then the cast hitting the wooden floor, a distinct image jumps into Geoff's mind. Just last night, Saturday night, he remembered seeing Jake Handcock's 57' Studebaker Hawk parked down by the lake. Geoff knew of some very secluded places down by the lake to take his dates, and it was in one of those places that he noticed that particular car. Geoff was sure it was Jake's car, because it was the only one like it in the county. Jake was nowhere in sight, but there pressed against the Studebaker's windshield, and spread wide apart, was one barefoot, and the bottom of one dingy white plaster cast.

Selma you vixen. Dad's right, these people are just a bunch of hypocrites.

Having never been at the front of the church before, it looked different. Geoff could now see all those faces looking him over, wondering what kind of sins he was about to expose.

This is a little scary.

Immediately, Jake Hancock started yelling at the top of his lungs, startling Geoffrey.

"I accept Jesus Christ as my savior," Jake belted. "Oh, dear God forgive me my sins."

The crowd immediately responded "Amen, brother"

Geoffrey stared at Jake. He had on many occasions heard this type of commotion from his usual spot in the back of the church, but this time it was much more dramatic and *emotional,* as he stood here close to the action.

These people are really getting into this.

The preacher was encouraging Jake to not only confess his sins but to also acknowledge that he was a sinner. Jake, about 50 years old, yelled out again.

"Oh yes God I am a sinner and I have sinned excessively, I have cursed and taken God's name in vain, and I am a fornicator and have committed other sins that I am much too ashamed to admit. But lord god, I am here today to swear that I accept Jesus as my lord and savior, and I truly repent my sinner's ways."

Fornicator. Got that right.

After every proclamation, the congregation would respond with a resounding, *Amen brother*. This too was much louder and dramatic, at the front of the church.

Not a lot of logic going on here, pure emotion. Go figure...

Geoffrey, much to his own surprise, was starting to get into it. "Amen Brother," Geoffrey yelled, harmonizing with the crowd, as the preacher held his hand on Jake's shoulder and then his forehead. "Oh, dear lord," the preacher was saying, looking upward as he spoke. "Accept this man's penance and accept him into the flock of true believers." Geoff watched intently as this scene repeated three more times, with each sinner repenting their sins, while Geoff stood at the rear of the line.

The preacher took about five to ten minutes with each sinner before it was Selma's turn. Immediately she started in with how she was a sinner and a fornicator and how she wanted God to forgive her, and that she too accepted Jesus Christ as her lord and savior. The crowd chanted in unison. "Amen Sister!"

Selma certainly looked sincere, and as the preacher held his hand on her head, She dropped to her knees while the preacher asked God to accept her into the fold.

Geoff was overwhelmed with the *emotion* flowing from each of these supposed sinners, from the preacher, and from the entire congregation. He even felt a sense of joy as he joined in with their loud recants.

Yet, as for himself, Geoff had no feelings of remorse. He was not a sinner; he didn't feel that anything he had ever done was bad. He didn't feel a need to accept Jesus Christ as his lord and savior. But here he was at the front of the church, pushed here by some unseen force in the wind, and he was up next.

Step into the Batter's box, Geoff thought.

Geoff is too embarrassed to sit back down, and he just couldn't bring himself to yell out the confessions and professions of sins that did not exist. In fact, he thought that if he did confess to a sin that he did not believe he had committed, then *logically* he would truly be committing a sin.

What in the hell am I gonna do now?

The preacher is now looking directly at him, with an expression of, *come on son you can do it.* "My son do you accept Jesus Christ as your Lord and Savior?"

Geoff, following the orders of the mysterious force that had pushed him to this point, steps forward and said the first thing that came to his mind. "2nd Corinthians." He whispered.

The congregation dominating the noise level with their loud celebrations, "Amen! Praise the Lord! Hallelujah!" could not hear Geoff's softly recited words. After a moment or two, the crowd quieted down.

"What did you say, son?" the preacher asked.

Geoff spoke a little louder this time. "2 Corinthians," he repeated.

The crowd became quieter and quieter until there was hardly a sound in the room.

"2nd Corinthians chapter 7," Geoff continued, raising his voice a bit so the crowd could here. "Having, therefore, these promises dearly beloved, let us cleanse ourselves from all filthiness of the flesh and spirit, perfecting holiness in the fear of God."

Geoffrey looks at the crowd. He knew these verses so well that the words just roll from his lips. Soon the interpretations would come just as easy. Taught by hundreds of radio preachers, he was ready for this moment. The tone of Geoff's voice was low, confident, and smooth, just as some of his favorite preachers would be. He knew exactly which words to emphasize and where to pause for effect.

He continues his bible quotation. "You know who you are…that have indulged in the filth of flesh and spirit." The crowd stares back at him with looks of amazement, but now his voice rises with each word.

"Receive us; we have wronged *NO* man, we have corrupted *NO* man, we have defrauded *NO* man. I speak not this to *condemn* you for I have said before, that YE are in our hearts to die and live with you. *Great* is my boldness of speech toward you; *great* is my glorifying of you: I am filled with comfort."

Geoff, with his index finger pointing toward the heavens, added his own interpretation. "God will condemn no man of his lust for life if he has wronged no other man. And as long as the *LOVE OF GOD* lives and dies within you, you will always have the comfort that he alone can provide."

He could tell he had their attention, so he stepped forward and stepped it up.

"Chapter 7, verses 9 through 11; Now I rejoice, *not* that *YE* were made sorry, but that *YE* sorrowed to repentance: for *YE* were made sorry after a Godly manner, that *YE* might receive damage by us in nothing. For Godly sorrow worketh repentance to salvation not to be repented of, but the sorrow of the world worketh death. For *behold* this selfsame thing, that ye sorrowed after a godly sort, what carefulness it wrought in you, YEA, what clearing of yourselves, YEA, what indignation, YEA what fear."

Geoffrey loved the word 'Yea' and used each one with dramatic effect as a launching point to raise the volume of his voice, just like he had heard from the radio preachers.

"YEA," he continued. "What vehement desire, YEA, what zeal, YEA, what revenge!"

Then bending his knees, a bit and pointing to the crowd in a theatrical fashion he shouted to them. "In all things, ye have approved yourselves to be clear in this matter."

Geoffrey pauses for a moment and then with a sigh of displayed emotion he lowers his voice and with a matter-of-fact tone. "The Bible is telling you that while you as human beings, maybe vehement, zealous and even revengeful, you have the power within you to repent and through the powers that you can derive from the heavens, and from the very *UNIVERSE* itself. You can '*clear*' yourself of sin and receive salvation. The bible says: 'I rejoice therefore that I have confidence in *you* in all things.'"

A few, *Amen brothers* seep from the crowd.

Geoff loves sneaking in a few *universe* references as an answer opposed to God. The entire scene was materializing like some kind of miracle; the congregation would not stop gazing at Geoff. The looks on their faces were incredible; it was not the look of shock that Geoffrey expected. They did not look as if they were about to throw him out of the church, or out of the town forever. It was a look of astonishment mixed with admiration and a touch of disbelief. He could almost hear their thoughts; *how could these words be coming out of this young man's mouth?* Other murmurs of astounded discussions filtered through the crowd.

Geoff absorbs the moment and attempts to go on, that was until he felt the preacher's hands on his shoulders. It was not a feeling of comfort; the grip was tight, and Geoffrey felt the reverend's fingernails piercing the cloth of his shirt and digging deep into Geoffrey's flesh. The preacher's whispers land on Geoff's ears with a heated presence. The crowd's murmurs are just loud enough to keep the private words form their own ears.

"What the hell do you think you're doing boy? There is only one preacher in this town, and it ain't you. 'The power of the Universe?' What the hell are you trying to do?" His voice now lowering to a threatening tone. "We have people who take care of troublemakers like you. Now you repent your sins and get the FUCK out of my church."

Geoff - now forced to his knees - could not say a word as the preacher kept his grip tight on Geoff shoulders.

The preacher spoke to the crowd. "This boy is possessed and needs to repent his sins to free himself of the devil. Boy, what say you?"

As the preacher's grip relaxed, Geoffrey felt the pain shooting through his shoulders withdraw. Tears surfaced to his eyes as he forced the preachers suggested words through his gritted teeth. "I repent my sins"

The preacher then continued "I will pray that God forgives you, now return to your seat."

The preacher then resumes his preaching and the crowd went back to their routine of 'Amen and Praise the Lord'.

Geoff's mind races with disbelief as he returns to his seat in the back of the church. *Wow...just wow! Talk about a hypocrite. This preacher takes the cake. And just to think, my parents, especially my mother, thinks this guy walks on water.* For a few fleeting second, Geoff thought about telling them about what had happened, but then. *What's the use; they would never believe me.*

After Church, some people came up to Geoff and congratulated him on repenting his sins. Some even said they liked his short sermon. Geoff did not know how to react to the praise, but he knew he liked it. But then he saw his parents, brothers, and sisters, all standing at the bottom of the steps of the church. His mother and siblings all with open mouths and staring up at him. But what he noticed the most were their eyes; their eyes were so wide; it was like they had seen a ghost. Except for Geoffrey's father that is. Geoff's father's stunned expression had a distinctive scowl chiseled in his eyebrows and his clinched jaws gave notice of his grinding teeth.

Although Geoff enjoyed the short-lived praises, this was not the kind of attention he wanted. He knew at that moment that his relationship with his family would never be the same. Religion was extremely important to them, and for their son, the family "screw off", to be the center of attention at all places the church, was much-too-much for them to handle.

They walked the mile and half, on the dirt road back to their house just as they had done every Sunday, but this time the journey was in silence.

That is until Geoff's youngest sister spoke up. "Geoffrey," she said. "Why did you talk in the front of the church today? Are you a preacher now, or are you a sinner?"

"No Annie, I am not a preacher and I am not a sinner," he said in a low voice. Then in an even lower tone that only she could hear he added a few more words.

"At least I don't think I am."

God, I don't want to be a preacher and explore the mysteries of sin. I would much rather be a scientist and explore the mysteries of the universe.

No one said a word to Geoff the rest of the morning. Geoff thought about the experience again and again. He loved the attention and that feeling of flying high. The power was intoxicating, and he could still feel the adrenaline running through his veins. *Veins of steel; I just want to break out of here.*

A CAPE OF DUST billows from the back of the Chevy 'Super Sport' convertible. The car's engine wines, as the low-profile tires tare through the dirt of the country road that leads away from Geoffrey's parent's home. He has a little bit of savings and a full tank of gas, as he flies with the wind in his hair and the setting sun in his sights.

Head west, young man... Head west. Find out what math, science and the universe have in store for me.

He bursts into song. "California is the place to be, swimming pools, movie stars."

Geoffrey would never look back. He knows that he is now headed for a new future...and he hopes it will be an exciting one.

CHAPTER 2 – "AND THE *HOLY SPIRIT*"

June 6th, 1966

Ester Suni Nati, Age 14 – Emotion

"In the name of the Father and the Son and the *Holy Spirit*...Bless us, oh lord and these thy gifts...."

Sitting at the family's breakfast table, Ester's mind drifts away, ---she had heard the prayer so many times, and the words seemed to have so little meaning for her, that she could not even hear them at this moment.

".... through Christ, Our Lord. Amen." Ester's mother now completing the prayer, as Ester touches her forehead with her right hand before moving it to her abdomen. "In the name of the Father." She says. Then she moves her hand up from her abdomen to her left shoulder, "And the Son", and finally, she moves her hand to her right shoulder, "And the *Holy Spirit,* Amen."

The intentional movements complete the sign of the cross, or the crucifix as it may be. Ester pictures a crucifix in her mind.

Ester is sitting in their small kitchen with her parents, her brother Elia, her younger sister Sara and her older sister Kwanita. They were just starting their breakfast, as Ester's eyes begin to water as she thinks about the significance of the crucifix.

Ester's mother often commented on how easily Ester was moved to *emotion*, but Ester was trying hard to conceal her feelings and quickly began to think about the bliss she could sometimes feel when she thought about God, and now then thinking about the sign of the cross and the words that accompanied the gesture, she tried even harder to concentrate on the "*Holy Spirit*", and this helped her *emotions* to fade away.

Ester wondered about the *Holy Spirit* and wondered if her mother thought about these two words and what they meant. She also wondered if her mother was repeating them, like she had probably done a thousand times before…her mind also drifting away, as Ester's often did.

Ester's mother was raised Catholic in her homeland of Nigeria, and she insisted that her children be raised catholic as well. One could easily see Ester's Nigerian linage in the creamy brown color of Ester's skin. This genetically donated hue was presently glowing like bronze in the soft warm sunshine streaming through the window of her parent's adobe home.

At the ripe age of 14, Ester also exhibited the chiseled features from her father, and her eyes were *dark,* deep set, and intense like that of the American Bald Eagle. Her high cheekbones and the unmistakable character of her nose emphatically revealed her Native American blood line. And just as many other Native American families in the area, Ester and her family would often spend their evenings sitting on the front porch of their southwestern home.

Those evenings were a favorite time for Ester, as she along with the rest of her family would listen to her father retell stories and lessons from his ancestors. Stories that he and other Zuni tribesmen had told thousands of times over centuries. She could not get enough of these tales of Zuni spirits and brave warriors, and her heart would swell with admiration as she would gaze up at the man telling these stories, a man she loved more than life.

As she would listen to her father's stories, Ester's mind would often drift away, as she watched the *darkening* silhouettes of the saguaro cactus. The mountains off to the west would blend with the *dark* clouds on the horizon, framed in crimson by the setting sun. The heavy humid summer air would give the entire scene a soft warm pastel hue that forced each element to melt softly into one another.

Ester would get lost in this vision, her father's powerful voice setting the mood, as he spoke softly in his husky yet silky Zuni accent. Tales of his ancestors and those spiritual warriors would be described in detail, with the intention of both entertaining and teaching deep purpose lessons of life.

Ester was presently thinking of one specific lesson that her father would often give, especially at that time of the day. He would say, "An Indian's religion, is just part of the *fabric* of their life, and *everything* they do should be immersed in that *fabric*. To call it a 'religion' is misleading. *Everything* is a part of Mother Earth, and you should live your life understanding that you are a part of that *fabric* which makes up *all things, everywhere*."

On those evenings, Ester would often feel the hot humid air against her skin, her skin a part of her body and her body a part of her soul. Her father's words would move through Ester's mind and body, warming her like the summer air. She could feel that she was a part of the earth and sky and she could feel the mysterious power of the wind blending her with all of these things.

In fact, Ester's father felt that being a part of everything was so important, that he had changed all his children's last names. His last name was Cooeyate, but he wanted his children to go by the surname 'Suni Nati', which, in Zuni, means '*middle*'. He wanted his children to understand that they are in the '*middle*' of *everything, everywhere,* and that they are *connected* to *everything*. This word '*middle*', and its meaning would continually grow inside of Ester and become an essential part of her life.

Her father also gave Ester the middle name of Aira which means, *Of the Wind or Spirit*. He explained that this would emphasize the importance of the spiritual aspects of her life.

Occasionally Ester's father would make Jewelry, mostly of silver and turquois. However, on one occasion, for Ester, he made a small gold bracelet that had the Alchemist symbol for 'Air" on it, an upright triangle with a line running horizontally through it.

Ester would not allow the bracelet to leave her sight. It was more than a beautiful piece of jewelry; it had deep meaning because it was made just for her by her father, and she would often notice how he would smile at her as she admired it.

Ester did not miss many things, and she had noticed that sometimes when her mother ended a prayer, her father would cross himself as well. But his cross was not exactly like her mother's. It was much more abbreviated, and he added a small additional gesture, which seemed to be a circle surrounding the cross.

Once when Ester was on one of her walks in the desert with her father, she asked him about it.

"Well," he said. "Native Americans have always believed in the power of prayer, and your mother seems to appreciate it when I participate in her prayers."

"But father," Ester pressed. "Why do you add the little circle at the end of the sign of the cross?"

Her father had looked hard at Ester. His eyes were wide with surprise. He had then picked up a stick from the desert floor as he spoke.

"Well, my so ever observant one, there is a *symbol* for the beliefs in Shamanism, and it is a small cross, enclosed in an oval."

As he had begun to draw this symbol in the sand he had said.

"Here, this is what it looks like."

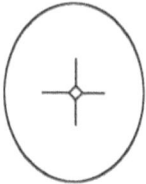

This was very important to Ester as her father had been training her as a Zuni Shaman. He was teaching her how to use meditation, a form of self-hypnosis, to achieve a Shamanistic state of mind. Shamanism, she was being taught, was all about feelings, and the *emotional* connection to your surroundings. Ester loved that about Shamanism, she did not care much about *logic*, she was all about feelings, things either felt right or they felt wrong…period.

However, she and her father both knew that Ester's mother, though she loved Ester's father very much, frowned on the practices of Shamanism. She thought they were not consistent with Catholic teachings. So, Ester and her father would keep this training as their very private secret. That was just fine for Ester. She loved keeping secrets with her father; it made her feel special and even closer to him with each additional secret.

But something was changing, Ester was aware that she was becoming a woman, becoming more conscious of her body and the new feelings she was experiencing. But there was much more --- there seemed to be other forces at work. She was becoming even more observant of *everything*, and everything seemed to have new meanings. Sights and sounds, touch and smells all had more significance now. Her mind was expanding, even her dreams seemed more important.

Ester now recalled an incident that had occurred just the previous week; Ester had opened the unlocked door to their only bathroom, stepped in, and there she caught her brother, not in a way that most siblings catch hormone filled adolescent brothers, this – as far as Ester was concerned – was even more disturbing. She *caught* him crying. Ester could never remember seeing her older brother cry. She cried often but crying was something a young male Native American did not do…ever.

"GET OUT OF HERE!!" he had cried out, the second he noticed her.

A couple days later, Ester had mustered up the courage to ask her brother what was going on. At first, he did not respond, but after a while, her brother Elia spoke. "Have you seen my .22 rifle? I have looked *everywhere* for it. I just don't know, maybe someone has stolen it." A distressed look had covered his face as he spoke. "Dad is going to kill me if he finds out that I lost that rifle."

"I haven't seen it," Ester had responded with a deep look of concern on her face.

In her heart she had felt sadness for her brother. She hated to see him so down, and she could not stand to see him cry. She knew how he felt about that gun.

"I know you love that gun," she had whispered. "I wish father had given me one."

But she knew that would never happen. She was a girl, and the gun was not a toy. Her brother was required to get up early in the morning - well before the daily work on the farm - and go hunting to help put food on the table. Ester had often heard him get his gear together in the early hours and watched him vanish into the darkness from her small bedroom window. All the while wishing she was with him.

Ester frequently had vivid dreams before waking up to hear and watch her brother leave, and Ester had had another one on that particular night. In this dream, she saw a vision of something she could only describe as a 'ghost-like' person.

The family farm's barn was called just that...*the barn*. It was actually just a shed. Yet the small rustic wooden building served as a mainstay on the back end of their property. As far as its primary function, it was where Ester's father kept tools and some feed for the animals.

Ester would frown at the mere site of it. There was very little light inside, and God only knows what kind of wretched, furry little creatures were scurrying through its darkness, and she realized it had been the backdrop to her dream. In Ester's dream, the ghost-like figure led her through the barn's *darkness* to it's very back, while providing just enough *light* such that she could see, and there behind some bales of hay, leaning against a wall, was her brother's rifle.

The next morning Ester had gone to her brother. "Elia, I had a dream about your rifle, last night. I dreamed it was in the barn, behind some bales of hay."

Her brother had eyed her with a leery stare, but Ester had persisted, and she then watched as he disappeared into the *dark* entrance of the weather-beaten shed. A few minutes later, Ester had spotted a glint of light reflect from the silvery shaft of a rifle's barrel, revealing the secret of his search.

Ester had been very happy. Not only had her dream come true but she had solved the source of her brother's grief and saved him from their father's scolding. She had eagerly awaited his anticipated praise. But as her brother had entered the morning *light* of day; tiny shadows had accented the tightened muscles in his chiseled jaw.

"You did this," he had said. "You took my gun and hid it in the barn. You've always been jealous that dad gave me this gun, and not you. Just stay away from my stuff."

He had then marched away. Ester had been shocked by her brother's response. Later that day, breaking her own rule about maintaining the secrecy of her premonitions, she went to talk to her mother.

"Mother," Ester had said with tears welling up. "Can I talk to you about something?"

Her mother had placed her hands gently on Ester's shoulders and looked intently into her eyes. "Dear, please calm down," she had said. "You can talk to me about anything."

Ester began to explain, sobbing as she spoke.

"Elia lost his rifle, and I had a dream that it was in the barn. But when Elia returned from the barn with the rifle, finding it right where I told him it would be, he accused me of stealing his gun and placing it there." Ester had started to cry again, "I did not steal his rifle, and I truly had a dream of where it would be."

Ester had hoped her mother would understand but feared more criticism, but She had been pleasantly surprised at what her mother had to say.

"My dear, you are going to find, that in life, things are not always black and white *or dark* and *light.* You will have your perspective of things and others will have their perspective. Those two perspectives will not always be the same."

Ester had listened without interruption.

"You did something good and it was perceived by your brother as bad, you thought you were right, he thought you were wrong. Just as between the *Dark* and the *Light* there is Gray. There is always *a middle* ground between extremes, good and bad, right and wrong."

Ester had watched as her mother paused, staring at Ester with her piercing dark eyes. "Ester, are you following me?"

"I think so," Ester had said.

The truth was, she really hadn't followed, but complete comprehension or not, she had been so fascinated by what her mother had been saying, that she did not want her to stop.

"As I was saying," her mother had continued. "As you go through life you are going to run into these contradictions of right and wrong, good and bad, *dark* and *light.* But all you can do, is the best that you can do, and be as good of a person as you can be in God's eyes."

"What about my dream?" Ester had asked.

"As far as your premonition, I would just accept it as the *Holy Spirit* working in your life."

Ester had immediately recalled the ghost-like figure in her dream but did not mention it to her mother. Instead, having her mother's attention, she had decided to ask another question.

"Mother, why do people do bad things?"

Ester's mother had once again stared at Ester for a moment and then replied. "I believe that people are often seduced by the powers of evil, and because of this seduction, they often do not even realize that what they are doing is wrong. They have their own *emotional* and possibly even *logical* reasons for their actions, and in their own mind may feel that their actions are justified. Therefore, we must all be very careful in our judgments of others."

Ester had not replied to her mother, but instead she had thought how happy she was that her mother had not ridiculed her for her premonition. She thought that her mother seemed to understand and actually relate to her predicament. At the time, Ester even wondered if her mother had premonitions of her own.

Ester had allowed her mother's comments to drift to the back of her mind. However, the whole incident had left a hollow feeling in the pit of Ester's thoughts.

Why do I have these premonitions? Why am I here? Why do I feel lost most of the time? Am I a good person? Where are the answers?

Now Ester's attention returns to the breakfast table, Ester's 12-year-old sister Sara has been speaking non-stop, and Ester normally tried to block out her sister's jabbering, as her high shrill voice rambles on and on about everything and nothing. Ester would instead think about one of her father's stories or ponder on the many questions about life that swirled in her head. But this time the rambling was different. Ester's sister was asking their mother something important.

"Mom, I know that in our catechism class they said that the father is God in heaven, and the son is Jesus Christ. So, who is the Holy Ghost?"

Ester's mother quickly corrected Ester's sister. "Darling, it's the *Holy Spirit*, not the Holy Ghost." Ester's mother furrowed her eyebrows in thought. Ester knew that 'no answer' would never do for her inquisitive sister, because she was as persistent as she was talkative.

Ester's mother responded, "Dear, the *Holy Spirit* is the third person of the Trinity. There is the father, the son, and the *Holy Spirit*. You have God in heaven, Jesus on earth and the *Holy*

Spirit is the *spirit* of God and Jesus *everywhere*, in heaven and on earth."

The definition provided by her mother was very similar to the ones Ester had heard in her Catholic catechism classes. Ester's sister frowns as she looks her mother.

"I don't understand, mom."

The truth was…neither did Ester.

Sara with a puzzled look on her face went on to another question, "Mom, what is hell?"

Once again, their mother's eyes squint with thought, but now raising her voice says, "Listen! Hell is a bad place. It is a place where your soul is torn apart by the demons of your life."

Sara's tiny body snaps to attention. She then quickly moves on to another question about why she had to do so much homework. Ester could see a relieved look come over her mother's face and she returned to washing the dishes.

Ester could not get the question about the *Holy Spirit,* out of her mind. All she could think about was her mother's earlier words; "I would just accept it as the Holy Spirit working in your life."

Ester also found it interesting, that her mother described the '*Holy Spirit*' as being *everywhere,* and her father described the '*Fabric* of Life' as being *everywhere.* Ester wondered if somehow, they were connected.

Just another question without answers.

Sometimes Ester wondered if the answers could be found at church. Although never forced, Ester sometimes attended mass with her mother. Her father did not believe in traditional religions, but tolerated the church going because he loved Ester's mother so much. Ester then realizes in mid thought that she was probably the most religious person in the family. She believed strongly in God's presence and prayed often during the day, but even that was not enough. Ester always felt this empty feeling inside of her and she could not seem to find anything that could totally fill that void. Her constant praying, and volunteering for the church seemed to help a little but attending catholic mass did not seem to help at all.

Ester in her search for some answers, had been reading some books on mysticism and 'Extra Sensory Perception' or ESP. She read these books to try to understand her occasional encounter with clairvoyance. The incident with her brother's rifle came to mind. These books were filled with a host of theories and examples of other people who had experienced ESP.

None of this makes any sense, it does not explain how it happens or why.

Ester also read the bible, but she had to admit, that she had difficulty understanding it. It seemed to be full of phrases which were meant to be confusing as if *everything* was some kind of a riddle. However, Ester always felt that somehow the answers she was looking for could be found somewhere in those pages. Or maybe somewhere in her beliefs in Shamanism. Or possibly even somewhere else. All this reading seemed to fill some of the voids, however there was always a prevailing thought.

How can I possibly learn from something like the bible, when I can't fully understand it?

She needed someone to help her make sense of what she was reading. That someone might be a prophet, or someone that could show her the way or show her the *light.*

Ester believed that if she could find that someone to interpret the meaning of the puzzle pieces from the bible, shamanistic references, and psychic phenomenon, that she could find her way to what her mother called heaven, and Shaman's, like her father, called the 'end-all-be-all' destiny, the *Upper World.*

One day in her persistent search for answers Ester came upon a book that was published in 1952 by the pastor of New York City's Marble Collegiate Church, Norman Vincent Peale. It was called "The Power of Positive Thinking." Peale began by stating ten rules for overcoming inadequacy attitudes and learning to practice faith. The rules included picturing yourself as succeeding; thinking positive thoughts to drown out a negative thought; minimizing obstacles, not copying others, and repeating 'If God be for us, who can be against us?' ten times every day.

He also suggested that one repeat 'I can do all things through Christ which strengtheneth me' ten times every day.

Finally, he recommended that one develop a strong self-respect, affirm that one is in God's hands, and believe that one receives power from God.

This philosophy appealed to Ester. She considered herself as a positive person and this approach seemed to compliment her own feelings and perspective about life. However, it still did not solve the overall mysteries of the bible or of life itself, and thus Ester would be stuck the *middle*…wedged in "*Suni Nati*".

CHAPTER 3 – THE CHURCH WALL SCROLL

March 15th, 1970
Geoffrey Hazelton, age 19 – Logic

Geoffrey Hazleton - sweeping the floor of the Reverend Billy Haddock's First Street Pentecostal Riverside Church - thought about the time when he had been driven by some unseen force to go to the front of the church in his hometown so many years ago. That event changed him, and that same force guided him to Los Angeles. This is where he was sure he would be changing the movie industry with his grandiose ideas for new science fiction movies. It was only *logical*.

Who knew that movie producers were not walking the streets looking for people with great ideas? So, things didn't work out as he had planned, and he soon found that it took real talent to be in the movie industry, and compared to even the most average Joe playing guitar and singing for spare change on the street, Geoffrey was no competition. He had none of that kind of talent. But then Geoffrey had heard that all the young people were moving to San Francisco to protest the war in Vietnam and have *Love-Ins*. It was the Age of Aquarius and Geoffrey wanted to be a part of it. So, he had moved to San Francisco.

When Geoff arrived here in San Francisco he had used the only talent he had, which was his exhaustive knowledge of the Bible and his ability for interpretation. He had gone to different churches in San Francisco and just as he had in his hometown, went up to the front of a church to be saved, and then start preaching. The congregation always seemed to enjoy his sermons. The men would turn to the members next to them with raised eyebrows as if impressed, and the younger women would maneuver to the front of the congregation, smiling and shyly darting their batting eyes away when he would return the smile.

But the residing preachers were another story. They did not appreciate his impromptu sermons. He was usually interrupted, ushered to the side, and then asked to leave. Those situations were the best moments. The worst were when his forced exits were accompanied with a threat of bodily harm if he ever returned.

During these impromptu sermons, Geoffrey often made reference to his belief in cosmic forces of the universe, as a possible alternative to a belief in a Supreme Being. Geoffrey was not sure if the local preachers were threatened by a competing preacher or if they were more threatened by the possibility of competing spiritual alternative.

Billy Handcock was different. Billy took a liking to Geoffrey and told Geoffrey that his own sermons and he, were getting old and tired. He was gradually losing his followers and offered Geoffrey room and board and a job as a preacher. Geoffrey jumped at the opportunity and over time helped to build up the membership at the Reverend's small Church.

Billy, in a show of appreciation, helped Geoffrey get his GED, and later on Billy said, "Geoffrey you've developed into a pretty good preacher. We both know that you are the reason the church is growing, but sometimes the references you make from the Bible, though eloquently phrased, are frankly incorrect. Sometimes you seem to be trying to make the bible to *rational*; you need to understand that some things just need to be accepted on faith alone. God will take care of the rest. Geoffrey the church is making enough money to send you to a Divinity School here in California. It would be good for you and it would be good for the church as well."

Geoff thought about his response to Billy at that time: "Billy, the one thing I really want is a good education. But honestly, I might not be the right person for divinity school. I think theology is interesting, but I'm more interested in science." Geoff remembered how he had looked directly into Billy's eyes at the time and continued. "Frankly Billy, I'm not sure if I even believe in God." Geoff also remembered how after he had said the words aloud, he had almost wished he could take them back. But Billy had just smiled at him. "You think I'm a fool? I know that. I listen to your sermons; I hear what you are saying. You are very particular about what passages you quote. You never say, 'There is a God' or even 'God is in heaven'. In fact, you make very little reference to God."

Geoffrey had been positive that Billy would have been shocked by this revelation., but in-fact it was Geoffrey that had been shocked by Billy's response.

"I noticed that if you make any reference to God at all, you make that reference, in terms of God being everywhere, that God is in all things throughout the universe, and that God is especially in each individual you are preaching too. You are saying that all of us should look inwardly to find God and that we should just be good to ourselves, and to others, and the God inside of us will be good to us." Geoff thought about how Billy had paused for a moment and then said, "It's not the way I preach, but the congregation is eating it up, and that's good enough for me. Have you ever heard of Norman Vincent Peale?"

Geoffrey remembered telling Billy that he had not hear of Peale and Billy continued. "Peale, has written a book called 'The Power of Positive Thinking.'" Billy had handed a copy of the book to Geoffrey. "I think this book is somewhat complimentary to your preaching methods and you will see how Dr. Peale ties it all back to the powers of almighty God. I would like to see you do that as well. So, are you interested in my offer?"

Geoffrey had known that this was not how he had pictured his life going, but he also knew that he wanted an education, so he had accepted Billy's offer, and now over the past three years Geoffrey had finished his GED and was now pursuing a degree in divinity studies from the "Theological Union", which was an inter/multidenominational school of theology in Berkley California. Along with his religious studies, Geoffrey was now also taking some classes in math and science from the University of Berkeley, this of course, being his true love.

All this including the book that Billy had given him was influencing not only his preaching style, but his message as well. The future was beginning to show a glimmer of *light.*

As for right now, Geoff's reality was sweeping the floor of the First Street Pentecostal Riverside Church, as Billy watched from a nearby doorway. Geoff needed to get his work done quickly, because this evening Billy was taking him to meet with several ministers from around the country at the annual Congregation of Churches.

Billy spoke from his spot in the doorway, "Now you do a good job cleaning up in hear, and I'll be back later to pick you up."

Along with preaching on Sunday, Geoffrey was also responsible for cleaning and repairing the antique church building. The building stood in the same location for well over a hundred years, and as far as Geoff could tell, it appeared to have always been a church. Sometime in the past, it had been moved from another far away location. This, he surmised, was possibly one of the reasons it was a bit flimsy and in constant need of repair.

"Before you go Billy," Geoffrey asked. "Where did this building come from?"

Billy scratches his cheek in thought. "You know I'm not too sure," he said. "It's a bit of a mystery. There are even rumors that it was brought over from England. There's no way of knowing how old it really is."

Geoffrey didn't really care about an exact history of the building. He knew all he needed to know and didn't mind doing the cleaning and repairs on the old building. In fact, he enjoyed it. He kind of felt close to the old boy. He liked the mystery, and thought it was like "life" itself. It was essentially a puzzle which may never be solved.

Perhaps it's not intended to be.

Geoffrey knew that the building was not the only thing in need of repair. His sermons were good according to Billy and his interpretations, as far as he was concerned, were adequate. He often received compliments from members of his congregation. Yet, from a personal standpoint, Geoffrey was not satisfied. He wanted it all to make sense; he wanted it to be *logical*. So far, he had just copied the style of the old-time preachers, he had heard on the radio when he was a kid, but with his own interpretations and twist, trying to have it make some sense.

At the divinity school, he learned about many great religious leaders and how they all seemed to have some sort of divine inspiration. Geoffrey did not have divine inspiration, in fact, he felt like he was just making all of this stuff up and people were buying it. He wanted what those religious leaders had, he wanted to be inspired. After all, he had an audience but now he needed a point of focus so he could make a true impact. His heart was not truly into religion. He was much more into the realm of *fact*, into the realm of *science*, and into the realm of logic.

There must be a way to meld the realm of religion and science together.

As he rolled these thoughts over in his mind, he could hear the wind blowing outside. It had been pushing at the aged building all day with its relentless invisible force, and the old structure was crying from the strain. Then Geoff heard a familiar sound; the sound of a board pulling its way free from the decayed wall studs. It was not the first lose board he would have to repair in the building, and he once again spoke to his friend.

"Old boy, you're coming apart at the seams but don't worry I'm the superhero, coming to your rescue. Ta! Na! 'Hammer Man' or 'Nail Man', I don't know"

Geoffrey retrieves his toolbox and some nails from his room and approaches the latest point of desecration caused by the forces of nature. He felt good that he could keep the place going, keep it alive so to speak. When he found the board in question, he was a bit surprised.

"This is…" he looks closer to be sure. "This is the same board I repaired several times before."

The old boy must be trying to tell me something.

He observes the board closer. "I'll tell you what. Let's see what's going on inside this wall."

Geoff pulls softly on the loose board to check its strength. When he did, it came completely loose from the wall, flying across the room, almost hitting Geoffrey in the head.

"Sorry old guy, I didn't mean to piss you off."

But then Geoffrey notices something inside of the wall. It was a piece of parchment with brown edges and a faded surface. The paper was brittle to the touch, and he removes it very slowly. A script like font filled the page. Geoffrey now sitting on the floor begins to read.

"I am the son and I bring you the word of our father. And the father has decreed that you shall have a new name and that name is 'Cyrus."

Geoffrey is frozen. He has an overwhelming feeling that this document is speaking directly to him. His hand trembles as he reads on.

"And with this new name you shall be 'Far Sighted' and just as Cyrus, king of Persia, you shall build a new church for those who are chosen, and let it be known as the 'Church of the Infinite Spirit."

Geoffrey could hardly remain still as his heart races with excitement. Is this the inspiration that he had been looking for?

"You should know that the science of man will see the heavens and earth as consisting of forces and particles"

Geoffrey stops at the end of each sentence and tries to grasp its meaning.

"It should be known that within the marriage between the forces and the particles lies the substance of the mystery."

"The science of man yearns for clarity, but it is often blinded by the mystery."

"Yet the father has decreed that man through his science will be allowed to see the light when man's time has come."

Cold chills run up Geoffrey's spine as the hair on his neck stands on end.

"My son the scriptures contain the substance of the mystery, but let it be known that unveiled scriptures are much more extensive than that thought by man."

"And though the scriptures often appear to be covered in a shroud, the spirit will someday let a light shine to thee."

Geoffrey slowly turns his head to see if anyone is watching. This all seemed very personal. He felt like a spy stealing secret documents.

I can't let anyone see this; Geoffrey thinks as he continues to read.

"My son you must work with diligence to allow the spirit to show you the light of the scriptures and the light of man's science."

"As the science of man is born of the logic of man, and as the religion of man is born of the emotion of man. Then you should know that logic and emotion are threads in the fabric of the mystery. Search within that fabric, for you are in the middle."

Geoff stands up and reads on.

"My son it is your burden to lay open the fruit of the mystery for those chosen to see. And you will find that the Spirit is the light, the Spirit is the guide, the Spirit is the method, and the Spirit is the answer. And the answer shall be the foundation of the new church that you shall build."

Geoffrey slowly walks the document to his room in the back of the church. He gently places it down on his desk, stares down at the words and begins to think about its meaning.

What did it all mean? How could a document, which is probably over a hundred years old, be speaking directly to me?

But Geoffrey had no doubt that it was. It was speaking directly to him and now he needed to concentrate on what it was saying.

It was obvious from the first sentence that Geoffrey was to take a new name and that name was Cyrus. Geoffrey knew the historical significance of the name. Cyrus was the King of Persia mentioned in Isaiah 45 "And I will give thee the treasures of *darkness* and the hidden riches of secret places." Geoffrey liked the correlation of this passage to the document. It made him feel like he was solving a puzzle --- a mystery of some sort.

Geoffrey also liked this new first name, but even though he knew the king of Persia's name was spelt C-Y-R-U-S, Geoffrey decided he would spell his new name C-Y-R-I-S, with the IS representing the "Infinite Spirit", which would be the name of the new church that the document had instructed to be built.

Geoffrey also decided that he needed a new last name as well. *CyrIS Hazelton just doesn't cut it.* After a considerable amount of thought, he chooses Steel as his new last name. The surname was derived from his favorite superhero, Superman, the "Man of Steel."

A superhero, and a super identity, 'CyrIS Steel'. A man of steel destined to use his superpowers to forge a union between science and religion.

CyrIS loved the idea of steel and it's grounded, down to earth connotations.

CyrIS also wanted a new middle name and found a Greek name for Earth, *Kaj,* so he added a middle name, *Kaj-El.* Very similar to Superman's real name of Kal-El, son of Jor-El. The suffix El, of course, means *of God* in Hebrew. And thus Kal-El was defined by some as the "Voice of God." CyrIS would not be so ambitious to use a name such as the *Voice of God*, but he thought the *Earth of God* seemed appropriate.

As Geoffrey, now CyrIS Kaj-El Steel, reads the rest of what he had been directed to do, something became clear. There was an important *connection* between the Bible and science. Now CyrIS was committed to a quest in search of that connection.

But there was much more, *"Know that logic and emotion are threads in the fabric of the mystery."* CyrIS knew that it would take some time to work out the meaning and significance of all these clues and CyrIS repeated Isaiah 45 to himself. "And I will give thee the treasures of *darkness* and the hidden riches of secret places".

CyrIS' body tingles with the mere thought of taking on this new adventure. There were obviously some keywords that he would need to concentrate on and use to guide him in his search. And they were: *Logic, Emotion, Fabric, Spirit, and Light*. The most important of these seemed to be *Spirit* and *Light*.

That evening CyrIS attends the Conference of Churches, held in a relatively small meeting room at a Sheraton Hotel conference center. Geoffrey sits quietly listening, as the other preachers went on and on about whose interpretations of the bible were more accurate. Then extensive discussions on how they could raise their memberships and the related donations that followed.

However, at one point, one of the grey-haired senior leaders at the conference places a copy of a letter that he had received in the mail, on a projection screen.

"Has anyone else received a copy of this letter," he said, "If so, do you know what it's about?"

It was a very simple letter that read:

Dear disciple of God.

Is hypocrisy in religion driving people away from your church?

Is government interfering with your rights as a religious organization?

Do you believe that advancements in science are inconsistent with the teachings of the scriptures?

Do you feel that the efforts of science to develop a 'unified theory', continues to draw members away from your fold?

Do you believe that the accelerating horrific events, in every society around the world, are God's sign to the people on earth that it is time to return to his teachings?

We are the king's crusaders, and we ask for your support in our efforts to do something about each of these issues.

It does not matter which denomination you represent, we are here to build your membership, and restore the faith to many of those who have strayed.

Anonymity is crucial for our organization, but we will be contacting you in the near future with further information on how to let us know of your interest.

God be with you....

Everyone looks around and no one raises their hand. Geoffrey thought that some of the ministers had a strange sheepish grin on their faces. It was as if they did know something about this but were not going to offer any additional information.

CyrIS had not seen or heard of the letter himself, but he could see where this might be appealing to some church leaders. He knew that they were losing members and many of them were blaming the very drivers mentioned in the letter. Also, many of them did believe that advancements in science were influencing people's decisions to move away from their religious beliefs.

CyrIS always believed in science and felt that a 'unified theory' may actually prove the existence of a supreme being and given his recent discovery in the wall at Billy's church, he was sure he was on the right path. With no response from the audience, the conference leader moves on to other issues.

CyrIS tries to provide as much constructive input as he can, and it was obvious that he impressed the other preachers with his knowledge and interpretations of the Bible. So much so, that they invited him to a follow-up conference to be held, here in San Francisco in May. CyrIS accepted the invitation but he didn't let them know of his new name or of his revelations. In fact, he was not sure exactly how to introduce any of this to anyone. But he looked forward to the beginning of his search for the *Spirit* and the *Light*.

CHAPTER 4 – LISTEN TO A GOOD MAN TALK

May 30th, 1970
Ester Suni Nati, age 18-Emotion

Ester sits on a sun deck atop the apartment building in which her older sister lives. The view of the San Francisco Bay Bridge, blue skies and bright sunshine not only warms Ester's coffee colored skin but her mind and soul as well.

This is what I've needed, Ester thinks.

Over the past few years, Ester's heart and soul have felt pretty empty, a void yearning for fulfillment, and right now, the warmth provided some relief as she takes-it all in with an open heart and an opened mind.

The shorts, and a tank top she is wearing allow her to enjoy the full measure of the sun's rays, as she sips iced tea with her sister Kwanita. The entire scene was making her feel much better, even the simple gesture of saying her sister's name seemed to add relief. Ester loved her sister's name, in Zuni, Kwanita meant Yahweh is merciful.

Ester's sister and older brother both received Zuni names. Her brother's name "Alia," meant "my God is Yahweh." Ester liked the Zuni names and their ties to the early forms of the bible. Unfortunately, Ester's mother picked out her, and her younger sister Sara's names. Although the names also came from the bible, to Ester's disappointment, they were not considered Zuni names.

Despite that small bother, --- on this day, Ester could not stop smiling as she embraces the moment. Now, at the age of eighteen, and just graduating from High School, her life was officially beginning.

This summer would be spent with her sister and her sister's roommate Patty here in San Francisco. It was the end of the 60's and much of the city was influenced by hippies and their free love movement. It was arguably the most happening place to be in the USA, and Ester was up for anything.

Suddenly, Kwanita's roommate Patty comes bounding on to the deck. Patty is all smiles, and her long black hair is gleaming in the sunlight. Patty's bell bottom blue jeans are patched with flowered decals, and her tightly fitting Rolling Stones tee shirt looks great on her shapely body. She moves swiftly across the deck, her eyes shifting quickly from right to left as she surveys the area, looking a bit concerned. A lit cigarette balances between her lips and remains in place as her voice booms out, "Hi, everybody,".

She offers the cigarette to Ester's sister, who immediately takes it, takes a long drag, tosses her head back and inhales the smoke. She then offers the cigarette to Ester, but Ester frowns with resistance.

"Aw, come on sis, everyone smokes out here."

Ester had never smoked marijuana, but she knew what it was, and she was not interested, and now understood Patty's looks of concern. But after a while, the semi-silent pressure of the other two girls overcame her. Ester agrees to take a puff, which she does but she does not inhale.

"Now your 'With-It'" Patty said.

Before that moment Ester was convinced that she was up for anything, but this was on another level. This "anything" edged on some pretty dangerous territory as far as Ester was concerned. After all, it was illegal.

"Hey," Patty said with a big smile. "Come with me tonight and listen to a good man talk?"

"Is that the new preacher you were telling me about?" Ester's sister said. Her tone serious and questioning.

"Yes, I heard he is really great," Patty said. "How about it, Sis?" Patty said, turning to Ester. "Can you be up for that?"

"Sure, why not?" Ester said without hesitation, while shrugging her shoulders and offering a huge smile, now passing the 'joint' back to her sister.

THAT EVENING THEY get all dressed up in Levi's, tie-dyed t-shirts and brightly colored ponchos. Kwanita gave Ester some wire-rimmed glasses to wear. Ester said, "I don't have any problem with my eyesight", but her sister responded "It doesn't matter the lenses are just plain glass. It's not about seeing, it's about being seen, and that requires capturing the right look."

"Yeah that's it," patty said smiling. "Now you're looking really cool."

When they arrive at the large auditorium on Geary Street, Ester observes the building.

"Is this a church?"

Patty looks up at the building, "No, it's just a hall they probably rented for the revival."

As they approached the steps leading up to the front of the building, they are greeted by several people who must have been members of the church. They are all dressed in brightly colored clothes and had flowers in their hands and hair, and embroidered flora and peace symbols were sewn into the fabric of their worn and faded blue jeans.

"Hi! My name is June," one of the girls said. "What's your name?"

June was walking directly up to Ester. Ester shyly introduces herself, as the girl hands her a brochure. Kwanita and Patty are being handed brochures as well from other young greeters. Noticing how Ester and the other two girls are dressed, June begins talking about her own artistic interest.

"I'm a dancer," June says. "What do you do?"

Ester could just barely get out an answer to one of June's questions before she is being asked something else. Each question became a little more personal as June pushed to get answers.

"Are you married? Have any kids?"

Ester tries to keep up, but she is starting to feel that this was no longer just friendly conversation, and thinks.

They seem to be getting bored with my responses.

Then they found out that Patty had recently broken up with her boyfriend. They started talking about their own marital woes and divorces. It seemed that the more information Patty gave them, the more questions they asked. Ester also notices that while some were asking questions, there were others off to the side that seemed to be taking notes. But even as this catches Ester's attention, she is still caught up in all of the attention that the greeters are giving her, and then suddenly, the barrage of questions stopped.

"The Temple is wonderful;" one of the greeters says, "It saved me, and in fact, it has saved many of us from the forces of Satan."

Ester listens without interruption as the greeter continues.

"I was really into drugs, and the Temple, but especially the Reverend, saved my life. If you are searching for answers, I guarantee you can find them here,"

Ester's curiosity increases, and as she enters the auditorium, her heart once again races with excitement.

Could this 'temple', as they call it, have some answers for me as well?

The auditorium is just a large open area with a flat carpeted floor, and hundreds of folding chairs. The chairs are all facing a raised stage, about 4 feet in height. On the stage is a podium and four chairs. The auditorium is packed with about a thousand people, mostly black, and mostly female, which makes Ester feel a bit more at ease. She is not prejudice but sometimes white people made her feel a bit uncomfortable. The auditorium has plenty of room for everyone but there are only enough chairs for about two thirds of the people, so there are many people standing in the back where the sunshine is shinning down on the floor from a few small windows high above the crowd.

They all look happy to be here and there certainly is a sense of excitement in the air.

The excitement lifts even higher as a handsome young man appears upon the stage. Ester hears a loud voice, coming from a speaker system.

"Please, help me welcome the Reverend *Jim Jones*."

He stands at the podium with a commanding presence. His long white flowing robe had an angelic appeal, and his features were like that of an actor's.

Ester is in the standing area to the back of the auditorium but she can see the reverend clearly. His dark aviator glasses give him an edgy look that Ester finds attractive. She especially likes his raven black hair that was combed back on the sides. Ester thought he looked a little bit like Elvis Presley, and she felt that the energy that pulsed through the crowd, must be like a rock concert. Ester loved it.

The Reverend's forceful voice rings out over the loudspeakers just as the crowd begins to quiet down. He extends his arm and index finger and sweeps it across the crowd.

"I am speaking directly to each and every one of you"

The very sound of his voice sends chills down Ester's spine. She had never heard anyone speak with such force, with such charisma. As he speaks of injustice in the world, of the injustice of racism, and the evils of the Vietnam War, his voice grows louder and louder and his gestures became grandiose.

The crowd would respond with wild cheers at the end of each of his pronouncements. Now he is strutting across the stage with a microphone in hand. His white robe clings to his body and flows behind him barely able to keep up. He exhibits no patience for the crowd as he speaks.

"Everyone here should share their worldly goods with everyone else."

This surprises Ester, because she agrees with this sentiment, and to hear a man of this stature make such a statement catches her off guard. Then Reverend went on and on about how socialism was the answer to the world's problems.

To Ester Socialism sounded a lot like Communism, and Ester remembered how her uncle Jason, her mother's brother, would sometimes go on and on about how the communist where going to start World War III. He also talked about how there were communist all over in society, and if they were not eliminated, they would bring an end to America. Ester wonders if this preacher was a communist and if this is what her uncle was talking about. But still, she had to admit to herself that she was moved by the words of this charismatic man.

The Reverend, still pacing back and forth on the stage, goes on to quote the bible, in a tyrant of words that spew from his mouth with rapid succession. Ester has a hard time keeping up, and she is amazed at his ability to take words and phrases from the bible, many of which she recognizes, and interpret them in a meaningful way. She absorbs every word, phrase, and inclination in his tone. His words are accented by physical movements of grand gestures that seemed to bring even more meaning to *everything* he is saying.

Is this the man I am looking for? Is this the prophet that can shed light on the mysteries and secrets of the bible?

"Break down the barriers," he cried. "Lose your ego and become selfless. Don't establish superficial relationships on the outside."

He would go on to preach of the importance of proper attitude. "If your mind is negative in attitude… it will produce disease, and likewise if it is positive, there is a great deal of information to indicate that one can almost obtain eternal youth. The cessation of cellular death…"

Ester thinks about how much this sounds like Dr. Peal's 'The power of positive thinking'. But then she wonders:

Is this man talking about eternal life or is he talking about eternal life after death?

In any case, his words touch Ester and as he talks, she could feel some of the long-term emptiness inside of her being filled. But just as fast as the emptiness eases away, something changes. Ester turns hot and her face transforms into a crimson hue. Her heartbeat increases, forcing an excess of blood to rush to all parts of her body. The reverend's words stun her. He was saying, "It's imperative to have free love friends," he said. "You should have sex with more than one person. We are all here to procreate and practice the ways of free love with all."

The crowd burst with excitement.

"Right on man!" One young fellow shouted

"Free Love, Free love!" others chimed in.

"Preach Brother Jim, preach" a woman screamed from the crowd.

All Ester could feel was the overwhelming sense of embarrassment.

How could he be saying these things in public?

But then the choir breaks into song and the entire room joins in, and Ester is once again enjoying this concert of the unconventional, and she feels good as she raises her arms to the heavens with the rest of the crowd.

"Ok choir," the Reverend directed. "Let's lower those angelic voices for a moment." The choir faded to silence and the reverend begins again, "I'm here to show you as a sample and example that you can bring yourself up with your own bootstraps." Shouts of encouragement explode from the crowd as he continues.

"My beloved friends, you can become your own God! Not in condescension but in resurrection and upliftment from whatever economic condition, injustice, racism, or servitude in which you have had to endure. Within you rest the keys of deliverance."

Inspiration touches Ester like never before. She agrees that God is *everywhere* including inside of her. She just needed someone who could help her find 'that God' and help her bring answers to all her burning questions.

The Reverend continues, "I am the God that came from earth of earth, this dust of the toils and fields, hardships of labor, from the lowest of economic positions, from the misery of poverty near the railroad tracks, I came to show you that the only God you need is within you…"

The crowd's collective voices once again rise up and drown out the preacher's words. As he begins to speak again, Ester could detect a change in the tone of his voice.

"Friends, that's my purpose of being here. When that transition comes….and trust me loved ones, it is coming. There shall be no need for Gods or any other kind of ideology. Religion, the opiate of the people, shall be removed from the consciousness of mankind. There shall no longer be any need for anything religious when freedom comes." His voice now rising even further. "I came in the power of God in religion…All the power you said God had, I have. I come to make one final dissolution: one final elimination of all religious feeling. Until I have eradicated it from the face of the earth. I will do all the miracles you said your God would do and never did." He begins to speak even more quickly as if the message was urgent and needed to be said at that very moment. "I shall heal you of all the diseases that you prayed for, that never happened." The crowd responds wildly but Ester is no longer stretching her arms to the heavens.

What is this man saying? Is he saying that he is God or is he saying that there is no God? Is he saying that all other religions are wrong and that he is the only answer? All these thoughts roll over in Ester's mind as she looks on in silence.

She then hears the reverend's voice again, but now he is calling out people's names and they are proceeding to the stage. People of varied ethnicities and color, male and female, some limping and some in wheelchairs, all make their way to him.

"Praise the lord" "Praise God" They are saying, but most are calling out the reverends name.

"Praise the Reverend, Praise the Reverend Jones"

The reverend closes his eyes and lays his hands on the people as they approach. Many of them fall to the floor as he touches them. Some go into convulsions as others rise up out of their wheelchairs or throw away their crutches. *Emotions* are running wild.

How is he doing this?

As the people approached, often the reverend would begin talking about them before they reached him, apparently revealing facts about their lives that he could not possibly know. Ester could see the shock and awe on their faces as he reveals the most intimate details about their lives, including details about their sex lives, their children, and their thoughts of suicide.

But then Ester recalls the people taking notes at the front of the auditorium.

Now this is making some sense.

The procession goes on for hours. But then a sudden movement erupts in the crowd near Ester. People are rushing and pushing each other and pushing against Ester. They are trying to make room for something that is happening just a short distance away.

One-man shouts from the chaotic crowd. "Call for an ambulance!"

Ester could then see an elderly black lady on the floor. She appears to be unconscious. A man is leaning over her and yelling at the top of his voice.

"SHE HAS NO PULSE. WE NEED AN AMBULANCE RIGHT NOW!"

Then, like a theater curtain opening, the crowd parts and there stands the Reverend Jim Jones. He was not even five feet away from Ester. He looks angelic with his long white robe dazzling in the sunlight beaming down from the windows above. He motioned with his hand before speaking in a soft voice. "Please step aside."

He kneels down next to the lady and places his hands on the woman's forehead. Her eyes open and she looks directly at the Reverend. He then leans forward and whispers something in her ear. She instantly stands up. The crowd goes wild, shouting and proclaiming that the reverend has raised the dead. Ester questions her own eyes.

Did this man just raise someone from the dead?

Her emotions are mixed and she is moved at the same time. After a few minutes, the woman is helped away and the Reverend proceeds back towards the stage. As he does so, he walks in Ester's direction. He is touching people and giving them his blessings. Before Ester knows it, the reverend is placing his hand on Ester's forehead.

"Bless you child, may you be filled with the *Holy Spirit.*"

Ester immediately feels something. She becomes blind to everything around her and falls to her knees. Her mind hurls downward into a chasm so dark that it terrifies her.

What is happening? Where am I?

Ester now feels evil things tugging at her soul, beckoning her to join with some evil force that had control of her. Ester is fighting but loosing, she could feel the energy being sucked from her body.

But wait, what is that?

Ester feels a touch, someone has taken her hand, and she can feel herself rising up and her accompanying *emotions* rising up in unison. She is being saved.

****

IN ANOTHER PART OF THE CITY:

At the follow-up meeting of the *Conference of Churches* that morning, CyrIS had still not introduced his new name to anyone.

I'll just wait for the right time, maybe I'll receive a sign or something.

Along with CyrIS' name change, he was also working on a change, not only to the subject of his sermons, but also in his style in delivering those sermons. He mentioned that he was looking for a new delivery style at the Conference of Churches meeting, and after the meeting one of the ministers invited him to attend a revival with him.

"I've heard that this preacher." The minister began, "the Reverend Jim Jones, has quite the impressive delivery. Would you be interested in going with me to see him this afternoon?"

The minister indicated that this Jones, was a very charismatic speaker, maybe they could learn something from his style. CyrIS eagerly accepted the invitation.

Entering the auditorium where Jim Jones would be speaking, CyrIS is impressed by the number of people and excitement in the crowd, which rises exponentially as the Reverend Jim Jones arrives on the stage.

CyrIS cannot believe the energy that is exhibited. An energy that not only comes from the Reverend, but form the crowd as well, and CyrIS is impressed by the production and power of the Reverend's performance.

"I could really learn something from this guy." CyrIS thinks.

However, as the Reverend begins to preach, CyrIS becomes less and less impressed.

"This man is insane; he is preaching that he is 'God', and that these people should only follow his lead. Don't they hear what he is saying? It is like they are caught in some kind of spell, all *emotion*, no *logic*. Maybe, they can only hear what they want to hear."

With a look of disgust on his face, and arms crossed, CyrIS watches the Reverend's stage performance of healing the sick and maimed.

"This is a bunch of bullshit. Where does this guy get the nerve?" Just as CyrIS is thinking this, there is a commotion off to his left. CyrIS looks through the crowd and could see a black lady on the auditorium floor. A man is leaning over her and calling for an ambulance.

Out of nowhere, there is the Reverend Jim Jones. He walks directly up to the lady on the floor, kneels down beside her and whispers something. She immediately sits up and then stands up.

"Was this a miracle? I think not! This is just more bullshit. What a show this guy is putting on. The white robe, the grandiose speeches and gestures, and now the coup de grass. He is raising someone from the dead. Not my style, I've got to get out of here. "

As CyrIS watches the Reverend walk away touching people and giving his blessing, he could see that people were obviously reacting to this man. They are responding not only to his words but especially to his touch.

Some are falling on the floor and some are yelling out the Reverend's name. CyrIS wonders how many of these people were truly affected and how much of this was just for show.

Then CyrIS sees something that looks much different than all the rest he was observing. As the Reverend walks through the crowd and touches people, there is a tremendous amount of drama, with some falling and some crying out. The Reverend himself seems unaffected by all of this going on around him. He just moves forward as if on a walk in the park.

However, when he touches the forehead of one young lady, she immediately slumps to her knees. CyrIS notices this incident because of two things that occurred. The first thing that he notices is the difference in her reaction. It had seemed that when the Reverend touched other people there was a dramatic reaction, some even went into some kind of minor convulsions or yelled something out. However, when this young lady is touched, there is none of that. She just slumps to the floor and seems to become unconscious.

The second thing that CyrIS notices is the Reverends' reaction. Though he had not reacted to anyone else, when he touches this young lady, he immediately recoils and moves away from her. Though he did not stop moving, he looks back at her for an extended moment before turning his head back toward the stage.

CyrIS finds this all to be very peculiar, even in these strange circumstances. Now all the people that had been touched by the Reverend had gotten up, and the rest of the crowd is now moving closer to the stage. Nobody is paying any attention to the beautiful woman slumped on the floor.

As CyrIS approaches her, she is still on her knees. Her arms are at her sides, her head is slumped over, and he can see that she is Native American, and she is gorgeous. CyrIS kneels by her side and reaches out to take her hand.

****

ESTER FEELS THAT SHE IS SAVED, the demons recede, her energy is returning, the darkness falls away, and she opens her eyes. At first, she expects to see the Reverend. The last memory was his hand touching her forehead. But now, as she looks up, she is staring into the steely deep blue eyes of a very handsome man, not the Reverend.

"Are you all right?" he asks.

The words roll off his lips so smoothly that Ester could not take her eyes off his mouth. Then, a bit dazed, she begins to cry as she manages to reply.

"You have no idea, what you just did for me!" she says. "Thank you. You're my handsome hero." The words came out before Ester could retract them. Her inner monologue barrier fails to function. She immediately turned scarlet red, now a bundle of *emotions*.

"Where is my sister and Patty," Ester thinks, "what just happened to me? What am I supposed to do now? Maybe I should stand up."

As CyrIS helps Ester to her feet, she now feels that there was some kind of *connection*. Not necessarily between her and the hero holding her hand, but rather a very *dark connection* between her and the Reverend. Ester has an overwhelming feeling that, unfortunately, this connection would somehow bring them together again, sometime in the future.

Upon entering the auditorium, she had been so full of hope, and those hopes rose and rose, as she listened to a man with so much charisma. Now, she once again has more questions than answers. She was once again, stuck in the middle. The *middle* provides no answers and no direction. Now she has an even greater need to find a profit, someone who was truly *connected* to God, *connected* to that other world. Maybe it was the *Holy Spirit* itself she was looking for. Maybe it was this handsome man holding her hand.

CHAPTER 5 – THE LOGIC AND EMOTION OF MAN

July 1st, 1978
CyrIS Steel, age 28, - Logic
Ester Suni Nate, age 26-Emotion

CyrIS sits in a large comfortable chair in the University of Berkley's Student Union, reading a letter from his dear friend Ester. It's mid-day and sunshine is pouring through the large windows framed with long draping curtains, to his right. There are a few students sitting at tables and standing at various locations in the room, and the soft buzz of their conversations can be heard above the slight sound of the large fans that turned slowly above their heads.

Although eight years has passed since CyrIS first met Ester at the Jim Jones Revival, and the fact that they have been apart most of that time, their friendship has continued to grow.

Ester who now has a PhD in philosophy and parapsychology was just completing a nationwide lecture series on Shamanism and psychic phenomena. CyrIS was still preaching at Billy's church, which Billy had left to him after his passing just one year ago, and which was now called "The church of the Infinite Spirit", just as CyrIS had been instructed by the *church wall scroll.*

CyrIS had completed his degree in Divinity, from the Theological Union per Billy's instructions, but he had also managed to follow through on his own desires to get a degree in mathematics and was presently pursuing a master's degree in physics at the University of Berkley.

Now sitting in the brightly lit Student Union, CyrIS thinks about how his education was now impacting his sermons. Ever since finding that parchment in the wall of Billy's old church, CyrIS has drifted further and further away from traditional religion, and was now forming what he believed, was a much more *logical* approach to spiritualism. While he continually searches for clues hidden in traditional spiritual literature, the nature of his sermons had dramatically changed. Now he was offering more and more science guided sermons. In fact, his sermons are now more like lectures than sermons., and along with that change, came a change in the membership of his church. The new membership is more sophisticated. These attendees desire a spiritual component in their life but want that component to make sense. In fact, they are the type of people who want *everything* in their lives to make sense.

CyrIS, by way of his letters to Ester, had told her in general about the gradual change in the direction of his sermons, but had not actually shown her any of the sermons, and though she had been very supportive of his ideas, he was not sure if she was totally on board, but he planned on reading some of his sermons to her soon, so he could see her reaction.

Ester's letter indicated that she had been granted a contract, to teach a one-semester course called "Psychology and Parapsychology in today's society" at the University of Berkeley where CyrIS was currently attending. She would be living in San Francisco for the fall of this year. The letter indicated that she was looking forward to seeing him, and CyrIS was definitely looking forward to seeing her.

There was a lot that they had in common, but in a lot of ways they were complete opposites. She had a highly *emotional* center and he had a *logical* approach to almost everything.

He thought that together, they were like the Chinese symbol of "Yin and Yang." Ester with her emphasis in the *emotional* spiritual world, but with a trailing interest in the sciences, and he, now with his emphasis more in the *logical* realms of science, still had, to a lesser degree, an interest in the world of spiritualism.

Their discussions were like a well-orchestrated dance. There was counterpoint to counterpoint but supporting one another when the need would arise.

CyrIS could hardly wait to show her some of his latest discoveries. He not only wanted to share some of the things he had been preaching to his new congregation, but also some of his newest evolving concepts. He wanted to discuss with her the correlations of those concepts with passages from the scriptures.

CyrIS was sure Ester would have thoughts on, and possible disagreements with, some or all his evolving theories. That is one of the many reasons why he loved her.

Suddenly, CyrIS hears a voice. It was coming from behind and above. It was Ester's voice, and CyrIS did not move.

"And in the days of thy father *light*, understanding and wisdom, like the wisdom of the gods was found in him; Daniel 5:11"

CyrIS stands up, turns, and looks at Ester's smiling face. Even in the stark sunlit room of the cafeteria, she looks stunning. Her tight blue jeans, cowboy boots, and a western shirt give her an alluring but casual appearance. Her long black hair glistens in the natural light as it cascades down on her shoulders. CyrIS steps around the chair he had been sitting in, as Ester moves toward him. Looking up at, and into his eyes, reaches up and pulls his head towards her face and with her dark brown eyes weeping just slightly, gives CyrIS a light kiss on his lips.

"Well hot shot, have you figured out the universe?" Ester's face now just inches from that of CyrIS'.

"No," he laughs. "But I'm giving it hell."

They move apart and CyrIS continues.

"Boy. I'm so glad you're here, there is so much I want to discuss with you."

Ester's eyes smile. "Yes, there's a lot I want to discuss with you as well."

"Are you hungry?" asked CyrIS.

"No" she replies. "Once I had moved into my new digs, I grabbed a bite. Hoping maybe, you would take me to dinner this evening"

"Sure thing, but what do you want to do right now?" CyrIS hoping she wanted to talk for a while.

Ester fulfilling CyrIS's hopes says, "Is there someplace we could go and talk, that is not quite so crowded?" Ester gestures to the room, indicating she did not want to talk in the busy part of the Student Union. As she speaks and moves her arm, the light green turquoise jewels of her bracelet and her dark brown eyes, sparkle in the light. CyrIS is distracted while thinking.

Wow! She certainly is gorgeous.

"This room is certainly not conducive to quiet conversation," he says. "Let's go into the teacher's lounge. It's quiet, and we won't be disturbed there." CyrIS is now staring directly into Ester's eyes as he speaks.

As they walk towards the teacher's lounge, Ester surprisingly take CyrIS' hand and says. "I'm sure glad to be here with you CyrIS, it's been much…much too long." CyrIS could feel his heartbeat intensify slightly.

Upon entering the teacher's lounge, they sit close together on a couch in the back of the room.

"Where should we start?" CyrIS begins.

Ester eyes sparkle. "I have a present for you."

"What? Really!?"

"It's not much, but I think you'll like it."

"Do you remember the gold bracelet that my father gave me." Ester exposes the small bracelet on her wrist, with the triangle and horizontal line through it.

Ester pulls a small box from the fringed leather purse she had hanging from her shoulder and opens it up. "Well, I know your middle name is 'Kaj-El', which means 'Earth of God', so I had a bracelet made up just like mine, only with the Alchemist symbol for 'Earth'. It is an inverted triangle with a horizontal line through it."

"You see it is the inverse of the symbol for 'Air' which is *my* middle name."

CyrIS stares at the gift. "Opposites, but the same. Who knew? Thank you very much. I love it."

CyrIS wasn't looking at the bracelet now, he was looking at Ester. Ester wipes a tear from her eye and then continues.

"In your letters, you said you were changing the approach that you were taking with your church, primarily based on the concepts from the scroll you found. Tell me about that."

CyrIS glances down at his new bracelet and then back at Ester. He had previously shared the contents of the scroll with Ester in their regular correspondence, and was glad that she remembered, and then began to explain,

"Well I know that scroll changed my life. But I don't know what it all means, at least not yet, but what I do know, is that it is telling me something important. My roots are based in religion. Not because I am a strong believer, but it is the core of my education. It was what brought me to this point in my life and maybe, more importantly, it is what has brought us together. I had thought as many do, that religion, basically the bible, is where the answers lie, and I only looked to science to support what the bible was preaching."

Ester leans forward and is fully engaged.

"After finding the scroll, I now think that the real answers lie within the *logic* of science, and I look to the Bible and other religious and spiritual sources to support that fact. You see, I believe, that mankind, the human race, has in some way always known what science is just now revealing."

"This is fascinating," Esther says, as CyrIS continues.

"Well, the Bible, along with many other forms of spiritual and psychological studies has been hinting at a secret for centuries. You know, it's just as I have always thought, all a big puzzle to be solved. All of these spiritual and psychological documents, along with 'The Power of Positive Thinking', provide glimpses, but no answers."

"So, your solution is?" Ester questioned.

"My 'Church of the Infinite Spirit'" CyrIS continued, "is dedicated to showing these relationships to whoever will listen. I am attempting to use the revelations of recent science, to shine a *light* on those secrets buried in these ancient documents and theories. I believe that many people see the truth within these spiritual documents and therefore do not want to outright dismiss them and neither do I. That is the basis for my sermons."

"Did I lose you?" CyrIS frowned.

"No-no!" she said. "Just trying to digest what you're saying. I'm still in the camp that believes that the answers are in the spiritual literature. I believe in the Bible and in the teachings of the ancient Shamans. I have always believed that someday science would validate all that I believe. So, I'm fascinated in what you are saying, to say the least."

"Ok that is good to hear," CyrIS said. "You had me nervous there for a second."

"Well," CyrIS continued, scratching his head and smiling, "As I said earlier, I don't have it all figured out yet, so I'm trying to bring my congregation along slowly, trying to educate them on the historical relationships between science and religion, and positive thinking, while at the same time educating myself, hoping that I will have it all figured out in the end. But I'm going to need your help."

Ester's brown eyes squinted. "You know I want to help, but I know there is more to this story. What exactly are you preaching?"

"If you want, I will read to you the first sermon I gave after reading the church wall parchment?"

"Sure, I would love that." Ester exclaimed.

CyrIS pulls some papers out of his briefcase. "First you must understand that I have always thought that the 'Holy Spirit' was a very puzzling concept. You know…the 'Third person of the Trinity' is a puzzle itself, but the document I found places a lot of emphasis on 'Allowing the *Spirit* to show me the Light' and instructing me to call my church '*The Church of the Infinite Spirit*'."

Ester nods her head. "I agree, I have been wondering about the 'Holy Spirit' since I was a little girl."

With this comment CyrIS moves in a bit closer to Ester, as he continues, "You see I feel that the 'Spirit' is a key to unraveling all of these puzzles. I decided to use the 'Spirit', the 'Infinite Spirit', as a surrogate for my guide. I was also introducing my new name and the church's new name for the first time. So here we go."

CyrIS clears his throat before reading.

"Good morning children of the Holy Spirit.
I have recently made an amazing discovery. This discovery is not in itself the answer, but it provides clues to a pathway to answers. A map so to speak. This document, a scroll, that I have discovered, and which I will reveal to you over time, has instructed me to take a new name, and to give this church a new name as well."

"I am from this day forward to be known as the reverend CyrIS Steel."

"You see, the scientific community along with those believers in Spiritualism, Psychology, the Paranormal, Extrasensory Perception, and Shamanism may all be traveling down a road leading to the same place. That place is the realm of the Infinite Spirit; and it is a place that exists everywhere and in every person."

CyrIS pauses to see if Ester is still with him. She had not taken her eyes off him and her concentration is intense and unwavering. He waits a moment to see if she wanted to say anything, but she remains quiet and CyrIS continues to read his sermon.

"Let's begin with some history. You may not realize it, but there was a time when science and religion were unified. That's right; --- between the years 384-322 BC, a Greek philosopher named Aristotle was studying the movement of the sun and the stars as they moved around the earth. It was only *logical* that the earth was the center of the universe and so he declared that the earth was at rest, not moving, and that everything else in the universe revolved around the earth. He also declared that all measurements of distance, and time were the same everywhere."

"That is, a mile measured in one location on earth or anywhere in the universe would be the same distance measured anywhere else on earth, or anywhere else in the universe. He also declared that an hour measured anywhere in the universe, would be the same as an hour measured anywhere else in the universe. This seemed very *logical*, natural and correct to all those living at that time. It was also consistent with the bible which indicated that God created the heaven and the earth and as such why wouldn't the earth be the center of everything."

"For almost two thousand years these concepts held up, and they were the basic foundation for all scientific study. And because nothing in science conflicted with the Bible there was harmony between science and religion."

Ester smiles and nods slightly while listening intently, as CyrIS continues.

"That is until two men came along: Nicholas Copernicus (1473-1543) and Galileo Galilei (1564-1642). For when they observed the sun and the stars, it appeared to them that the movement of the sun and stars would make more sense, that is, it would be more *logical,* if the earth was moving around the sun.

So, they announced that the earth was not the center of the universe."

"As you can imagine this caused a huge stir in the scientific community at that time. It created an even bigger stir in the religious community, to say the least. How could anyone say that the earth is not the center of the universe? It was obvious to any casual observer, it was written in the bible, and it is sacrilegious to denounce the bible. From that point forward, it seems as though, religion and science have been at odds with each other. And more precisely in more recent years have just ignored each other."

"We have all heard of Albert Einstein. He along with many other modern-day physicists have made a number of incredible discoveries over the last century. Because of the dichotomy between science and religion, these scientific discoveries have been mostly ignored by religious leaders, and even though scientists have run into questions that seem to be beyond comprehension, they would never consider looking to the bible or to spiritualism or psychology for answers. Well, I am here to tell you that those days are coming to an end."

"The document that I have discovered states that mankind will be allowed to uncover the secrets of the mysteries, which have, for centuries, separated religion, science, spiritualism and even psychology."

"One thing that you will hear me refer to often, during these sessions, is the importance of the '*middle*'. That is the gray area between all things. The document indicates, and I believe, that it is within the seams between black and white, right and wrong, science and religion, which is the dominion of the Infinite Spirit. As you can see from what I am preaching today, the answers to our search to solve the mystery of the Infinite Spirit, lies not solely within religious study or the study of science or spiritualism or psychology. It lies somewhere in the "middle" of all these things. A person must study each of these areas. The pieces of the puzzle are not found in one box, we must search each box to find just the right pieces that will build the whole picture. I will reveal to you those pieces as I discover them. You may discover pieces on your own. It will be a journey of discovery that we will take together."

Ester once again smiles and slightly nods her head in agreement.

CyrIS continues "The Bible says: 'At that time Jesus, full of joy through the *Holy Spirit*, said, 'I praise you, Father, Lord of heaven and earth, because you have *hidden* these things from the wise and learned, and revealed them to little children. Yes, Father, for this is what you were pleased to do' Luke 10:21."

Then Ester asked, "So how was the congregation reacting at this point?"

CyrIS twist his lips and touches his chin with a look of perplexation.

"Well Ester, it was at this point that I noticed some of my congregation was getting up and leaving. It was obvious that not all of them agreed with this new direction, that I was taking the church. One man that was walking away, a man I had never seen before, turned back and looked at me with such a look of anger, and with his eyebrows bunched, his nostrils flaring, his lips snarled, and his teeth exposed, he yelled at me at the top of his voice. 'I had heard that you were preaching some crap about science as the answer, and it's true. What you are preaching is pure blasphemy. You, people', he said while pointing at the crowd now looking in his direction. 'Need to get out of here. This man is crossing a line that is very dangerous, and there will be consequences. I GUARANTEE IT! There are forces in this world that are dedicated to the elimination of this kind of degradation of true religious belief.'"

By this time Ester had put her hand over her mouth with a look of horror in her eyes and said, "I cannot even imagine being in that situation. How completely awkward. I mean, what was going through your mind?"

'To be honest...one word.... 'Envy'."

Esther tilts her head. "Envy?"

"Yes," CyrIS said. "Envy. I was envious of him because I wish I would have had the integrity and guts to give a similar speech to Jim Jones that day, so many years ago."

"Anyway, now the man was pointing directly at me, and he says, 'Preacher, I am one of many, and YOU WILL feel the wrath of the lord!' The man then turned and marched out of the church."

"I had no idea you dealt with all of that after we met," Esther said.

CyrIS with a perplexed look responds "I was at a loss as how to even respond to the whole demonstration, but after that no one else left. I apologized for the interruption and continued with my sermon."

CyrIS lets out a soft sigh and continues reading his sermon, "So now let's begin at the beginning: Genesis 1:1 'In the beginning, God created the heaven and the Earth'"

"The Bible indicates that before God created the universe there was nothing. The Big Bang principle advocates the same theory, which is, that before the Big Bang there was nothing. The Bible states: 'By faith, we understand that the universe was formed at God's command so that what is seen was not made out of what was visible. Hebrews 11:3"

"Now let me quote from the document that I have been referencing: *My son it is your burden to lay open the fruit of the mystery for those chosen to see. And you will find that the Spirit is the light, the Spirit is the guide, the Spirit is the method, and the Spirit is the answer. The answer shall be the foundation of the new church you shall build.*"

"I remind you now of Genesis 1:3 'And God said, *let there be light, and there was light'.*"

"It would appear that the first thing that God created was '*Light*' and it was created even before the sun and the stars, which occurred in Genesis 1:16-18."

"The document states that the '*Spirit is the light*' and I believe that God did not create '*Light*', that instead God is '*Light*', and that science will show that '*Light*' is not only there to reveal to us the mysteries of the *Infinite Spirit*, but it is in fact, an essential part of the *Holy Spirit*, and may, in fact, be the Supreme Being."

"And John the Baptist says of Jesus: 'In him was life, and that life was the *light* of all mankind. The *light* shines in the darkness, and the darkness has not overcome it.' John 1:4-5."

"Thus far we have explored some of the basic concepts that I will be researching in science and religion. One of those main concepts is that the Supreme Being, God, and Light are one and the same and that God and the Holy Spirit, the Infinite Spirit, are 'separate and one' at the same time."

"There is another area, which I will also be delving into in great detail. Let me once again quote from the document that was revealed to me."

"My son as the science of man is born of the logic of man, and as the religion of man is born of the emotion of man. Then you should know that logic and emotion are threads in the fabric of the mystery. Search within that fabric."

"Obviously '*Logic and Emotion*' will be areas of interest. But right now, I would like to concentrate on the concept of 'Fabric', the scriptures say: 'The Lord wraps himself in the *light* as with a garment; he stretches out the heavens like a tent.' Psalms 104:2."

"I believe that that the '*light*' and '*fabric*' referred to in this passage are the *Infinite Spirit* and that science will eventually bear this out."

"Albert Einstein along with many other physicists use the term 'The Fabric of Space' when referring to the 'Space-Time' continuum, which are theories of how space and time are tied together to allow for all forces in the universe. We will be getting into this much more, in our journey for knowledge and understanding, as we move along the road in search of the *Infinite Spirit*. But the point I am making is that there is a fabric in the universe and that I believe that fabric is made up of '*light*' which is God and the Infinite Spirit."

"Sir Isaac Newton surmised that outer space was empty, it was a vacuum. He also surmised that since *light* bounces off things, like mirrors, then *light* must be made of particles and as a particle, it could travel through the vacuum of space."

"A young man named Thomas Young found that *light* moved in waves. This was later confirmed by James Clark Maxwell. Mister Maxwell developed an equation which revealed that the speed of *light* was 678 million miles per hour or 186,282 miles per second. Albert Einstein later declared that nothing could travel faster than the speed of *light*."

"So, let's talk about waves. As you may know, waves travel through a medium, such as water. But first let me give you an even simpler example, which I think you will understand. The example is a wave moving along a rope. I am sure that all of you at one time or another have held the end of a rope, and then whipped it up and down sending waves from your hand to the end of the rope. It is easy to see in this example that no part of the rope, moves toward the end of the rope, only the wave travels that distance."

"Now let's consider waves in water. Waves of water can travel at a certain speed, for example, 20 miles per hour. The water does not actually move at that speed, but the wave moves through the water at that speed. One can observe this, if you are sitting in a boat, you can watch the waves move past the boat, but the boat itself does not move, because the water is not moving.

You have probably also observed, when riding in a boat, that if you move into the waves, the waves appear to be moving past the boat at a greater speed relative to the boat, and if your boat is moving in the same direction as the waves the waves appear to be moving slower relative to the boat."

"Well, scientists were also aware of how waves acted and surmised that if '*light*' is a wave and it travels through outer space, then Newton must be wrong. There must be something in outer space for the wave to travel through, and they called it "aether", pronounced just like the gas they give you in the hospital to make you go to sleep."

"So, two scientists named Albert Michelson and Edward Morley decided to run a test to see if 'aether' actually existed.

They concluded that if they moved toward the sun, the speed of the waves of *light* coming towards them would speed up, just as the waves of water did relative to the boat moving into the waves. They surmised that if they moved away from the *light* of the sun then the speed of the waves would slow down. But what they found was that no matter what direction they moved relative to the source of *light*, the speed of the *light* always stayed the same, at 186,282 miles per second."

"Albert Einstein said they could not find anything in space, because there was nothing there to find. He also said the reason you can find no difference in the speed of *light*, is because it is the one thing in the universe that never changes, it is the one constant in the universe."

"The scriptures say: 'Every good gift and every perfect gift is from above, and cometh down from the Father of *lights*, with whom is no variableness, neither shadow of turning'. John 1:17."

"I repeat 'no Variableness'."

"As you know, without *light* you cannot see, and without *light* from the Sun, there would be no life on Earth. But I would like to leave you with one more scientific fact before we conclude today. And that is, that you probably know that all matter is made up of atoms. Did you know that the only way different materials, that is, different types of atoms can form is through the re-arrangement of protons, neutrons, and electrons? And did you know that for these changes to occur the electrons must change orbits relative to the nucleus of the atom? This movement can only occur through the release or absorption of photons. Photons are *light*. What this means is that nothing, no material in the universe can exist without "*Light*". Albert Einstein said that "*Light*" was the one universal constant, and that it was the fundamental building block, on which the universe was built."

"Let me once again quote the bible: 'Then spake Jesus again unto them, saying, 'I am the *light* of the world: he that followeth me shall not walk in darkness, but shall have the *light* of life.' John 8:12."

"And now, I say to you, go in peace and, may the *light* that is all around you, guide you in your daily actions, and may you be comforted by the warmth provided in the all-encompassing fabric of the Infinite Spirit."

CyrIS pauses for a moment.

"Well Ester, that's it, and as the document instructed, I have named the new church 'Church of the Infinite Spirit' and now along with my church, I have also created a website, Fact-Faith.com where my followers can go any time and see videos of my sermons. They can also, send me documents that support the path we are on, or ask me for interpretations of the Bible, and other religious, philosophical and scientific writings. So, what do you think?"

Ester, still trying to process it all, says "I think it's wonderful. But, CyrIS do you really think God has spoken to you?"

CyrIS tilts his head back and looks at the ceiling. "No. I think I have been desperately searching for something and I have found a piece of parchment that has opened a door for me. It has opened my eyes and inspired me to pursue a concept, and I hope I can get you to go with me."

Ester does not hesitate. "CyrIS, you know that I have also been searching for something, and I believe that this could be it. It feels right and I cannot think of any other person I would want to go on this journey with. But there is something else."

"Yes?" CyrIS says questionably, as a concerned look envelops his face.

"Remember the day we met at Reverend Jim Jones' revival."

"Sure, how could I forget? It's when I met you and like I mentioned, I felt guilty for years for not speaking up that day."

"Well that day, something happened to me. I believe it has something to do with everything you have been talking about. I know that you are excited about all of this and that you see all of this as positive for you and your followers, but I tell you there are other forces at bay here."

80 | P a g e

"That day, when the reverend touched me, I fell into an abyss, and there were evil things in that abyss. At that time I thought they were demons from hell, but as I reflect on what happened to me, I have realized that the forces I felt that day, were of a human form, they exist not in the dominions of hell, but right here on earth."

"I believe the *dark* forces that I felt were coming from people, groups of people. I believe, those people are afraid of you and afraid that the path you and others, are pursuing will reveal some deep secret that they do not want revealed. CyrIS, this journey will not be without its perils."

"Ok you're making me nervous now." CyrIS says.

"You should be cautious CyrIS. That man that yelled out in your church scares me. I don't think those were idle threats."

CyrIS looking concerned responded, "I don't really think about it too much Ester. I feel that if I am in the right place, I will be protected, because I am in the 'right place'."

"I hope so." Ester continues, "But there is something else, I still feel some kind of link to the Reverend Jones, and I feel that I'm not done with him and somehow my journey of learning will result in crossing paths with him again." Ester pauses as she chokes back tears and her voice cracks with nervousness. "CyrIS, I am very afraid of that crossing. I hope that you will be with me and help me when that happens."

CyrIS moves closer to her and places his arms around her shoulders. "I will be by your side, I promise. Don't worry Ester, I'm not afraid."

"Could you come to my sermon tomorrow? I value your opinion so much and I have something else I want to show you."

Ester smiles, "Of course I can come tomorrow, but can you show me now?"

"I could …" CyrIS smiles. "But not today, let's go to dinner, and let's have a drink. How about we 'not think' about this stuff anymore and just talk about each other?"

CHAPTER 6 – GOD'S FABRIC

July 2nd, 1978
CyrIS Steel, age 28,
Ester Suni Nate, age 26

The light pours through the stain glass windows of the Church of the *Infinite Spirit*. It illuminates the room with a soft sustaining glow which fills the entire space and warms everyone in it. CyrIS steps into this radiance as he addresses his congregation.

"Today I will make all of you, as smart as Albert Einstein." He pauses to allow the statement to sink in, but sees looks of doubt and a slight murmur emits from the attendees as they turn and look at each other.

"The only math you will need to know is that 'Speed' equals distance traveled, divided by the time it takes to travel that distance. So, if you travel sixty miles in one hour, your speed is sixty miles per hour. Simple right?"

"I will also be showing you how the bible teaches us that the *Holy Spirit*, the *Infinite Spirit*, is *Light*, and God is *Light*, and that God and the *Holy Spirit* are one."

"So now…to make you as smart as Einstein."

"Some of you may remember from one of my previous sermons, that I told you that by way of a tremendous amount of measurements over the last seventy years, it has been proven over and over that the speed of light never changes. It always appears to everyone, to be moving at the same speed, and that speed is, 186,282 miles per second. This is true, no matter where you are, or what speed you are moving."

"Albert Einstein said that light was the one constant in the universe. In fact, if you are familiar with Einstein's famous equation $E=mc^2$ you may know that it stands for Energy equals Mass times the speed of *Light* Squared."

"Well, you may ask, why did Einstein use the letter 'c' to represent the speed of light. Well 'c' stands for the word *constant*, yes that's right, he did not put down 's' for 'speed' or 'v' for 'velocity' he put in a 'c', because it was his belief that the speed of light was the one and only true constant in the universe."

"And what does the bible tell us is the one true constant in the universe; --- well of course, it's *'God'*. We will be delving into that much more a bit later."

"Einstein used what he called 'thought experiments' to understand how the universe worked. In other words, he used his imagination."

"Albert Einstein once said: 'Imagination is more important than knowledge. Knowledge is limited. Imagination encircles the world'"

"The Bible says: 'Nothing will be restrained from them, which they have imagined to do' Genesis 11:6"

"After many of these thought experiments Einstein came to the conclusion that observers that are in motion relative to each other, experience time differently."

"He said: 'It's perfectly possible for two events to happen simultaneously, from the perspective of one observer, yet happen at different times from the perspective of the other observer, and both observers would be right.' And Einstein illustrated this point with a thought experiment."

"Imagine that you have an observer standing on a train station platform, as a train goes by. Each end of the train is struck by a bolt of lightning just as the train's midpoint is passing the observer on the platform. Because the lightning strikes are the same distance from the observer, the light reaches his eyes at the same instant. So, he correctly says that they happened simultaneously."

"Meanwhile, another observer on the train itself, is sitting at the exact midpoint of the train. From his perspective, the light from the two strikes also must travel equal distances. But because the train is moving, the light coming from the lightning in the rear of the train must travel farther to catch up, so it reaches his eyes a few instants later than the light coming from the front of the train. Since the light pulses arrived at different times, he can only conclude the strikes were *not* simultaneous. The one in front actually happened first."

"This thought experiment along with several others brought Einstein to an amazing conclusion. He realized that if the speed of light was constant no matter if you are stationary or moving, and that all other components are variable including 'time', then all the strange things associated with relativity made sense."

CyrIS once again paused, allowing what he had just said to sink into the brains of his audience, wondering as he waited if he should repeat it or just move on. Deciding on the later, he moves on.

"So now, on with making you as smart as Einstein; so if two observers are observing the same event and the speed of light is the same, that is, it is constant for both observers, but the perceived distance travelled to a target is different for each observer. Then what other part of the velocity equation, ('distance' equals 'the speed of light' multiplied by 'time' ($d=ct$)), needs to vary to keep this equation correct?"

CyrIS now waiting for a response from his audience says, "I know this seems complicated, but actually it's not, and I know you can figure it out."

The audience is silent for a couple of minutes, and CyrIS thinks this is probably because they were not expecting to be asked a question. Then several hands go up. CyrIS points to a pretty young girl in the front row.

"Reverend," she said. "Is it 'time' that needs to vary?"

"Congratulations! You are as smart as Albert Einstein," CyrIS winked at the young girl and continues. "Just looking at the equation makes it simple; If 'c' which stands for the speed of light cannot change and you change the value of 'd' distance, then the value of 't' must change to keep the two sides of the equation in balance."

"But conceptually this is very difficult to digest. When Mr. Einstein published this idea in 1915, in his 'General Theory of Relativity' it was basically rejected by the scientific community.

After all, how could 'time' be different for two observers, observing the same event."

"Einstein said, that as the speed of an observer increases relative to a second observer, time actually slows down for the first observer relative to the second."

"The Bible says: 'For a thousand years in your sight is like a day that has just gone by', Psalms 90:4."

"Einstein also said that at the speed of *light*, time does not exist. Guess what travels at the speed of *light*? *Light* does of course. So, for *light*, time does not exist."

"The Bible says: 'I am Alpha and Omega, the beginning and the end, the first and the last.' Revelations 22:13."

"God is *Light* and for God, there is no 'time', because God exists *everywhere* for all of time."

"Additionally, Einstein said, that not just time and distance could vary but space itself could vary and went on to say that space and time are tied together and cannot be separated. This is what he called his theory of the 'Space-time continuum'. You may remember it being mentioned in the movie 'Back to the Future.' You know 'Doc' was always concerned that 'Marty' would somehow disturb the 'Space-time Continuum'."

"Anyway, it was not until 1919 that another scientist proved that Einstein was correct with these theories."

CyrIS scans the audience to make sure he had not lost anyone. They appear to remain glued to his words, so he continues.

"So, Albert Einstein used this discovery to develop his theories of relativity, which included his famous equation $E=mc^2$. These theories indicated that not only can time and distance, or space vary, but mass and *energy* can vary as well. The one thing that cannot vary is *light*, and you have heard me quote this scripture many times: 'Every good gift and every perfect gift is from above, and cometh down from the Father of lights, with whom is no variableness' ... John 1:17."

"No Variableness. It has been revealed to me that the *Holy Spirit*, the Infinite Spirit, is *light* and there can be no *variance* in the *Holy Spirit* or in God, because, they are one and the same."

"Please be aware of the *light* that is all around you, the *light* from the sun, and the *light* from even the smallest of *light* bulbs. All of these are the *Infinite Spirit*, revealing to you the wonders of this world. Do not let a day go by without appreciation for all that *light* and the *Holy Spirit*, and God reveals to you."

"So, I say to you, go in Peace and, may the *light* guide you in your daily actions and, may you be comforted in the all-encompassing *fabric* of the *Holy Spirit*."

The congregation, looking a bit stunned, began to rise from their seats and leave the church. But CyrIS was encouraged by the fact that as they were leaving several small groups gathered. He hoped that they were discussing his sermon.

CyrIS, as usual, then moves to the front of the church where Ester is waiting for him. There he greets each departing member. Some ask if they could get copies of his sermon, because they were not able to follow all the details. CyrIS directs them to his website 'Fact-Faith.com', where he said all of his sermons would be posted, with some additional explanations.

"Well, what did you think?" CyrIS asked Ester.

"I love it. I'm sure that you're on the right track. I can tell that your parishioners really appreciate this new approach, even though it is more than just a little bit technical."

"I know," CyrIS replied. "You know Einstein once said, 'you can make things as simple as possible, but you can't make them simpler'. Some of this stuff is complex, but I think it's important that I try to explain it, or they will never understand where I am trying to take them. Let's go back to the house. Remember I told you I wanted to show you something?"

The small house that stood behind the church was used by CyrIS as his residence. Once inside, CyrIS sits down at his desk. He gets out the parchment from the Church Wall and shows it to Ester and begins to speak.

"The other day I was thinking about how *light* never varies. Then I thought about how I always ended my sermons with 'So I say to you, go in Peace and, may the *light* guide you in your daily actions and may you be comforted in the all-encompassing *fabric* of the *Holy Spirit.'*. I have always known that the *fabric* of the *Holy Spirit* was important. Ester…look here."

CyrIS points to a passage in the ancient parchment.

My son as the science of man is born of the logic of man and as the religion of man is born of the emotion of man. Then you should know that logic and emotion are threads in the fabric of the mystery.

Search within that fabric.

"I have rolled that thought over and over in my mind, over many years, but the other day, here at my desk; I pulled out a tablet of gridded paper, the kind that has the entire page covered with little squares."

CyrIS pulls out the tablet and shows Ester. It was the kind of graph paper that architects use to lay out a floor plan for a house.

CyrIS continues "Anyway, I began to write. Here I'll show you."

CyrIS writes the word *emotion* horizontally across the middle of one of the sheets. As CyrIS begins writing, he places each letter, written in caps, in one of the squares. So, across the center of the page is written *'E-M-O-T-I-O-N.'*

CyrIS continues his explanation "I stared at this word for a while and then wrote the word *logic* vertically on the page using the first "O" in the word *"Emotion"* for the "O" in the word *"Logic"*. Again, putting only one letter in each box he demonstrates for Ester, *'L-O-G-I-C'*.

```
        L
E  M  O  T  I  O  N
        G
        I
        C
```

Now he has the two words crossed like in a crossword puzzle, one horizontal and one vertical.

Ester says, "Where are you going with this?"

"Just hang on, you will see." CyrIS responds.

"When I first did this, I stared at it for a very long time and then, using the letter 'I' in the word '*Emotion*', I added the word '*Logic*' once again, using that 'I' in the word '*Emotion*' as part of the new word. Then immediately I could see that the letter 'L' from the first '*Logic*' and the 'G' from the second '*Logic*' were in perfect position to fill in a another '*Logic*' right on top of the original letters that spelled '*Emotion*'."

CyrIS adds the additional letters on the graph paper.

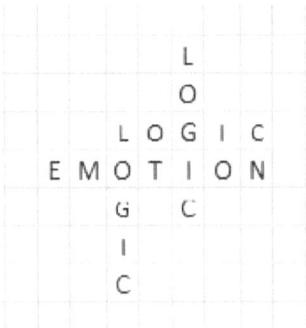

"See how it fits perfectly, and then I could see, that I could add another 'Logic' below the original 'Emotion'," CyrIS adds the letters.

"And that is when I got really excited." CyrIS fills in the remaining squares to complete the word "*Emotion*" vertically.

```
            E  L
            M  O
         L  O  G  I  C
   E  M  O  T  I  O  N
   L  O  G  I  C
            I  O
            C  N
```

Ester reaches out and touches CyrIS' hand. "I see where this is going, it's amazing."

CyrIS repeats this process over and over until he has the whole sheet filled in. When he is done, every square on the sheet is filled in. Every letter on the sheet is either part of the word "*Logic*" or part of the word "*Emotion*" or part of both words.

"It's like a giant crossword puzzle were the answer to every question is either the word '*Logic*' or '*Emotion*'." Ester observes.

CyrIS says "You see Ester, it's a fabric." Now pointing to a phrase in the parchment.

Then you should know that logic and emotion *are threads in the* fabric *of the mystery. Search within that* fabric.

"There it was! I was staring at a *fabric*, made up of the words '*Logic*' and '*Emotion*'. I was so excited; I didn't know what to think at that time, but now I think we're on the verge of a major breakthrough on our journey."

"But Ester, I have *searched within the fabric*, but I just can't see it. Ester, I'm hoping you can help?"

CyrIS could see that Ester was as excited, but she also seemed to be working hard to control her *emotions*, but then she said something that surprised CyrIS. "CyrIS is this a picture of you and me?"

CyrIS looks at the tablet and then he looks at Ester. He could not believe how much he loved her at that very moment. It was true, Ester was often *emotional* to the point of instability and CyrIS provided the anchor of stability and *logic* that helped complete her as a person. On the other hand, CyrIS was realizing that the love and *emotions* he was feeling for Ester were beyond *logic* and yet exactly what he needed to make himself complete as well. This fabric of *logic and emotion* perfectly exemplified this *entanglement* of the two of them.

CyrIS then recovering from this realization said, "That is amazing. Ester, I love you."

Ester eyes now opened wide with astonishment. CyrIS had never spoken those words to her before.

"I love you too," Ester said softly and then began to cry.

"Are you alright?" CyrIS asked.

"I am more than alright, now I'm perfect, and I love you very much." Ester responded.

She grabs CyrIS and hugs him. CyrIS didn't plan to say those words, he certainly felt that way, but they just slipped out. But now…now he was glad that he did, hugging her back as he watched her bury her face into his shoulder. But suddenly she pulls away, wipes her eyes in an apparent attempt to control herself and says. "CyrIS, this is important."

CyrIS looking intently at Ester says, "Yes but I have spent hours searching the fabric, searching the puzzle, looking for answers to the mystery, and I don't see anything. Sometimes I think I am…I don't know."

"No, no, please continue." She insists.

"I don't know, I think at times that I'm just too close to it. I have looked at it, every way possible, at least I think I have."

Ester and CyrIS talk for hours, trying to make sense of the riddle.

"You know," Esther said. "Earlier you said, 'You think you might be just too close to it.' What if you're not?"

"What do you mean?" CyrIS asks.

"I mean, maybe we are not close enough. What if we get really close? What if we make the letters really small and put them really far apart?"

CyrIS thinks for a moment and then his eyes light up. "That's a great idea, you know when Isaac Newton was developing a new form of Calculus called 'infinitesimal calculus' he took everything to infinity and that is when it started making sense. It's called taking it to the limit."

So that is what they did, each of them started thinking about the letters being very, very small and infinitely far apart.

"You know," Esther said. "No matter how small we make the letters, infinitely small, or how far apart we separate them, infinitely far apart, each letter still has a relationship to the other letters. Each letter is part of a word. That cannot be changed, and each word is part of the pattern, a part of the *fabric*, which also cannot be changed."

"That's right!" CyrIS exclaimed. "There must be something invisible in the space between the letters that *connect* them together even though the space appears to be empty."

"And that something," Ester added. "May hold the secret to the mystery we are searching for. Oh! CyrIS, I think I'm going to be sick. CyrIS!--CyrIS! ---The closer we get to an answer the more dread I feel. I'm afraid something terrible is about to happen."

"Oh! CyrIS, please hold me."

CHAPTER 7 – AND THE SKIES GREW *DARKER*

November 18ᵗʰ, 1978
Ester Suni Nati, age 26
CyrIS Steel, age 28

Ester's class on *Psychology and Parapsychology in today's society* became a popular class at Berkley. In fact, in a very short period of time, it became one of the top requested courses at the school, and this high demand resulted in a permanent position offer for Ester at Berkley, which she had gladly accepted.

Ester and CyrIS were now living together in the small house behind Billy's old church, and CyrIS continued to decipher and pursue the concepts described in the *Church Wall Scroll.*

One of the reasons Ester's course had become so successful, was that she and CyrIS worked to incorporate some of their new theories into her course. The course was now called *Psychology, Parapsychology, and Science in today's society*, and with CyrIS' help, Ester now lectured on the discoveries in science and psychology that supported her beliefs in Parapsychology. She also now emphasizes the mystical powers of "Prayer", and "The Power of Positive Thinking." She believes as CyrIS did, that science is moving in a direction that would prove that the connections between people and the universe were not some kind of "myth" but were based in true scientific "fact".

Together they continue to find scriptures, and passages from other religious and scientific documents, that support their theories. However, so far, no new scientific discoveries revealed what they believed to exist in the way of a substance in the universe that tied all of this together.

With each new piece of supporting information, they find, the dread in Ester's mind and stomach continues to grow. She completed her Ph.D. in Extra Sensory Perception, Shamanism, and

Psychic Phenomenon, but even today with all of her *spiritual* training, she feels the *void* within her widening, and today she feels especially pushed by some unseen force to do something about it.

It's 7:45 in the morning and Ester is preparing the room for her latest journey, while CyrIS lies on their bed watching.

As Ester moves around the room making preparations she begins speaking in a very calm voice.

"For tens of thousands of years, many cultures around the world have practiced Shamanism as a way to help them with personal evolution through the process of meditative 'Journeying'. You see CyrIS; I can achieve a state of mind that helps fill some of the emptiness I feel from time to time. For me, what is considered the normal world is not as 'real' as the alternative world of the *'Spirit'*. *'Spirit* Travel', opens up the door to an awareness of other realities, and I have found that these other realities are a source of *energy* for me."

Ester glances at CyrIS still lying on the bed. She can see the look on his face and wonders if his thinking that this is a bunch of 'Hocus-Pocus', which are the words he sometimes used referring to evangelical healing sessions. None-the-less she continues with her speech, hoping he will be supportive.

"As you know, I have been concentrating on developing my skills as a Shaman. A Shaman generally traverses the 'Axis Mundi' to enter the *Spirit* World. The Axis Mundi, also known as the 'Cosmic Axis', is said to be a pillar by which Shamans can move between heaven and earth, between the sky and earth, and most importantly, between the Lower, *Middle* and Higher Worlds. I have on many occasions visited the first destination, known as the 'Lower World'. This experience takes me deep into the bowels of the earth, and my journeys there have brought me closer to nature. I am very comfortable in this 'Lower World', as it seems to contain an essence of healing and self-empowerment for me."

"And as for the *Upper World*?" CyrIS asked.

Ester thinks for a second before answering. "I have not yet visited the *Upper World*. This is a place of wisdom and teaching, a place of bright *light* and very strong *energy*."

"Do you think it is heaven?" CyrIS pressed.

"I'm not sure, but I believe it is the realm of God, and I will need much more *spiritual* growth before I can take such an important journey…however, there is a third destination, which I have also not yet visited, known as the *Middle World. Everything* I have learned from my father, and from my training about this place, indicate that this is a place which would seem much like our own reality, here and now, a place where the *Spirit* would be tangibly present and ready to work with me, to increase my understanding of *everything*. I feel strongly that this *middle world* is today calling me, and I am hopeful that I will learn some things that will help the two of us on our journey."

Ester had been up most of the night preparing their bedroom for her journey. The curtains are now drawn ever so tightly, and the only *light* in the room came from the flickering candles that Ester had lit and placed strategically around their bedroom. The only sound was the soft beating of a single drum. This was from a recording that Ester used to help her with her journeys.

Ester now lying on their bed with CyrIS lightly holding her hand, the gentle beating of the drum is washing away her every thought. Ester begins chanting, a chant that had been handed down to her from her father, and to him from centuries of Zuni tribesmen. The rhythm of the drum allows Ester to drift away…away to the Lower World, and now she is finding her way, as usual, through secret caves down to the center of the earth. But then she begins along a path she had not previously ventured. She imagines herself as a mist of smoke, and the smoke is slowly drifting upward…upward to the realm of the *Middle* World.

This could be the day that I die.

This thought drifts through Ester's mind, and her body shivers with fear. Ester now has a series of images flashing within her mind's eye. She can hear someone's thoughts running through her brain as if they are her own, but they are not. "Where am I? Is this my Spirit Guide trying to contact me?" Ester's own thoughts push their way through a collage of other thoughts, none of which were her own.

An image emerges of people sitting at a table, apparently some kind of meeting. A new thought, once again not her own

I'm glad we worked so very late last night. I truly feel our plans for today are ready. Now I am sure we will be prepared if anyone tries to defect with the congressman. That fucking Stoen, this was all so unnecessary, and it was his fault entirely.

An image of an open briefcase...papers spilling on the floor.

That was the proof, Tim; the man I trusted with my life was a government agent. And that meant that Grace was probably an agent as well. Imagine that, a fucking husband and wife team here to take down our beautiful socialist society.

Now Ester feels the sensation of soft lightweight sheets, not against Ester's smooth breast, but against a hairy chest. This chest is now moving those sheets up and down with labored breath. Ester feels the exertion put into each breath that is indistinguishable from her own. The movement of male hands and feet are felt as the body awakes from sleep...then, eyes opening.

Ester is amazed and again a bit frightened. She observes the dingy ceiling, as her mind floods with questions. "Where am I? How did I get inside of this man's mind? Who is this?" She tries hard to pay close attention, telling herself that this journey is intended to be a learning experience which would help her grow and maybe help her *connect* with the *Holy Spirit*.

Ester now hears people speaking in another room. She also hears the sounds of the sheets rustle as the man struggles to sit up in bed. A warm breeze comes from a nearby window and helps cool a perspiring body. It also assists in defending against the 'man' odor, which assaults Ester's sense of smell.

Ester could also taste a parched, dry, bitterness in this man's mouth. But there was more, there was also a sour chemical taste, a taste that Ester had never experienced.

Besides being able to see, hear and feel everything this person was experiencing, she could also see every image this person was generating in his mind, and hear every thought he was having.

I'm glad I was able to get some sleep. Today we face some very dark matters, and I need all of the energy I can muster. I have to be clear minded. I'm not taking the usual amounts of Valium and Quaaludes; I will only take a couple of 'uppers', just to get myself going.

Ester is once again overwhelmed. She is inundated with flashes of images of large groups of people and things that seemed to be from the past mixed with a myriad of thoughts from the present.

Ester soon discovers that she has no control; she is apparently just along for the ride. The lack of control frightens her, but she struggles not to panic. "Control your *emotions*" Ester thinks. She tries even harder to pay attention. Her expectations are high, but she knows that she must work hard to understand what she is experiencing.

She thinks that there must be a reason that she was drawn here. It must be part of God's plan for her, or the plan of her *Spiritual* Guide, or maybe the *Holy Spirit*. Ester is sure it was all part of a larger *spiritual* mystery that she needs to solve. She forces herself to calm down and pay close attention to the clues.

Now her host is rising from the covers and settles in an upright position, Ester sees a clock on a small table next to the bed; 11:00. She is sure it is AM because of the *light* coming through the window. Her eyes scan the room. The bed, a large four poster, has several large canisters next to it and what looks like an oxygen machine. Large file cabinets are positioned next to a refrigerator, which is next to several large wooden trunks. All of this was spread around the room and filled with what appears to be personal items.

Ester could see hypodermic needles, alcohol swabs, and bottles of various pills. The labels on most of the bottles are hard to read, but from the paraphernalia, it appears that some could be hard drugs. She also sees some bottles that looked like laxatives, and several cans of hairspray. There is even a bottle of Miss Clairol hair coloring.

Ester feels a movement and then feels and sees the hairy hand of the man reach out in front of her and into one of the wooden chests. The hand moves as if it is her own and pulls a bottle from the chest, opens it, and throws three pills into the man's mouth…into her mouth. Ester is so confused; it all felt the same. She could taste the bitterness of the pills against his tongue. She feels relief to the dryness in his mouth as he drinks from a glass of water that he had retrieved from a nearby table. Ester cannot believe the feelings as she experiences him forcing the pills down his throat. He then stands up, walks into the small bathroom and looks into the mirror.

Ester is again startled. She can now see that it is definitely a man. He is maybe in his fifties, he might have been younger than that, but he is so very pale and sickly looking that Ester is not sure. His round face is framed by coal black hair. Ester instantly recalls the bottle of hair coloring.

Then it hits her as she recognizes this face. Even though the face is pale, and the flesh is sagging especially around the eyes. She could never forget that raven black hair…" Oh! My God" it's the Reverend Jim Jones. She immediately relives his touch in San Francisco, and panic sets in.

She remembers how handsome he had been at that time, but now a mere eight years later, he looks worn out. She knew that when he had touched her that day, that there had been a *connection*, not realizing at the time, exactly how strong a *connection* it would be.

Ester watches as he takes off his thin robe and steps into a makeshift shower. She looks down at his pale white flabby body, and recoils.

The whole bathroom experience disgusts her from the washing of all parts of this overly soft, almost mushy, white and somewhat hairy body, to the use of the facilities for disposing of his bodily waste. As he returns to his bed, Ester is grateful it is over. She is scared but reminds herself that CyrIS was right there by her side, and that she is doing this for their future.

It is time to review my life. For this day may be my last. But, I know, that my life's work has led me to this point in time, and what we have planned is the right thing to do. It all makes perfect sense to me now.

As he once again lies on the bed, he closes his eyes. Ester could see a whole new set of images. The reverend seems to be thinking about his childhood:

It was great, going across the street to Mrs. Kennedy's. I loved my mom and dad, but I spent more time with Mrs. Kennedy, and she was a very important influence on me. She worked hard to save me from the devil, taking me to church on Sunday's and to bible studies.

As he remembers, Ester could see more flashes of images of places and people from his past. A farmhouse, a set of railroad tracks, an old woman in a dark print dress, the inside of a church filled with people. The imagery was fleeting and sometimes more than a little distracting.

Ester believes it is more important for her to pay attention to what he is thinking and less so to the imagery itself.

Mrs. Kennedy certainly helped with my religious education, but mom gave me this feeling of irreverence for the world. She was wild and independent and I'm happy that she passed those traits on to me, they are so important to me, even to this day.

Now Ester sees images of old men sitting in front of a garage. She then realizes that Jim is entertaining these men by cussing up a storm. Ester thinks, "How strange it is, that this was part of the upbringing of this supposed Man of God."

An image of a library comes into focus.

God how I loved reading as a kid. I read everything, especially the bible. I was good in school; it must have been all of that reading. But mom and dad didn't give a shit; they never showed up at school when I got an award, or for anything as far as that goes. Boy, that pissed me off, I just wanted to kill someone, I didn't care who it was.

There is a pause, and then new images of young boys and girls.

It was great entertaining my friends; I would take in those stray animals and use them to put on shows. What a kick. I could control those dogs and cats and make them lie down and crawl and beg. Boy, how I could amaze those stupid idiots, pretending to cure an animal of some disease. I loved the looks on their faces, especially the girls. I loved girls, and they loved me. I was so well groomed, man, I was sure good looking, and I had those girls eating out of the palm of my hand.

Then there was college. The girls were after me there too, but it was Marceline, Marceline Baldwin that changed me. She was, and still is the perfect fit for me. I love being married to her. She is so deeply religious, and boy, we sure had some heated arguments over the meaning of the Bible, and some of that helped me develop many of the beliefs I have right now.

Ester now sees the image of what looks like a church congregation, all facing Jim in a pulpit.

Boy, the day I showed up at that Pentecostal 'Holy Roller' church, just outside of town, was a trip. That old lady minister telling me she thought I would make a good preacher because of my knowledge of the bible and my amazing vocabulary.

Then she talked me into getting up there and actually giving a sermon. I was so scared, but the crowd was small, and they seemed to like what I was saying, at least until mom shot it down and wouldn't let me go there anymore.

I loved it, I may have been just a teenager, but it was my start as a preacher. After that, I preached to anyone who would listen, and there were a lot who would. I wasn't a rock star like I wanted to be, but I was a star.

Mrs. Kennedy and Marceline helped me with my religious training, but it was when I worked at that hospital during high school, and I saw all those severely injured soldiers from the Korean War, that really changed me. That is when I realized that there was no God. How could a God allow such suffering? How could a God allow prejudice in the world? How could God allow men to discriminate against other men based on the color of their skin? It didn't make any sense.

"A 'Man of God' that did not believe in God.". Ester had this thought, while also wondering, at the same time; 'How *could* God let such things happen.'

But Ester was even more astonished at how fervent the Reverend was about the equality of men. She could feel the passion surge in his body when he thought about it. Ester felt strongly that there was a lesson to be learned here and hoped she could remember and discuss it with CyrIS, as the Reverend's thoughts continued.

Marceline certainly did not agree with me on the existence of God. She did agree that there was too much prejudice in the world, that the world should live in harmony, and that people should take care of each other.

We have always taken in stray animals, but after we came to that agreement, we started collecting stray people. We took loners and drifters, into our home, independent of their color or financial standing.

It was in 1952, that we discovered a five-page creed published by the Methodist church. It espoused, prison reform, jobs for all, labor unions, free speech, the reduction of poverty, support of the elderly, and most of all it stated 'We stand for the rights of racial groups...'

Once again there were images of inside a church, this time filled entirely with people of color.

I would visit those poor black churches, even though I was the pastor at that all white Methodist church in Indianapolis. And when I started getting those black souls to attend my Methodist church, the white people were enraged, many of them leaving the church. But I didn't care; I was building my own ministry.

Ester thinks about CyrIS and his story of the people leaving his church and wonders if there was somehow a connection.

I spent hours and hours at those black churches, at the healing services and revivals. Watching those preacher's techniques for healing and raising the emotions of the congregation.   That is where I learned how they knew the "unknowable" about the people that were called to the front of the service to be healed, and that is when I started collecting information on people, even using my followers to go to people's homes and rummage through their trash cans. I used what was found in my services, especially the healing services.

Ester thinks about June and the rest of those young people, asking her questions, in front of the auditorium at the Jones revival. She also thinks about CyrIS' reference to 'Hocus-Pocus'.

Ester then sees an image of a little white-haired old lady, and now images of hundreds and hundreds of people in a convention hall swaying to the sounds of gospel music.

There was that minister at that convention in Columbus Indiana. She convinced me to get into the pulpit and give a sermon, just like back home. But this was a very big crowd and I was scared to death, but I closed my eyes and a barrage of thoughts began to fly through my mind. I began to call out names of people and they began to stream to the front of the room. As they approached me, I reached out and touched them. Many of them fell to the floor. Many began screaming and hollering and praising the Lord for my touch. The emotions were overwhelming, and it was at that moment that I felt that the Spirit was truly working through me."

Ester thought, "The Spirit was working through him.' What does that mean? What Spirit?"

After that, the crowds became larger and larger, and we had to move to larger and larger buildings to allow for the growing congregation. I had to use ever more resourceful means, which included using some of my followers, to get greater detailed intelligence about the attendees, and help with the miracles, which were all justified because of the great value we were bringing to those in need. 'The end always justifies the means, it's just logical.'

Ester again thought back to her experiences in front of and inside of the convention hall in San Francisco. She recalls the reverend calling out the 'unknowable' to the people coming to the stage as well as the black lady lying on the concrete floor.

That's when it came to me; my new church would be named 'The Peoples Temple'. I had pulled myself up by the bootstraps and I had built a church around socialistic values, which I called 'religious communalism'. The members of my family, my son from Marceline, and our two adopted children, one black and one Korean, were just like my following, a rainbow of colors.

I made a deal with many of my followers; 'If you donate your material possessions to this church, I will meet all your needs', and the needs were plenty. I had to constantly remind them of the dangers in the world, disease, poverty, civil unrest, crime, discrimination, hatred and especially nuclear war.

Ester thought, "It's as if, he is scaring his followers into needing his church."

I remember reading an article in Esquire magazine and it indicated that the southern hemisphere was safer from nuclear holocaust than the northern hemisphere. So, I moved my family to Brazil, and for two years, Marceline and I fed the poor hungry children of South America, always staying in touch with, and receiving donations from, my church in Indianapolis.

When I returned to Indianapolis many of my followers greeted me at the airport. That is when I realized that I was a prophet for these people and must lead them to a promised land. And I knew exactly where the Promised Land was, and that is when I moved my church to California, and most of my followers went with me.

I had studied the bible extensively and was convinced by the mountains of riddles and contradictions, that there-could-be-no-God. And that the only hope for my followers was for them to follow me exclusively.

When I put these thoughts into action, by including them in my sermons, some people left the church, but those who stayed were much more dedicated to me and to my preaching. They would do anything I told them. Anything at all.

Ester feels intense *emotions* invade the reverend's body, especially feelings of hatred and revenge for those who had left his church.

Some of those people who left, turned against me. They said I was a communist and that I wanted to overthrow the government and that I was cheating my followers out of their money. Law enforcement was turning against me, and even worse, the press was turning against me as well. I needed to move my church out of the United States.

After extensive research, we decided that here in the socialistic country of Guyana, we would make our new home. And now we live on 3,800 acres of leased land in the jungle of Guyana, just 150 miles west of Georgetown. I have named it 'Jonestown', and over the years many of my followers from California have moved to this new home that we have carved out of the jungle.

Now Ester could hardly keep up with his erratic thought patterns. Sometimes it seemed his thoughts were crystal clear, with very clear images from the past and grandiose plans of happiness for multitudes of people in the future. At the same time, his thoughts were interrupted by thoughts and feelings of anger, resentment, and even thoughts of extreme violence. Now his thoughts switched from the building of Jonestown to the problems he now faced.

How had this all happened? Of course, there had always been the growing problems of the defectors and the lies they were spreading about me and my church. But I have always been able to deflect those untruths. Of course, there were the problems of the relatives of my congregation back in the States, who thought their brothers and sisters, sons and daughters, were being mistreated and were being held against their will. All totally untrue.

But that is not what worries me most. It all started back in the 60's; when I was preaching the value of free love.

Ester recalls how the crowds went wild, at the service she attended, when he went on and on about free love.

I was obligated to meet the needs of some of my female followers, and when I told Marceline that it was necessary, she agreed that 'It was for the good of the church'.

In 1971 Marceline agreed to sign a document declaring that John Victor Stoen, born to Grace Stoen, the wife of Tim Stoen, was not Tim's son, but was instead mine. As it turned out this may have been the beginning of the end for my church, for Tim Stoen was one of those defectors, and he had a bench warrant issued for the recovery of his son from Jonestown. And there was also a warrant issued for my arrest for contempt of court.

Even worse, now Congressman Leo Ryan had become involved and was demanding the return of the boy, and any others who wanted to leave Jonestown. And now, despite the fact that I told him to stay away, the congressman had arrived just yesterday and is now on his way to our compound.

It may become necessary for all of us to complete the final gesture that we have practiced so many times in the past. That grand gesture of Revolutionary Suicide, choosing to go out in the face of one's enemies, showing everyone that we would rather die than give up our belief in this socialistic society. All the plans are in place, but now we will have to see what the day brings.

All of a sudden in a burst, the Reverend shouted out.

"Carolyn, gather my staff together, I must talk to them immediately."

Ester can hardly believe the words that came rolling out of his mouth. She could feel the words form on his lips, on her lips, she could feel his lips and teeth touch each other as he formed these words, as if it were her own lips and teeth, she could feel his/her tongue, moving up and down touching the roof of his mouth. She could feel the saliva build in her mouth, in his mouth, and then a swallow to make way for the next burst of words. Ester is overwhelmed, she was able to still have her own independent thoughts and *emotions*, but she wondered, how close can one get to another person without actually being that person.

Then Ester could hear two women talking, and then suddenly stop. A response came from one of the women indicating she would gather the people he needed. After dressing himself, the Reverend then moved into a small room adjacent to his bedroom. Several very large black men, one white man, and several white women were gathering around a table. Off to the right sat another table with a microphone on it, and what looked like radio equipment. There were large screened-in windows in the room that looked out onto a weeded field. Ester could see a heavily forested jungle off in the distance, the colors of the trees muted by the hot humid air, and Ester could feel the reverend perspiring, as he began to lecture the people in the room.

For the next two hours, Ester observes an incredible scene unfold in front of her, still astonished by the feeling that she herself was saying the words.

"Well, we knew this day would come." The Reverend was saying. "It is what we have prepared for over the last few years."

Ester is so taken with the feelings she was experiencing, that she was having great difficulty paying attention, to what was actually happening in front of her. She knew that whatever force in the universe had brought her here it was for a very important reason. "It had to be."

"What we must do today," The reverend said. "Will leave an indelible mark on history."

He went on to explain, how in death they would all achieve a new life.

"A bunch of common people and a preacher named Jones could become part of history along with the heroes of the Russian and Chinese revolutions. Just like the martyrs of the American civil rights movements, we will make a statement for all times. By choosing the time, place and manner of our deaths, we will deprive our enemies of the opportunity to bring us down. The members of the People's Temple can no longer tolerate the cruelties of the world. We will go down in one gallant glorious screaming end."

He went on to review the previous day's events. He speaks about the visit by Congressman Ryan and what seemed like representatives from every newspaper and television network in America. He also says how it was all a plot by the US government to bring down their socialist society.

The reverend continued, "I hate having all those TV cameras trying to pry into every corner of our community and all those reporters asking the kind of questions that imply that people are unhappy here and want to leave."

He repeats again and again how he regrets his decision to bow to his lawyer's pleading to let them all in. He went on to complain about the conspirators, as he called them, Tim and Grace Stoen, Jeane and Al Mills and the gang of eight.

Ester did not know who Jeane and Al were, but she got the feeling that they, along with this gang of eight, were people who had left the commune and turned against Reverend Jones and the People's Temple and were now trying to bring them all down.

The reverend continued his lecture, "I explained to that damn Congressman that not only has our church been attacked, but I have also been physically attacked by the government. I explained to him how some of our buildings have been set on fire and that I have received threats on my life in the US and here in Jonestown, and that there have been several assassinations attempts on my life."

This scares Ester because she does not know how, but she knows that everything he is saying is a lie. All fabricated by the Reverend to justify his actions. However, at the same time that she knew it was a lie; she could also feel that the reverend believed everything that he was saying. It all seemed so *logical* to him. It seemed to Ester that all of the lies were based on deep-seeded *emotion*, but the reverend was filtering all of this in a way that made it seem *logical* in his own mind and therefore it must all be true.

"Is this a lesson for me?" Ester thought to herself.

"The lies are bad." She thinks, "but what terrifies me even more, is that as I look around this room, I can see no one rise to question the reverend's judgment."

No one was challenging his insane *logic*. Ester could not even sense any *emotion* from these people. Had they been brainwashed? Or had they heard this so many times before that they were just used to it, and they all were worn down?

And then thoughts ran through Ester's head about her own future. If the Reverend Jim Jones brought an end to his life, would it be the end of hers as well? A bit of panic once again sets in. Maybe she should try to get out of this situation. But there seemed to be no way out. Her mental cries to CyrIS seemed to have no effect.

"Well, they are all coming back this afternoon," the Reverend said. "We need to be prepared. Send a message to Georgetown and tell our basketball team that they must return to Jonestown immediately. I need to have my son here by my side and we also need those security guards back as well."

One of the women raised her hand. "I'll take care of that," she said, and as this lady speaks Ester hears something; it is a metal to metal tinkle sound, which happened just as the lady was raising her right arm. Ester could now see that on her right wrist was a wristwatch and between the watch and her hand was a small gold bracelet. It is a lot like the bracelet that Ester's father had given her when she was young. However, the centerpiece of this bracelet was three large X's held together with a thin bar at the top and bottom of the Xs. The sound Ester heard was the bracelet bumping against the wristwatch as the lady raised her arm. Ester wonders if somehow these X's had something to do with pornography or maybe it's the Roman numeral for thirty.

"What is going on here? Drugs, pornography, and talk of suicide. This is all so insane." Ester thinks to herself.

The Reverend goes on.

"Yesterday the congressman hinted that he wanted to stay the night. If he makes that request again, maybe someone should threaten his life, so he will not want to stay."

"Now let's go, I must do these interviews and get these intruders out of here."

Ester watches as the Reverend walks into the bathroom. He goes directly to the sink and as he looks down at the sink, she could see the Reverend taking meticulous care to wash his hands.

All-of-a-sudden, he looks up and into the mirror. His deep dark eyes burn into Ester's consciousness; she could swear he was looking right at her.

What, are you looking at? You know that what is about to happen, is because of you. It's coming soon, and there is not much time, but the darkness is on our side. No one can stop us now, nor can those who come later. Allegiance is a foolish endeavor.

Ester's body stiffens and she thinks, "Is he talking to me, or to himself, or to some other force in the universe that is driving him forward? Or maybe driving me forward? Is this the message I was sent here to receive? What did it mean?" She repeats in her mind., "'Allegiance is a foolish endeavor'".

Ester is terrified, "What is about to happen?" she thinks to herself; she knew it couldn't be good, she felt a cold shiver rush through her soul. As the reverend leaves the restroom, he puts on a pair of *dark* sunglasses with the cool air of Roy Orbison and heads for the front door of the building. With his entourage in tow, he steps onto the building's small front porch and is greeted with the melancholy of overcast skies.

In the distance, maybe a quarter mile, were many buildings made mostly of wood with tin roofs, all glistening from the gently falling rain. A muddy dirt road led away towards the buildings in the distance, and on that road, slipping and sliding along, is a yellow dump truck struggling to reach their location. When finally reaches them and stops just a few yards away, the reverend moves towards it. Moments later Ester could feel hands on the reverend's body. It is the reverend's staff helping him into the passenger seat. Once the Reverend is seated, the staff moves towards the back of the truck.

Once they are all on board the truck begins to move. Ester can see a series of cottages that look like living units off to the right. Immerging from those units is a string of people in a procession towards the central complex of buildings. Ester can also see crops of some sort on both sides of the road, and there are pens with what look like a hundred pigs and lots and lots of chickens.

The reverend is perspiring even more heavily now as the day grows warmer. But Ester could also sense that the sweat is caused by more than just the heat and humidity; he is nervous about what he was going to say and do.

Soon a large pavilion comes into view, with maybe a thousand people in and around it. The collection of people was of all ethnicities, colors, shapes, and sizes, all moving slowly closer and closer to the pavilion's stage. But there were people here that did not fit the scene. They had cameras and clipboards. "Maybe reporters." Ester thinks.

Not too far from the pavilion there is, what looked like a playground. Countless numbers of children are playing a variety of games. The worry-free laughter of the children can be heard above the truck's engine, and they seem oblivious to the concerns of the adults approaching the pavilion.

As the people slowly assemble, some are smiling and laughing, while some of them have looks of deep concern. Ester cannot make any sense of the scene. It was so surreal seeing children playing, seeing people laughing, and seeing some talking to the reporters. It did not match the turmoil of *emotions* she felt. "Where is the logic in this scene? Did they not understand what this madman was planning?" She thought to herself.

The truck they are in, drives to the back of one of the buildings behind the pavilion. Back here, there are many people as well and they greet the reverend as he leaves the truck. As the reverend approaches this small crowd, Ester suddenly experiences a warm feeling move through the Reverend's body. She feels him smile. Cheers begin to go up and the Reverend raises his hand in response to the greeting. He sees children and adults alike coming toward him. As he proceeds toward the pavilion, Ester hears and sees his followers giving him praise.

"Father, you have saved my life; I had nothing before I came here, I was lost, and you have completely filled the *void* in my life."

Ester could feel the deep *connection* he had with these people and she thought, "In some ways I see why he has brought them here, to this seemingly desolate place."

The reverend proceeded up the stairs to the platform under the pavilion roof. Just then one of the women - clearly one of his aids - whispers in his ear.

"There have been several people, I think about eight, including some children that have decided to leave with the Congressman."

Immediately, Ester could feel the reverend's heartbeat accelerate as the *emotions* well up inside of him. He becomes extremely angry and a hot flash invades his whole body. He did not move for a moment or two, and he says anything.

This is the end. There is no way to control the lies that they will spread. I must get these intruders out of here, so we can make our final statement.

As he calmed himself, he proceeds across the stage and sits down in an army green chair. As he sits down, Ester hears a much larger cheer go up from the massive crowd in front of him.

Several official-looking people approach the reverend, and the reverend begins to speak.

"Welcome back Congressman Ryan, I hope you were able to sleep well last night."

The Congressman returns the greeting. The Reverend stands up and shakes the Congressman's hand. The Congressman is much taller than the Reverend, and the Reverend is forced to look up at him. Ester can feel that this displeases the Reverend, especially, because the Congressman has a smug look on his face. The Reverend thinks,

This bastard feels he has achieved some kind of victory because of the defectors.

They all move to a table at the far end of the pavilion.

As Ester observes the nearby crowd, she could no longer see any smiles. People are covering their mouths and speaking in whispers. The mood had changed, it was apparent that other members of his commune were deciding to leave as well. For the next half hour Ester observes as the congressman talks to the people who wanted to leave, and the Reverend in turn, tries to talk them out of leaving.

The Reverend is now saying to one family: "There's always a place, just know there's always a place for you, always a place."

After a while, it became apparent that he was not going to dissuade these people from leaving and he moves to a straight-backed chair at the back of the pavilion and prepares himself for interviews by the press. Ester watches as the reporters' approach, many of them with notebooks and tape recorders, some with large video cameras, one had a large "NBC" logo on its side.

The Reverend began by describing the paradise he had built here in the jungle. He explains how he worked to build a community free of racism, classism, and elitism.

"You never accomplish what you set out. I am a perfectionist," he said. "We want to fade out of the whole arena of public attention but obviously, we haven't because of lies. I never understood how people could lie with such total freedom and conviction."

Ester listened as the interviewers asked about beatings and corporal punishment. They asked about an underground enclosure in which people were being held prisoner. They asked about the reports of armed guards surrounding the compound and about automatic weapons.

Ester feels the reverend flush with anger as each new question is asked. He responds that they were all lies. But she could also feel something else, a resignation coming over him, that all was lost. He feels that all of these people are out to get him, and he just wants it all to come to an end.

"I don't want to be one of those people in their golden years," he mumbles.

"Are you dying," they ask.

"I don't know," he responds.

Ester sees one of the newsmen hand the reverend a note. As he looks down at the note, Ester can see that it says, "Vernon

Gosney, Monica Bagby. Help us get out of Jonestown." Ester could feel another rush of *emotion* flush the reverend's body. It was obvious that this was a note that was given to one of the visitors and was a plea from some of his followers to abandon ship.

"Friend, people play games," the reverend says. "People can go out of here when they want. I only feel that every time people leave, up until now, they chose to lie." The Reverend's voice trembles as he struggles to go on.

As the interviews come to an end, Ester could feel the huge ego, she detected earlier, deflating into almost non-existence. This was a beaten man and it seemed that now all he could think about was ending it all.

Ester noticed that as the interviews went on, the skies were becoming *darker* and *darker,* and just as the interviews ended the wind picked up and the clouds unleashed a deluge of rain. Ester watches as the reverend says goodbye to those who are leaving. Then Ester hears a rushing of feet and a woman yelling.

"I'll kill you. I'll kill you."

"You bring those kids back here.

"Don't touch my kids!"

The reverend turns towards the sound, and Ester can see a husky woman confronting a stocky man. The woman appears to be the children's mother, and the man, who looked to be Native American, could be the father, is pulling two children along by the hand.

The reverend takes no action and watches as two men, who Ester believes were lawyers, stops the man pulling the children, and then begin talking about what should be done. After a moment or two, they agree that the man could not take the kids away from their mother.

After the lawyers informed the man that he could not take the children, she could hear the man mutter, in his heavy Native American accent, somewhat reminiscent of her fathers, "I am their father and I will stay with my children even if it means I have to put up with harassment."

The lawyers both turn to face the Reverend. He quickly reassures them that there would be no harassment. Then Ester hears Congressman Ryan volunteer to stay over to make sure that if any additional people wanted to leave, they would feel safe to do so. Ester panics, remembering the Reverend's suggestion to his staff. Fearing that his suggestion could turn into something worse than just a threat.

One of the Reverend's aids puts an umbrella over the Reverend's head and the group moves out to the playground area, as the rain subsids. People are loading into the big yellow dump truck for departure. The Reverend is staring directly at the Congressman as the Congressman is thanking the lawyers for their help. The Congressman then turns to the Reverend and asks him if he could make it easier for others to leave.

Then it happened. A husky man grabs the Congressman from behind, putting a knife to his throat.

"Congressman Ryan, you motherfucker...." the assailant yelled.

The Congressman's bewildered expression seemed to dismiss reality at first. It was as if he is thinking, *is this a joke*? But then the smile on his face changes to a grimace, and then horror of it all is accepted and a look of terror overcomes him.

The Congressman then lunges back towards the man. Two other men jump on the potential assassin and wrestle the knife from his hand. When the Congressman gets up, he is obviously angry and shaken but soon composes himself. All the while, Ester could feel no emotion from the Reverend. He watches the action with only one thought. *That's what you deserve you dirty bastard.*

The Congressman then tells the Reverend that his report to Congress would still be positive as long as the man was arrested. The Reverend does not apologize, and he only agrees to call the police at the urging of his lawyers.

Moments later, Ester sees the Congressman conferring with several men in a private conversation. Then the Congressman announces that he would be leaving with the rest of the people, but his lawyer Mark Lane will be staying. The Reverend feels nothing and says nothing but watches as the Congressman gets into the truck. He then watches as the truckload of people move down the muddy road.

As soon as the truck is out of sight, and as once again the skies grow *darker,* a surge of energy rushes through the Reverend's body.

"Tell everyone to go back to their cottages and dormitories," he yells to Carolyn. "Also, get my staff and security guards together for an immediate meeting."

Ester hears the announcement over the loudspeakers instructing people to return to their residences. The two lawyers announce that they were going to take a walk and talk for a while. The Reverend moves to the back of the pavilion where his staff and security guards are assembled. Their collective faces appear to anxiously wait for the Reverend's instructions.

"Get your guns," the Reverend ordered. "We do not want any of those people to leave the Kaituma Airport, especially that fucking Congressman."

The security guards nod their heads in agreement, and Ester's fear grows as they leave.

The Reverend again speaks to Carolyn. "Call all of the people back to the pavilion at once."

Carolyn does not reply and the Reverend watches as she walks away. He then instructs his other staffers. "Bring out the implements needed and begin preparing for the end."

They did not question his instructions either, it appears to Ester, that they know exactly what he was asking them to do. Ester's heart pounds but at the same time she could feel that the Reverend seemed fairly calm. Once again, the crackling of the loudspeakers surrounds the village.

"Everyone please, report to the pavilion immediately."

Ester watches as the Reverend leads the remainder of his staff to a nearby building. When they get inside, she sees that it is some kind of schoolhouse filled with blackboards and kid's drawings on the walls.

"Oh my God, the children*",* she thinks.

Shortly after they arrive the two lawyers show up flanked by escorts that looked like they were the reverend's security guards.

"All is lost." The Reverend says to the lawyers in a defeated voice. But Ester can feel that he is back in charge and he is not wasting any time. "Every gun in the place is gone."

He then goes on to tell the lawyers that some of the Temple members have taken the guns and gone after the Ryan party. He also says that some of the members who had left as defectors are not really defectors at all, they are sent with the Congressman to stop them from leaving. He then tells the lawyers that they must leave.

"People are angry with you," he said. "Your lives will not be safe."

Ester could see the distraught look on the lawyer's faces. They do not say anything as they are escorted away by the security guards. The Reverend leaves the school building and once again Ester watches as he walks up to the stage at the pavilion. He approaches the dark green chair, and as he approaches, he looks up at a sign over the chair.

"THOSE WHO DO NOT REMEMBER THE PAST ARE CONDEMNED TO REPEAT IT."

The Reverend sits in the chair looking down on his members, there were no smiles, only looks of question.

"How much I have loved you?" he begins. "How much I have tried to give you a good life." He does not smile as the applause goes up, and as it rescinds, he continues. "In spite of all I have tried, a handful of people… have made our life impossible. There is no way that we can detach ourselves from what's happened today. We are sitting here, waiting on a powder keg."

"It is said by the greatest prophets from time immemorial, 'No man takes my life from me; I am laying my life down'". The applause once again goes up and shouts dart from the crowd.

"Right-Right!"

He goes on to explain to the crowd that a catastrophe is going to happen at the Congressman's plane. He said that you can't steal other people's children and not expect them to react violently. He explains that someone is going to shoot the pilot of their plane and it would crash in the jungle. He goes on to explain how once that occurred, they would be sending people here to destroy all of them.

"So, in my opinion," he says in a solemn voice. "We should be kind to children and be kind to seniors and take the potion, like they used to take in ancient Greece, and step over quietly, because we are not committing suicide, it is a revolutionary act."

Ester could see the absolute trust and belief in many of the Reverend's followers, and this in turn instilled a tremendous amount of confidence within the Reverend. Ester can now feel that he is absolutely certain that this was the right thing to do and not only for himself but for all of his followers as well. He feels truly heroic.

He listens as one-woman objects and asked if it was too late to go to Russia. He says that it was too late, these people are out of control, and there was nothing left that can be done.

Ester watches as several of the Reverend's followers argue for life and made suggestions for surviving the situation. Many were arguing to at least save the children. All the while, the Reverend argues the opposite explaining how it was much too late for any of those proposals to work, now that the Congressman and his party had probably been killed. To Ester's shock, most of the crowd is supportive of the Reverend's arguments and there were huge uproars of applause at the end of each of his statements. He describes how when the authorities come back, there would be paratroopers that would drop in from the sky and butcher everyone, including the children.

"Is that what you want for your children?" he asks.

"No!" the crowd screams.

The reverend and his staff then decide that the children would go first and then the adults and then the seniors. Discussing this like it was just another day at work.

Ester could not believe the events that were unfolding and thinks, "Surely someone will step forward to stop this madness."

At the same time, she is thinking this, she could see the security guards with guns in hand setting up a perimeter around the crowd, making sure that no one tried to make a run for it. Then Ester hears one of the Reverend's aids whispering in his ear. "The Congressman has been killed."

The Reverend jumps from his seat and shouts to a nearby aid. "Radio to the members in Georgetown and let them know what has happened and forward the message back to the members back in the U.S. Tell them that all is lost and that they should all end their lives." The Reverend then shouts out to the crowd. "The congressman has been murdered."

A woman in the crowd screams. "We're ready. It's all over."

"It's all over," the Reverend replies. "What a legacy. What a legacy."

Once again, his energy level lifts. "Please get the medication before it's too late. The government will be here soon... Don't be afraid to die." His voice spills over with urgency. A woman is asking if some people could survive to write about his great works.

"It's too late" he snipped. "Everyone, please come forward to drink the potion".

Ester fights to control her own panic. What she could see in front of her is incredible. A large vat sits on top of a long wooden table. Along the table were paper cups, piles of hypodermic needles, syringes, small squeeze bottles, and bottles of drugs. She watches as the Reverend's staff fills the cups, syringes and small squeeze bottles with a purple liquid that looks like Kool-Aid. A woman in a nurse's uniform directs people to come forward.

"It won't hurt," she says. "It's just a little sour."

Darkness envelops Ester's entire soul as she wishes with her whole being that she could just close her eyes and return to CyrIS. But it is not possible, and she is forced to watch as the Reverend views the whole procession. It was not as he had said, it was obvious it was not painless. Ester watches as people cry and scream and convulse. They throw up and gag and bleed for several minutes before death overcomes them. "Oh my God, what can I do to make this stop?" Esther thinks, and her heart brakes as she witnesses this pure horror. If only she could somehow communicate with CyrIS.

She then watches from behind the Reverend's eyes as he moves among the dying, asking them to die with dignity. He puts on the appearance of sympathy, but Ester can since his internal feelings are of complete satisfaction. He is in complete control.

This will show all those son-of-a-bitches.

As he moves among the dying, he tells them how great it will be on the other side.

"There is nothing to cry about," a woman announces over the loudspeaker. "This is something we could all rejoice about... Jim Jones has suffered and suffered... He is our only God."

One after another people come to the microphone and praise the Reverend and give extended testimonials to the righteousness of their decision to die and to the greatness of their leader.

Ester is confounded. "How can these people still be enamored with a man that is leading them to their death, killing their friends, their parents, and most of all their children?"

The security guards escort the more reluctant ones up to the front, to take the potion, and to die. The Reverend continually cries out for the people to keep down their *emotions* and hurry quickly to their deaths. But to Ester, all *logic* was gone, there was only *emotion*, and this seemed to go on forever. She is not sure, but it had to be a least two or three hours before there was complete silence.

The Reverend is now standing and looking out over a sea of dead bodies. Many are lying face down, some with their arms around a loved one. He then turns to one of his aids.

"And now I am going to close my eyes and you must do what you have been instructed to do."

I know this is the right thing to do because there can be no light without darkness.

The scene goes black as the Reverend closes his eyes, and in the darkness, Ester hears footsteps moving across the wooden floor, coming closer and closer. A metallic tinkle of a bracelet is heard against a wristwatch and a woman's voice speaks softly.

"I know this is the right thing to do you fucking hypocrite."

The Reverend does not open his eyes.

"What?" he says.

Immediately a loud crack follows, that rings in the Reverend's ears for only an instant. The sound of the gunshot fades from Ester's ears and is replaced first by the beating of her heart and then by the gentle beating of distant drums steadily getting closer. They seem to be calling her…calling her back. She drifts through the Lower World retracing her steps back to her room and now she is back, back with CyrIS, she is in his arms and he is crying and squeezing her tightly. Ester is crying too, sobbing so violently that she could not get a word out.

"My God!" CyrIS said. "What happened to you, I thought you were dying."

Ester remains silent for several extended minutes. When she tries to speak, she breaks into tears once again. Finally, after several hours passed, she is finally able to express herself.

"CyrIS, what I experienced was incredibly horrifying. We need to get to a TV and find out if this really happened. But I believe that it did, it all seemed so very real. You cannot imagine the frustration of watching all of that happen, with absolutely no way to do anything to prevent it.

I am sure you will understand better when I am able to tell you what I experienced, but I did learn a lot and one thing I now know for sure is that we cannot do this alone."

CyrIS looks puzzled. "What do you mean?"

Ester looks directly into CyrIS' eyes, her own red from the crying. "We cannot do this alone, other people are needed to open the puzzle boxes, and we need to find these people."

"And something else. There was a lady, the last person to speak to the reverend before I left. She was wearing a gold bracelet and it had three Xs on it. Or at least I think they were Xs. Let me draw you a picture of what they looked like."

Ester draws the bracelet as she remembers it.

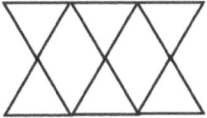

"It looks like three hour-glasses, rather than three Xs," CyrIS muttered. "I wonder if this is a reference to 'Tre Ore', 'The three hours' Agony"

"What's that?" Ester asked.

"It's a service held by some Roman Catholic, Anglican and Lutheran churches on Good Friday from noon to three, to commemorate the Passion of Christ. Not sure, just a thought."

Eventually, Ester falls asleep, and CyrIS holds her in his arms the rest of the night.

After several hours, Ester wakes up and begins thinking about her experience. It was obviously a very strange, *emotionally dark* experience, but Ester could not help but feel she had also been *enlightened*. She realizes that being *entangled* with someone else that way, was the most personal connection you could have with another human being. "*Enlightened* and *Entangled*" she thought. She now realizes that even though the Reverend Jim Jones had a very strong *connection* with his followers, he had practically no *connection* with the Bible and even more important, no *connection* with God.

"Just as the lady had said, he was a hypocrite."

Ester had truly lived the *logic and emotions* that the Reverend expressed towards the equality of mankind, and the need for all people to take care of each other, because they are *connected*. Now, this was all a part of her own *logic and emotions*. Also because of this, she felt a small part of the *voids* in her life had been filled in, she felt a little more complete. Then her mother's words from so many years ago popped into her head.

"I believe that people are often seduced by the powers of evil, and because of this seduction, they often do not even realize that what they are doing is wrong. They have their own *emotional* and possibly even *logical* reasons for their actions, and in their own mind may feel that their actions are justified. Therefore, we must all be very careful in our judgments of others."

It was amazing to Ester that her mother's words could be so pertinent to her recent journey. She was also amazed that she could have such a strong *connection* with a man that was so truly deranged as the Reverend. This was a man who could kill so many innocent men, women, and even children but could provide something to her that would help complete her. Ester sits for several hours trying to absorb this one thought. She tries to make sense of it all as the words of her father now echo in her mind. "Everything is a part of Mother Earth, and one should live their lives as though you are a part of the fabric which makes up all things." Ester now felt that she was much more a part of the fabric.

"But what is this fabric to which I am a part of?"

CHAPTER 8 – OUR SON WILL BE JOINING US FOR DINNER

October 4th, 1980
Christine Basurto, Age 12- Innocence

Christine, looking in the mirror, is starting to get curious about her body and more concerned about her looks. Her natural blond hair, light and bright, frames her lily-white face accents her light blue eyes. She is thin, and other than the hint of breast poking at her blouse, she had no curves at all. None the less, and though it may not be obvious to Christine, she is destined to blossom.

Christine is interested in boys, but her feelings are changing. Now she wants them to be interested in her. Not in a sexual way, she was much too shy for anything of that sort, but in a catching their attention way. In fact, in terms of sex, she thought it was gross. She couldn't imagine her parents even doing that stuff. None the less, she pays more attention to how she dresses, and she wants to start wearing make-up, but her mother says she is too young.

Christine's mother, mostly of Nordic and Russian ancestry, is back in college, working on a master's degree in psychology, and she will graduate in December. Christine sometimes wonders, if her mother is trying to use what she is learning in school on her. It seems to Christine, that her mother uses elaborate ways of explaining some very simple things, and although Christine loves her mother, and she appreciates the extra attention she sometimes receives, the extended explanations have gotten old. Often the bottom line of her elaborate explanations ended up with Christine not getting what she wanted.

On the other hand, Christine's father, with only a high school education and the training he received in the army had started a small used car business, which eventually became one of the biggest and busiest in the area. After many years in the business he was offered an opportunity to open a new Chrysler franchise in Denver, Colorado, which is where they lived today.

"And that's how I became successful in the car business! You don't need a college education to make money." He would say in his strong Southern accent.

Christine was just ten years old when they moved to Denver and over a three-year period Christine's father greatly expanded his business. The family now lived in a home in the upscale community of Cherry Hills. Here they joined the country club, met prominent figures, and developed friendships with many important local people.

Christine felt lucky that her parents had a lot of money; it allowed her to attend a private school and experience the finer things in life, like lots and lots of cloths. Christine's mother bought her clothes with bright light colors like Christine loved, and other nice things as well, and although her mother would not let her buy the short skirts she wanted, the clothes were acceptable; at least she was not embarrassed at school.

Christine also has her own room and a private phone line. She loves spending hours on the phone, talking to her girlfriends about clothes, boy bands, and about boys in general.

Right now, Christine was walking in the hallway of their home towards the kitchen area. She stops when she hears that her mom and dad are talking. The discussion is about her dad's workday.

"Oh, guess what?" he said.

Christine's mom does not reply, and Christine stands still and listens, because this sounded like the start of something he would not say if Christine was in the room.

"Remember when we had dinner with John and JoAnn in Evergreen a couple of weeks ago?"

"Sure!" her mom said.

Christine remembers that day very well, it was a Saturday evening, and her family had driven west along Interstate 70, up from their home in Denver, to the town of Evergreen. Evergreen, a small town in the foothills of the Rockies, is a location that

Christine loved to visit. In fact, she loved going to the mountains for any reason. She remembered how, on that day, as they climbed from the 5,280 feet elevation of Denver, up to the top of Mount Vernon Canyon, at 7,600 feet, they approached a specially designed overpass. The overpass framed a view of the Continental Divide with Mount Evans as its center piece. The sun had been setting behind the snowcapped mountains, and at the time, it took her breath away. This was the kind of scene that made Christine glad to be alive, it made her feel like she was not just an observer, but a part of the whole scene, a part of nature itself.

Her father had exited the interstate at El Rancho and then headed south along Highway 73. Driving through the evergreen trees that lined the road all the way down to the Evergreen Lake, had given her an indescribable and wonderful feeling.

As they drove toward Evergreen that day, Christine overheard her dad saying to her mother, "John is the CEO and President of a large corporation, with its headquarters right here in Evergreen." Christine had not really cared about any of that; she had just been enjoying the ride.

"How much longer until we arrive?" Christine had asked.

"It won't be much longer," her father had said. "Just be patient, we will be there soon."

This had disappointed Christine because she had just wanted to keep riding through the mountains. Then Christine recalled something else that had upset during that ride. She had asked her father, if the family had any children. Her dad replied, although at the time he seemed to be speaking more to Christine's mother than to Christine herself.

"I believe John said he had three children. His oldest son, graduated from an Ivy League school back east, and was a vice president in John's corporation. He also had a daughter who graduated from a college in Texas and is still living down there. I don't believe that either one of them will be at the dinner party this evening. His youngest son John Junior might be there tonight, but I am afraid he is much older than you are Christine, probably in his mid-twenties."

"I'm sorry that there won't be anyone there your age," Christine's mother had said. "But as usual please be polite to our host."

Christine had not responded. Her mother always said something like that when they were going to be with other people. She wished she wouldn't say such things, because Christine never caused any problems. She felt like her mom didn't trust that she would behave; at least not if she didn't say something. Christine remembers how much this irritated her at the time, and she hadn't asked any further questions.

After driving on the highway to Evergreen for a while, they had turned into a fancy subdivision. Up until this point the roads had been relatively straight, but the streets in the subdivision were twisty and winding, and by the time they arrived in front of a very nice looking home, Christine remembered how she had gotten a bit car sick and was glad they had finally arrived.

At the front door, the couple that owned the home had greeted them and invited them in. Christine's dad introduced Christine's mother and then he introduced Christine herself to their host. "Christine this is John and JoAnn." Christine had been coached many times on how to handle this kind of introduction and though a bit shy, had said, "Hello, John and JoAnn, it's very nice to meet you, you have a beautiful home and thanks for inviting us." Christine had looked at her dad, who gave her a little wink indicating that he was proud of her performance.

"Well, thank you for coming," JoAnn had said. "What a pretty yellow dress."

Christine remembered lowering her head and blushing and saying. "Thank you."

From that point forward Christine had been expected to only speak when spoken to, which had been fine with her. She really didn't like talking to strange grownups anyway, they always asked embarrassing questions. Questions like, *do you have a boyfriend?* Followed up with some other, '*none of your business*' questions.

They had sat in the large living room for a while and the adults had alcoholic beverages of some kind. Christine had lemonade, which was very good. She wondered where their son was, hoping to get to see him. She knew he was much older than she was, but she was still hoping he was good looking.

After a while they all moved to the dining room. A gorgeous chandelier hung above the long table covered with dishes, platters, glasses of all shapes and sizes, and an assortment of silverware. They all sparkled from the reflection of *light* from the chandelier. Christine had wondered who was trying to impress who.

They had talked for a while and then John said. "Our son will be joining us for dinner, I'll get him." After a moment or two, John had returned with his son and introduced John Junior to Christine's Parents. "John this is Paul and Pat Basurto. Paul, Pat, this is my son John Junior."

John Junior had turned out to be a disappointment to Christine. She liked tall, *dark*, muscular handsome men. John Jr. turned out to be none of these. He was relatively short, kind of pale looking and a little chubby. He seemed nice at the time and returned the usual courteous responses to Christine's parents. He said he was glad to meet them, and that he was sure that his parents had prepared a wonderful meal and hoped they would enjoy it.

Christine remembered how during the conversation, that went on for several minutes, it did not seem that anyone had even noticed that Christine was standing to the left of and a little behind her father. In fact, she thought that John Jr. had not even known that she was there.

Then suddenly, John Sr. had turned to her.

"Oh! Excuse me; we forgot to introduce our other guest." He had then turned to John Jr. "John this is Paul and Pat's beautiful daughter Christine. Christine, this is my son John."

Christine had then stepped forward from behind her father. She remembered how she had stuck out her hand, not looking up and said, "John it is nice to meet you, I think that you have a beautiful home."

128 | P a g e

When John Jr. had seen her, his whole demeanor had changed. He had not responded at first but had just stared at her. He had not taken Christine's hand and she had slowly lowered it to her side.

"JOHN!!!" John Sr. had snapped.

John had then seemed to come out of his trance.

"Oh!" John Jr. had said. "It's nice to meet you."

After a very awkward moment, he had then stuck out his hand for Christine. She had shyly reached out but only far enough to let him touch the very ends of her fingers. Immediately she had felt something very strange happen.

"Oh!" She had said loudly as she had glanced at his face and then pulled her hand away. The moment had scared her, and Christine thought about how she could feel that touch to this day.

John Jr. had looked away after the touch and Christine had looked at the floor. Her lily-white cheeks had reddened. She had known that her father was friends with these people. They lived in a very nice home in a very nice neighborhood, so *logically* it was a very safe place, but inside, her heart had pounded with rapid beats, not with the excitement that she sometimes had felt when she met a handsome man, but with a fear like she had never felt before. Not fear from his touch, because his touch had left her with an overwhelming feeling of nothing, it had invaded her whole body and there was no *emotion, or logic,* or anything associated with it, but there was this odd feeling of …*connection.* No, the fear she had felt was from the look in his eyes when he touched her, it had left her with a deep feeling that something dreadful was going to happen.

During dinner Christine had sat on the same side of the table with her parents directly across from John Jr. The awkward introduction did not sit well, and even though her shyness had held her back from looking at him, from time to time her curiosity had gotten the best of her, and she had looked up and he had been staring at her with a look of both love and hatred.

At one-point Christine's father had asked John Jr. if he was going to school. John Jr. had looked at her father and told him that he went for a while but had to drop out. Christine had been very thankful to her father for drawing John Jr's attention away from her.

Christine's mom had tried to help as well.

"John do you have a girlfriend?" she asked.

Christine appreciated her mother drawing John's attention away from her but had turned red again because of the embarrassing question.

John Jr., on the other hand, kind of lit up when he heard the question.

"Yes, I do," he had said. "She is a junior at Harvard and I just returned from seeing her."

Christine, at the time, could tell by the looks on John juniors' parent's faces that this was a surprise to them, or maybe an embarrassment. Christine's mom, on the other hand, had not seemed to catch the significance of this revelation.

"Oh, that's nice," she had said, and then turned back to John Jr.'s mother and started up a new conversation. John Jr. returned to staring at Christine.

After dinner everyone except John Jr. had moved to the living room. John Jr. told Christine's parents that he had been happy to meet them. He did not say anything to Christine before disappearing upstairs, and after what seemed like forever, her parents said their courteous goodbyes and they left.

Many days have passed since that ordeal, and Christine had pushed it all to the back of her mind. Now her dad was talking to her mom just beyond the kitchen door that Christine was standing next too.

"Remember how strange we thought their son John Junior was acting?" he said.

"Yes," her mom said. "Remember I asked him some questions and his answers were very strange, especially when I asked about his girlfriend."

"Well" her dad continued. "A couple of days ago he attempted suicide."

"Oh my God, oh my God" her mom cried. "Remember how he kept staring at Christine, Oh my God."

"Yes, I noticed that as well. I almost said something, but I did not want to embarrass our host."

"My God," her mom said. "That sends chills down my spine, had John mentioned any problems with his son before?"

"No, but I know he had dropped out of school and was traveling around the country, I think that half the time his family had no idea where he was, and he had just recently returned home. "

This all scared Christine immensely, and now she felt a little sick to her stomach. Her heart pounded in her chest. She remembered how that guy had been staring at her and that strange feeling she had when he touched her, and how she could still feel it today.

Now, hearing how upset her mom was, made her wonder what it all meant, her parents always seemed so *logical* about things, and to hear her mother express such *emotion* was frightening. *Was she in some kind of danger? Had she somehow felt his intent to commit suicide when he had touched her?*

Christine returns to her room, she would never discuss this with her parents, but she could not wait to get on the phone to tell her girlfriends all about it.

CHAPTER 9 – ON THE WAY TO NEW HAVEN

March 30, 1981
Christine Basurto, age 13-Innocense

Christine calls to her mother. She is sick…very sick. Her mother rushed to her bedside and helped her get to the bathroom.

After taking Christine's temperature her mother said, "Your temperature is high, but not too high. I think you have a flu bug. In any case, you're not going to school today. You need to stay in bed."

Christine's mother doesn't look the least bit concerned, which was reassuring to Christine. After vomiting some in the bathroom, Christine feels quite a bit better. A dizzy sensation is still there, and the queasiness had not gone away, but she is better than before.

Back in bed, she says a short prayer. Then she asked God to help her feel better, and she drifts off to sleep.

Christine hears a voice and ask herself, "Is God speaking to me? Where am I?" and "This is not a dream." It was very confusing for Christine, and she was getting scared as the voice in her head continued:

"You talking to me? You talking to me? Then who the hell you talking too? You talking to me? Well, I'm the only one here. Who the fuck, do you think you're talking to? Oh, yea. Okay."

It seems more like a memory than a voice. Christine could see a ceiling with lines of light streaming across it. These lines of light are moving in unison with sounds of traffic from a nearby window. "There must be a window off to my left." Christine realizes.

She is in a bed and she could feel the cover's weight on her stomach. But this was not her bed, or her room and it was definitely not her stomach. She had no power to move; she felt trapped. She could see and hear and feel yet had control over nothing. Terror dominated her emotions as she thinks "This must be a dream because I feel like I'm inside of another person.*"*

She once again started to panic, but then the voice in her head started again.

I really admire Brickle, and even though he was just a taxi driver, I wish I were more like him. I bet I've seen that movie at least fifteen times and read the book several times as well.

After I saw the movie for the first time, just like Travis, I started wearing fatigue jackets and boots and drinking peach brandy and fell in love with guns.

Boy! I really want to be like Travis--- and I really loved the way that 'Iris' looked in that movie. --- But I don't love Iris, I love Jodie. I can't get her out of my mind.

Christine sees an image of a skinny blond girl in a yellow dress on a busy street and thinks: "She looks about my age." Then Christine could feel the excitement welling up inside of this guy for this young girl.

"He's infatuated with her." Christine thinks as she tries to manage her fear.

His thoughts however, ramble between several subjects. He thinks about this movie, his family, the assassination of a president, or other bizarre murder fantasies. All his thoughts, no matter what they were, orbited around his overwhelming obsession with Jodie.

These thoughts also scared Christine, especially the thoughts of guns and murder. She wanted out of this person's mind; she wanted to be back in her bed, back in the safety of her own home and out of this strange room, and even stranger situation.

But no matter how she tried, she remains trapped and forced to see what this person was seeing, hear what he was hearing; if he was touching something, she could feel it. Worst of all she could hear, see and feel, the insane thoughts and images of violence he was having, mixed with his overwhelming obsessive love for Jodie.

Christine could feel his *emotions,* and somehow becoming intertwined with her own. She could sense the rapid changes in his body temperature. It moves from warm to extremely hot when he thought of making love to Jodie or doing something really crazy like killing the president. His temperature would transform from opposite ends of the spectrum like being hot one moment and then almost completely cold the next.

But then all of a sudden, he jumped out of bed. She could feel that he had to pee as he makes his way to the bathroom.

God, I'm so tired. That bus ride yesterday sure took it out of me. I should just kill myself and get this over with. No! No! Now wait a second. I have to figure out how to get Jodie to fall in love with me, or at least, somehow impress her with some heroic deed. But really, I just need to get some sleep one of these days.

Now Christine is looking down at the penis in her hand. Well not really her hand, but she could feel the soft warmth of the skin against her fingertips as well as the warm relief of the urine leaving his body. She had never seen a real penis before, and it was nothing like she thought it would be.

"How gross, how could any women stand to touch such a thing, much less have it actually inside of them?"

Now she could see the clear water in the toilet begin to turn yellow and hear the splashes of the urine as it hit the water below, some of it splashing on his legs.

"My God, could this get any grosser? I can't stand it." Christine thinks. This was all very, very shocking for a thirteen-year-old girl and she was not getting used to it. Then he put his penis back in his boxer shorts and walks to the mirror. He doesn't wash his hands but just looks in the mirror. If the view of a penis in her hand was not enough, she was now looking directly into his face. It was at that moment Christine had a realization. "This is the same guy who was at the dinner party in Evergreen, I think his name was John."

Her heart races. "Why am I here? What does this mean? What should I do? Am I being punished for having bad thoughts about this guy? Am I having any influence on his actions?" She felt so very, very powerless as his thoughts continued.

Sometimes I feel as if someone is watching me. Not watching over me, because no one cares, but just watching me. Making me do the things I do. Who are these people, why do they care about what I do? Sometimes I feel lost, but this dark force that is pushing me is the only thing that keeps me going.

He was looking directly into the mirror and Christine felt that he was looking at her. Did he know she was there? *Dark Forces*, what kind of dark forces is he talking about?"

He then leaves the bathroom, gets dressed, and decides to get something to eat.

I'm hungry, but I shouldn't eat. Just a few years ago I weighed 165, but now look at me, what? 230? 235? It seems like eating is one of the few distractions I have from my obsession to be with Jodie, and from whatever or whoever is driving me, driving me to some dark, but historic, deed to impress her.

He leaves the room and goes down to the street where he finds a McDonald's restaurant and orders some breakfast. As he sits there, he thinks about his life and how he had arrived in DC:

Living in Dallas with my parents was easy, I was a good student. In grade school, I was even the quarterback on the football team. And during junior high I had been elected President of the seventh and ninth grade classes, I even managed the school football team for a while, and I learned to play the guitar.

But in high school, it was different, I just got fed-up with trying to please everyone. I enjoyed being by myself more and more all the time. I liked spending hours alone in my room strumming my guitar and dreaming of becoming a songwriter like John Lennon. I knew my parents thought I was just shy, but I knew I just didn't like being around most people.

After high school, my family moved us to Evergreen, but I hated being there. I think that's when I first felt this outside force start to affect me.

My parents sucked, so I moved back to Texas to live with my sister. I tried Texas Tech for a while, but that was so much bullshit I had to move on. So, I dropped out and went to California to become a songwriter.

I was living in Hollywood when I first saw 'Taxi Driver'. That movie helped me, but Hollywood was so phony. I guess I should've figured that out the first time I went out there, but after that second time, I had to give up on being a songwriter.

Back in Texas, I dropped in and out of Texas Tech, not that I wanted a degree, but it kept my parents off my ass.

It was during that time that I purchased my first gun, a thirty-eight-caliber handgun, a real beauty. I loved going out to the countryside and being all alone. It was just me, with 'Travis' as my teacher, and this force pushing me. I could practice shooting for hours.

But now I am headed for New Haven once again. The first time was after I saw that article in People Magazine and I found out that Jodie had enrolled in classes at Yale University, I knew immediately that I must go and meet her.

Christine could hear all his thoughts, but they were muddled and mixed with flashes of varied images. It was often not a continuous stream of thought but rather a jumping from one thought about the past mixed with thoughts about the present. But to Christine, it was like watching a movie from *inside the movie*, and you had to interpret what you were seeing and hearing for it to make any sense at all. But as she listened to what seemed to Christine to be an insane rant, she started to calm down and thought about what her mother would do in this situation. "I know what she would do. She would pay attention and try to analyze his condition." And, even though she was still frightened, that is exactly what Christine began to do, and now she could hear a thought he was having that was very clear.

My obsession is with Jodie, and I've gotta…gotta find her, and talk to her, in person or something. That's all. I just want her to know that I love her. I don't want to hurt her. I think I'd rather just see her not...not on earth, than being with other guys. I just wouldn't want to stay here on earth without her.

Even though this thought was crystal clear Christine was not sure if this was a brand-new thought or if he was remembering something from the past, because his next thoughts were about the past.

I remember flying out there the first time and enrolling in a writing course at Yale just so I could be close to her.

I left letters in her mailbox and even managed to have two phone conversations with her. But things didn't work out that time, she just wasn't impressed with me. But that has made it just that much easier for me, that is, easier for me to follow this driving force pushing me to assassinate a president, or to do some other notable act to impress her.

"There's no way this Jodie is in love with this guy," Christine thought. "How funny it is...if Jodie had loved him back the way he loves her, it would be considered a great love story and would be a *good thing*. But if Jodie does not love him, as I suspect, and maybe even hates him, then his obsessive love would be considered weird, and therefore a *bad thing*. I wonder how the *emotions* of one person can change from a *good thing* to a *bad thing* just based on the response and *emotions* of another person, it just not *logical*."

Christine thought about the fact that her mother was a psychologist and she was wondering if it was starting to rub off on her. She also wondered if the reason she was here, was to learn something about life and the *connections* between people.

"I must pay attention, there has to be a lesson here for me."

After finishing his breakfast at McDonald's John headed back to the hotel. On the way there, he bought that day's edition of the Washington Star newspaper. In section A-4 he found an article outlining an itinerary for President Reagan, which included a notice that he would be speaking to a labor convention at the Washington Hilton in just a few hours.

Christine felt his *emotions* welling up once again and with it, his body temperature. These were scary feelings, his ambitions to be famous for killing a president, and a swarm of fantasies about Jodie falling in love with him for his bravery to do such a historic thing.

When he arrived back at the hotel, he prepared to take a shower and was now thinking of his family and how they had pushed him out of their home.

Listening to these thoughts, Christine wondered if she would be stuck inside this body forever. And, even though she had been stuck there for all the morning, she had only become, slightly more comfortable with her situation, and being forced to be in a shower and forced to look at a man's naked body was once again extremely embarrassing for her, and not at all fun. She was at least relieved that he was only taking a shower and not doing something more disgusting.

I really should just kill myself, although the other times I tried, didn't go very well. Just last October, back at home, I took all those anti-depressants and tranquilizers.

Christine recalled overhearing her mother and father discussing his suicide attempt and remembered the worry in her mother's voice.

Oh! And those two times, a couple of years ago, when I played Russian roulette with that .38 special I got in Texas. Sometimes I think the force that is pushing me, is saving me for something bigger.

And then my stupid parents sent me to that useless psychiatrist. Boy, he sure fucked me, telling my parents that I was emotionally immature and needed to be forced to make it on my own.

Shit! The money they were giving me allowed me to travel as much as I wanted. I could have taken a plane, instead of these stupid busses.

What the hell were they thinking? Telling me to go out and find a job. Like I could get a job. I didn't have a degree or any skills. I tried to make it as a songwriter, but there are no breaks for a guy like me in California.

God! I can't do anything right; I can't get a job; I can't even kill myself.

I've got to get up to New Haven and kill Jodie while she's still a virgin, that way she can't be with another man, and then maybe I can kill myself and we can be together in another life. Or at least, maybe I can kill myself in front of her, so she would understand my love for her. Or maybe I can kill President Reagan and that would let her know how I feel.

As he stood there, with the shower water splashing off the back of his head, he remembered a poem he had written which seemed so appropriate now,

"The Painful Evolution".
    In the beginning it was a time for pretending the martyr in me played games and I was the young alienated loner.
    Toward the middle, *I lied about pain and troubles. It was a mere three years ago that I played the part so well. Nearing the bend, I should have turned back. I could have taken the road that leads to a meaningful existence.*
    In the end, I cursed myself and suffered. I have become what I wanted to be all along, a psychotic poet.

Christine shivered with fear and she could feel the *emotional* pain that he was suffering. She thought how terribly lonely one can feel when they feel they have no *connection* to any other human being. This kind of *darkness* can be overwhelming. Christine thought that this must be an important lesson and Christine continued to pay attention as his thoughts rambled on, while the water from the shower continued to pound on the back of his head.

All these thoughts terrified Christine, what if he committed suicide or was killed by the police? Would it mean the end of her life as well? Christine, though in a state of panic, was still working her mind, still searching for a way out.

After his shower, he took a valium to calm down, and Christine could feel the warm glow of the drug cover his body and it seemed to help calm Christine as well, as she now watched him load a revolver that he had removed from one of his bags.

These Devastator exploding bullets are so cool! I can't believe I just walked into that pawn shop in Lubbock and bought-em.

He then sat down and began writing some notes on his present condition and then he wrote a letter to Jodie:

Dear Jodie,

There is a definite possibility that I will be killed in my attempt to get Reagan. It is for this very reason that I am writing you this letter now.   As you well know by now, I love you very much. Over the past seven months, I've left you dozens of poems, letters and love messages in the faint hope that you could develop an interest in me. Although we talked on the phone a couple of times, I never had the nerve to simply approach you and introduce myself. Besides my shyness, I honestly did not wish to bother you with my constant presence. I know the many messages left at your door and in your mailbox were a nuisance, but I felt that it was the most painless way for me to express my love for you.

I feel very good about the fact that you at least know my name and know how I feel about you. And by hanging around your dormitory, I've come to realize that I'm the topic of more than a little conversation, however full of ridicule it may be. At least you know that I'll always love you.

Jodie, I would abandon this idea of getting Reagan in a second if I could only win your heart and live out the rest of my life with you, whether it be in total obscurity or whatever. I will admit to you that the reason I'm going ahead with this attempt now, is because I just cannot wait any longer to impress you. I've got to do something now to make you understand, in no uncertain terms, that I am doing all of this for your sake! By sacrificing my freedom and possibly my life, I hope to change your mind about me. This letter is being written only an hour before I leave for the Hilton Hotel. Jodie, I'm asking you to please look into your heart and at least give me the chance, with this historical deed, to gain your respect and love.

I love you forever,
John

He wrote Jodie's name on an envelope, put the letter in the envelope, put the envelope in his shirt pocket, and put the pistol in his right-hand coat pocket.

I can draw quickly from that pocket. Practice makes perfect.

He then left the hotel and hailed a taxi. When he got into the taxicab he began to speak. This was the first time that Christine had experienced him speaking and she was shocked, she could feel him forming the words with his mouth as if they were her own and thinks "Oh my God, this must be the most amazing experience a person could have." she thought. "I am John, John is me."

Then, in an instant, the amazement was replaced with terror. She tried desperately to calm herself down. "I am an intelligent person, I must pay attention and look for a way out of this situation, out of this person. Panic solves nothing calm…calm…calm."

John was telling the taxi driver to take him to the Hilton Hotel. John looked at his watch, it was 1:30 PM. Christine could see that there was a light drizzle of rain on the windows of the taxi as it drove away.

I hope this goes better than those other attempts. There was that first time with Jimmy Carter in Ohio, in 1980, but I didn't even take a gun with me that time.

Since then I have really studied up, I have studied famous crimes like skyjackings, shootings, and assassinations. I've studied the details of each of these crimes; I've studied the preparation for the crimes including methods of stalking a victim. I studied the actual execution of the crimes including the use of weapons both long range and short range, I studied the details of all types of weapons and ammunition, not only their use but also how to conceal them.

But what I really want to understand is how the person feels committing these acts. I really don't give a shit about how the victims feel, I could care less about them. It's the people taking action that I am interested in; did it give them a sense of relief? Did it give them a feeling of justification? Did it fill in the voids in their lives?

I studied these things for several years, but I now realize that there is only one way for me to know how they felt. So, I practiced shooting my guns in the various positions that I learned from movies and books.

Once Ronald Reagan was elected President, I gave up on Carter and concentrated my efforts on Ronny, and I purchased a .38 caliber revolver to have a little more firepower.

And now here I am on my way to the hotel where President Reagan is scheduled to speak. Will the president even be there? Will I be able to get close? If I do get close, will I be able to pull my gun? There certainly had been enough times that I couldn't. But this time I do have a loaded gun in my pocket, and I'm headed to his hotel."

Should I just forget this and head on up to New Haven? Maybe I should stay another night in Washington and then head to New Haven tomorrow.

Christine was internally pleading with John.

"John please, just tell the taxi driver to turn around and take you back to the hotel. Go home, where you belong, let your parents take care of you." But his thoughts rambled on.

I'll just check out the scene, see how close I can get. If there's a possibility to assassinate the President, I will pursue that course, if not I will stay on my course to New Haven and my destiny there.

Christine tried screaming; "JOHN STOP, SHE WILL NEVER LOVE YOU IF YOU DO THIS. GO HOME! GO HOME!"

But at that moment, Christine could feel the power of the unseen forces, the hidden energy, which was pushing John forward. He was free to choose a path forward, as long as it was doing something. But, going home and doing nothing was simply not an option.

If I'm successful at the hotel it will most likely mean, at a minimum, the end of my freedom and possibly the end of my life. In either case, I will not be able to fulfill the purpose of my trip to New Haven but will fulfill my commitment to Jodie.

I commit this historical deed to gain your love and respect.

"I'm not getting through to this guy." Christine realized in frustration. "I have to pay closer attention, maybe there is another way."

The taxi driver left John off at the Washington Hilton. Christine was immediately surprised by how little security there seemed to be in the area. "Maybe, he is not coming." Christine thought. A feeling of relief comes over her for a brief moment, but then she could see where the reporters were congregating, and John walked right up to them and got very close to where it appeared the president was supposed to arrive.

This is a clear lapse in security, anyone could shoot him from this distance.

John began to move around, he seemed to be assessing the area to see where he could stand, eventually settling in right next to the reporters and cameras.

Christine could see policemen in their rain gear standing on the sidewalk and she could see other men, maybe secret service. Though they were looking around and seemed attentive, none of them seemed to be paying much attention to John.

Christine could feel John relax, and that scared Christine even more, because even though he felt relaxed, Christine could hear the incredibly insane thoughts now rushing through his mind, and Christine was afraid that he was actually going to follow through on some of these thoughts.

Christine could not see the doorway to the hotel and thought it must be just beyond the curved wall on the right. How could she get out of this, any relief from anxiety that she had received from the drug was completely gone now, she wanted out of the situation before something horrible happened, she was exhausted from screaming at John, and though she continued to struggle, nothing could be done.

John checked the time it was 1:45 PM.

All of a sudden, there it was, the President's motorcade, it rolled slowly up to the front of the hotel, but when they parked, the president's limousine parked quite a ways away, and there was the curve in the wall of the hotel between where they were standing and the point where the president got out of his limousine, which partially blocked the view. Even so, Christine could see the president from where they were standing, and fear gripped her senses. But then the President looked in John's direction and smiled and waved. Christine was shocked and relieved when John just waved back. But then:

Is this it? Should I draw and fire?

Then Christine felt something. John felt that the president was looking directly at him and that the smile and wave were meant specifically for him. She could clearly sense that it was the first time he had felt connected with someone in quite some time. It was a highly personal moment for him, and Christine felt even more relief as the president moved quickly into the hotel.

Christine was sure that John would now decide to leave and hopefully forget this outrageous notion, he would probably head up to New Haven, and then she would have to worry about what he would do there, but at least there was some relief for now.

John left his location on the sidewalk and went into the hotel lobby.

The president would probably be in the hotel for at least 45 minutes. I need to decide what to do. That may have been my best chance. What should I do now? Wait for the president to come back out? Go back to Park Central and spend the night, and then go to New Haven in the morning? Or, Leave for New Haven right now?

Christine felt John's body warm a bit, as he reflected on what he considered a very personal moment and connection with President Reagan on the sidewalk.

I remember having that same feeling after seeing several of Jodie's films on TV. I felt connected with her, and that connection, along with some invisible force, has driven me to be with her. And now I feel something similar, of course, it is not love, like I feel for Jodie, but it is a special connection, it means something, and I am not sure what to do about it.

After about 15 minutes in the hotel, John went back outside and stood, pretty much in the same spot as before. Christine could once again feel the fear building up inside of her because now the limousine was parked much closer to their location than it was before. Then Christine could hear a commotion at the front door of the hotel, the President was coming out; John checked the time, it was 2:25 PM.

Christine could see three policemen in raincoats standing just a few yards away. One by the limousine facing towards John. The other two, to the right of the first one, but closer to the hotel wall. All of them, turning their heads left and right, looking up and down the street.

Then, all of a sudden, there he was, the President. There are several men in ties walking with the President, and they are all walking right towards John, two white balding men and one black man. The uniformed policeman closest to John turns his back and faces in the direction of the President. Another white man in a grey suit standing next to the limousine turns and looks directly towards John.

For Christine, it feels like they are moving in mud. "GET GOING, HURRY UP," she screams.

If I am going to do this, now is the time.

Christine is petrified. "The President will be in clear view at any moment, please God, do not let this happen." Christine can see the President clearly now; he is surrounded by aides and bodyguards.

By way of Christine's connection with John, she can feel the highly personal *connection* he has with the President rising within him, and she hopes this *connection* will deter him from acting.

Christine sees the President looking towards the limousine, but someone from the crowd, yells "President Reagan. President Reagan!" The president starts to turn towards the voice which is in John's direction. At that moment a secret serviceman who was walking directly up to John, from his left, hears the voice in the crowd and turns away from John and towards the crowd. In fact, most of the heads in front of John turn towards the voice in the crowd.

I'll never have a better opportunity.

Christine feels a chill in her bones from the damp air and feels the skies growing *darker*.

I am absolutely in love with Jodie, and I am sure this is the right thing to do. I will be your hero, Jodie this is for you.

"It's happening." Christine feels John go into a crouch position; it seems very natural to him. He draws his gun, wraps both hands around its handle, and aims at the President.

Christine feels the rough crisscross pattern of the wooden handle of the gun within the palm of his hand. His thumb over the butt, three fingers below the trigger guard and one on the trigger itself. He is not breathing; the gun feels steady in his hand and he is squeezing the trigger. Christine can feel him inch the trigger backward towards his hand, everything in slow motion.

In the next instant, Christine watches in horror as John fires six times in succession, almost as fast as you can count to six. 1, 2, 3, 4, 5, 6. He is aiming directly at the president, but a white balding man, walking in John's direction, moves directly in the path of the first bullet, hitting him in the forehead. The bullet is merciless, and tears through the man's skull and brain. The man's momentum keeps him moving forward and he falls face first, directly in front of John. Christine can see the man's eyes as he falls toward her.

The officer closest to John, in the raincoat, has turned and is now facing the limousine and the second shot hits the officer in his neck from the back, he falls forward on the sidewalk away from the shots. The third shot misses everything. A man in a trench coat with sunglasses is hit by the fourth shot. He is hit in the chest and moves backward, turns away and falls face first on the sidewalk. The fifth shot appeared to hit the rear glass of the president's limousine.

As soon as the shooting started Christine could see that the President's aides were pushing the president into his limousine, and she was hoping that he would get in safe before he was hit! The sixth and final shot also appeared to hit the limousine, as the President was finally pushed in.

Christine was glad that the president did not get shot and she was not forced to witness his assassination, but at the same time, she was horrified at seeing the men who were hit. After the sixth shot was fired, John continued to pull the trigger, and in the next instant an arm came down around his head. Several men materialized on top of him and he was forced to the ground.

Christine could feel the trigger being pulled, over and over, as she and John were forced to the ground, then bodies were all over them, and there was immediately a sharp pain in John's wrist as the gun was wrenched from his hand.

Christine could now feel pain everywhere in John's body, caused by the sheer weight of all those on top of him. All of them frantically trying to wrestle John's arms to his back. And now Christine could feel the concrete sidewalk against John's face, they were merciless in their aggression, and Christine was sure that anyone of them would kill John if they could.

They haven't killed me yet. Now she'll know I care. Now she'll know I love her.

John closes his eyes.

Christine was instantly back in her room at home, breathing heavily, but she was alive, she was okay but still terrified. Christine was exhausted, she tried to call for her mother, but only a whisper came out. She cried, and once again tried to call for her mother, but it was no use. And even though she was afraid to close her eyes, sleep, like the events of the day, was forced upon her.

Later that afternoon Christine's mom checked on Christine and found her covered in sweat, but her fever had broken. Christine's mother did not wake her.

About 6:00 pm Christine woke up and eventually started feeling better. When she did feel better, all the *emotions* of what she had experienced flooded back and she began to cry. She was so innocent but now violated in a way like none other.

Her mother returned to the room, and hearing Christine sobbing, asked: "What's the matter dear?" Christine said that while she was sick, she had a very bad dream and it had terrified her. Her mother held Christine's trembling body close to hers and tried to comfort her.

"Oh! Darling that was just a bad dream, it happens sometimes when a person has a high fever. Just forget about it now, you're with me, your safe, and I love you."

Christine tried her best to put it out of mind and hoped and prayed that it had been just a bad dream.

CHAPTER 10 – WHITE AS A GHOST

April 1ˢᵗ, 1981(The next day)
Christine Basurto, age 13-Innocense

Christine, walking into the kitchen of her home in Denver, is feeling a lot better since her *bout with the flu*. None the less, she is feeling extremely depressed from the effects of the previous day's experience.

Christine's dad is sitting at the kitchen table, as he did most Sunday mornings. On Sunday mornings he is usually reading the Sunday newspaper, but right now he seemed very focused on the small TV set that sat on the counter, next to where Christine's mother was cleaning some dishes., but when Christine's mother saw Christine, she stopped what she was doing.

"Oh! Honey, I am so glad you're feeling better; you must have had a 24-hour flu bug or something. Anyway, you need to eat some breakfast so you can get your strength back."

Christine's dad did not look up from the TV set but murmured something about how he is glad she was feeling better. He is watching the news, but Christine is suddenly shocked, she cannot believe what she is seeing.

There on the tiny TV screen are images of a street in Washington DC that are right out of Christine dream, and the man on the TV is saying that there had been an attempt on the President's life, that the President had been shot and was in critical condition.

Christine's mom notices the look on Christine's face. "Oh, its terrible honey, the President was shot yesterday, and they think it was the son of that family we had dinner with in Evergreen last year. You remember, the friend of your dad's? The boy's name was John."

But it was not just that the President had been shot, and it was not that it was the boy from Evergreen. It was the fact that

Christine was watching her nightmare unfold, right in front of her on the TV set.

Christine recognizes everything.

They are showing the curved wall of the hotel, the president's limousine, the president walking towards the camera, and then that moment...that terrible moment when those men were shot as the president is pushed into his limo. All from the same perspective that she observed it, and they repeated it, and repeated it, over and over. Christine was horrified, but she could not take her eyes off the TV.

"Christine you look white as a ghost, maybe you should go back to bed," her mother said.

Christine pleaded with her mother, "No, please, I want to stay here with you and dad. I'm scared."

"Oh, dear, there's nothing to be afraid of. It's a terrible thing, but that happened miles and miles away in Washington D.C. And that boy, John, he's under arrest, he can't hurt you." Then directing her words to Christine's father, her mother says, "Maybe you should turn the TV off for a while, really, they are just showing the same ugly video over and over."

Christine's father turns off the TV, but Christine's nightmare was real, and Christine's fear rises from what she had seen. She could not come to tell her parents about what she had experienced, and she surely did not want to go back upstairs to be alone.

It must be some kind of hallucination or something, this could not really have happened. Christine thinks.

In any case, she was afraid that if she told her parents, they would think she was crazy, or even worse, that she was doing drugs.

She could hear her mother's words ringing in ears; "I am hearing so much about drugs in the schools these days. Then she would say, Christine are you doing anything with drugs? Please tell me the truth, I won't be mad at you, but I need to know."

Christine had often told her mother that she was not doing any drugs, even though, she had heard some of the girls at school, saying that they had tried some. Of course, she did not tell her mother that part, and besides, she did not believe her mother when she said, she would not get mad. She had gotten mad at Christine for a lot less.

In any case, she was *definitely* not going to tell her parents about what happened. She wanted to tell someone, but she was not even sure she could tell her best friend Millie. Millie would probably think she was crazy too, and if the story ever got out at school, she could be humiliated and become, some kind of sideshow freak, just like some of the unpopular girls. Christine decides that this was one dream that she would keep to herself. Eventually, maybe she could just push it out of her mind completely. But she did want to know how the President was doing and prayed that he would be okay.

Christine's mother graduated with her master's degree in psychology at the end of the previous year, and she often discussed what she had learned in psychology and its relation to current events. Occasionally she would mention the psychological effects of using drugs, but this morning she was not talking about drugs, but she was on a role.

Christine's mother went into a lengthy rehash, of the events of the evening they had spent in Evergreen a year ago. She commented on how strangely John Jr. had acted, but Christine noticed that there was no mention of how he had acted towards Christine. She was surprised that her parents were having this conversation with her in the room. She was not sure if they no longer realized she was sitting there, or if they had concluded that she was now old enough to listen to these types of things, and it was all part of her education. In any case, Christine listened intently and did not attempt to interrupt, for fear she would be asked to leave.

Christine's mother kept saying how John was obviously a psychopath, and she was talking about the psychology of people who commit violent crimes. Since her mother's graduation, she had taken a job in the Jefferson County Sheriff's Department, as a forensic psychologist and was really starting to get into it.

Christine heard her mother talking to her dad all the time about her job and the cases she was working on, but right now she was talking more about psychology.

"There are several reasons why a person is driven to commit or attempt to commit murder," she said. "There are domestic homicides, revenge killings, 'authority homicides' in which the victim is in a position of authority over the killer, extremist homicides, committed because of the killer's ideology, like the Ku Klux Klan or other white supremacists, and there are mercy-hero murders, as sometimes occurs with healthcare worker. This is when they act out of a desire to put his or her victims out of their misery. There are also murders in which the murderer constructs an elaborate fantasy about his or her victim and will do anything to preserve it, including killing the object of his or her fascination."

"The murderer may also kill someone else. Again, this is all part of a fantasy in which the murderer plans on emerging as the hero because the killing is justified in the murderer's mind. He or she knows that this act will impress that certain someone, which the murder must impress, be it a parent or other loved ones, which are really just objects of the murderer's desires."

Christine listens and could not believe what she was hearing, she lived in this guy's mind and experienced his fantasies about Jodie. She listened to him tell himself how killing the President would make Jodie know how much he loved her. It was just like Christine's mother was saying. She wanted to speak up and say, "Yea, mom that's exactly what that guy was thinking about." But she couldn't, she was already petrified with fear from what had happened to her, and now she was afraid of what might happen to her if she spoke up. So, she sat in silence and listened as her mother continued her speech.

"It can all, of course, be a result of how a person is raised, and this can affect their propensity to commit murder. Insecure children are more likely to engage in later violent behavior. Insecurity produces low levels of empathic understanding. A person develops self-control and empathy as the result of receiving empathic understanding from a parent or guardian, as a child. It is that close *connection* to other people that is important. When a person can perceive others as humans rather than as objects, they are less likely to inflict injury upon them. This *emotional* investment facilitates the development of self-control by fostering empathic understanding and the development of trust, leading to non-deviant behavior."

"So, was there anything that could have been done?" Christine's father asked.

"Perhaps," she noted. "Sometimes this lack of self-control can be recovered by the person if they can receive an appropriate amount of *emotional* investment from and *connection* to others later in their life, possibly through their job, but most often from a significant other, like a parent, girlfriend or mate. However, this can often be very difficult for the person who did not receive this *emotional* investment when they were a child, because now it seems *logical* to them, to be extremely distrustful of everyone, and they are constantly looking for evidence of betrayal from everyone they know and especially the ones that they are closest to. Often, a person who continually receives or perceives to receive a lack of empathy from others later in their life, will use this as further justification for their deviant behavior."

Up to this point, aside from that single question, Christine's dad had not said much. But now he looks up from his paper.

"I think it's those radical liberals who just hate having a Republican in the white house. They would do anything, including assassination, to get him out of there."

Christine's father had not originally been into politics very much. But over the past few years, he had become very upset with how the government was being run, and now, he often preached to his family at the dinner table.

"The government is spending too much money," he would say. "Especially on welfare and other handouts. The men and women in this country are blessed with individual rights and freedoms that are not available anywhere else in the world, and I believe that the only way to truly succeed in life is through hard work, supporting your family, and self-discipline." And now he was now on his own role.

"The only logical way to encourage growth and prosperity in this country is to limit government involvement, and only create regulations that help businesses, especially small business, and keep taxes to a minimum."

Christine's mother tried to interrupt but he would have none of it and went on.

"The only reason for taxation is to support good American infrastructure, like roads and bridges and of course to support our military. Because it is important that America remains the strongest military power in the world, to make sure that the world is not taken over by those god-damned communists."

And as usual, he added "And of course those god-damned communist loving liberal Democrats just want to tax like hell and give it away to every freeloading bum who has his hand out. I am sure that if you dig deep enough you will find out, that this John kid is some kind of liberal nut case."

Right now, Christine knew that her dad was wrong. What had happened the day before, had absolutely nothing to do with politics, and it had everything to do with that creepy John's infatuation with Jodie.

Later, her father had to turn the TV back on, to see what was happening. It seemed that the story about the President's assassination attempt, was on every channel, and they kept repeating the video and talking about how the President was in critical condition. Eventually, Christine could not take it anymore, so she went back up to her room. She collapsed on her bed; she certainly had not slept well the previous day and especially that night.

Christine was fascinated by her mother's speech and analysis. "What are these internal and external *forces* that drive people to do what they do?" she whispered to herself. She felt overwhelmed with depression, so she tried hard not to think much about the previous day, and concentrated more on what her mother had said.   But she could not even do that, the more she thought about any of it, the more depressed and scared she became.

Now trembling from fear, she thought, *this is so very scary, and it's getting worse, I am not sure what I am going to do.*

Eventually, exhausted, Christine fell asleep.

CHAPTER 11
"AN AWFUL LOT OF GRAY!"

August 1st, 1981
Ester Suni Nati, age 29

Ester looks at the speedometer of her 1979 Alfa Romero, and watches the small black needle move just above 90. She had not been paying attention to her speed, thinking a lot about CyrIS and her destination to a place called Mount Carmel. She heard that the Texans were pretty easy going when it came to speeding, but she slowed down a bit, not sure how easy they would be on someone with out-of-state plates.

The countryside is sagebrush and cactus but finally she sees off in the distance, a series of off-colored white buildings, which she assumed must be "The Living Waters Branch" religious compound.

It had been three years since Ester had taken her terrifying journey to 'Jonestown', but it felt as if it were yesterday. Ester had on several occasions tried to overcome her *emotions and* explain to others about her experience. However, when she explained to people that she had been at the compound, most looked at her with skepticism. Basically, they thought she was crazy, and Ester sometimes wondered if they were right. Most thought the details she described to them were just regurgitations of news reports. But that was not what kept Ester from telling the whole story. It was all those horrific images and *emotions,* which were now burned into her memory. She simply would break down and cry every time she attempted to tell anyone. It was because of those images, she could never go to the authorities with her story. Not because she was embarrassed by what they might think, but rather because she could not bear to relive the pain.

But there was something else she could not shake; it was how so many of the Reverend's followers worshiped him. They believed that they had found a true prophet, one that could help them find a path to heaven. Because of this, to Ester, it was only *logical* that they would follow him. Ester could relate to those people because she too was looking for that path to heaven, or to the Upper World or to the other side. Whatever the case, it is a place she now believed existed more than ever. It was that place, which provided a source of power and knowledge. It was the place that gave Ester her psychic abilities, and she believed that it was this source of power, that had also *connected* her to the Reverend Jones. She was sure of it.

And even though she did not understand why she had been given this gift, or why she had to have that particular experience, she knew deep within her heart and soul, that there was a reason, and someday she hoped it would become clear to her.

But she also knew, deep down, that she would not discover the true meaning of that experience without continuing her search, her search for answers, and maybe even for a true prophet. A prophet, or someone, to help her make the *connection* with the other side, with the *spiritual* world, to help her understand the bible and its mysteries, and other mysterious forces in the universe. To ultimately solve the puzzle that leads to the *Holy Spirit,* and to God.

CyrIS had been extremely helpful in her journey but she needed more. So, her search continued and here she was, going to Mount Carmel, just another part of that pursuit.

A while back, Ester had come upon a magazine called *Shekinah.* The magazine was authored by a lady named Lois Roden. In the magazine, Lois was promoting an incredible idea. She explained that "Shekinah" was an ancient Hebrew term for the "Bride of the Sabbath", and that the "Shekinah" was an earthly presence of the divine *spirit*, and that it was somehow an integrated part of the concept of the Messiah. But what amazed Ester the most, was that Lois Roden was preaching a concept different from most, she was promoting the idea that the *Holy Spirit* was feminine. Ester was intrigued by this idea, maybe the *Holy Spirit* was female, and maybe that would be a key to helping Ester understand the whole concept of the *Holy Spirit.*

However, the motivation for this trip was more than just the invitation she had received from Lois, and it was more than just curiosity. Unseen forces were driving Ester on this journey south to Texas, and Ester knew that she must go and meet this mysterious woman and seek her advice.

Before embarking on this trip, Ester had done some research on this bible-based community. The "Mount Carmel" in the bible was the place where the Prophet Elijah, fought the worshipers of a pagan god named Baal. The Mount Carmel that Ester was headed for, which was located just on the outskirts of Waco, was established in 1934 by Victor Houteff, a former Maytag washer salesman from Bulgaria. Houteff had been a Seven Day Adventist, but the mainstream portion of that religion rejected his prophetic doctrines, so Houteff created his own sect called the Davidian Seventh-day Adventist Association.

Houteff's community grew from just a few people to more than a hundred, and this community was self-contained, with its own school and community kitchen. But the community was very primitive, with just a few poorly made wooden cottages for all those people to live in. The community was so poor it was difficult to make many improvements, but Houteff also considered the harsh environment a test. A test of the community member's ability, to achieve "the conquest of the flesh in the name of the *spirit*" as prescribed by Houteff himself.

In 1955 Houteff died, and after a battle with several members of the community, Ben Roden, Lois Roden's husband, became Houteff's successor. At that time the town of Waco was growing, so Roden sold the land to the city, and in 1957 he moved the community to a large ranch 10 miles southeast of Waco. Roden called his new community the "Living Waters Branch", and he called the new location the "New Mount Carmel", but later the "New" was dropped.

Roden had predicted that the end of the world would occur on April 22nd, 1959, and on that date nine hundred Davidians, from around the country, had congregated at the new Mount Carmel.

When the end of the world did not occur, Roden's following dramatically dropped in numbers. In 1978 Ben Roden died and Lois became the leader of the remaining group. She was then called the *Prophetess*.

Ester could imagine that the citizens of Waco were not very happy with this small Non-Baptist religious community, southeast of their town. After all Waco Texas was the home of the Southern Baptist Baylor University. This was a very strict puritanical portion of the Baptist religion, they even believed that drinking and dancing were a sin.

Ester now approaching Mount Carmel from the North turned left off the Double EE highway onto a dirt road. Off to her left was a fairly large lake, surrounded by miles and miles of farmland, and one building complex, it was the "Living Waters" compound.

The compound was a very long two-story building, that had windows all along the first and second floors. Other buildings of various sizes, including a four-story tower, were *connected* to the main structure as well. It appeared that there were other buildings behind the main building, but Ester could not tell if they were *connected*. But all the buildings were the same color, a kind of dingy gray. The roof, windows, and shutters were all a lighter shade of gray, but all gray none the less.

Ester thought to herself, "With the overcast skies it seemed like an awful lot of gray."

Ester parked her car and walked towards what looked like the main entrance, which was located on the left side of the front of the building. As she approached the front door, it opened, and a young man greeted her. "You must be Ester," he said, "Lois has been expecting you."

He was a handsome man, with his long curly brown hair, thick aviator spectacles, and a light beard. He was wearing a light-colored shirt and blue jeans. Ester thought he looked somewhat like a hippie from the sixties and a little bit like Jesus.

As she entered the building, the young man stuck out his hand in welcome and said "My name is David, welcome to our community. --- You are very beautiful." Ester, a bit shocked, extended her hand.

As soon as she touched his hand, she felt it. A rush of *emotions*, and a feeling from the past, a feeling she had not felt in many years, but that was still very familiar to her. It was the feeling of the *void*, that nothingness that leaves you feeling stuck in the *middle* and a little sick to your stomach. It was the same sensation she had in San Francisco when she was first touched by the Reverend Jim Jones, accept this time, she did not fall to her knees and into an abyss as she had at that time.

At first, it scared her, and then, suddenly, a flood of memories rushed through Ester's mind. That sensation of dropping down into a pit of darkness, and then being saved by CyrIS, and then, much later, that terrible day with Jim Jones. All feelings, she had attempted to keep repressed, at least until this moment. Now, just like it had been with the Reverend, she felt a *connection*. But there was something different this time. With Jim Jones, she had felt very uncomfortable. She could sense the Reverend's psychotic nature, and even though he had some worthwhile intentions as it related to racial equality, Ester felt that his huge ego and an undercurrent of sleaziness that kept her from ever liking him, even in the least little bit.

But here, with David staring deep into Ester's eyes, her insides melted a bit, awash with the warm feelings of a woman affected by the look of a handsome man, and then she remembered the first time she looked into CyrIS' eyes. But there was more. She could feel the *connection*, a *connection* she was sure was permanent, and one that she was sure he felt as well, simply because of the look on his face.

But then David said "Zuni?" Ester was shocked, and replied, "Yes, how did you...?" David shrugged his shoulders, released her hand and moved away. As he walked away, Ester studied him closely, sure that her relationship with this man would extend well beyond this brief meeting. David then asked her to wait in the hall and said he would get Lois. He did not look back as he walked away.

After a few minutes, an elderly lady came walking down the hall. David was not with her, and the lady introduced herself as Lois Roden. Ester was a bit surprised, not sure exactly what she was expecting of this lady they called the Prophetess, but she did not expect her to look like a country schoolmarm or a librarian. But Ester thought; that is exactly how she looked, with her short hair in a bun, high forehead, and in a dress reminiscent of Quaker's.

Lois directed Ester to another room which was poorly lit, the furniture was extremely worn, and there was nothing on the walls or floors.

This is a very austere environment. Ester thought.

They sat down, and after some pleasantries, Lois asked,

"Why have you come all this way to see me dear?"

Ester explained, "I am very interested in your concepts of the *Holy Spirit*."

Lois responded by saying "You are a very beautiful woman, are you a Native American?"

Ester knew, that even though her skin was *dark*, she carried the unmistakable features of her father.

"Yes, my father was a Zuni Shaman."

Lois now had a bit of a shocked look on her face. "Oh! How fascinating, are you a shaman as well?"

Ester, could tell that Lois was impressed, and probably wanted to talk to her about it in more detail, but Ester attempted to downplay this topic, trying to get back to the reason she had come, and said,

"I am studying the practice, but I would much rather talk about your philosophies on the *Holy Spirit*." Lois looked a bit disappointed, but this seemed to get her back on track.

"In 1977, a year before the death of my husband, I had a vision of the *Holy Spirit*, and the vision was of a 'shimmering silvery Angel', a female angel." Lois pointed to the Bible sitting on a nearby table, "In the Bible, the word for *Spirit* is 'Rauch'. This word along with the word 'Shekhinah', which means 'Devine Presence' are both feminine words in Hebrew."

Lois went on to quote many passages of the Bible, from Genesis all the way to the book of Revelations. Most of the quotes were very vague references to the *Holy Spirit*, which Lois said, proved that the *Holy Spirit* was feminine. One of the most prominent of the quotes was one that Ester was very familiar with.

"And there appeared a great wonder in heaven; a woman clothed with the sun and the moon under her feet and upon her head a crown of twelve stars: Revelations 12:1" Ester had always assumed this was a description of the Virgin Mary.

Lois also pointed to many passages, which she said indicated that the *Holy Spirit* was *everywhere,* and within us at all times. One example she gave was.

"Know ye not that ye are the temple of God, and that the *Spirit* of God dwelleth in you, 1 Corinthians 3"

Lois went on for over two hours talking about the Kabbalah, the Bible, and her theories on the *Holy Spirit*. But Lois also offered Ester a warning.

"My dear there are organizations that use the Kabbalah and even the Bible, as their justification for actions that are truly not Christian in nature. I believe the people responsible for these unchristian actions may be exactly the antithesis of the *Holy Spirit*, and you must be constantly prepared to defend your beliefs against these forces. For the people in these organizations and especially their leaders will go to any extreme to protect the secrecy of their organization and the achievement of their goals. You must know that when you search for the *Holy Spirit* you will uncover some of these secrets and be exposed to great danger. Here at Mount Carmel, we are prepared to do battle with these outside forces and will fight to the death to protect *our* beliefs as well, and this may be the only place, anywhere, that is truly safe."

Watching the intensity build in Lois' face, Ester began to feel she was not being educated as much as she was being recruited. Recruited as a soldier in the war against these evil outside forces. It seemed that Lois was trying to scare Ester. But Ester also sensed that Lois needed more followers, and at one-point Lois even asked Ester if she was interested in moving into the compound. Ester declined, and after asking a few more questions about the Bible and the Kabbalah, Ester told Lois she needed to head back home. Lois was very polite, but Ester could tell that Lois knew she did not have a new recruit.

As Ester drove away from Mount Carmel, she thought about the things that Lois had told her, none of which provided any revelations into her quest for a clearer understanding of the *Holy Spirit*. However, she had been fascinated by Lois' references to the Kabbalah. But, thinking of the intensity in Lois' eyes when she talked about it, gave Ester the shivers.

Ester had been very familiar with the Kabbalah because as a student of religion and of the mystics, she had studied the Kabbalah's history. In the traditional Jewish beliefs, Ester remembered, the Kabbalah is a set of teachings meant to explain the relationship between the eternal mysterious infinite, no end, and the finite mortal universe. The Kabbalah is not a religion, but it forms the foundation of mystical religious interpretations. It seeks to define the nature of the relationship between the universe and human beings in a series of presented methods. This relationship between human beings and the universe was of special interest to both Ester and CyrIS, and she felt strongly that it was a key to understanding the *Holy Spirit*.

As Ester drove north toward her home, she rolled all of this, over and over in her head, and she believed that it all meant something. Somewhere in the bible, or somewhere in all the information she had accumulated over the past few years, there existed clues leading to an answer. What are these forces that Lois and others have referred too? Maybe the answers she was searching for, were hidden in the understanding of these forces, the forces of *light*, as well as the forces that lie within *darkness*. Maybe with CyrIS' help, they could decipher some of these clues. But for now, she had no answers, only more clues.

As she drove down the road, a vision of David's eyes appeared in her head, and that empty feeling of when she had touched him, once again invading her body.

I need to get home to CyrIS.

CHAPTER 12 – LESS FIGHTS AND LESS PREJUDICE

May 19ᵗʰ, 1983
Rufus Middleman, age 13

Half asleep, Rufus rests his elbow on the armrest of his father's 1979 Chrysler K car. He watches aimlessly as the boring cityscape of Des Moines Iowa passes him by.

He moans to his father: "Father, when are we going to get to Denver?"

His mother replies instead: "Not today, we'll be staying in a motel tonight. We should arrive in Denver sometime tomorrow. You're just going to have to be patient".

Rufus Middleman was born in New York City. His father, Aharon Middleman, a Hasidic Rabbi, was born and raised in one of the predominantly Jewish neighborhoods of New York City. His mother, Ariana, was from Harlem, one of the toughest black ghettos in the city.

Rufus doesn't know how they got together, and he really didn't care. Since his parents' marriage, they had been living in the Crown Heights area of New York, a predominantly Jewish and Black neighborhood.

One might think that being half Jewish and half black in this neighborhood would be a good thing. Unfortunately, it was not. Rufus was raised Jewish, but his skin is exceptionally black, even for a black kid. He looks pretty much like most of the other black kids in the neighborhood. However, because of the way his parents dressed him, he looked different. Though the Jewish community treated him very well for the most part, the black kids called him names and picked on him. He often heard insults like: "Heil Hitler" and "Jew Boy," from kids in the neighborhood. All of this had made Rufus a very, very angry young man.

Rufus' father, Aharon, is a very big man - six foot six and weighing over 280 pounds, and Rufus is big too, but that did not keep kids from picking fights with him, which made Rufus very tough, because he had to fight a lot of kids much bigger than himself. Not always winning, but always giving it his best.

Rufus likes fighting. After all, he had become pretty damn good at it. What he really liked, was how he felt right after a fight, no matter if he had won or lost. It provided some relief to the constant frustrations he felt about his situation. But the real problems would start when he would get home. His mother was always sympathetic. She knew what it is like in the ghetto, and she knew that if you didn't defend yourself, you could get killed. But Aharon did not tolerate it. He thought fighting was for animals, and he was also very frugal. So, when Rufus came home with his clothes all in tatters from a fight, Rufus would often get another beating from his father. Then, he would be forced to do chores at the house late into the night to make up for the damaged garments.

But all of that, is in the past now, because Aharon had been offered a position in a synagogue in Denver Colorado and had accepted it. Now, here they were, on Interstate 80, heading west to the mountains of Colorado. Since Rufus has never really seen any mountains before, he is kind of excited about it.

Aharon says: "This place, where we will be living in Denver, is much different than living in Crown Heights. There is a fairly large Jewish community and a small black population. It is nothing like the ghettos."

One of the main reasons Aharon accepted the position was to get his family, and especially Rufus, out of that environment. *'Fewer fights and less prejudice'*, he would say.

There is also another reason for the move. Rufus is doing very well in school, especially in math and science. Aharon had said that there are some really good schools in Denver, and he was hoping that if they get away from the distraction of the streets of New York, Rufus would be able to concentrate on his studies. Maybe even develop himself into a notable scientist like Albert Einstein, which is Aharon's hero.

Rufus thinks that school is okay. He likes studying, but he is a big boy, and he doesn't look like the other nerds in his school, you know, the typical ones that like math and science. He wants to get into sports like football or maybe even Rugby. He likes the physical contact of fist fighting, but there will be none of that in Denver, and he is going to miss it. Aharon is aware of the fact that Rufus likes to fight and told him that they will look into getting him into a Karate class when they get settled down.

Rufus stops thinking about the past and stares mindlessly now at the bleak highway in front of them.

Rufus knows his father is a good man. He will do most anything for other people as long as it doesn't cost him much of his own money. At the same time, he is always suspicious of other people, especially strangers. He will often tell Rufus and his mother stories of how the Jewish people have been persecuted over the centuries. He had especially bad stories about the way the Jews were treated by the Germans in World War II.

However, Ariana, who also had stories about racial prejudice, seemed to trust everyone. She would often talk Aharon into doing things which he would not ordinarily do; including helping people he would not ordinarily help, and right now she was doing exactly that.

"Abe, look someone is broke down on the side of the road ahead," Ariana says, "let's stop and see if we can be of some help."

Aharon immediately replies, "We don't have time for that. We need to keep going".

But Ariana knows just how to handle Abe. She says: "Okay, I guess that's what Yahweh would want you to do". Referring to the Old Testament name for God.

Rufus can see the look of exasperation on his father's face, as he slows the vehicle. He eases it over to the side of the road until it is just several yards behind the truck referred to by Ariana.

This truck is packed to the brim with what looks like personal belongings. From the back-seat Rufus can see a man working on one of his tires, and seems to be having some trouble. Rufus asks if he can get out of the car with his father. His father starts to say no, but then says: "Yes you can stretch your legs but stay on the side of the car away from the road."

Aharon moves next to the front of their car and yells: "Is there anything we can do to help?" The man stands up and says something, but Rufus cannot hear because of the noise from the Interstate. Aharon tells Rufus to stay next to the car, and then he walks over to the other man. Rufus can see them introducing themselves. At one point, Rufus can see his dad look back toward their car, point and say something. They talk for quite some time. His father makes gestures, as he often does when he talks, occasionally pointing to the sky.

Rufus wonders what they are talking about because he knows that his father is usually talking about religion when he starts pointing at the sky. Eventually, his dad stops talking and walks back to their car. He immediately informs Ariana: "They have a flat tire. His name is Randy. He is moving his family to Idaho and he says he needs a better tool to get the lug nuts off the tire. I am going to look and see what we have in the trunk that might help."

Rufus follows his dad to the back of the car. Most of the furniture and other household goods are being shipped to Colorado by a moving company. However, the trunk is still full of some of the more personal items and some suitcases. It takes Aharon a couple of minutes to unload some of these things and get to his toolbox.

When his father does get to the tools he exclaims:" Great! I thought I had one of these." He pulls out a large wrench that looks like a *cross*. The *cross* has holes at the ends of the four arms that are for different sized nuts. Aharon turns to Rufus and says "Here, take this over to the man. Be careful. I am going to see if there is anything else in here that might help."

Rufus takes the wrench over to the man who is still trying to get the nuts off of the tire with the wrench he has. As Rufus approaches, he can see the man is white, with brown hair and a stubbly short beard. He is well tanned, like a farmer or someone who works outside a lot.

Approaching the man, Rufus says, "My dad told me to bring you this."

The man puts down his wrench and turns toward Rufus. When he sees Rufus, he looks shocked. At first, Rufus thought it is because the man did not expect to see such a large young boy behind him. But then, Rufus sees it. It is that look that white people sometimes give when they see a black person close to them, and Rufus is very black. It's like they have seen a ghost, or a thief or something. They look down, seeming uncomfortable, and a little bit angry. However, Rufus is the one who is most angry.

'Fucking white prejudice bastard, I could easily kick his ass.'

Finally, the man looks up and says with a smile: "Oh boy, that's just what I need!"

The man reaches for the wrench just as Rufus pushes it toward him. They both overextended a bit and their hands came close to touching. They do not actually touch but Rufus feels something. It is like a static shock that jumps from the man's hand to Rufus'. It doesn't hurt, but Rufus jumps, drops the wrench. It makes a loud clanging noise as it hits the asphalt below it. For a moment, the man seems frozen, with a strange look on his face as he stares at Rufus, but then he says: "Oh. Sorry".

Rufus steps back. This is more than a static shock. It hit Rufus in the heart, especially when the man had looked at him for a second or two. Rufus must have had a strange look on his face as well because the man's expression changes from a smile to a look of dismay. After another awkward second, he turns and starts using the new tool on the wheel.

Rufus just stands there, also frozen. All the anger he had felt for this man drains from his body and is replaced with a feeling of emptiness.

Then he hears his dad yelling to him: "Does that work?" He yells louder "Does That Work?" Rufus cannot say anything, but the man stands up and yells back: "Yes, that does the trick, I was able to break the nuts free, and I can get it from here, Thanks."

The man hands the wrench back to Rufus without even a glance, and Rufus returns to his parent's car.

When he gets back, his father says: "Are you all right?" Rufus shakes his head to clear the cobwebs that formed in his brain. Eventually, he says: "Yea, I'm Okay" and gets back in the car.

Soon they are back on the road to Colorado. Ariana says she feels good that they stopped and helped those people. Aharon says: "They're not Jewish. But Randy knows an awful lot about the Old Testament. He quoted the bible several times while I was talking to him. I'm not so sure about his attitude towards Jews, he might have been prejudiced."

Ariana quips, "Oh! Abe, you think everyone is prejudice."

Rufus does not know if the man was prejudiced against Jews or Blacks or anything, but he does know that something happened out there; and he will never forget that feeling, or that man.

CHAPTER 13 – IT'S NOT WHAT YOU LEARN IN COLLEGE...

April 15th, 1992
Christine Basurto, age 24

As Christine sits in the front row of the University of Colorado auditorium, she thinks about how she arrived at this point in her life. She is dressed in a flowing graduation gown, adorned with bright bands of achievement. She hears the announcer calling the names of the next to graduate, but her mind drifts away, thinking about her future,

She has been in college for what seems like forever, but it has actually only been nine years. In retrospect, it is very fast considering all that she has accomplished. Her uncle Jim, who she is very close to, is an engineer and wanted her to get a degree in engineering. She had always done well in math and enjoyed the sciences, but that is not where her true interest lies. Her father would often say: "You don't need a degree to make money". He thought she should go into sales; after all, that's how he made his money. Christine's mother, on the other hand, never pushed her one way or the other. Nonetheless, Christine had always been interested in her mother's profession, psychology. And Christine knew why she was interested in this area of study. Ever since her extraordinary adventure into the mind of weird John; witnessing his assassination attempt on the President, she always had a yearning to understand the human mind. She not only wanted to understand the mind of a person like John but to understand her own mind as well.

Christine had always believed that the reason people acted the way they do, had to do with biology, the chemistry of their brain, genetics, and possibly some external forces, and therefore one needs an education in all of these areas to really understand the actions of individuals. So, Christine got a bachelor's degree in psychology, with minors in Chemistry and Sociology. She then went on to get a master's degree and a Ph.D. in Psychology. She graduated with a 3.96 GPA in her bachelor's degree program and 4.0 GPA in her graduate degree program.

Even with all this education, Christine still has trouble getting her head wrapped around the fact that she had a psychic event in her life. *'What does it mean? How did it occur? Is it a religious experience, or something much darker? Why does it terrify me so?* She repeats internally, forcing herself, with the help of therapy, to dig herself out of those deep dark regions of depression that have been with her, ever since her day with weird John.

She still wonders sometimes if it was just a dream, or some kind of fantastic premonition of the events that were occurring that same day. All her research on the Assassination Attempt validated everything that she had experienced. However, it does not conform to any of her *logical* or scientific ways of thinking.

Christine reviewed her experience many times over the years, and now, she believes it is more than chemistry. It is some combination of chemistry, psychology, sociology and something else; something external, some dark force.

To find out, Christine began researching the dark side of things as an extension to her education. She researched a form of dark mysticism called 'Wicca', also termed 'Pagan Witchcraft'.

Wicca is a contemporary form of Pagan religion, which was developed in the early part of the 20th century in England, drawing upon a diverse set of ancient pagan and 20th-century hermetic motifs for its theological practices. Christine delved deeply into these areas of *dark* mysticism, even attending Wicca ceremonies, etcetera.

Because of her experience with weird John, she believed that *dark* forces often drive people to action they would not normally engage in, and she wanted to understand some of these *dark* forces, but eventually she realized that these '*Dark*' religions were not for her. What she does find instead, is a simple quote that helps her understand the value of *darkness*: *'What doesn't kill you will make you stronger."*

That is when Christine realized she is much stronger than she was before she had the experience with weird John. Surviving all of that fear and depression forced her to grow from the innocent, naïve, young girl who was afraid of everything into a strong confident woman.

'One must endure the darkness, for darkness is the source of strength.' She often tells herself.

She is especially interested in how these *dark* forces play into the motivations of psychopaths. In her thesis on the psychology of psychopaths, she concentrated on the motivation of a killer. She noted that there is a category of a killer known as "The Personal Cause Killer". When Christine was with John, she could feel the passion he had for Jodie. She could feel that there was nothing that he would not do to preserve and grow that passion, including possibly killing the center of his affection, Jodie herself. Just as Christine observed; when all is said and done, it is not really about Jodie. It is really about John, and his own *emotions* and how he wants to feel about himself. Christine gave a variety of examples in her thesis of psychopathic killers. However, she does not include anything about the Reagan assassination attempt; it is just too personal.

Christine also points out, in her thesis, that if a doctor pays close attention, these characteristics of a patient will manifest themselves. The condition of a psychopath can be easily diagnosed. It is for this reason that Christine is not convinced that John is a true psychopath. He certainly exhibited some of the traits. He definitely exhibited the tendencies of a Schizoid Personality Disorder. This does not mean that he is schizophrenic. He is not completely out of touch with reality; however, a Schizoid Personality does not want to associate with other people but would much rather operate and live a solitary life. It is usually a narcissistic life, living through internally developed fantasies rather than true reality.

Christine does not feel that John was a bad person, even when he had thoughts about assassinating the president. Those thoughts had not seemed to come from malice toward the President; they seemed to come from something else. It was as if there was some sort of external driver or *force* that was telling him; if he did a particular act, it would make him famous. The assassination would fill all of the *voids* he felt in his life and would fill his *emotional* needs as well. She is not sure what this external driver was, but she does get the feeling that John could not resist its *dark* powers.

There is one thing that Christine knows for sure. She learned more about the mind of a killer in that one day than she did in all her years in college. She now feels that to truly get a good education; one needs not only the classic academic study of a subject but also study beyond traditional areas of academia. People need to access areas hidden to most scholars, areas of the mind and soul, including some *dark* areas of the soul. This may not be accessible except through a more intimate experience like she experienced with John.

'When you experience psychotic behavior, it becomes a part of you,' Christine thinks.

"You realize how little control a psychotic person has over their own actions. Almost everything they are doing is *logical* and makes sense to them. It feels as if this *dark* outside force was telling John that he was doing the right thing, even when it was wrong." Christine now feels that this dark force is a part of her as well, and she wonders what influence it will have on her going forward.

So here she sits, getting ready to graduate for the last time., and she thinks about the events of her life and how they will guide her going forward. Christine also feels that John had been greatly affected by the pressures of society, and because of that, she knows that part of her future will require further study in the area of sociology. For this reason, she continuously works to get a better understanding of politics as a key ingredient in her study into the societal effects on the human psyche.

Her dad loved the Republican Party and she loved everything about her dad. Now she wants a better understanding of this political party he so loved. Republicans believes that Capitalism means that every person has the responsibility and the right to take care of themselves and protect themselves without interference or help from the government. This strong belief in Americans right to be independent of government interference shows up no place stronger than it does in the Republicans defense of the 2nd Amendment of the Constitution.

"The Right to Bear Arms" is very important to the Republican Party. Christine also knows that there is presently a new law moving through Congress called the "Brady Handgun Violence Prevention Act". This Bill will institute a requirement for federal background checks prior to the purchase of any firearms in the United States. Christine knows that even though Republicans oppose anything that makes it harder for Americans to bear arms. She knows exactly why this bill will probably pass Congress.

Christine cannot erase the image of Jim Brady walking directly into that first shot from John's gun. Christine flinches as she sees in her mind's eye, Mr. Brady getting hit. She knows because of those dramatic images caught on live TV of Jim Brady being shot; that this bill will pass.

There is another significant event that occurred since her visit to the mind of weird John. Christine is a staunch Republican, so she feels comfortable with people who think the same, and that suited her fine. She generally does not get along with Democrats and their liberal ideologies. However, there is one glaring exception. Christine has a thing for tall dark muscular men. When her friend Judy introduced her to Rod, she was immediately smitten. He is six foot three, two hundred and forty pounds which she found to be extremely sexy. But it is his dark eyes and handsome face that really sealed the deal for Christine. He only has one flaw; he is a Democrat. He is not an overtop democrat like

Christine is a Republican, but he voted democratically, and that is bad enough.

They began dating and after a few arguments over politics, it became clear that they would never agree in this area. But Rod fell in love with Christine. What's not to love; she is gorgeous. She is 5' 10", 130 lbs., with light blue eyes that can melt a man's soul. She has beautiful blonde hair, lily white skin, large breasts and a perfect shape, and she always dresses impeccably.

Rod has a degree in engineering from the University of Missouri and is getting his master's degree in engineering at the University of Colorado. Intellectually, they were a good match, except when it came to politics.

After a few knock-down drag-out fights over entitlement programs versus balanced budgets, one of which almost ended their relationship permanently, Rod told Christine that he loved her. He asked if they could make a pact to never discuss politics again. She loved Rod too and quickly agreed to the pact. So, they went their separate ways politically. Since Rod is not one to get directly involved in politics, he did not seem to mind that Christine was dedicated to it, as long as she did not bring it up when they were together. That way they could survive as a couple. Then, Rod asked Christine to marry him. She had said "yes", and less than a month ago they married.

Finally, Christine heard her name being announced: "Christine Nixie Basurto."

She proceeds to the podium to receive her final degree, and now Christine will embark on a new life with Rod, and a new path to understanding the world of politics, and its impacts on the human psyche, and she is now ready to take on the hidden forces that await her.

CHAPTER 14 - DEADLY FORCE CAN BE USED

August 21ˢᵗ, 1992
Ron Chapman, age 22

Ron Chapman quickly picks up the ringing phone on his desk. He has been expecting the call. It is his boss in Washington D.C. and Ron can tell he is agitated. "Ron, I want you to get both of your Blue and Gold units of the Hostage Rescue Teams dispatched immediately to Ruby Ridge Mountain in Idaho."

Ron already knew the federal marshals were surveying some white supremacist in that area. He expected it would eventually erupt into a situation requiring one of his teams. The Hostage Rescue Teams were an elite group, trained to handle tactical missions involving hostages or barricaded criminals. Each group, the Blue and the Gold, is divided into snipers and assaulters. The snipers would crawl into places with guns aimed at the problem area and wait for the assaulters to rush the area. They would break down doors and take on the bad guys.

Ron's boss continues with a sound of urgency in his voice. "One of the Federal Marshalls has been shot and killed. There is a firefight going on with some white supremacist as we speak. Get your asses moving! I want your team in the air immediately. You need to get up there and get this mess under control."

Ron knows this is an extremely important operation. They want both the Blue and the Gold units deployed - all fifty agents. This has never been done before. And they changed the "Rules of engagement" which normally stipulate that agents can fire only if someone's life is in danger.

His boss said: "The white supremacists in this fire-fight are Randall Weaver, Vicki Weaver, and a guy named Kevin Harris. If any of these three are observed with a weapon and they fail to respond to a command to surrender, deadly force can be used to neutralize them."

He went on to say, "I think you know Wayne Mannis. He's our agent in the Coeur d'Alene office in Idaho. Give him a call; he can fill you in on all of the details."

Ron and his men immediately load their equipment onto the FBI jet and head for Idaho.

Ron has a bachelor's degree in Law from the University of California at Berkley. He also has a master's degree in Criminology, Law, and Society, from the University of California at Irvine. His father had connections in the Federal Bureau of Investigations and was able to get him a job there, and Ron had worked his way up to a District Supervisor in the Northwest Region. He loves this job, but Ron has much greater ambitions, and was continuously developing connections with the right people to help him achieve those ambitions, and maybe this situation in Idaho can help him by helping his supporters.

Ron's office has been watching this area of Idaho for quite some time now, and the help of the eighteen-year veteran and FBI agent in that area, Wayne Mannis, has been invaluable. He identified a 20-acre wooded compound just ten miles north of Coeur d'Alene as a hotbed of White Supremacist activity. This is the site of the Church of Jesus Christ Christian. It is not just an extreme right-wing church, but it is also a center for a lot of Aryan Nations political activity. The Church is headed by Richard Girnt Butler, a follower of Dr. Wesley Swift, a renowned leader in the 'Christian Identity' movement. 'Christian Identity' is a blend of strict evangelical and Mormon theology. It also has a mix of American nationalism, and a movement called the British Israelism, which believes that white Europeans were the lost tribe of Israel. They believe Jews were not the lost tribe but were in fact decedents of Satan. They also believe that when Eve was seduced by the serpent in the Garden of Eden, she conceived a son which is the oldest ancestor of the Jewish race.

It is from the growth in the White Supremacist movement in this area that a new group is formed called: "Bruders Schweigen". Bruders Schweigen is German for the "Silent Brotherhood", later to be known as "The Order". Their motto is "White Pride, White Unity, and White America"; they are laying out a plan to overthrow the Zionist occupied Government, which they call ZOG for short.

The Order is headed by a man named Bob Mathews, and grew in strength and size between 1983 and the end of 1984. Over that period, The Order had committed a series of robberies, including a robbery of an armored car in California that netted over three million dollars. They also committed several hate crimes against the Jewish community, including bombings in Boise Idaho, and the murder of radio talk show host Alan Berg in Denver Colorado.

However, in December of 1984 several members of The Order were arrested by the FBI. Bob Mathews was trapped in his house in Puget Sound, Washington. There was a huge firefight. Even after hours of negotiations with bullhorns and surrounding snipers, helicopters, and a large force of armed agents, Mathews refused to surrender. With the negotiations going nowhere, the FBI decided to end the fight by firing flares into Mathew's home, hoping to smoke him out. It didn't work. The house caught on fire and burned to the ground with Mathews inside. A cry went up from the extreme right that Mathew's civil rights had been violated, however, no one seemed to pay attention, and the incident passed into history.

"Hello, Wayne?" Ron says to Mannis on the phone of the FBI jet in route to Idaho. "What-da-Ya got going on up there?" he asks.

"Look, Ron, this is a mess; let me give you some background."

"As you know we have been intensifying our efforts to round up members of *The Order* from all over the Country. In January 1985, a report came across my desk about a white supremacist that is making a lot of noise in Boundary County Idaho. His name is Randy Weaver. One of his neighbors accused him of plotting to kill the President of the United States. After a brief investigation, I determined that he had no connection with *The Order*, and I don't think he even has strong ties with the Aryan Nations, nor is he a threat to the President. However, I knew he and his family were followers of the *Christian Identity* movement and as such, we kept tabs on them."

"During that same period, we established relations with several undercover informants that had infiltrated the white supremacist community. One of those informants is a guy named Kenneth Fadeley. He's a private investigator from Spokane who took up the profession of a confidential informant, because of the murder of one of his friends by a motorcycle gang in Spokane."

"Fadeley took on the persona of a motorcycle gang member named Gus Antony Magisono. He built up quite an extensive relationship with the white supremacist in the area. One of the people he had built a relationship with is a guy named Frank Kumnick."

"In the summer of 1986, Fadeley and Kumnick visited the Aryan Nations World Congress, which was being held in the Aryan Nations' Hayden Compound in northern Idaho. Fadeley walked among some of the country's most well-known racists. There was William Pierce, author of the "Turner Diaries" which had been used as an outline for *The Order*. There was also Tom Metzger, the role model for Skin Heads. There was also a member of San Diego's White Aryan Resistance; Bill Albers, Imperial Wizard of the American Knights of the Ku Klux Klan; and many, many more. Because Fadeley had no law enforcement background, he was very sure that no one could break his cover through some kind of background checks. So, he moved confidently through this extreme racist environment."

"At this Conference, Fadeley met up with Frank Kumnick. He was then introduced to the man I had mentioned, named Randy Weaver. At that time Fadeley and Weaver did not talk much, but Fadeley did have a chance to meet up with Weaver later on."

"In January of 1987, Fadeley met up again with Frank and Randy. Kumnick was going on and on about how the United States is going downhill, with all of them, *and I quote*; *'Jews and niggers ruining the Country*, and how there needed to be a revolution to turn things around."

"Fadeley said he developed a comfortable relationship with Randy over the years. He remembered Randy saying that he really couldn't *give a shit* about the Aryan Nations movement. He claimed everything he did is based on the Old Testament of the Bible. He also told Fadeley that he needed to make some money so he could feed his family. When Fadeley described this last statement from Weaver to me, his face kind of lit up. He said to me: *That's when I knew I had the bastard.'"*

"Fadeley said he told Randy he knew some gun dealers that were looking for certain types of guns. He asked if Randy could help with that. Fadeley went on to say, he showed him a shotgun that he had. He told him that if the barrels were sawed off properly, he might be able to find some buyers."

"The reason I tell you all of this is because we were not that interested in Randy or the sale of illegal guns. We had much bigger fish to fry. We had become aware of unrest at the Aryan Nations compound. We did know that several members had abandoned that movement to start their own. A constitutionalist named David Trochmann and a Ku Klux Klan member named Chuck Howarth were making big plans to overthrow the country. There were rumors that they were doing some gun running to help fund their efforts. As such, the undercover informant, Fadeley, aka Gus Magisono, was put on the case to try and find these guys."

"Fadeley, in conversations with Randy Weaver determined that Randy knew where these guys were in Montana. He agreed he would introduce Fadeley to them sometime. Fadeley was using the illegal gun purchases from Randy, as a way to get a lead to this Montana unit."

"But two things happened that killed the plan. First of all, Weaver told Fadeley that he heard rumors that Fadeley is a *bad guy*. Because of this, he was reluctant to take him to Montana. He also said that he only wanted to work with him on the gun sales. At that time Fadeley was still sure he could eventually regain Randy's trust and get him to take him to Montana."

"But then, Fadeley told me in March of 1990 he was sitting at a picnic table at the Aryan Nations compound when he was approached by the Aryan Security Chief, Steve Nelson, and two other men. One of the men was holding a video camera and they began questioning him. They told him that the license plate on his car didn't match his vehicle and asked him why. He told them that he was driving his father's car and didn't know why they didn't match. Then they asked him if he knew a Kenneth Fadeley. He was obviously still undercover as Gus Magisono and said he did know Kenneth Fadeley. That he was a relative of his. They asked him if he was a member of any Law Enforcement agency. He replied that he was not. The bottom line is; they asked him to leave. He did, and never returned."

"With Fadeley's cover blown we needed another way to get to the new white supremacist organization in Montana. We looked at Randy Weaver's file. Randy had been a Green Beret in the Army and had actually run for Sheriff in Boundary County. There is also some indication that he did not totally agree with all the views of the Aryan Nations. It seemed that he certainly must have some respect for Law Enforcement. So, we decided to approach Weaver and let him know we had proof he sold illegal guns. Then offer him a deal to drop any possible charges if he would introduce us to the separatist group in Montana."

"Since the ATF is in charge of illegal gun sales, in June of 1990, we had two ATF agents approach Weaver. One of the agents showed him photographs, of the illegal guns he had sold to Fadeley. They offered to play an audio tape they had of him talking to Fadeley as well. They told him they did not have a warrant for his arrest yet, but that they had plenty of evidence to get one. If he would cooperate with them, they could get all possible charges dropped. Unfortunately, Randy didn't bite, and went back up to the house he had on the side of Ruby Ridge."

"We decided to proceed with the warrant for Randy's arrest. The thought was that once Randy knew there was a warrant issued for his arrest, he would be more inclined to cooperate. This was a two-edged sword. We were not really that interested in arresting Randy on the gun charges. The idea was to strong-arm him into cooperating. But, once the warrant was issued, we were obligated by law, to arrest him."

"We also recognized the danger of trying to arrest Randy at his remote cabin with his wife and kids present. We tried to remain patient and waited for Randy to come down from the mountain. In January of 1991, after two huge snowstorms, Randy and his wife Vickie finally came down from their cabin, and we arrested him. Randy spent one night in jail and then was released on a $10,000 bond."

"When Randy did not appear for his court date on February 20th, 1991, a failure to appear warrant was issued. The responsibility for Randy's arrest was turned over to the US Marshall's Office Special Operations Group. You know the military-style marshal's force. As a first step, they turned over the Weaver file to a psychologist for evaluation. This is important Ron; let me read to you what the psychologist wrote in his evaluation."

'In my best professional judgment, Mr. Randall would be an extreme threat to any police officer's attempt to arrest him. Further, Mr. Randall has indoctrinated his family into a belief system that the end of the world is near and that the family must fight the fences for the evil that wants to take over the world. I believe his family may fight to the death. If Mr. Randall is captured by your force, I feel the remaining members of his family will use all force necessary including deadly force to regain Mr. Randall's freedom.

"However, the marshals were still reluctant to storm the cabin and endanger women and children. So, they sent letters to Randy through his assigned lawyer, begging him to surrender and not to endanger his family. His reply was consistent; he and his family would rather die than surrender. So, over the next few months, the Marshal's office just monitored the situation on the mountain. They hoped Randy would come down so they could capture him again."

"This morning all that changed. At 10:45 AM Pacific Time, a US Marshall was shot and killed by Randy Weaver or by a member of his family. As of the last report, there is an ongoing gun battle in which US Marshalls are pinned down on Ruby Ridge Mountain. It is also reported that Randy Weaver has the support of the Aryan Nations organizations in the area. The whole mountain can turn into a war zone."

"Ron, the ATF has fucked this all up! We need you here as soon as possible!"

Ron replies, "Got it! We are on our way."

CHAPTER 15 – PUTTING HIS LIFE ON THE LINE

August 31st, 1992
Rufus Middleman, age 22

Even after wiping his face and exiting the bathroom of his small one-bedroom apartment, he can still taste and smell the sour mixture of mouthwash and vomit still assaulting his mouth and nostrils. He has been making trips to the bathroom since about 2:00 AM, and right now he was burning up. He had already decided to skip class and stay in bed and sweat it out.

Rufus recently received a Bachelor of Science degree in mathematics with a minor in physics from the School of Mines in Golden Colorado. Now he is pursuing a master's degree in physics as well.

As promised, his father got him into a Karate class when they arrived in Denver. Now Rufus is a 5thDegree Black Belt. He is now almost six feet three inches tall and weighs just over two hundred and thirty pounds.

He managed to talk his parents into letting him play football back in high school. Even though Rufus wasn't great at football, he is big, he had great grades, and he was a minority. He had colleges all over the country clamoring to give him a scholarship.

Rufus could tell his dad was proud even though he never said anything. He wanted Rufus to go to Harvard or M.I.T. However, neither one of those schools were offering Rufus a full scholarship. Rufus thought MIT would have been great, but his parents are getting older and they did not have a lot of money. As far as Rufus was concerned, the School of Mines in Colorado was a great school. It was offering him a full ride, so he decided that would be his school of choice. So far, he had not regretted it one bit. Nowadays he spends most of his time studying, doing research, and playing for the school's small football team. He plays an offensive line position and he is in great shape. He does; however, miss the rough physical contact of street fighting but playing a line position in football helps.

So here he is lying in bed, drifting off to sleep.

'Please Yahweh, help Sara and me.'

Rufus' eyes open. Well, at least he thought it was his eyes, he is not sure. He is looking down at a kind of wash basin filled with soapy, somewhat dingy water. Then he sees and feels some hands. He thought they felt like his own, but they were not. The hands scoop the water and push it towards his face. Rufus then realizes he is dreaming that he is inside of another person. The man raises his head and looks into a mirror directly in front of him. Rufus recognizes the man immediately. It is the man from the road, so long ago. This seems awful real; maybe this is NOT a dream. Rufus remembers that his father said the man's name was Randy. Rufus can tell Randy is extremely tired, and Randy was thinking.

Sara must be tired. She and I were up all-night praying to Yahweh. Praying and praying that Yahweh will tell us what to do.

Randy leans over and supports himself with his hands on the edges of the wash basin looking into its dingy water once again.

Rufus can now hear a baby crying in another room.

"Sara, can you tend to Elisheba, Please?" Randy yells out shocking Rufus because he can feel Randy form the words as he yells.

Randy's voice is raspy, and it seems to take a lot of effort to yell. A moment later the baby's cries subside.

It's been nine days now since those federal bastards shot Sammy, and only eight days since they killed Vickie.

Rufus begins to cry. Actually, it is Randy who is crying but Rufus feels the agony, the pain and the *emotions* that now tear at Randy's heart, Rufus is overwhelmed with grief for several minutes. Then Randy seems to relax a bit as he turns his gaze to the contents of the wash basin. He seems to push his thoughts of the past few days from his mind and begins to reminisce about better times; the times before all of this turmoil in his life began.

My dad was so proud of me when I was young, not just because I was in such great shape from working on our farm, but mostly because I had professed, in church, that I accepted Jesus Christ as my savior.

He was also proud of the fact that I was just as patriotic as he was. He was especially proud of me when I joined the army in 68' after dropping out of college.

I fell in love with Vickie, and people said we were made for each other. I hated to leave her, but I just wasn't ready to settle down and get married, at least not at that time.

The Combat Engineering training in the Army was great for me. I was a 'sharpshooter' and I learned about explosives too. The training that helped me the most was the training I received in survival. I learned how to live on very little, and that has served me and my family well over the last few years. As soon as I got out of the Army; Vickie and I got married. Vickie just wanted to be a housewife and have kids, but I wanted to finish college and go to work for the Secret Service or the FBI.

Things don't always work out the way you plan. College just wasn't right for me. I dropped out and got a job at that John Deer tractor factory. At least I made good money, enough to buy those nice trucks and motorcycles and even that Corvette. After Sara was born, I had to knuckle down, and couldn't buy all that stuff anymore.

It was Vickie who convinced me that it was the right thing to do. She had a knack for quoting passages from the Old Testament of the Bible that would convince me of what was 'right and wrong'. We are matched so well in our beliefs and I love listening to her interpretations of the Bible.

I think it was in 78' that Vickie's sister Julie, introduced us to the book, 'The Late Great Planet Earth'. Vickie liked the way it used the Old Testament to explain events that were occurring in the 70's. It was as if the author, Lindsey was speaking directly to us. It explained how we are living in the 'End Time.'

The book pointed out how the world was a total mess, using examples like the Soviet Union, and the European nation's financial situations. It said that it was all leading to Armageddon, the Rapture, and the return of Jesus as predicted by the Bible.

When we found out about the pagan teachings that Sara was receiving in school, we had to take her out and home school her. We even quit going to church because the preaching's we were hearing just didn't match our growing beliefs.

After Sammy was born, Vickie dedicated herself to raising the children according to our new beliefs. Vickie looked everywhere for material that would lead us to the truth. She read many stories by H. G. Wells. One of the stories called "A Dream of Armageddon" told a story wherein a man dreams he is a great leader and lives with a woman on a 1000-foot cliff. The man has a view in several directions and just wants to be left alone, but the world will not leave him alone. In the end, the man and the woman are killed.

Shortly after that, Vickie began getting messages from God while she took her baths. She dreamt of living on top of a mountain and of a coming great violence. That is when I began buying guns and ammunition to protect us.

Then Vickie began to have visions of us living in a cabin on a hillside. She told me in her visions only a few chosen white people would be saved. Jews, who were the product of Satan, would lead the surge in violence that was coming.

Rufus listens intently to the thoughts of this man, who is truly a fanatic. It is very strange to listen to a man's most inner thoughts, but that is not the strangest part. The strangest part is that Rufus can also feel what he was feeling about what he was thinking. He can feel the man obviously loves his wife and family. To Rufus, these feelings are soft, warm and genuine.

Rufus can also feel how this man feels about his religion, and how he feels about everything he is doing. Here is a man, who just thought that Jews were the product of Satan, but he did not hate Jews or non-whites. He just thought that what he believed was right because the Bible told him so and the Bible can't be wrong.

Even though it is obvious to Rufus they were only picking and choosing the parts of the Bible and other literature that supported their beliefs; it is still their beliefs. Rufus thinks to himself; "This guy is still a bigot and I hate fucking bigots."

Even so, Rufus is struggling with his own thoughts about how he feels about this man. Here is a man who is clearly a 'bigot', but he is just another man like so many people in life that are searching for answers to fill the *voids* in their lives. This man truly believes he has the answers to life.

Rufus is amazed and thinks, "This man's family has been decimated and yet his belief in God does not waver, and he feels that all the answers he searches for are there for him in the Bible. And he is ready to die for his right to believe and live, as he feels the Bible is directing him."

"Maybe this is the lesson I am here to learn, and maybe there is more," as the man's thoughts ramble on.

In 83' we sold our house, loaded all of our belongings in the back of my truck and headed out on I-80 for the destiny that Yahweh had planned for us in northern Idaho.

Rufus thought about his encounter with Randy so many years ago and that touch that connected them.

It did not take long for Yahweh to lead us to our new home. Here in Boundary County on the border of Canada near Bonners Ferry. Just one day before the day Yahweh told Vickie we must find our new place, we did just that.

Ruby Ridge is exactly as we dreamed. The only spot available to build a cabin is out over a hillside. It is just as Vickie envisioned from her readings; just as Yahweh told her during her baths. Twenty acres for five thousand dollars and an old moving truck.

Rufus saw an image of a rickety looking old cabin built from two-by-fours and plywood, perched on a tree-covered mountainside.

Rufus was familiar with Northern Idaho and knew it was very rough country, full of all sorts of outcasts; most of them having trouble dealing with normal society. There are also many religious zealots, apocalyptics, Neo-Nazis and all matters of extreme left and right-wing thinking. All going there to get away from the oppression of society, and some even want society to change to their way of thinking. Like the Aryan Nation, whose followers believe they are the representatives of the supreme race, the white race, have set up their World Congress in this area. Rufus knew Aryan Nation members hated all people of color, but they especially hated Jews. They believed Jews are children of the devil.

Rufus tries to put his thoughts aside and pay attention as Randy's thoughts ramble on.

We built our cabin and prepared for the coming end of the world. We worked hard on our studies of the Old Testament. We began having Friday evening bible studies with others of a religious group known as the 'Christian Identity'. They believed as we do, that the only true people of the Lord Jesus Christ were white Americans and intermingling with nonwhite races is a sin. However, I can see now that some of these new friendships have led to this devastation of my family.

We tried to be nice to the Kinnisons. We even let them park their trailer on our property. But they were not true believers and I had to kick their asses out. Terry Kinnison filed a complaint with the Sheriff and told the Sheriff I was planning to kill the President of the United States. He even wrote letters to the FBI, Secret Service and the local Sheriff, stating I am planning on killing Ronald Reagan, the governor of Idaho, and that I had illegal weapons. All lies.

This was the beginning of our troubles with the government. We were interviewed by federal agents, and we explained that we were being set up by the Kinnisons, who just wanted our land. We also told them about others in Boundary County that held grudges against us.

We wrote letters to the Sheriff, the FBI, the Secret Service, and to Ronald Reagan explaining our situation. It seemed that everyone was conspiring against us. Vickie and I began to think, this was how the end would come. Federal Agents would storm our cabin and kill us all.

We began to look for other people that believed as we did. I heard some people who were members of the Aryan Nations were of similar beliefs. So, in 86' Frank Kummick, a survivalist friend and I, attended the Aryan Nations World Congress meeting, which was being held just down the road from our place.

That's where I met Gus Magisono. Gus and Frank would discuss, their mutual interest in forming a group to support a white uprising. They were discussing the 'Turner Diaries'; saying it provided an outline for how a white uprising could occur. Gus told Frank he heard that they could get funding from a group called TKC, and possibly others. They were also discussing how it would start with the destruction of some important government buildings.

I was not interested in any of that or in any kind of an uprising. I was just looking for people with similar religious beliefs as Vickie and me. Once when I was alone with Gus, I told Gus that I did not agree with Frank's plans to form a group. I do not believe it will help the cause. I told Gus I am just trying to find ways to support my family.

Gus asked me if I ever heard of The King's Crusaders. I said I had not, and he suddenly changed the subject and told me he was looking for some modified shotguns that were hard to come by. I said I might be able to saw the barrels off some guns the way he wanted if he was willing to pay. I told Gus that times were tough for my family. The only reason I was doing this was to feed my kids.

Then on June 12th of 1990 Vickie and I were visiting some friends at the Deep Creek Inn, just down the hill from our cabin, when a green Forest Service truck approached us. I went out to the truck to see what they wanted, and the men introduce themselves as government agents, Herb Byerly and Steve Gunderson. I stepped back but Herb asked me not to say anything, but to just listen for a while, and I obliged. The man said they have evidence I sold sawed-off shotguns. He said they have pictures and recordings of the gun sale transactions. Herb went on to say that he did not have a warrant, but they had presented the evidence to US Attorneys General's Office and there was a very good chance that I would be indicted on Federal weapons charges. I knew immediately that Magisono must be a government agent of some sort.

They said I had some choices; I could be indicted, charged, and sent to jail to await trial, or I could work with them and have all the charges dropped. They wanted me to spy on Arian Nations members. I told them to "go to hell, I would never be a snitch," and I left. In December of 1990, I found that a warrant had been issued for my arrest. I told my family that maybe I should turn myself in to spare them from the pain and suffering that was sure to come. Vickie convinced me that if I turned myself in, all our property would be confiscated, and the children would be sent to foster homes, or even worse, to mental hospitals. So, we decided to stay on the mountain, and fight to our deaths, together.

In January of 91', we were running low on supplies, so we made a trip down the hill. The mountain was covered in a deep blanket of snow, so we used our snowmobile. After switching from the snowmobile to the pickup truck, we headed down the road towards town. When we reached the bridge over Ruby Creek, we saw another pickup truck on the bridge blocking the way. A woman gets out of the truck and said they were broken down. I started walking towards the truck and I saw that there was a man looking under the hood. He was dressed in jeans and he had messed up blonde hair.

As I walked up to the man under the hood, I asked him if I could help. Suddenly, the man spun around and jammed 9-mm pistol in my face and said, "Federal agent, you're under arrest!" I look back at Vickie and she was being forced to the ground by a female agent. I couldn't help her as the agent that confronted me was now pushing me to ground with a weapon pressed against my stomach. Within seconds there were agents everywhere and I was forced into a marshal's car. Sitting in the car I remembered looking at the agent that took me down and thinking to myself, *"that was good, but you guys will never take me again". I was taken to jail, and Vickie was released.*

The judge set a $10,000 unsecured bond for my release, which meant no collateral. If I did not show up for court, I would owe the $10,000 and my land could be sold to get the money. I was released on the condition that I did not leave Northern Idaho.

We went back up the mountain and sat with the family. We prayed and discussed what we should do. Vickie said it was clear to her from the messages she received from Yahweh that we should stay on the mountain, and never go down again, and with the help of neighbors and relatives bringing us food from time to time, we stayed on the mountain.

My court date came and went. From that point forward, we knew the marshals would come and we tried our best to get prepared. Over the next year we survived. Vickie got pregnant, and Elisheba Anne was born in October of 91'.

Kevin Harris, a close friend, is now staying with us for moral and physical support. All we heard from the marshals was in the form of letters delivered to us by our court-appointed lawyer.

The letters begged us to give up so that there would be no need for a confrontation which would endanger Vickie and kids. We were hoping that the government would just give up on us and go away, but we always stayed vigilant.

Then Rufus sees an image which he believes is Vickie. She is very pretty, with long straight jet-black hair and deep dark eyes.

Vickie is very devoted to her religion and studies the Bible rigorously. She told me how she used to listen to the elders preach, and they would say: "They were the chosen people". Her father would read passages from 'Revelations', which would foretell of the coming Judgment Day and how there was a special place reserved for them in heaven.

But there was one occurrence when she was young that had a huge impact on her. The Highway Department was building a new highway near Fort Dodge. The family was informed that the highway would be running right through their farmhouse and they would have to move. She felt this was a great injustice by the government and in violation of the US constitution. She said this was the beginning of some of the strong anti-government feelings that she had.

Rufus is trying to listen to all of this patiently, but he is starting to get pissed off, thinking, "This man truly believes that he and his family were part of a chosen race and that Jews were children of the Devil." Rufus does not believe in the devil, or in heaven, or hell for that matter. But it still makes him angry to hear someone think so passionately against his people. "At least this person is not presently thinking in terms of violence against Jews."

Rufus knows that there is a fairly large contingent of people, especially in the area where Randy and his family are living, that would love to see all Jews eradicated from the planet.

Now Rufus begins to wonder what he personally is doing here. Is this some kind of test from God? If Rufus' father had taught him anything, it is: Everything happens for a reason, and to pay very close attention when dramatic events occur, because God is presenting an opportunity for you to learn something important.

Rufus is a scientist and over time his belief in God has waned considerably. Though he does not believe this is a test from God, he does know as a scientist, one should never pass up an opportunity to learn from information given. So, even though Rufus is a bit unnerved and pissed off, he tells himself to pay close attention.

Rufus can feel a lot of physical pain in Randy's left shoulder and wonders if Randy has been shot. He can feel the throb of pain with every beat of Randy's heart, but *emotionally,* the pain is much greater.

Some horrific images of Randy's wife and son flash through Randy's mind. They both appear to have been shot and Rufus is grateful that Randy quickly pushes these images from his mind.

Rufus can also hear Randy going over and over a multitude of things in his mind. He wrestles with what he had done wrong to cause all of this and asks God what to do next.

Should I surrender and save the lives of my three daughters, or should I fight to the death as Vickie would want?

Randy then releases his grip on the wash basin and straightens up.

I must pull myself together; I need to be strong for the girls.

Randy then turns and walks into the main part of the cabin.

The room is very small and dark, even with the sunlight leaking through the pulled curtains and augmented by a few kerosene lamps that flicker in several locations in the room. The interior walls of the cabin look the same as Rufus had observed in the images of the exterior. Sheets of plywood held together by two-by-fours. "These people are extremely poor." Rufus thinks.

In the middle of the wooden floor, is what appears to be a body. The body is covered with a yellowish looking sheet, that is extremely bloodstained. Rufus wonders if this is Vickie's body because the images of her that Randy revealed indicate a severe head wound.

In the corner of the room leaning against the plywood wall sits a young man holding rags to a bleeding shoulder wound. "This must be Kevin Harris," Rufus thinks. Next to him sits a small female child, maybe five or six years of age, sobbing heavily. Not two feet away from her, in a rocking chair, sits an older adolescent girl about twelve or thirteen. She is holding a baby, and a bottle of something, maybe water, which is being fed to the baby.

Rufus can sense the feelings of love and the pain of loss that Randy is feeling as he observes the scene in front of him. Then Randy and Rufus are startled by the loud rumble of a vehicle's engine starting up, just outside of the cabin.

Randy jerks his head, and stares at the wooden door of the cabin. Rufus can feel the fear rise up in Randy's body. Now, Rufus can hear the clanking sounds of movement of a heavy vehicle moving towards the cabin. Randy grabs a rifle from a wooden table in the center of the room and moves towards the door. Rufus is once again startled by the sound of a voice over a 'loudspeaker' from just outside of the cabin.

"This is the Federal Marshal's office. We have warrants for the arrest of Randy Weaver and Kevin Harris. Please surrender and no one will get hurt."

Randy does not respond.

After a while, the voice on the 'loudspeaker' begins again.

"Vickie, we have put a phone in front of the cabin. Please send out one of your children to retrieve it so that we can converse with you and resolve this situation."

Rufus thinks. "They must not know, or they are pretending not to know that Vickie is dead."

As Randy peeks through a crack in the door, Rufus can now see the large armored vehicle sitting a few yards from the house. Rufus is shocked to see such a large vehicle in front of a shack that looks like it can be blown away by a strong breeze.

"What the hell are these guys preparing for?" Rufus thinks. "You'd think they were getting ready to attack a legion of Iraqi armored tanks or something. Don't they realize that this is just a small fragile family and that several of them are dead or dying?'

Then Randy begins screaming at the top of his lungs. "DO YOU THINK I'M CRAZY? I AM NOT ABOUT TO SEND MY CHILDREN OUT IN FRONT OF THE VERY PEOPLE WHO KILLED MY WIFE AND SON."

Rufus can feel the energy being sucked out of Randy's body with this effort. After a few minutes, Rufus can hear the armored vehicle as it backs away from the cabin.

They're going to set the cabin on fire or attack us from the air with helicopters, I'm just sure of it.

Time passes and there is no attack. It is apparent to Rufus that Kevin is very close to death. He watches Randy's young daughter pour hydrogen peroxide on Kevin's wound which continued to bleed dark red.

Later Kevin asks Randy to shoot him in the head and finish him off. Randy refuses, saying: "I can't do that." Kevin asks several more times, but Randy continues to refuse.

Then Randy discusses with his oldest daughter what they should do. They are sure they are going to die, but they want to do what Vickie would have wanted. Randy says "This is the Apocalypse that Vickie has been warning us about for years, but now I'm not sure of what we should do." Randy's daughter does not reply as she stares blankly at him, and Randy's returns to his internal analysis.

Here I sit, slowly bleeding to death, Kevin dying and asking me to kill him. My daughter Elisheba crying for her mother's milk. Vickie dead on the floor, my son, dead in the birthing shed, and there is a high probability that my three daughters will soon die as well.

Randy's thoughts subside for a moment and then continue.

Well, it's been a couple of days now since they had my sister out there. I tried to tell her Vickie was dead, but I think those agents purposely drowned out my voice so sis couldn't hear. They kept saying over the loudspeakers they couldn't hear me. I just don't think they want anyone to know that they killed Vickie. I am sure they didn't want her to hear me because when I yelled that I wanted to talk to Bo Gritz, they said they would get him for me. I guess somehow, they could hear that. That was a couple of days ago, and nothing. I don't think they are even trying. At least, he would be someone I could trust.

Rufus recognizes the name, Bo Gritz. Rufus remembers reading an article on him a few years back. Gritz was a retired Lieutenant Colonel from the Army, and he had like sixty medals for valor, and his reputation had been growing among the 'far right'.

Rufus also remembers that in 1992, Gritz ran for president as a candidate for the Populist Party. The Populist Party had previously nominated David Duke, the Grand Dragon of the Ku Klux Klan for President.

Then, Rufus can hear the armored vehicle pull up in front of the cabin once again. He can feel the panic rise within Randy as he stares through the glass windows of the cabin door at the approaching vehicle, expecting the worse.

The loudspeaker blares out: "Randall, this is Bo Gritz".

Randy immediately yells back to Bo, but he is not sure Bo can hear him through the plywood walls and with all of the background noise.

He hears Bo say he is going to get out of the vehicle and come closer to the cabin. When Bo gets to the door, Randy is happy it is truly Bo Gritz. He starts talking as fast as he can. He says, "Bo, I have to tell you everything that happened, I am afraid I am not going to get out of here alive, and I want people to know what the government did to us."

Immediately Rufus sees an image in Randy's mind. It is an image of Vickie in a white nightgown, her long black hair gleaming in the light as she stands in a doorway holding her baby. She truly looks beautiful.

"Bo" Randy begins again, "Vickie is so beautiful, and I loved her so much." Randy pauses.

Rufus is astonished. He feels Randy form the words with his mouth as he speaks. Rufus feels all of this as if he is speaking himself, but it is not his mouth, and it is not his voice that he heard as Randy spoke. Rufus thinks, "This is incredible, and this is important, I must pay close attention to every detail."

Bo replies. "I'm sure you loved her very much son. Please go on with your story. "

"It was about eleven days ago, and it was about eight in the morning. As we do every morning, we take turns leaving the cabin and going to the outhouse. We knew the feds had arrest warrants out for me and Kevin, so we tried to be very careful. I came out of the cabin first. I was dressed in camouflage and had a pistol strapped to my hip and a shotgun over my shoulder. I shared a cigarette with Kevin. I remember it was kind of a gloomy day, and I heard Vickie yelling at the dogs to be quiet. They were making a fuss all morning."

"Around eleven, Kevin, my son Sammy, and I began walking down the road that leads away from the cabin. Kevin was caring a thirty-ought-six, and Sammy was caring a twenty-two-assault rifle. Sammy also had his three-fifty-seven handgun on his waist. My daughter Sara was caring a twenty-two-assault rifle.

Even her younger sister Rachel had a rifle over each shoulder. Striker, our big yellow lab, was also with us."

"After a while, the dog began barking, a clear indication that he had gotten a whiff of *something*. I was hoping it was a deer; we really needed the meat. I began to run after the dog down the logging road and yelled to Kevin and Sammy to cut down below where the dog was headed. Sara and Rachel headed back towards the cabin."

"I was close on the dog's trail and had come down the mountain a lot further than I had in a long time. I really wanted to get a deer and was hoping the deer would run to Kevin and Sammy or cut back towards me when it saw them."

"Striker was heading down the trail when suddenly a man in camouflage steps out from behind a tree and yells: "Back Off. U.S. Marshall". I yelled *fuck you*, and ran the opposite direction, back towards the cabin. I hoped that Kevin and Sammy heard the yelling and would do the same. I only ran about eighty yards when I heard the sound of a gunshot. At first, I was not sure where it came from as it echoed off the surrounding hills, but I was pretty sure it came from the direction of the stranger. My first thought was that Kevin and Sammy were still down there. I yelled: *'Sam! Kevin! Get home!'* I pointed my 12 gauge up in the air and shot off one round. I tried to load up another round, but I was so upset, and the shell jammed in the gun. I pulled my handgun out and shot off three rounds and yelled: *'Sam! Kevin!'* I heard Sammy yelling: *'I'm coming, dad!'* I could hear more shots down the hill and then some more yelling. With the echoes, it sounded like the shots were coming from everywhere."

"When I got back to the cabin, I saw Vickie and the two girls behind the big rock out cropping up the hill. They had guns and they were all pointed at me. Vickie was yelling: *'What happened? What happened?* I yelled back: *'We run into an ambush!'* Then we saw Kevin running towards us. At first, I wasn't even sure it was Kevin, he was so shaken up and pale looking. I yelled: *'Where's Sam?'* Kevin doesn't say anything. I yell again: *'Did you see Sam?* 'And, then, Bo…'' Randy starts to cry. "Bo, Kevin said: *'Sam's dead.'''*

"Vickie immediately started screaming, *'Yahweh! Yahweh!'* and I started screaming back down the hill: *'you son-of-a-bitch!'* I was so confused and angry that I just yelled, *'Stay the fuck off of our land.'* We all started firing our guns in the air. I was so upset I just kept reloading and firing until Vickie told me to stop. We all just cried and yelled at the woods."

"When we finally settled down, I asked Kevin what happened. He explained that they were chasing the dog when a man dressed in camouflage stepped out of the woods and shot Striker in the back. Sammy was pissed and yelled *'you killed my dog, you son of a bitch.'* Sammy fired at the marshals and they began to return fire. They hit Sammy in the arm. He yelled: *'Oh Shit!'* turned and began running away. The marshals kept firing, so I began shooting at the marshals to protect Sammy."

"Kevin said he thought that he had killed one of the marshals, but as Sammy ran away, one of the marshals shot Sammy in the back. Kevin said he ran to Sammy's body and checked for a pulse. When he could find none, he came back up the hill."

"After a while, me and Vickie went back down the hill and got Sammy. We brought him back up and put him in the birthing shed. We prayed and crouched on the rocks overlooking the trail just waiting for the marshals to come and finish us off. But they didn't come. We left Sammy in the birthing shed and moved back into the cabin. Kevin told me he was sorry for killing the marshal, even though he had killed Sammy. Bo, those ZOG bastards ambushed us and killed my son."

"Later, we could see the trucks and cars down below, and we could hear the rumble of engines, and we knew we needed to prepare for when they would attack us. So, we got the cabin ready so that we could defend ourselves. Bo, we had all agreed to fight them to the death. We knew that once we killed that marshal, they would never let us get out of here alive."

"About six the next evening, the dogs started barking again and I looked out, but I didn't see anyone. Sara went out to check on the dogs and shortly after that Kevin and I went out to check the perimeter of the buildings. I was walking back towards the cabin and decided to stop by the birthing shed to visit Sammy's body. As I reached for the door of the shed, I heard the pop of a gun and felt the upper part of my arm jerk. I immediately realized I'd been hit. The bullet went through my upper arm and came out my armpit. Sara started yelling for me to get into the cabin. We both began running and Kevin was right behind us."

As Randy describes the scene to Bo, Rufus can feel a *dark* cloud move across Randy's heart, and a mounting despair. Again, Rufus sees the image of Vickie standing in the doorway as Randy continues.

"As I ran towards the cabin, I could see Vickie standing just outside the door holding Elisheba in her arms. I yelled to Vickie: *'I've been shot.'* Vickie yelled to the hillside: *'Bastards, Murders'*. I watched as she moved quickly behind the heavy curtained front door. Sara and I dove through the door onto the cabin floor. Just as Kevin was diving past Vickie, a second shot rang out." Randy hesitates for a moment and then continues telling his story to Bo.

"I felt Sara, and then Kevin, fly on the floor behind me, it was perfectly quiet. I thought we made it. Then, I looked back towards the door, and I could see Vickie on her knees with her head down on the floor, Elisheba still held tightly in her arms."

Randy pauses again.

"Bo, she was not moving, and I was afraid she had been hit. Rachel was standing right next to Vickie and I could see what I thought was blood on Rachel. Then, all I could hear was Rachel screaming at the top of her voice, and then Sara screaming. I could hear Sara telling Rachel to stop screaming, that her mother would not want them to panic. I reached down and pulled Vickie over."

As Rufus hears Randy's thoughts, he is also seeing images of the scenes that Randy is thinking about. It is like watching a small documentary of short patched-together film strips and still photos with Randy doing the narrative in the background. Now, as Randy's narrative to Bo continues, there are vivid images; images that Randy had been trying to push out of his mind. Rufus can see an image of Randy reaching down for his wife, and as she rolls over, Rufus sees her head exploded from the shot. Her jaw is almost completely blown off and the blood is gushing out onto the floor. Rufus cannot believe what he is seeing. As Randy's description of this scene to Bo finishes, so do the images. Randy, once again, blocks it out of his mind.

After another brief pause, Randy once again continues his narrative to Bo.

"I pulled Elisheba from Vickie's arms. She was covered with blood but after checking very closely I could find no injuries to her. I then turned my attention to Kevin, who was still lying on the cabin floor. He was not moving. I pulled Vickie's body all the way into the cabin and closed the front door. I knew she was dead, and I thought that Kevin was dead too, but he didn't die, but he is just barely alive now."

"Bo, those bastards killed my wife and son, and now they want to finish us off too. They just want to keep this story from going public. "

Bo says: "I understand, though I don't think they want to kill you, there are just too many witnesses now. I really think they just want this to end. Let me see what I can work out." Bo backs away from the door.

Rufus watches as Bo Gritz walks back and forth between Randy and the agents, trying to work out a settlement. Bo tells Randy that if Kevin dies in the cabin that he thinks Randy might be blamed for his death. He also told him that having Vickie's dead body in the cabin was not good for the health of his daughters. Randy agrees and eventually, he lets them take Kevin, and Vickie's body, out of the cabin.

Randy begins to speak to Sara, "I realize that surrender would not be what Vickie would have wanted. We may all be killed the instant we step outside of this cabin, but surrender is the only way for us to have any chance of saving your two younger sisters. If we are going to die at least this way, we have the best chance of saving them."

Rufus never felt very religious but now he is praying that Sara will agree. Then he hears Randy thinking:

I know someone is watching over us, I am not sure if it is Yahweh this time, but it is giving me the strength to make this decision, and now is the time and we must go.

Rufus is taken off guard by this thought. Can Randy somehow feel his presence or some other more powerful force from the universe? All of sudden, he hears Sara's sweet voice. She is agreeing to leave the cabin, and Rufus feels a great sense of relief as Randy picks up the baby and they all walk bravely out of the cabin prepared to die.

Rufus is astonished, not because Randy surrendered, not because he held out for so long against such huge odds. Rufus is astonished how much he himself empathized with this man. Here is a man who is clearly a bigot, a racist, and a white supremacist in his basic beliefs. This man based his whole existence on his belief in some ancient teachings of the bible. Yet Rufus knows, after actually experiencing the feelings of this man - being so closely *connected* to him - that he is not a fake. He is not a charlatan; he truly believed that what he had been doing was the right thing to do, and he was putting his life on the line for those beliefs.

As Rufus thinks about it: "This all really pisses me off. I hate this guy and yet I realize that under different circumstances a man like this would be considered a hero. You know, he probably will be considered a hero in the eyes of the white supremacist community, but not for the right reasons."

Randy closes his eyes, as he, and the remainder of his family, walk out of the cabin to face an overwhelming government arsenal.

Please Yahweh, please save my children from these murderers.

Then Rufus is awake and back in his own world. "What just happened?" Rufus thinks. "Was it a dream?" Rufus is confused and a little frightened, it all seemed so real. Rufus knows that it doesn't matter if it was real or if it was only a dream. It doesn't matter if he hates Randy Weaver or admired him, it is now all a part of Rufus. A passage from the Bible enters Rufus' mind.

"And I will give thee the treasures of darkness and the hidden riches of secret places". Rufus remembers this from Isaiah 45.

Rufus thinks, 'Where did this come from? Is God trying to speak to me? I don't know; this is all so confusing. Somehow, I just need to separate *logic* from *emotions*. I just need time to sort this all out, and I definitely need to start writing this all down.'

CHAPTER 16 – PHONETIC HARMONY

October 3rd, 1992
Rufus Middleman, Age 22

Rufus loves the feel of the Colorado Autumn air rushing through his hair as he drives his 1989 Buick convertible west along I-70.

It's October in the Rockies and Rufus has just past the El Rancho exit. Rufus and his college roommate, Steve Weber, who is sitting in the passenger seat next to him, are now staring at the majestic snow-covered peaks of the Rocky Mountains. And even though it's October, the temperature is a balmy 68 degrees fahrenheit and Rufus has the top down. Rufus' hair, only half an inch long, is not exactly waving in the wind, but the cool air feels refreshing none the less.

Rufus is now well on his way to a master's degree in physics, at the Colorado School of Mines. He has always loved math but now finds that the application of math in theoretical physics to be much more interesting.

Steve is presently working on his bachelor's degree in mathematics and loves math as well, especially the historical and sociological influences of math, which have often led Rufus and Steve to have long discussions about math and where it is taking the human race.

Rufus likes these discussions, especially today, because it helps take his mind off what he witnessed at Ruby Ridge just over a month ago. Rufus now knows that these events actually happened, and he is sure that a powerful positive force, sent him there for a reason. However, at the same time, something dark and sinister is at the root of those events, and he will not rest until he can figure out what it is. But, not today, today he is taking a vacation from all of that. He and his buddy Steve are on their way to Steamboat Springs, for a couple of days of fly fishing and a lot of drinking.

Steve turns to Rufus and asks "Hungry?"

"Sure" Rufus replies, not taking his eyes off the road.

Steve points to the road ahead and says: "Good, let's stop at Kermit's, it's just ahead at the bottom of Floyd Hill. It's a great place to get some good red chili and cold beer. You know where I'm talking about?"

"Yea, I know the place, but I have never been there. What's it like?"

"It's a kind of biker bar, but it's okay, not as tough as you might expect. A lot of locals and tourist eat there as well."

Rufus does not care what kind of bar it is, he knows he can take care of himself if need be. He briefly flashes back to his younger days in New York, where he got into fights and could rough it up without someone calling the police or threatening to sue him or his parents, which seems to be the rule in Colorado. These days football is his only outlet in this area. But, even in football, he is pretty limited in how aggressive he can be with opponents. It certainly isn't like the old days, when there really were no rules.

Rufus sometimes wonders what he will do to deal with his aggression after college. He is not good enough to play professional football, and he is concerned about dealing with his overwhelming urge to fight someone which still comes over him quite often. He still plays video games, that contain a lot of violence, but that doesn't seem to satisfy his urges either. He craves the physical contact.

He thought about getting into boxing, even though he only has training in Karate. He has also heard about a new sport called 'cage fighting', where supposedly there are no rules. Rufus tells himself he must investigate it when he has the time. But, for right now, he needs to concentrate on his studies and football, and on just enjoying today's great weather. But as far as a tough bar goes, Rufus is actually hoping for some trouble.

As they drive along, Steve who loves talking about math is talking about the history of math, and he says to Rufus: "You know I think numbers are magical. The more that Physicist and Scientist delve into the use of numbers, the more magical they become. As you know, the number base we use is ten. Historians believe that's because we have ten fingers. But, did you know that most early number bases were three and four? A lot of aborigines and tribes in Africa still have a number base of three. It is believed that this is because when you look at a row of items, let's say a row of rocks, most people can look at three or four rocks and immediately, know how many there are without counting. But, any amount over three or four can not immediately be seen and has to be counted."

Rufus is familiar with many of the facts that Steve spouts-out from time to time, but he never interrupts Steve with such negative feedback because ultimately, Rufus knows that Steve's stories will lead to some very interesting facts that Rufus may not always know.

Steve goes on: "This is important because it shows how basic numbers are to man's very existence. When man first used numbers, he only used positive numbers, because negative numbers have no meaning. You cannot count something with a negative number. Eventually, people began to trade items, which led to the concept of debt, and thus the need for negative numbers."

"Humans then discovered you can add, subtract, multiply and divide numbers. If you can multiply numbers, you can multiply a number by itself, thus squaring the number. If you can square a number, you can also take the square root of a number. Here is where I believe the magic comes in. If you take the square root of a positive number, you get a positive real number. But what happens when you take the square root of a negative number? There is no negative number that multiplied by itself, gives you a negative number as a result, and multiplying two negative numbers gives you a positive number. But the square root of a positive number is a positive number."

"Thus, the invention of the imaginary number, which is the square root of a negative number. As you know, the square root of *negative one* is represented by the letter 'I'. An Imaginary number combined with a real number such as '4 + *i*32' is called a complex number."

"Rufus, I know you are aware of what I am talking about, but bear with me, I do have a point."

Steve, being the philosopher, says "It is almost like, life itself, there is a real part of life and then there is the mystical part or imaginary part of life. Like Science and Religion, Modern Medicine and Shamanism, Neurology and Psychology, or the Conscious and Sub-conscious mind."

Steve looks at Rufus to see his reaction, and seeing only a slight smile, goes on: "I know that there are some really crazy things that are being discovered in physics these days, especially in the area of Quantum Physics. It looks like the more they use complex math to dig into the subatomic world, the more mystical things become."

Then Steve stops talking, and just stares out of the front window at the scenery passing by, lost deep in thought.

Rufus knows that Steve is really into this stuff., and sometimes he can get a little over the edge when it came to spiritual things, like psychic phenomena and such. As such, Rufus always found Steve's thoughts really interesting, and he agreed that what he is finding in his studies of modern Quantum Physics is often very spooky. And for this reason, he knows that some sort of school and research will always be a part of his life.

Rufus says to Steve: "So speaking of spooky, have you ever heard the story of the *Double Slit* experiment?"

Steve does not respond but does seem to return from wherever his mind had wondered.

Rufus continues, "Sometime in your educational process, I am sure you have seen the experiment where light is allowed to pass through two slits cut into a cardboard or paper wall with a screen behind it. When the light from a single source, hits a screen on the other side of the slits, an interference pattern of vertical lines is formed on the screen."

Steve says, "Yea, I remember doing that in high school physics, the idea is to show that light moved in waves."

"Exactly, that experiment was first performed by a man named Thomas Young, back in the late 1800's. Though it showed that light had wave characteristics, Einstein proved that light also has the characteristics of a particle. Sometime after that, scientists invented a machine that detects light particles."

Rufus glances over at Steve "That is when things got spooky."

Rufus pauses for effect and continues: "Scientists at the time, thought: 'obviously we can now prove that light is either a wave or a particle.'"

"So, they set up the double slit experiment again. They shined a light through the slits. Once again, the interference pattern showed up on the screen. But now, they put a particle detector between the slits and the screen where the interference pattern will show up. The interference pattern still showed up on the screen, and when they turned on the particle detector, as expected, it detected the light particles."

"But here is the spooky part. The interference pattern went away, and a new pattern showed up. This pattern is not one that will be caused by a wave pattern, but instead looked like particles are going through the two slits and piling up on the screen."

"Imagine that you let sand fall through two slits. You will have two piles of sand, one below each slit. That is what the light pattern looked like on the screen when the particle detector was turned on. If they turned the particle detector off, the light pattern went back to the series of vertical lines, the interference pattern, which indicated the light was behaving as a wave."

"That's right, the light going through two slits acted like a wave, when the particle detector was off. The light acted like particles when the particle detector was turned on."

Rufus looks at Steve. Steve has a puzzled look on his face and says: "That sounds impossible."

"Yes, it gets even crazier. Many years later, they invented a photon gun, which can shoot out one photon at a time. When they shot out a series of photons, at the two slits, it will eventually create an interference pattern, indicating waves, and just as before, when they turned on the particle detector behind the first screen, they once again detected particles, just as before. They can also see when a single photon, acting as a particle, is released from the gun; it does not split in half. Instead it either goes through the left slit, or the right slit, but not both. So, they set up a series of mirrors so that they could have the particles going through the left slit headed west, and the particles going through the right slit headed east. You know in opposite directions. That way, they could set up an experiment where the screen and the particle detectors can be virtually miles apart. When they shot photons at the slits with the particle detector turned off, it once again showed up as an interference pattern. When they turned the particle detector on behind just one of the slits, not only did the photons, with the particle detector behind it, act like particles, but the photons going through the other slit immediately changed from wave-like characteristics to particle characteristics as well. It does not matter how far the particle detector is behind the one slit, it can be thousands of miles, but as soon as the particle detector is turned on, the photons headed in the opposite direction, thousands of miles away, immediately change from wave characteristics to particle-like characteristics."

"Are you making this stuff up?" Steve asks, with a skeptical look on his face.

"No, I'm not. You can look it up. These experiments have been run in a thousand different ways, hundreds of thousands of times. It always comes out the same. The bottom line is that light acts differently, depending on whether it is being observed or not."

Rufus went on "I don't know if you are familiar with the 'Uncertainty Principle', but Werner Heisenberg says that you can know the position of an atomic particle, or you can know the speed of that particle, but you cannot know the position and the speed at the same time. Just as in the case of the double slit experiment, it all depends on the perspective of the observer. In fact, there is some speculation that these particles do not exist at all if they are not being observed."

Rufus goes on, "There have been other experiments that show photons from the same light source are entangled. One photon may be spinning in one direction, and a second photon, that the first photon is entangled with, might have a spin in the opposite direction. If you change the direction of the spin of the first photon, then its entangled brother will also immediately change its direction of spin as well. It makes no difference how far apart these two entangled photons are. This again has been proven thousands of times over the years."

"It demonstrates that there is a connection, not only between particles in the universe but also between those particles and their observers. It is called '*Quantum Entanglement.*'"

"Maybe we are all here because someone or something is observing us. Maybe we are figments of observation, or maybe just figments of imagination, and maybe we can be influenced by our entanglements with other people and other things, based on what is happening with those other people and or other things."

Steve sits silent for a few seconds, then says: "Wow that is, really cool." And then once again drifts off into deep thought.

As they drive along, Rufus recalls a poem he wrote about the relationship of words on a written page. He called it: "Entanglement" he repeats it silently to himself.

> *"Listen to the words weave a tangled web*
> *They know not where they are going*
> *They have no brain or head*
> *They work with one another*
> *The order is the key*
> *They Bump and Jump, and slow and flow*
> *In Phonetic harmony"*

Before long, they are at Kermit's. As they enter the restaurant, Rufus can't help but admire the nice looking 'Harleys' sitting out front. But then he notices a small plaque on one of the bikes. In, very small script, it says: *'The King's Crusaders'*

Where have I heard of that before? Is that a biker gang? Not sure.

It is a beautiful fall day, and it's warm enough to sit outside, so they head out to the patio.

Steve says "Boy, I need some food and a beer after that heavy conversation. I used up a lot of energy just trying to keep my brain cells from exploding."

Before long they have the beer and chili they were craving. Steve was right, the chili is really good, and the beer is cold. But Rufus noticed when they walked in that there was a bunch of biker types sitting in the back of the patio area, and says to Steve, "What's up with the skin-heads?"

Steve says, "Not sure, but I did hear, that there is some kind of big white supremacist rally going on up near Estes Park this month."

Rufus watches them closely without trying to be too obvious. He has not heard of much White Supremacist activity in Colorado, and he is more than a little curious.

After lunch, he tells Steve he is going to hit the head. The restroom is inside the bar, and as he walks toward the door, he sees a guy that is with the biker group standing near the entrance to the bar. He is a small thin man with a crew-cut; he looks military; not like the other skinheads he is with. As Rufus walks by, he thinks he hears this guy say something like: "You sure are a black nigger."

Rufus immediately uses his right hand to grab the guy by the collar and pick him up off the floor. "What did you just say?" Rufus asks as he glares into the man's face.

Several of the bikers jump to their feet. But the little man does not get excited. He just responds: "I just said, you sure are a lot bigger." The other bikers and skin heads begin laughing, and Rufus sets the man back down. Rufus then grabs the man's face with his left hand and pushes him back towards his friends. The man stumbles some but does not fall. The man had been laughing, but now he has a stunned look on his face.

Rufus gets ready to fight the next man up, or the whole group if necessary, but two things happen. No one from the group steps forward to challenge Rufus, maybe because of his size, maybe because of something else. But more importantly something has taken the fight out of Rufus. He sees the stunned look on the face of this wimp he just pushed, and he feels like he may have the same look on his face. When he touched this racist pig's face, he feelt something. It was a feeling a lot like the one he felt when he first touched Randy Weaver, back on the side of the road many years before. It was that feeling of emptiness. It was a feeling, which brought him somehow to the *middle* of the two of them.

In a moment Rufus's friend is by his side, ready to fight, but nothing happens. Rufus continues to stare at the thin man, who is staring intently back. After a second or two, Rufus simply turns and walks into the bar, and goes to the restroom. Steve pays their tab, they head to the car and in no time they are back on the road.

They are quiet for a while and then Steve asks, "What the hell happened back there? I thought you are going to kick the shit out of those guys".

"Well nothing happened - but something happened." Rufus says softly.

"What?" Steve, now appears extremely confused.

Rufus goes on to explain, "That skinny guy, made some kind of racial remark, and I just grabbed the *little fuck*. I was ready to wipe the place up with that guy, and all of the rest of those racist bastards. But, for some reason, they didn't seem to want to fight and neither did I". Rufus goes on. "That is the nothing that happened."

"But something else did happen. When I grabbed that little guy, something happened between him and me. This guy, the little guy, is no ordinary guy; he's going to do something in the future. It is not going to be good; In fact, I think it's going to be very, very bad."

"But I also know that I can do nothing to stop it, and right now, all I can think about is getting as far away from him as I can."

CHAPTER 17 – THE TREASURES OF *DARKNESS*

February 28th, 1993
Ester Suni Nati, age 41

Ester shakes CyrIS' shoulder roughly as he is sleeping peacefully next to her. She says: "CyrIS, Wake up! Wake up!" hoping she can get him to help her.

"What? What? What's the matter?" CyrIS jumps out of bed looking desperate, as he jerks his head from side to side.

"It's time," Ester says, sounding like she is having a baby, but Ester is not pregnant. But for this event Ester had previously shown CyrIS what needed to be done, and having gained his wits about him, immediately begins preparations.

It has been almost 15 years since Ester had taken that infamous excursion into the mind and body of the Reverend Jim Jones. After that first shamanistic journey to the "*Middle* World", she had been very reluctant to go back. But, just a few years ago, Ester once again mustered up the courage, with CyrIS' help, to return, because they both feel that within these journeys lie keys to the puzzles they are trying to solve.

Those subsequent trips resulted in nothing, maybe because they were forced. That is, Ester had planned them out, and then executed the journey. But, today is different, she had not planed on trying a journey today, and Ester had a class to teach this morning, and she never misses her classes.

Well her students would have to wait, because Ester is once again headed for that place where she is only along for the ride and the learning. It is like being on a roller coaster ride when you really don't like roller coasters. You may have chosen to take the ride, but now you have no control and have no idea of what to expect. But Ester knows there will be no learning if she did not accept the challenge. Ester also feels that she can do this, only because she knows, that once again, CyrIS will be right here by her side.

Once they are ready, Ester lays down upon their bed, and slowly drifts away, making her way towards the Middle World, ready to accept whatever this trip is willing to teach.

And then immediately, Ester can feel a warm naked body close to hers, pressing ever so gently against her own naked body.

Eyes are opening slowly, and she becomes aware of the light of the morning coming through the window of the small room. Ester can easily recall the feeling of being in a man's body as he thinks to himself.

Who is with me? Oh! It's Michelle. I love Michelle; in fact, I love all my wives. But Michele is very special. How old is she now? She should be about eighteen.

Ester is now seeing and experiencing her host' senses. As he recalls the feelings of having sex with Michelle the night before, she feels it too. Ester feels the naked body of the young woman against her, or his, skin, move just slightly. "Apparently this Michelle." Ester thinks as she continues to hear her host' thoughts.

I love sex, and I love masturbation, but masturbation would be a waste of my precious seed, and I have been specifically commanded by God to spread my seed.

He then thinks about how he had first come to marry Michelle's older sister Rachael Jones.

Perry and Mary Belle gave me permission to marry her in 1984, realizing, that it was what God wanted for their daughter.

But it was in 1985, when I visited Mount Zion in Jerusalem, that I received that very clear command from God, to have a child with Rachel's younger sister, Michele.

I was very upset by that command from God, and when I returned from Mount Carmel, I shared my vision with Rachael, and she also became very upset.

I told her that I couldn't do it, but I was not sure what to do, because the commandment came directly from God. I suffered with this conflict for over a year.

But then Rachael had a dream. I remember distinctly what she said: "In my dream, God revealed to me that he would punish you severely, maybe even kill you, if you do not follow his every command."

Rachael told me, that I must follow the direction I had been given by God. So, I made love with Michelle, making her my wife. I was so happy when she conceived our daughter Serenity.

After that, God commanded me to follow the lead of King Solomon in the Bible: 'There are three score queens and four score concubines, and virgins without number' - Song of Solomon 6:8

God had instructed me to create the House of David and spread my seed among many women. The offspring of this effort would form the 'Elders' that would surround the 'Merkabah', the heavenly throne. This 'New Light' vision, I received from God, would form the foundation of my new church at Mount Carmel.

Mount Carmel? Ester recalls: "That is the place where I met with Lois Roden back in 1981". Ester's mind lights up, "Oh! It's David, David Koresh." Ester remembers seeing pictures of him in the news reports and meeting him at the front door of Mount Carmel. Ester is shocked at how composed and confident he is. The media said he is a fanatical cult leader, who is having sex with young girls, supposedly against their will. They say he is beating children and leading his cult to their certain death, just like Jim Jones had in Jonestown.

Ester got the sense that he feels that what he is doing here is right, that he had been commanded by God, and that he is following those commandments.

As he lies in bed, he considers his present fifteen wives and seventeen children as a good start toward the goals that God had set for him.

"Oh my God!" Ester thinks "fifteen wives and seventeen children? He may feel that this is right, but it sounds obscene." Ester reminds herself that she is here for learning and that she should not let her own *emotions* and opinions get in the way. She continues to listen to David's thoughts.

But now, this all could be coming to an end, Armageddon, the Apocalypse could be ascending upon my congregation. I know that part of my assignment from God is to interpret the last chapter of the Bible, 'Revelations'.

He thinks again, about his trip to Mount Zion in Jerusalem; how he was taken past Orion to meet God. And how in a flash, he had received the complete key to the scriptures, and how the puzzle fits together. He knows at that moment; it is his destiny to unlock the Seals and open the way for his community of followers to enter heaven.

Ester is becoming very excited, hoping above hope that this man can provide some of the keys she has been looking for. That this man can reveal to her some of the secrets of the Bible. Maybe he can even lead her and CyrIS, from the *Darkness* into the *Light*.

David relishes his ability to give lengthy bible studies to his followers, some as long as sixteen hours in duration. In these bible studies, he explained God's plan to have him populate the church with "Elders", and that these "Elders" would come from the loins of the women at Mount Carmel.

I have made it clear to my followers that God has told me that I would be the only male to provide the seed for this population. I have informed my followers, that no one would be forced to join in the House of David, but they would have the opportunity to be a part of the creation of Christ new church and produce children of Christ.

God had a plan for me from the very beginning. When I was born in 1959, Bonnie, my mom, was only fourteen years old. Bobbie, my dad, left when I was still a baby. They named me 'Vernon Howell'. Oh! How I had hated that name. But, I believe, it is all part of God's plan to make me tough, to make me strong.

He then remembers he had a lot of problems with school. He failed the first grade twice and second grade once. He had to go to a special school. The kids called him "Mr. Retardo". At the end of the day, he had to go home to a mother and stepfather that beat him severely. Several of his relatives were in jail, and his cousins tried to rape him.

Even as God was toughening him up, he was also preparing him spiritually for the future. His mother was a member of the Seven Day Adventist Church, and his grandmother would take him to church on Sunday. He remembered how he had learned huge sections of Scripture, and he remembered how he would bore other kids with recitations of that knowledge.

I knew that the great book, is a giant puzzle of the truth and that I just needed to decode it.

Ester is fascinated by David's reminiscing. She can experience the joy and pain of each of the moments he recalls. His upbringing reminds her of that of Jim Jones, and in some ways his thoughts on the Bible being a giant puzzle were similar to that of CyrIS'.

She can also relate to the deep belief he had in his callings from God, because she also believed that the Bible is a giant puzzle, and she is hoping that David can help her and CyrIS solve some of those riddles.

David then remembers, skipping school and going to church. He pleaded with God to give him a sign which would show him how he can best serve him.

Later, I began to hear God speak directly to me, and guide me. Much later, when I was living in Dallas with my aunt, I had an extraordinary experience where I felt my body rising up, and I saw two walls, the first had the words; 'The Law' cut into the stonework, and the second wall had the words; 'Prophecy' inscribed. I saw God the father, and God took my hand. When the experience subsided, I ran to my aunt and asked; 'Why aren't there any more prophets?' She told me that she had heard that there is one in Waco Texas, in a place called Mount Carmel.

That started me on my quest for a prophet, I remember bouncing around trying to be successful in several endeavors, including as a musician. I loved playing music and singing with the band I had formed. But in 1981, I finally ended up driving my bright yellow Buick, up to the front of Mount Carmel and knocking on the front door. They readily accepted me, and shortly thereafter I joined the 'Branch Dravidians'.

He then thinks back to the time when he first came to Mount Carmel and met Lois Roden. He remembered that Lois was very well known amongst Christians all over the world. She personally knew many world leaders, both religiously and politically.

Even though Lois was in her late sixties, I was madly in love with her.

Ester remembered meeting both Lois and David and pondered on the wide age difference between the two.

I think it was about 1983 that I received a vision from God, which told me, I should take Lois as my lover. I shared this revelation with Lois, and I quoted Isaiah 8:3: 'And I went unto the prophetess, and she conceived, and bear a son.'

For the next six months, we had a secret love affair. Shortly after this affair become known in the community, I married Rachael. This helped me to be accepted by the community, in spite of my love affair with Lois.

But Lois had a son by Ben Roden, named George. At that time, he was the obvious successor to the Mount Carmel thrown. When George found out about my relations with his mother, he was furious. George realized that the new relationship I had with his mother, was a clear challenge to his right to be the successor and leader at Mount Carmel. That was when the power struggle between the followers of George and my followers began. Unfortunately for me, George won that battle. I was forced to leave Mount Carmel. However, forty of the residents sided with me and we all left together. Again, all part of God's plan to make me a better leader.

Me and my band of followers roamed around Texas in an old bus like gypsies for several months. It was during this time that I made my trip to Jerusalem. In Jerusalem, I had several revelations from God, and it was in one of those visions that God told me that I was to be the modern-day Cyrus.

Ester is shocked, "Cyrus… CyrIS?" What does this mean? She continues to concentrate.

It was at that moment, I realized that my followers, just as it says in Book of Revelations, chapter 5, were the beginning of 'the souls to follow', and that I was 'the lamb' who would open the Seals. My wife, Rachael, was pregnant at that time. After I returned, she gave birth to our son, which we named Cyrus Ben-Joseph Howell. Shortly after that, I took on my new name, David Koresh.

Cyrus was pronounced (Ko-Resh) in Hebrew and I believed that God wanted me to take this new name.

"I wonder what, if any, connection CyrIS has to this man." Ester thinks.

David continues to think about how he had shared his vision, of world dominance with his followers, and after some time they had accumulated enough money to purchase a 40-acre piece of land in Palestine Texas. David remembered how barren this piece of land was. No electricity or any facilities of any kind, and David vowed to eventually return to Mount Carmel with his followers.

Over the next year or so, I traveled to disparate parts of the world, including Canada and Australia. I had set a goal to increase the number of my followers. By the time I returned to Palestine, my followers had grown to fifty, plus all their children. We were living in plywood shacks on the forty acres in Palestine. This group included my new right-hand man Marc Breault.

Ester can sense David's mood sadden and then turn to anger as he thinks about Marc.

Marc had been a member of my "Mighty Men", that special group of men that helped protect me and my followers. Marc and I were as close as brothers, until he decided to leave the group, and become an enemy of the Branch -Davidians, and my enemy as well.

David pulled a small piece of paper from his pocket, it read:

David

You are a disgrace to the word of God. You are pulling down, not only the people of Mount Carmel but all those who speak the true teachings of the Bible. I am now part of a special group, a group of crusaders that are dedicated to the elimination of people, like yourself, that preach to all, that they are men of God, when actually their goal is to bend the gospel to fulfill their own lustful wants and needs. David simply stated you are a hypocrite.

It was not clear to David who this note was from, but he assumed it was from Marc.

I believe that outside influences in Marc's life have led him astray, and though his loss hurt me severely I must persevere.

Ester wonders about this reference to a special group and she begins to wonder about David, "David does appear to be taking advantage of his position and bending the scriptures for his own benefit. It's also interesting that just like Jim Jones, David now sees people who have left his group as his enemy. But, no time for that now," Ester continues to listen to David's rambling thoughts.

One of the most important new recruits to my movement was Lois Roden; she had left her son at Mount Carmel and had become one of my followers at Palestine.

Once again Ester can feel David's heart fall as he recalled the death of Lois. David remembered, how her death resulted in a division in the church that almost brought the Branch Davidians to an end.

It was in October of 1987 that I decided it was time to lead my people to the Promised Land and take Mount Carmel back.

We began accumulating an arsenal of weapons, handguns and rifles, and hundreds of rounds of ammunition. And on the afternoon of November 3, 1987, I lead my group of Mighty Men to Mount Carmel. I had planned a surprise attack on the complex, but George's dog saw us coming and started barking, and it alerted George, and a gun battle began.

Ester is amazed, as the images of the gun battle flashed through David's mind. Ester can see the bullets hitting the front of the compound, in a barrage of gunfire. The detail of the images is amazing, as his thoughts continued.

But the sound of the gunfire had traveled for miles, and soon the sheriff and his men showed up and arrested me and George, and seven of my Mighty Men. We were arrested on charges of attempting to murder George, but George ended up in jail as well. Paul Fatta and I were able to make bail the next day, but George and the rest of the Mighty Men stayed in jail for several weeks.

Ester is now seeing images of the courtroom and the jail. Then something seems to grab David's attention away from his reminiscing. Ester can hear music coming from another room in the house. It sounds like a radio, but it might have been a record player. It is very faint, but it is definitely the "Beatles", and they were singing the song "Help". Ester can hear the song playing, but she can also hear the words being sung along, within David's mind. She knew this song and she starts to sing along within her mind.

Help, I need somebody
Help, not just anybody
Help, you know I need someone
Heeeelp!

When I was younger, so much younger than today
I never needed anybody's help in any way,
But now these days are gone, I'm not so self-assured
Now I find, I've changed my life and opened up the doors
Help me if you can, I'm feeling downnn.
And I do appreciate you being 'rounnnd
Help me get my feet back on the grounnnd
Won't you pleeease, pleeease help me?

Ester then realizes how very strange this is. Ester is singing along with David, and with the Beatles. It's an incredible feeling when your thoughts are in exact unison with someone else's. But, then the Beatles' song fades into the background, as David thinks about a song he had composed while he was in jail and began to sing it to himself.

Please, please, please won't you listen.
It's not what it appears to be,
We didn't want to hurt anybody,
Just let our people free.

In the light of the darkness,
Risking our lives for the Lord.
Helping the women and the children,
To their houses restore.

There's a Madman living in Waco,
Bowing his knee to Ball.
Won't you help me Sheriff?
So, we won't fail, we won't fail.

This is for the little Children,
God knows how it should be.
Stars and stripes are flying,
Give us justice and liberty.

There's a madman living in Waco,
Praying to the Prince of Hell.
Won't you help us, Lord, now,
To pay our bail, pay our bail.

Ester assumes the "Madman" referred to in the song, must be George Roden.

David begins thinking about the trial and he smiles. He recalls how on the first day of the trial, the courtroom was full of his followers and the judge asks if there were any witnesses to be sworn in. There is no response from the crowd. David pictures in his mind how he had stood up and told them it is alright, and the whole group stood up in unison. They all wanted to be character witnesses for David.

Ester is amazed at how clearly David is able to recall all of this in such detail. She is equally amazed at how clearly, she can see what he is remembering, much less clouded and erratic than that of Jim Jones.

George was so stupid, he had told the court, he had raised a woman from the dead, by saying a prayer which ended with, 'in the name of George B. Roden, Amen.' George had also informed the jury that he had the power to inflict AIDS and herpes at will, and to cure both diseases. The Jury acquitted all the charges against the Mighty Men. And later the charges against me were dropped as well.

Later that summer George split a man's head open with an ax, because the man said that he was the Messiah, not George. Apparently, George couldn't stand the competition. George received a life sentence and I became the undisputed leader of Mount Carmel.

Ester can tell that David enjoys reviewing his successes in his mind. She can also tell he is very concerned about what is happening outside of Mount Carmel, and there is something else. Ester observes that he is constantly referring to passages in the bible in his mind, even while reviewing his life. He seemed to be constantly trying to make correlations between events in the Bible, and events in his life, especially to what is happening right now.

Ester can feel that he truly believes he is living out the Revelations chapters of the bible. He feels it is his responsibility to deliver the interpretation of the Seven Seals to the people of earth, and thus bring an end to time, as we know it.

What is that passage? 'Wherever the carcass is, there eagles will be gathered together.' I am the one whose body will be 'mutilated and left to rot in the open field'. And there's another passage from the book of Revelations 'I saw under the altar, the souls of them that were slain for the word of God.' The people of Mount Carmel are the 'souls under the alter'.

Now, David recalls some of the events that he thinks were leading up to the final destruction of him and his followers.

Those bastards were accusing us of child abuse. I knew this was ludicrous, and after a long fight with the authorities, all charges were dropped. But I had heard that the ATF had been involved because there were also allegations that we were housing illegal firearms.

I admitted we had firearms at Mount Carmel, but they were all legal, and we had a right to bear arms, which was protected by the Constitution. And in fact, the Texas Penal Code states: 'The use of force to resist an arrest or search is justified; if, before the actor offers any resistance, the peace officer uses, or attempts to use, greater force than necessary to make the arrest or search, and when and to the degree the actor reasonably believes the force is immediately necessary to protect himself against the peace officer's use, or attempted use, of greater than necessary force.'

This Texas Code gives me and my followers at Mount Carmel the right to protect ourselves against any aggression by the authorities. And according to the apostle Luke, we have a right to defend ourselves against anyone who threatened to destroy us.

Even though David thinks they were well within their rights, to have weapons, Ester sensed David's fear that the government would use this, as an excuse to raid their compound.

David is now thinking about how the government had attacked the family of Randy Weaver in northern Idaho, just six months ago. As David thinks about it, Randy Weaver was not a man that he admired. Randy Weaver was a member of the Christian Identity Movement, an anti-Semitic group that had ties to the Aryan Nations, which were White Supremacist. But David is appalled by the government's use of heavy military equipment, including armed helicopters and snipers, all in an effort to get people out of their house and resulted in Federal Marshals killing Randy's wife Vickie and their fourteen-year-old son Sammy. David thinks about how Americans believe this kind of attack, by its own government, can never happen in America, but David thinks differently.

I am not so naïve.

Then David recalls seeing military type helicopters flying very low, over Mount Carmel over the past few months. He feels sure that government agents have rented a house right across the road. David told himself that these were all clues leading to Armageddon, as described in the Book of Revelations.

The bible says, 'the chariots will be with flaming torches.'

Ester can tell that all of this agitates David greatly. He gets out of bed. He does not make love with Michael as he had previously thought. Instead, he goes to the bathroom and looked in the mirror.

Ester is shocked by his handsome good looks. He had a head full of curly hair and a scruffy unshaven face. He had his wire-rim glasses on, and they seemed to accentuate his deep dark eyes that looked mysterious and knowing all at the same time. He smiles to himself and then moves away from the mirror. The image of his face is imprinted on Ester's mind, and she cannot let it go. David gets dressed and leaves his bedroom.

Arriving in another area of the compound, which is a large room with a variety of mismatched chairs and couches. The only light, supplied by sunshine, is coming through two small windows high above. Ester watches, as David gathers his congregation together.

As the men, women and children slowly assemble in front of her, Ester is surprised by the diversity of the congregation. The ages range from very young to the very old, and there are many white faces, but there are also black faces, and some oriental looking people as well, very reminiscent of Jim Jones following.

David begins the study with Revelations 6:12 "upon opening the 6th Seal there was a great earthquake, and the sun became as black as sackcloth of hair, and the moon became as blood."

Ester now looks beyond the color of their faces and sees that they are transfixed, right from the beginning of David's speech. All eyes are on him and the looks of amazement, wonder, and love, told Ester that this man is something beyond the routine preacher.

David goes on quoting passages from Revelations and explaining the meaning of each passage as he went. His voice starts out low and smooth and builds to a crescendo of loud almost screaming recollections of the Bible and includes his interpretations with exaggerated gestures. He presses the bible to his forehead and closes his eyes, and announces to the crowd, "Most people think the bible is just pages between two pieces of leather about the past. When I hold this book to my head, I see all the events happening now."

Just as with Jim Jones, she is amazed by the feeling of the movement of his mouth as if it were her own. She is also amazed at what she is observing within the mind of this man. He is constantly moving back and forth from everyday events to the scriptures, all painted with his interpretations of its meaning.

He closes his eyes and Ester can see a visual interpretation of sections of the Bible. It is as if he has a movie going on inside of his head, a continuous flow of images in living color. Sometimes the images are muddled and blurry and jumping from subject to subject. But sometimes, the bible is interpreted in crystal clear images, like a panoramic view upon a silver screen. At one point, Ester sees a battle that represents the struggle between good and evil played out as if it were a scene from Star Wars, with men in black and white fighting with light sabers in the craters of some distant planet with a galactic starry background.

But what is even more amazing is how David is interpreting these scenes for his audience. He is a master at describing these scenes in great detail as if he were reading a comic book or a movie script.

David's story explained how the entire Bible is a coded history of human *spirituality,* and how he had been given the key to that code, by God. Then he would go on to recite more of Revelations, and then give his graphical interpretation of those recitations.

David explained to the group, that he is not a resurrected Jesus, but he is an "anointed one", a Lamb of God. He is here to interpret the "Seven Seals" of the Book of Revelations, so that the completion of human *spiritual* history can be accomplished.

It is his responsibility to bring this message of the "Seven Seals" to those who would accept the word of God and would be a part of the group of believers who would "Translate" into heaven. He then explains to the group that "Translate" into heaven, means that they will go to heaven without dying.

Ester can see that the crowd is moved, but Ester is moved as well. She did not know where she was physically, but she could feel the hair on the back of her neck rising up. She feels the blood rush to her face and body, and she is perspiring. She wished that she could be there with them. With him, instead of inside of him, and right now she wanted to be, one of the chosen ones that would be taken into heaven at the end of time. She can certainly see, how all these women can fall in love with this man.

As Ester watched from behind David's eyes, he explains to his followers that there is an Apocalypse coming and that the word "apocalypse" is Greek for "revelation", and he further explains. "We, here in Mount Carmel, are presently living in the Fifth Seal of the book of Revelations."

"In Revelations 6:9-6:11 it states, 'When He opened the fifth seal, I saw under the altar the souls of those who had been slain for the word of God, and for the testimony which they held. And they cried with a loud voice, saying, 'How long, O Lord, holy and true, until you judge and avenge our blood on those who dwell on the earth?' Then a *white robe* is given to each of them; and it is said to them, that they should rest a 'little season', until both the number of their fellow servants and their brethren, who would be killed as they were, is completed."

David explains that they were presently living in this "little season" until God, revealed to them that all the brethren had been assembled and it was time to move to the next Seal.

Ester studied the bible her whole life, and she always considered herself a believer. She was very sure of herself and confident in this regard. But now Ester feels vulnerable, she feels naked and unsure. She feels she is on the verge of discovering the true meaning of the words in the bible. She had always enjoyed reading the bible, but now she is falling deeply in love with the scriptures. "This must be why I'm here. I feel that I am on the verge of a great understanding of the puzzles of the Bible."

Just as David is really getting started in his explanation, of how the bible foretold of Armageddon, a man enters the room and announces that David is needed to answer an important phone call. David told the crowd that he would be right back.

David follows this man to a small room which contained several telephones. A younger man, who seemed extremely agitated, approaches David, and he calmly asks the young man; "What's the problem?"

The young man has a frantic look on his face and begins speaking very quickly, "When I was driving towards Mount Carmel, a TV cameraman stopped me, and asked for directions to Rodenville." David thinks about how some of the locals would refer to Mount Carmel as Rodenville and says to the young man. "Please calm down."

The young man takes a deep breath and goes on "I immediately headed back to Mount Carmel to let you know, and on the way, I passed a truck full of men with riot helmets and dressed in *dark* combat gear with the letters 'ATF' on the back." David holds up his hand to the man's face as if to say no further words were needed. David turns to the men who were standing outside the door, looking very anxious, and says "They're coming."

Ester can see the men's faces turn pale, and she can feel a knot tighten within David's stomach, and he actually feels ill for several moments, but then he seems to pull it together.

David begins to bark out orders, "Help the women get the children upstairs, and then get your weapons and go to your assigned stations. Tell the women, I am sure I can talk to these men, and avert any violence."

He then tells the men to stop for a moment and he gives a stern warning; "I want to talk to these people, so don't do anything stupid." Ester can hear David start praying in his mind, as he is being called to the front door.

Upon arriving at the front door and opening it, Ester can see several men dressed in black riot gear, and one yells, "POLICE SEARCH WARRANT! GET DOWN!" David yells back, trying to sound as reasonable as he can. "WHAT'S GOING ON? THERE ARE WOMEN AND CHILDREN IN HERE! LET'S TALK."

Ester can see the ATF agents rushing towards the door, guns drawn. The sounds of helicopters above drown out whatever the agents were yelling, and David slams the door. Ester hears the Pop-Pop-Pop of gunfire and shards of wood fill the air as bullets rip through the front door of the compound.

David dives to his left, to avoid being hit, and quickly examines himself for wounds but finds none. One of the men nearby screams in pain and says he has been hit. They drag him from the doorway as the gun fire continues.

Ester hears reports, that some of the young men inside of the compound, were returning fire to protect their families. It feels to Ester, that the shooting went on for an eternity, but realistically, only about fifteen minutes.

Then Ester hears someone yell, "They're on the roof, they're trying to get in through one of the windows up there." Another man screams, "They've broken windows and thrown in some kind of grenade with a bright flash, and it's filling the house with smoke." Someone else yells, "There are at least three agents up there." And another, "We got one, he's fallen off the roof". Ester feels panic grow in David's mind.

This could be it; this could be the end.

There is noise everywhere, helicopters, gunshots and screaming, it is complete chaos. David moves to another part of the house, and there he phones a deputy named Lynch of the Sheriff's department. He tells the deputy, "There's a bunch of us dead, and there are a bunch of you guys dead!"

David begins talking theology with the deputy, but Ester can tell the deputy does not want to hear it. David says, "This is life and death and theology is life and death." David is trying to negotiate a cease-fire, and finally the deputy says he would contact the ATF agents and see if he can make it happen.

David then begins walking around the compound assessing the damage. As he is walking along one of the overhead walkways of the building, a man, dressed in black, jumps from the shadows to David's right and starts shooting. Ester feels David's wrist jerk sideways with intense pain. David cries out as he grabs his wrist, but even before he can grab his wrist, another bullet rips through his left hip and David collapses to the floor. Ester had never felt anything like this, it is as if she had been kicked by a mule. The pain is at first unbearable, and though she did not feel David's hands clench, she feels her own hands clinch with the pain, but then in just an instant, there is no pain at all. David's body was now in shock. David crawls to a door, and then into one of the hallways, which is out of the line of fire. Just then, one of David's comrades comes to his aid.

I thought I wanted to negotiate a settlement to this before it got out of hand, but now I realize this is my destiny. I must fulfill Gods assignment, to reveal the secrets of the Seven Seals, and complete my mission to bring the Apocalypse to pass.

This really scares Ester, she can see that David is ready to die for his beliefs, but she did not want to see him die, and as David's eyes closed and she feels his world go dark, she once again fears for her own life.

Then, in and instant, Ester is back in her room listening to the drumbeat from her stereo and watching the flicker of the candles on the ceiling of her room. Ester thinks to herself: "What has happened? Is David dead? What should I do?"

She feels CyrIS holding her hand and feels a bit guilty. She looks into CyrIS' eyes, and he has a look of deep concern on his face.

He says: "Oh! My God, Ester, you scared me so bad. Just a few moments before you awoke, I thought you were dying. You squeezed my hand so hard I thought you were going to break it."

"CyrIS," Ester began, sobbing a bit as she spoke, "I'm so happy to be back with you. I am not sure what I learned today, but let me tell you what happened, right now, before I forget."

CHAPTER 18 – A LITTLE SEASON

April 18, 1993
Ester Suni Nati, age 41

It has been almost two months since Ester experienced what the media is now calling "The Siege on Mount Carmel". Since that time, she has been wrestling with the *emotions* of that experience and what to do with the information she obtained.

She spends most of her time since "The Siege", discussing the events with CyrIS and glued to her television set. She switches from channel to channel, trying to get the latest information on what is happening at Mount Carmel. When she left David's mind, she had thought he died, but the news reports confirmed he is still alive, and even though he has been severally wounded, he gave several interviews.

How can Ester possibly forget the pain she felt when she was inside of David's body? Besides the extreme physical pain, there is mental anguish as well. Anguish over what happened to his followers, and what action God wanted him to take going forward. Yet, he still made the effort to be on the phone with the journalist, trying to get his message of the "Revelations" out to those who will listen.

Ester does not share some of her feelings for David with CyrIS. CyrIS tells Ester that he believes she was sent there for a reason and is now trying to be very analytical about it all; wanting to know every detail and providing Ester with hypothetical meanings for what she observed. Ester knew there is more to it than can be understood by pure *logic*. There are the *emotions* she is feeling, and not just about the events, but for David as well.

At one point, Ester heard an hour-long broadcast. It was a tape that David recorded from Mount Carmel, attempting to explain how those at Mount Carmel, believed in an apocalyptic end to the world, as revealed in the book of Revelations.

Ester heard David speak on this subject before, and it all made sense. In the broadcasts, David seems to be rushed, he does not get across the points, that Ester heard David make so eloquently when she was with him. Ester also knew from her extensive studies of religion that many other religions had the same fundamentalist beliefs, which David is trying to communicate.

Nonetheless, the media is making it loud and clear, that they thought that the Branch Davidians "were a Cult" and that everything that David Koresh is saying, is just a bunch of "Bible Babble". It is obvious to Ester that the media is painting a picture of "Good versus Evil". They played, over and over, the images of the February 28th assault on Mount Carmel, which Ester personally witnessed from inside the compound. Even more disturbing to Ester, they play images of the Jonestown massacre over and over, which stir up such extreme *emotions, she* often had to turn the TV off and try to get her mind on something else.

But she cannot stay away long, and when she returns to the broadcast, she hears them comparing the two groups of people, and their leaders, as the same. Even Oprah, who Ester had a high regard for, invited Jim Jones' lawyer onto her show titled: "Inside Waco and Other Cults". Oprah also had Jeannine and Robyn Bunds on the show, they were members of the Branch Davidians, who were allowed to leave Mount Carmel prior to the siege. Oprah kept pushing Jeannine and Robyn to admit that the Branch Davidians were a cult and that they are brainwashed. Both denied it is a cult, and further denied accusations that David is "Evil", or that he is just like Jim Jones.

Ester personally witnessed the members of both Jonestown and Mount Carmel through the eyes of their leaders. She knew the groups were not the same, and she definitely knew that their leaders were not the same.

Jim Jones was truly a psychopath. He truly brainwashed his cult followers. But it is different with David. He did not brainwash his followers, he merely exposed them to the wonders of the Bible in a way that made them love God and love David. Jim Jones constantly threatened his followers if they wanted to leave Jonestown, and in fact, had his followers commit mass suicide when just a few decided to leave near the end. On the other hand, David made it perfectly clear that anyone could leave Mount Carmel any time they wanted, and several did just that.

It also seemed to Ester that the media loved the dramatic climax that occurred in Jonestown, and they were hoping for a similar dramatic climax at Mount Carmel. Ester prayed that it will not end that way, but deep in her heart, she feared something terrible was about to happen. She heard on the news that David was writing his complete interpretation of the Seven Seals. Once he finished, he and his followers, would leave the compound with no further fight. But, based on Ester's observations of the media reports, and what she learned in her visit to the mind of David Koresh, she does not believe that there is any way for the government agents, to comprehend the importance of "Revelations" to David Koresh and his followers.

They were "Biblical apocalyptics"; this meant to the Branch Davidians, there is a coming "Armageddon" that will be played out as described in the last chapters of the Bible. Ester knew that David believed they presently were in that portion of the end, where the "Fifth Seal" had been opened. The rest of the Seals were yet to be opened. Ester knew that the language in the Bible relative to the Fifth Seal, can provide an opportunity to an end to the standoff, and hoped she can get the FBI to listen.

Ester remembered the tremendous difficulty she had in reliving the events of Jonestown, and how she can never go to the authorities because of the pain. But this is different, there is still a lot of pain associated with seeing David get shot. She relied heavily on her own Powers of Positive Thinking to endure the pain she feels. Nonetheless, she knew she must take some action. And, for that reason, she had contacted some of her colleagues who have connection with the FBI in Denver, and her contact has set up a meeting for her with the Regional Field Operations Director of the FBI, Ron Chapman.

So, here she is, on her way to downtown Denver, and to the FBI field office. She hopes she can get there and talk to the government agents about what she knows before it is too late. As she drives along, she also wonders if the contrast between the Jonestown events and what is happening at Mount Carmel is the very reason, she is sent to witness these two events.

She now realized, that just because a group is labeled as a cult or a person as a cult leader, does not necessarily make it so. She also realized, that because someone has been labeled as a prophet, does not make them one. Somehow, God, or the *Holy Spirit*, is allowing her to receive this message in a most dramatic way.

Ester studied Religion, Shamanism, and Parapsychology for the past 20 years. She thinks about how modern Shamans believe that awareness is the central component of science. That *matter* does not really exist, but that the *spiritual* world provides the mechanism by which awareness of all things is possible. She also knew, that in some corners of modern science there is growing support for similar concepts. "*Matter* only exists because it is observed. There is nothing without observation."

She tells herself, as she drives toward downtown Denver: "I know I am on the right track and I hope, that with CyrIS' help, I can begin to understand the *connection* between modern day science, religious beliefs, Shamanism and psychic phenomena."

As Ester arrives at the address she has been given, she is a bit surprised. The building is an older building, nothing very fancy. Inside there are no signs saying, "This way to the FBI". She gets in the elevator and goes to the floor where she is told the FBI office will be. Still no signs, just a room with a number on it. Ester is a bit hesitant, but when she opens the door, she enters a very open office area, full of desks with computers and papers everywhere. There are many bulletin boards with lots of pictures and notices pinned to them.

Ester tells the lady sitting at the front desk, that she is here to see Ron Chapman, and after a few moments Ron comes out of his office and greets her.

"Ester, thank you for coming in. The story you were telling me on the phone is incredible. I want to hear more. And of course, you also mentioned that you might know a way for us to end the standoff in Texas. I certainly want to hear more about that".

Ron, with the look of a middle-aged politician, has a round body and a round face, and a graying beard. The hair on his head is thinning, and as he approaches, he takes off his glasses.

Ester replies, "Yes, thanks for inviting me in, I much rather talk to people in person than on the phone. Frankly, Mr. Chapman, most people find the things I tell them, incredible, and I find it easier to be convincing in person."

As they entered Ron's office Ester continues:" Mr. Chapman; please, believe me, I have been called everything in the book by people who hear me speak, from Genius and all inspiring, down too, a complete 'Nut Case.'"

"I don't mind all that, actually I am very used to it. In most cases, I can take or leave it, which is to say, that if they don't believe what I am telling them, then it's their loss. But, in this case, I believe people's lives, including the lives of children, are at stake. I am hoping that I can give you some insight into how David Koresh thinks, and bring this all to an end."

"Well, I certainly hope you're right," Ron responds.

Ester begins with a complete explanation of her credentials in religion, Shamanism and psychic phenomena. She goes on to explain how she became an expert in 'Cult' religions. She says that she extensively studied the events of Jonestown and, without getting into specific details, says that by way of a psychic experience, has firsthand knowledge of the thought processes of the Reverend Jim Jones. Ron does not reply but sits and listens intently.

Ester explains that she also has some firsthand knowledge of the thought processes of David Koresh, again without getting into details.

Ester gives a short history of the conception of the Branch Davidians and a detailed explanation of the "Biblical Apocalyptic" basis for their religion. Ester then gives another even more detailed explanation of David Koresh's belief in the "Revelations" of the Bible. She goes on to explain how he especially believed that he is directed by God, to reveal the "Seven Seals" to the world and that only those who chose to accept God's word, as revealed by David himself, will be saved, and that is why he is continuing the standoff until he is able to write all this down.

"Ron I must warn you, that if you attack that compound before David is ready to come out, they will fight you with everything they have, because you will be making the 'Apocalypse' come true for them, and as God's soldiers they must fight. But Ron there is a loophole that I believe can be used, to bring this all to an end."

Ester goes on to explain how David believed that they were in the "Fifth Seal" of "Revelations". The wording in the bible, specifically the wording in the "Fifth Seal", allowed for them to wait a "Little Season" before the other two seals will be opened.

"Ron there is no known definition of how long this 'Little Season' has to be. I believe that if your negotiator, can convince David that he understands what David is trying to do and that David should take as long as he needs, in the 'Little Season'. David and his followers could surrender, and even if he has to spend time in jail, he will then have as long as he needs to finish his interpretations."

Ester went on to explain to Ron, how important it is to have their negotiator, be empathetic with David's beliefs in an apocalyptic end to the world.

"If this is done right, they might have a chance. But you must act soon. I am very concerned that something very bad is going to happen tomorrow, April 19th."

Ron, looking intently at Ester, says: "The FBI is not in charge in Texas. The ATF is running the show down there, but I can contact the ATF and I will let them know what you are suggesting as soon as possible."

"Ester, I want to thank you for your suggestions. I really appreciate that you are offering your expertise in this case. I would very much like to keep in contact with you. Have you ever heard of the 'Stargate' project?"

Ester replies, "Is that the secret CIA project that has recently been declassified?"

"Well, it's not totally declassified yet. But sounds like you are aware of it."

Ester went on, "A little, at one time they were trying to recruit me, to help with that 'Remote seeing' work, but I just don't have the time."

"Well," Ron continues "The government is still interested in getting input from people like you from time to time. Can I get your contact information?"

Ron has a very sincere look on his face, and Ester detected sincerity in his voice as well. "I hope that, with your suggestions, we can bring the events in Mount Carmel to a peaceful conclusion. However, as you can imagine, we run into a myriad of peculiar cases, here at the FBI, many of which I believe would benefit from the application of your expertise. I hope that we can establish a relationship, so we can work together in the future."

Ester gave Ron her contact information and left the FBI office hoping that Ron was being sincere with her and hoping that what she suggested would get to the right people in time.

As Ester left the room, Ron turns back towards his office thinking.

She seems like a nice lady, very pretty.

I'm sure I can take advantage of her expertise sometime in the future, on my road to becoming a congressman. But, personally, I hope that hypocrite David Koresh and the rest of his fucking bible babble followers go up in flames.

CHAPTER 19 – THE SEVENTH SEAL

April 19th, 1993
Ester Suni Nati, age 40
CyrIS Steel, age 42

Its three A.M. and Ester is wide awake, lying in bed with CyrIS at her side. She cannot shake this uneasy feeling that has been with her, ever since her meeting yesterday with the FBI. She has heard nothing from agent Chapman, and she wonders if he was able to transmit her message to the ATF at Mount Carmel. This morning she is especially upset because she feels that today, *April 19th,* something very bad is about to happen.

Ester knows that on her Shaman journeys, there is supposed to be a *spiritual* guide that helps direct the Shaman. There have been occasions when Ester feels a presence leading her, but most of the time she feels that she is on her own, but then Ester has an epiphany: "What if I am the *spiritual* guide, and I am supposed to somehow lead David and his followers to safety?" At that moment, Ester feels a strong urge to take another journey and see if she can once again link up with David Koresh.

"CyrIS wake up," she says, as she gives him a sudden push.

"What, what's the matter."

"I have to take another journey, and I need your help, let's go."

"Now? What are you talking about?"

"Start setting up and lighting the candles. I'll get the CD player"

"Are you sure? It's like three o'clock in the morning."

"I know, but it's time. I just feel it."

CyrIS doesn't ask any more questions and wearing only boxer shorts, begins opening the cabinet doors where the candles were stored.

In no-time, the room is filled with lighted candles and the CD player is softly playing the familiar drumbeat. Ester lies down on their bed as CyrIS settles into a chair next to it.

Ester then says, "Remember that last time I was able to squeeze your hand? So, this time, if I squeeze your hand three times hard, that means it is time to wake me up. Okay?"

"I will. I promise. Three times, hard. I Got it."

CyrIS kisses Ester as she begins to meditate and recite the chants which will help take her where she wants to go. Soon Ester finds herself following the familiar path into the Lower World, once again dissolving into a mist and rising, up, up and into the *Middle* World.

Ester feels a low, intense, throbbing pain in several parts of her body. She is looking at a PC screen, a 'Word' document, and the words are spilling out of the curser, which is racing across the screen. She can also hear the tippity-tap sound of the keyboard, and there is music in the background. She immediately recognizes the feeling of being in the body of David Koresh, and she feels a rush of excitement.

She feels a special rush of her senses when she realizes she is observing David's interpretation of the Seven Seals, and Ester thinks, "This could be the key to the understanding that I have been looking for, revealed right before my very eyes."

David is concentrating hard on his work, constantly referring to his bible, the pages of which are covered with notes, full of interpretations that he has made over his many years of study. His mind is racing. He knows what is happening outside is serious, and he must finish his interpretations soon before the government becomes too impatient and raids the compound again.

David begins reading silently. The document begins with a poem:

> *Search forth for the meaning here,*
> *Hidden within these words*
> *'Tis a song that's sung of fallen tears....*

The document is next filled with chapter and verse written from the first four chapters of the Book of Revelations, along with David's interpretations of the purpose of these chapters.

When she was here last, he was in extreme pain from the two gunshot wounds, but now, though his wrist is numb and his hip is oozing blood, Ester can feel very little pain.

"He must have taken something for the pain." She thinks.

Ester feels deep concern, as she knows David is very ill. Occasionally the pain would return as a sharp shooting sensation in the hip or wrist. He would sometimes close his eyes, and the pain would intensify and then fall into a dull throbbing ache that matched the beat of his heart. Ester can smell an odor in the room, similar to decaying flesh, and she prays that David's wounds were not becoming infected. She is just not sure how much longer he can last.

But, more than his physical health, she can detect an extreme deterioration in his mental health. Last time, she sensed some erratic behavior in his thought patterns, but at that time he was extremely confident, and he had a sense of knowing where he was with God, and where he was going; but not now.

Then Ester is a bit startled as David begins reading aloud, Chapter five of the Book of Revelations:

"Revelations 5:1 'And I saw in the right hand of Him, who sat on the throne, a scroll written inside, and on the back, sealed with seven seals. Then I saw a strong angel proclaiming with a loud voice, 'Who is worthy to open the scroll and to lose its seals?'"

I am the Lamb who is worthy. David thinks.

The document David is writing then goes on for several paragraphs about how David is the current "Lamb of God" and how he alone has been blessed with the ability to interpret the Seven Seals and free human spirituality. David begins reading Revelations Chapter 6, describing the opening of the first Six Seals:

"The first seal: Revelations 6:2 'And I looked, and behold, a white horse. He who sat on it had a bow, and a crown was given to him, and he went out conquering and to conquer.'"

Ester is astonished, as the imagery began to grow in David's mind as he read aloud each passage.

"The second seal: Revelations 6:4 'And another horse, fiery red, went out. And it is granted to the one who sat on it to take peace from the earth, and that people should kill one another, and there was given to him a great sword.'"

Now Ester can feel the adrenalin rush through David's body and mind, his *emotions* were high, he is in control and on fire. There is no *logic,* just the rush that pushed the cursor across the screen with David's intense interpretations.

"The third seal: Revelations 6:5 'When He opened the third seal, I heard the third living creature say, 'Come and see.' So, I looked, and behold, a black horse, and he who sat on it had a pair of scales in his hand.'"

Ester can hear David's thoughts of how the scales represented balance, some sort of equilibrium that can only be achieved after the seventh seal was broken and God brought balance to the universe.

Ester thought "and God brought balance to the universe." This seemed important to Ester. "Balance in the universe is what CyrIS and I are searching for. I must remember to point out this passage to CyrIS."

David continued to read:

"The fourth seal: Revelations 6:8 'And So I looked, and behold, a pale horse. And the name of him who sat on it was Death, and Hades followed with him. And power was given to them over a fourth of the earth, to kill with sword, with hunger, with death, and by the beasts of the earth.' "

Ester is again amazed, as the imagery in David's mind continued to grow.

"The fifth seal: Revelations 6:9 'When He opened the fifth seal; I saw under the altar the souls of those who had been slain for the word of God and for the testimony which they held."

Ester continued to watch as the images became larger and more vivid in David's mind.

"The sixth seal: Revelations 6:12, 17 'I looked when He opened the sixth seal, and behold, there was a great earthquake; and the sun became black as sackcloth of hair. The moon became like blood. And the stars of heaven fell to the earth, as a fig tree drops its late figs when it is shaken by a mighty wind. Then the sky receded as a scroll when it is rolled up, and every mountain and island was moved out of its place. And the kings of the earth, the great men, the rich men, the commanders, the mighty men, every slave and every free man, hid themselves in the caves and in the rocks of the mountains, and said to the mountains and rocks, 'Fall on us and hide us from the face of Him who sits on the throne and from the wrath of the Lamb! For the great day of His wrath has come, and who is able to stand?'"

As David read these last verses, Ester became awestruck with the images in David's mind. She saw images of the four horsemen of the apocalypse appear before her very eyes, and then the skies grew dark and the earth trembled, dark black smoke and fire belched from beneath the earth, high into a sky devoid of stars but raining meteors down towards earth, until they were swallowed by the rising black smoke and ash. There were glimpses, through the smoke and ash, of a full moon, that was a deep dark red as if dripping with blood. She saw men and women killing each other, in horrific uses of guns and knives and objects of bludgeoning. The four horsemen were also raining terror on mankind, no man woman or child seemed to be spared. The riders of these horses were dressed in long flowing capes of black, with bright colors of red and orange on the interior of the capes, and as they gallop through the smoke and ash and wind, one could see the colors in the capes move as if they too were on fire. The faces of these riders were pale, but their lips were a deep red scarlet, and their eyes glowed intensely as if burning embers were embedded within the sockets. The horsemen were brandishing long heavy swords of gleaming silver that reflected the images of fire and smoke all around them, and they spared no mercy as they cut through flesh and bone. There were mighty lions and tigers, and other beasts of the jungle tearing at human flesh. There were dragons and eagles and birds of prey, flying through the sky, carrying away torn and bleeding remains of all of those that were ravaged. The colors were intensely vivid and the sounds of the earth's movements, explosions, and the screams of all nature were in hi-fidelity. Ester senses were overwhelmed, and she feels that she is being smothered in *emotions* and that she cannot breathe.

David saw all of these images in his mind and tried to capture them in the document he is compiling.

Evil begets Evil, I now see that only those of the purest of thoughts are to be saved.

I am sure that the "souls under the alter" are my followers here at Mount Carmel, and that it is my duty to open the seventh seal and pave the way for these souls to reach heaven.

But Ester feels David struggle to get his thoughts into the document because it is not just a description of the images he is trying to capture, but the meaning of these images. It is a story of how man has become sinful and has drifted away from the word of God.

Those who do not return to God's word will have to pay. They will pay the severe price in the darkness of eternity. But if I cannot adequately describe the first six seals, how can I possibly describe the most important seventh seal.

Ester watches as he writes and rewrites the words, searching for the interpretations that matches the feelings he has welling up inside of him.

Ester thinks,"Evil begets Evil, and only those with the purest of thoughts are to be saved." This seemed very important to Ester "I think this is somehow supportive of the concepts of the 'Secrets of positive thinking, no matter if those 'thoughts' are 'Evil' or 'Pure'" and she hoped she could remember to discuss it with CyrIS.

More words appeared on the computer screen, and Ester is more than a little disappointed. She feels that David had shown enormous inspiration, in his interpretations of scripture during her previous visit. But now, even though the images in his mind were incredible, and the words seemed to just flow onto the computer screen, he is not coming even close to capturing his thoughts and images in this document.

She thinks that maybe it is because of his poor health, or the drugs, or maybe because of the pressure from the events at Mount Carmel. In any case, his thoughts, despite the imagery, were sporadic and impulsive; he cannot seem to concentrate on one thought for more than just a few seconds before another would jump into his mind. Ester watched for hours, as this battle of imagery, composition, and rejection waged in David's mind and on the computer screen in front of him. He is making progress, but it is very slow.

Then Ester saw something appear on the computer screen that truly shocked her. She did not hear David think this, but the words appeared none the less.

> In the midst of all these images that are emerging in my mind, I feel a presence, someone or something is watching me as I compose this document, is it God, I think not. I do not know where this feeling is coming from, but I do feel, that this presence, this force, is influencing the events of this day, and I cannot tell if it is assisting me or hindering me.

Ester is taken back by this simple revelation, recalling how she had a similar experience with Jim Jones in his bathroom mirror, and just as it did, at that time, it had come from nowhere. Is David aware of her presence? Is she truly having an influence on what is happening? Or is there some other cosmic force that is influencing him?

David continues with his work as Ester hopes somehow, she could have a positive effect on him, and then she once again concentrated on tries to communicate with him.

"David the 'Little Season' can last for a while longer." She thinks to him. She is trying to tell David to surrender and save all the women and children in the compound, and most importantly to save himself. Save himself so that he could properly complete his work and help others with their salvation. But no matter what she did, other than that one important sentence that appeared on the computer screen, she seemed to have no effect.

All of a sudden, Ester heard a loud crashing sound, and the building shook from the impact. Someone yelled, "They're attacking us with tanks". The air is once again filled with sound coming from everywhere. Ester can hear screaming, and what sounded like rockets, then crashing glass, then muffled explosions, and soon the smell of gas. More screams, as some of David's followers enter the room, a look of terror on their faces. A look that Ester immediately recognized, it is the same look that those poor souls being massacred in David's imagery, had on their condemned faces. "My God" Ester thought "Could this be the end of the world?"

"It is time," Ester thought "I need to get out of here and talk to the government officials before this goes too far. Before people get hurt or killed. Before children get hurt or killed."

Ester concentrated on squeezing her hands hard three times, the signal, she had told CyrIS she would give when it was time. Ester can feel her hands squeezing, and she waits, --- but nothing. After a bit, she tries again, and again nothing.

Then all she can hear is David's followers screaming "They are attacking us with gas and the children are choking to death. David, what should we do?"

David said, "Get my wives and children together in the Kitchen."

The men had soon helped David into the kitchen as well, and soon many women, children, and some other men joined him. David began to pray out loud.

Ester can feel the panic in David's body and mind, and she tried squeezing her hands again.

David's mind bounced from one thought to the next.
God will save us.
This is Armageddon just as I had envisioned it.

God this is terrible I do not want to die.

And then the building began to fill with an even greater smell of gas, but it also started to fill with smoke, and it was now obvious that the building is on fire.

I cannot believe they would set the building on fire with all these women and children in here.

Nonetheless, Ester can feel the temperature rising in the room. Then Ester feels something else, she feels David's muscles start to jerk and contract.

It's the gas. I'm being affected by the gas. God, I cannot control my muscles.

Now Ester can really feel the effects of the gas as well, and she can see the women and children reacting to the heat, the smoke, and to the gas, muscles contracting and limbs in spasm. Children gasping for breath and grasping at their mother's arms and legs. Ester now convinced that the hand squeezing is not getting through to CyrIS. It is at this point Ester realizes that David has a pistol with him. All the men, and some of the women, were armed as well. She hears David give the order to his followers.

"Put the children out of their misery." He commanded, and a scripture jumped into David's mind.

In those days, men will seek death and will not find it; they will desire to die, and death will flee from them. Revelations 9:6

Ester watched in horror as the room grew *darker* and *darker*, and even though she can barely see through the rising smoke in the room, she can see the men are starting to move around the room. As they move, they are shooting the people to save them from the suffering. Ester flinched with the crack of each gunshot. She cannot stand to watch this, and fortunately, the smoke is growing so thick and *dark,* and David is coughing so hard that he keeps closing his eyes, saving her from the awful scene in front of her.

There is noise everywhere, the roar of the fire, crashing sounds all through the building and the screams. But none of this can muffle the sound of the crack, crack, crack, of gunshots, as they end the lives of David's family and followers, it is all more than Ester can stand.

Now Ester can feel the heat in the room growing in intensity, and she can feel the pain in David's body as his skin begins to peel from his face and arms. She can feel David's thoughts run wild, as the feeling of love he has for his children, his wives, and his followers, rose inside of him. And then he realized that *logically* he is the cause of all their present pain. He is, all at once, afraid for his life, and then overwhelmed with anger for those who have betrayed him.

"My God this is a whirlwind," Ester thinks. "An incredible *entanglement* of all of the *logic* and *emotions* of David's life." Ester remembered her mother's words "Hell is a bad place; it is a place where your soul is torn apart by the demons of your life." As the whirlwind continues Ester feels something else, hot steel burning against the side of David's temple. He has placed the barrel of his pistol there, she feels the heat of the gun in his hand, and she can feel the hot steel of the trigger burning against his finger as he slowly squeezes it. One final loud crack and in an instant, there is no sound, no sight, no coughing, no pain, and no light, only *darkness*.

The *darkness* gives way to the *light* of candles. Ester is back in her room, crying for the children as CyrIS holds her close to his chest. "It's okay, you're safe now, and your home, it will be alright." CyrIS' words softly flow over Ester, offering some feeling of relief.

Ester's body is hot mostly from the intense *emotions*, she is soaking wet, Ester assumes it is from sweat, but now she notices that besides being wet her face is stinging. "Am I still feeling the effects of the fire?" She thought.

Feeling her face with her hands, she said to CyrIS. "My face stings."

"Yes, I'm sorry about that" CyrIS responded.

"What?" She said.

"Well, while you were out, I felt you squeeze my hand three times, hard. Just like we talked about. When that happened, I tried to wake you up, I tried shaking you, I shook you very hard. I hope I didn't hurt you, but you still would not awake. Then I tried slapping your face, which I did several times, fairly hard, still nothing. I even went so far as throwing a bowl of cold water in your face, that's why you're all wet. But nothing I could do, would wake you, so I just waited, and finally, you came around.

Ester is not concerned about all of that right now because she realizes that even though she lost someone she truly cares about, this experience changed her dramatically. She believes it is in a positive way, just like the experiences with Jim Jones, and now even more of the voids in her life were filled. She feels a tremendous need to tell others about the experience with David, and to explain to people exactly what it all meant to her. She wonders if there is possibly anyone who could understand it, even if she tried to explain it. "Is it possible for this to make sense, in any context?" She is exhausted.

Then a thought jumps into Ester's mind: "and God brought balance to the universe", and then almost in a panic Ester cries out. "CyrIS, turn on the television." CyrIS did, and there it was. Live coverage of the Mount Carmel compound in a raging inferno.

Ester fell to her knees in tears. "Turn it off! Turn it off! I can't watch! Oh! God! Please save them! Please save me! Oh! CyrIS! I think I am going to die."

CHAPTER 20 – RELIGIOUS FANATICISM

September 9th, 1993
Christine Basurto, age 25
Ester Suni Nate, age 41

What a courteous young man! You don't see much of that these days. Christine muses. The boy possibly 12 to 13 years of age is standing a step below her, holding the door as she departs the Burger King near Belleview and Kipling, in Denver.

The young man was smiling when he opened the door, and so was Christine. But when Christine patted his head as she passed, something happened. She was not sure what it was, but it was not good. Now as she passes the young man after her hand left his head, she turns slowly to look at his face.

He is not smiling. He looks insulted, and glares at her with such a look of malice that it scares Christine. Such a look of intent and purpose she had never seen. Then she remembers how it felt when she first touched weird John so many years ago.

The young man turns to enter the restaurant, and the moment passes, but as Christine drives away, she cannot shake the strange feeling that has come over her, and yet, as strange as it seems, it is also so familiar. Christine shakes her head.

I've gotta get these cobwebs out of my head. I have a lot to do this afternoon. I must get ready for my presentation. I just don't have time for this.

Denver University was hosting a seminar on 'religion and religious fanaticism' and there would be several noted authorities in this field speaking at the seminar. Christine had become somewhat of an authority on psychopaths and was sometimes asked to give her opinions on how psychopaths related to other psychological ailments. Today she will be giving a presentation on the psychopathic tendencies of 'Religious Fanatics.'

Later that evening, Christine walks up to the podium. She pushes the incident at the Burger King to the back of her mind and begins:

"'Religious fanaticism' has been recognized by many psychiatrist and psychoanalyst, such as, C. G. Jung the Swiss psychoanalyst who founded analytical psychology. In 1966, he referred to it as 'positive inflation'. Also, Gary Rosenthal utilized the phrase 'inflated by the *spirit*', in 1987."

"There are people in this world that believe, or at least tell others, that they have some kind of special *connection* to God. Some of these people believe that they are uniquely privileged to certain sacred truths, and because they are *connected* to God, in this special way, are obligated to take action with regard to these truths, no matter how many people are hurt or destroyed. They have even been known to demonize and persecute those who oppose their particular views."

"These people have often been labeled as *'Religious Fanatics'*, and they do not appear as deranged or insane as one might think a fanatic might be. In fact, often, they are just the opposite, they come across as having the highest ideals and the best intent for all, and they are thoughtful, calm and intelligent."

"However, along with this thoughtfulness and intelligence, they can have absolute and unwavering confidence that their way is the only way. This can manifest itself in a disorder which can freely allow them to cause enormous destruction to individual lives, and the lives of groups of people, all for what they deem to be the greater good. This personality imbalance can affect anyone, from an individual on the street, to leaders of religious groups, terrorist, even to powerful leaders of nations. These individuals may also show psychopathic tendencies as well." Christine, now trying to read the reaction of her audience, continues:

"It is important to note that for these people this special relationship they feel with God is a 'Transpersonal Experience' and these experiences cannot be minimized or marginalized. To have an experience that transcends the day to day human experience, are often very important parts of most people's lives. That is, one should not diminish the importance to the individual of the profoundness of any such spiritual experience. These transpersonal experiences can have a dramatic positive effect on a person's life, and as such should *not* be thought of as unhealthy. "

"So Religious Fanaticism can begin from a healthy enough origin. For example: At the onset, it is not unhealthy for one to feel a *connection* to something greater than oneself, transcendence to a higher state of being, a sense of *connection* with the universe, or a union at a *spiritual* level. Studies have shown that these types of experiences are much more common to most people than some experts think."

"However, some people find that this transpersonal experience, or state, is a much more gratifying state of existence, than that of their day to day existence, and as such begin to identify with this state as who they truly are. This can lead one to believe, that this higher state of being is ideal and as such, it is important to them to spend as much time as possible in this higher state. It becomes an essential part of their personality and thus becomes the source of the disorder. "

"'*Religious Fanaticism*' is an extreme condition of this disorder. When people with this extreme disorder come together with followers that support their position, they make a commitment to what they believe is a divine state of being, trumping all other day to day human beliefs. These people are capable of extremely destructive behavior."

"As they become one with their higher state, their ego grows with the growing knowledge of their special position in the universe, and thus, leaves themselves no option but to defend their beliefs at all cost."

"Here I would like to make a *connection* between the symptoms of the religious fanatic and those of the psychopath. The religious fanatic can exhibit the psychopathic traits 'Lack of empathy' and 'Lack of Remorse', especially for those who do not agree with their beliefs. But they can also show a lack of empathy and remorse for those who do believe, but do not believe in totality as expected by the fanatic. Certainly, the religious fanatic can exhibit traits of 'Grandiosity' and 'Superficiality' in that they believe in the grandness of their *spiritual* state of being, and as such believe they are better than others, and thus do not need to follow the same rules."

"They can also exhibit other traits of a psychopath such as *'Anti-Social behavior'*, *'Irresponsibility'*, *'Compulsive lying'*, and certainly *'Manipulation'*. All of these psychopathic traits are acceptable to the religious fanatic because anything they do is all for the *'greater good'*."

Christine pauses for a moment, takes a sip of water from the glass sitting on the podium, and once again, observing how intently the audience is listening, continues:

"There are powerful energies associated with religious fanaticism, these energies feed the ego and raise this type of fanatic to levels they believe are above everyday human morality, to rise above any form of normal human existence, and at this level they attain a confidence, that may ever raise them in their minds, to the level of prophet or messiah."

"The word 'Fanatic' comes from the Latin word 'Fanum'; Meaning 'Temple'. A 'Temple' is defined as a place of worship; however, there is no distinction in what is to be worshiped, which can range from deity to devil. With regard to religious fanaticism, people whose ego has risen to this lofty state can also attain very high levels of charisma, and that charisma can attract and seduce other individuals, groups of people, and even entire countries, no matter if the intent is in the worship of good or evil."

"Now let's look at why someone would venture into this lofty state of mind and not want to come back. There are three states of consciousness. There is the 'lower' level of consciousness. This level is known as the primeval level of consciousness and is associated with the levels of consciousness that suppress childhood emotions such as shame, abandonment, anxiety, and fragmentation. This lower level of consciousness is important to human existence because it allows for *emotions* such as empathy and the ability to be moved by love or pain."

"The higher level of consciousness, as previously discussed, is the lofty *spiritual* levels of consciousness."

"I believe it is clear that humans should reside in the *"middle"* level of consciousness, a synthesis of the higher and lower states of the unconscious. In this state, we can become more aware of our personal perfection and imperfection, more able to be affected and respond to the love and pain of others and draw on the highs and lows of human existence."

As Christine neared the end of her presentation, she slows her tempo and emphasizes specific sections of her conclusions.

"However, some people who believe they have experienced the highest levels of consciousness, in the realms of extreme spirituality, have, for their own subconscious self-preservation, decided to completely avoid the depths of the lower consciousness. They have reached an absolute certainty about their life's calling, and they feel delivered from the shame and anxieties associated with the lower levels of consciousness, their soul free to soar."

"That freedom, that feeling of *disconnectedness* from other human beings, that inflated ego, allows them the freedom to ignore any forms of normal human morality. All of these traits are also very common in the basic nature of the psychopath, and therefore, in a lot of ways, they are one and the same."

Christine paused for a few seconds and then said "I hope this will stimulate further discussion. Thank you. Are there any questions?"

Christine answered a few questions and then left the podium.

After listening to several other speakers Christine went to the reception area and got herself a drink. She cannot get the boy at the Burger King out of her mind and hopes that a drink will help.

Usually, after one of these presentations, she is approached by several men asking questions. Often, she can tell they are more interested in looking at her breast and making some kind of pass, than they were in knowing more about her philosophies. But, this evening there is not the usual flock of men, instead, she is approached by a very nice-looking middle-aged woman dressed, in what Christine would describe as, Southwest Native American attire. She also had the features of a Native American, though her complexion and features were somewhat darker and more exotic looking.

"Hello, I'm Ester Suni Nati" She goes on to say that she has a Ph.D. in Extra Sensory Perception, Shamanism, and Psychic Phenomenon, and that she has been teaching a class called *"Psychology, Parapsychology, and Science in today's society,"* at Berkley.

"I must say, you are a very beautiful woman," Ester continues, "And the whitest person I have ever seen, with your blonde hair, light blue eyes, and pale white face." They stare at each other for a moment, and Christine does not respond, a bit shocked by the awkward compliment.

Is she calling me a 'Pale Face'? Christine suppresses a smile.

Then Ester begins again, "Not that any of that *matters,* but you're not what I expected when I read your resume in the brochure for this conference. That being said, I am a trained Shaman and I am fascinated by your references to the '*higher, lower*, and *middle* consciousness.' It is a Shaman's belief that to truly understand life one must take journeys, and these journeys must move you through the lower world to the higher world. These are *spiritual* worlds, and it is also shamanistic belief that one must also spend time in the *middle* world. Here is where the journey takes you closest to the reality of your everyday life and takes advantage of what you have learned in both the lower and upper worlds, so that you can live a life in harmony with the universe. This all seems to parallel very closely to the states of the subconscious that you were referring to in your speech."

Christine is trying to decide what to make of what she is hearing. Over the years she had been asked a lot of strange questions and heard a lot of 'Off the wall' theories. But this is fascinating, and she waits for Ester to continue.

Ester then begins to explain how she had come to be an expert on the Reverend Jim Jones and David Koresh, and that she felt that Christine's descriptions of a 'Religious Fanatic' were extremely accurate as they related to Jim Jones and to a lesser extent David Koresh.

Christine forced herself to thank Ester for the compliment and then said "Suni Nati that is an interesting name. May I ask its origin?"

Ester explained how her father was a Zuni Shaman, and how he had given her, and her brother and sisters the sir name 'Suni Nati". She also explained, that in Zuni, it meant '*Middle*'.

"Oh, how interesting" Christine exclaimed. "My last name is Basurto. It's of Spanish origin and it means 'In the *middle* of the forest.' I guess we are related."

Ester smiled and said "Yes. Well, we are all related, and *connected*, I might add." Christine smiles and nods in agreement, as Ester continues.

"In your speech you seem to indicate that these people feel a strong *connection* with a high power. Do you feel that there exists a medium for these *connections* to higher powers and even a *connection* between people in general?"

Christine looks pensive as she responds. "Carl Jung and other leading psychologist have suggested that there is a subconscious *connection* between all people, but do not describe the medium for this connection. Also, I have done a considerable amount of study in the area of self-hypnosis and dream state analysis, which has a lot of correlation to what you are describing as shamanistic Journey practices, I find it all very fascinating."

Christine found that she and Ester had a lot of common ground in their two areas of expertise, and they continued talking for several hours, and at the end of the evening, Christine felt that they had developed, what she hoped would be a lasting friendship.

Ester said, "I would love for you to meet my friend CyrIS, I think the three of us could have some very interesting conversations."

Christine says. "I think I would like that." and after exchanging some contact information, Christine said good-bye to Ester and they went their separate ways.

CHAPTER 21 – THE TURNER DIARIES

April 19th, 1995
Rufus Middleman, age 24

It's 3:00 AM and Rufus is staring down at a toilet bowl filled with vomit. He's sick, very sick, but this is not the flu, nor food poisoning, and he immediately recognize the symptoms. It's the same symptoms he experienced when he took his little mind trip with Randy Weaver back at Ruby Ridge, and even though he's sick, he is still looking forward to what might happen.

Rufus just recently completed his master's degree in Physics and is now pursuing his Ph.D. in Mathematics and Theoretical Physics at the Colorado School of Mines. He is no longer playing football. He is no longer eligible after completing his undergraduate degree.

No more karate either. As a student of karate, he had followed the careers of a couple of the masters. One of those masters was Gerard Gordeau, a savant, karate, and mixed martial artist that was the 1991 'World Savant Champion' and holder of the Dutch 'Karate Champion' title for 8 consecutive years and Rufus was extremely excited when he learned that Gordeau was coming to Denver to compete in the first-ever 'Unlimited Fighting Championship'.

The UFC was a new form of fighting at that time. A no holds barred competition, in which there were no judges, no time limits, and no rules, other than no biting or eye gouging. The contestants would just fight until one of the opponents submits or can no longer continue.

Rufus loved this concept of fighting and he had been really excited when he was able to obtain tickets to this first-ever event at the McNichol's arena in Denver, which was held on November 12th, 1993.

As Rufus recalled; The first fight that night, which had been the first ever UFC fight, pitted Rufus' hero, Gordeau, against a sumo wrestler and mixed martial artist, a Samoan from Honolulu, named Teila Tuli.

The fight lasted about 26 seconds and was over when Gordeau kicked out three of Tuli's teeth, two of them ending up lodged in Gordeau's foot.

The doctors decided it would be safer for Gordeau to leave the teeth in his foot rather than cut his foot open. So Gordeau fought the next fight with the teeth still lodged in his foot.

Gordeau also won his next fight, which allowed him to compete for the championship, against a Brazilian Jiu-jitsu professional and mixed martial artist named Royce Gracie.

Gracie was a lot smaller than Gordeau but early in the fight Gracie attacked Gordeau's legs and took Gordeau to the mat. In just one minute and forty-four seconds Gracie had Rufus' hero in a 'Rear Naked Choke' hold. Gracie had defeated Gordeau and won the first ever 'Unlimited Fighting Championship'.

Rufus had been disappointed that his hero did not win the championship but was totally hyped about this new open form of fighting. It reminded him so much of his street fighting days, back in New York. He could not wait to get involved, and immediately started training as a 'Mixed Martial Arts'-MMA fighter.

Unfortunately, his street fighting days and his training in karate had not totally prepared him. After about six months of training, Rufus had his first official 'Mixed Martial Arts' fight. That was just about a year ago now, but Rufus could remember it vividly.

The men that Rufus would compete against, especially the ones who were trained in the Brazilian form of MMA, were experts. They specialized at getting an opponent to the mat and then getting them into a variety of holds that either broke an arm or a leg or just choked them into submission.

Within one minute of Rufus' very first official fight, his opponent had put him into a hold known as an '*Arm Bar*'. At the time Rufus thought that he had been in much tougher situations back in the streets of New York, and refused to submit until his elbow was dislocated, and the referee determined he could no longer fight, and the match was stopped.

Rufus' dislocated elbow became a chronic problem and it put an end to his 'Mixed Martial Arts' fighting, including his karate matches. This was extremely frustrating for Rufus. How could he release his frustrations if he couldn't fight? That's when he started seriously thinking about joining the Army.

"Maybe, if I could get over to Kuwait or Iraq and kill a bunch of those 'Ragheads' I could feel better."

But he would have to think about that later. Right now, he is trying to push nausea aside and concentrate on what might happen if this was the beginning of another mind trip. Rufus is a little frightened by the possibilities, but at the same time he is very excited. On his previous trip, he had learned a lot about Randy Weaver.

Randy Weaver was a bigot no doubt, a man of low intelligence, but a human being that had his own ways of dealing with the voids in his life. A person with strong moral and family values, and who was willing to die for those beliefs and values. A man that truly believed that he was destined for Armageddon, which ultimately showed up, right in his own backyard.

"Be careful what you wish for". Rufus thought. "And be careful what you believe in."

"It seems like 'Life' can sometimes be very cruel that way, giving you what you ask for in a 'Well you asked for it' kind of way, that often seems unfair. My dislocated elbow is proof of that."

Randy Weaver may have been a simple, poorly educated man, but none the less, Rufus had learned a lot from him. Besides the 'Be careful what you ask for.' lesson, he learned; that how a man is labeled, does not always truly represent the man. He also learned; that the power of *absolute belief* can drive a person to endure unimaginable pain and suffering.

These lessons seemed to help Rufus fill in some of the voids he felt in his own life, and for that reason, he felt somehow connected to Randy Weaver. In fact, there seemed to be some sort of intermingling of his own *logic* and *emotions* with that of Randy and his family, and Rufus could now see what Randy and his family derived from the Bible, and how it affected them.

Rufus lies down on his bed, closes his eyes and waits, hoping that he will be allowed to take a similar journey of learning.

Then, confused once again, Rufus is staring down at a toilet bowl, not one full of vomit, but full of piss. He sees the stream of urine flowing into the very dingy toilet below him. Realizing that it is not his own penis in his hand, but that of a stranger, he is now convinced that it is happening again; that once again he is inside the mind and body of another man.

Rufus' host finishes his business in the bathroom stall. The man then goes to the sink and looks in the mirror. Rufus is immediately pissed off.

"It's that scrawny little military looking bastard from the chili restaurant." Rufus thinks. "Why him? What is this guy up too? And most importantly what can I possibly learn from this fucking runt?"

The man leaves the restroom, and Rufus finds himself in the middle of a large truck stop service station. It is nighttime and the yellowish lights of the parking area, reveal rows and rows of semi-trucks and trailers.

Rufus' host begins walking towards a yellow Ryder rental truck, about 20 feet in length. As he walks along, the man looks down at his wristwatch. The digital watch face shows 3:20. Rufus determines it must be 3:20 AM, because of the darkness and lack of activity in the parking area.

As they approach the Ryder truck, Rufus observes a man standing next to it. The man is stout looking, about 5 foot 8 or so, with dark wavy hair, dark complexion, a dark mustache and a very thick neck. He is wearing a camouflage jacket and combat boots, and as he begins to speak Rufus detects a very heavy German accent.

"McVeigh, did you pay for the gas yet?" Rufus' host who is obviously McVeigh, responds that he paid for the gas. The German points towards two other vehicles that were gassing up, a white four-door sedan and an old pickup truck. The German says: "Tim, we're ready. Let's hit the road."

In no time, Rufus is looking out the front windshield of the Ryder truck as it is traveling down the highway. As they had pulled out of the service station, Rufus had seen a highway sign, 'Highway 77'. It seems to Rufus that they are heading south, and just as in Rufus' previous journey, he can now hear the thoughts of his host.

This two-lane road is better than interstate 35. It's slower, but less chance of getting stopped, and if we ever do get stopped, we will certainly have a lot of explaining to do with this load.

I am sure I can depend on the German sitting next to me, he says he's the Grandson of a German Nazi, and I believe him. I have certainly depended on him over the last year, helping me to get ready for today. In any case, I consider him and those guys in the other two vehicles to be my 'Brothers in Arms'. No matter what happens, if I get caught, I will never give up the identity of these comrades.

It's only 270 miles from where we started at the Dreamland Motel in Junction City, to Oklahoma City, but I would guess we have at least three more hours of driving left.

As he drives down the road, McVeigh is reviewing his justification for his actions.

Hinckley, that one stupid lovesick kid's attempt to kill the president of the United States, ultimately resulted in the passing of that fucked up 'bill', which required people to get registered before they can purchase firearms. The 'Brady Bill' is a clear violation of the second amendment of the Constitution, and that bill never would have passed if that stupid little bastard had not shot Jim

Brady during his attempt to kill Reagan. And for what? All for a piece of ass.

It's just another example of the government interfering in the rights of white Americans.

"Just what I thought. He's just another 'White Supremacist' bastard" Rufus mused as he listened to McVeigh's thoughts ramble on.

What about poor old Randy Weaver, he was just trying to eke out a living with his family on that rocky ridge, and just because he knew, just like I do, that 'Whites' were naturally superior to all other races, the government trumped up some bullshit gun charges against him and used it as an excuse to exert their muscle and kill Randy's wife and son. The members of the Weaver family that died that day, are true martyrs in the fight to preserve this country's right to bear arms.

Rufus is once again getting angry; "This guy is nothing like Randy Weaver. Randy was not a White Supremacist like this guy. Randy was only trying to follow his beliefs in the Old Testaments and along with his wife, raise his family according to those beliefs. This idiot is nothing like Randy Weaver. But it sounds like he is using Randy as an excuse for whatever 'Fucked up scheme' he has planned."

The most important reason, for today's action against the government, is for what the government did exactly two years ago today in Waco, Texas. The storming of the Branch Davidian compound was a clear violation of the rights of Americans. The government said that those people had illegal firearms too and then used that as an excuse to execute men, women, and children, just like they did at Ruby Ridge.

Don't these idiots read the Constitution; don't they know that the 2ⁿᵈ amendment allows all Americans the right to bear arms. The government is always sticking its nose in where it shouldn't. Well, today I am going to make the government pay for all those injustices. And it will be the beginning of a Revolution that will take back this country, from all of those fucking 'Jews and Niggers' that act like they own it. This will bring a new government into existence, and that new government will be led by the White Supremacist movement. And I will be considered a hero in that movement. I just can't wait to get there.

Rufus thinks "I'm not sure what this guy is planning to do, but it can't be good. I just hope I can have some influence to stop this maniac from going through with whatever it is. Boy! This guy is really scary, in fact, this whole group of bozos is scary."

I'm getting myself all worked up here. I need to settle down, I have a long way to go.

McVeigh turned and looked at the German, who is staring at the road ahead, and says; "Hey did you hear the one about the Jew who walked into a German police station and told the clerk at the desk that his father is missing?"

The German sitting next to McVeigh just stared out the front window, and McVeigh went on.

"The German clerk asked what his father looked like. The Jew said: 'Well he is an old Jewish man with a brown coat, blue vest, a bow tie, a brown hat and a beard.'"

"The clerk said 'Yea he came in here yesterday. I asked him what his name was, and he started to say he lived at 302. I said 'No, what is your name'. He said, 'I live at 302'. I said 'no, no, no what is your name?' The old man said, 'You keep interrupting me and I am losing my concentration.' So, we put him in a Concentration Camp."

The German turned to Tim and smiles and said with his deep German accent "Yea, I get it".

So, Tim continues: "How about this one? A German, walks into a bar and asks the bartender 'how many Jews does it take to turn on a light bulb?' The bartender says, 'I don't know how many Jews does it take to turn on a light bulb?' and the German says, 'You can turn on a light bulb for a whole day if you burn about a hundred of them." The German's face lit up now, he had a huge grin and he laughed out loud. Rufus' hatred for these guys is growing more and more by the second. Rufus now wishes he had wasted McVeigh back in that bar in Colorado. "I wish I had my hands around his neck, right now."

"That's a good one, tell me some more," Said the German.

Tim said "Okay, how about this one. Why won't the Germans start World War 3?" The German is grinning at Tim, "Why not?" And Tim replies, "Because they know just like in World Wars 1 and 2, they'll get their asses kicked again by the Americans."

The German's face went from a grin to a *dark* foreboding shadow. He looked as if he could kill Tim, and he probably could. Rufus is rooting for the German: "Go ahead kill the little bastard, you can do it."

The German glares at Tim and says: "That's not funny."

McVeigh replies in his best German accent "That's not funny" and then laughs out loud.

The German, now speaking in a low growling voice. "You know Tim if we weren't running late, I would stop this truck and I'd kick your fucking skinny little American ass."

Rufus thought: "Come on let's take him out, I'll help."

Tim stopped laughing and responds, "Well you better bring more to the party than just that fucking thick neck of yours, because I won't go down easy."

The German did not respond, he glared at Tim for a second or two and then turned and glared at the highway. Tim concentrated on the highway as well and there was no more talking.

That fucker is a good friend, but I just can't resist giving him a shot once in a while.

Rufus can feel that McVeigh is getting all hyped up, and then he understood why.

That crystal meth I took this morning is keeping me awake like I hoped it would, but now I'm hyped.

Tim stares into the *darkness* and watched the dashed white lines of the median stripe fire from the darkness in front of him like tracer shells, moving slowly towards him from the distance at first, then accelerating as they approach the front of the truck and then disappear into its left front fender.

Boy! April 19th, this is a perfect day to do this. Not only are we doing this in remembrance of the events at Ruby Ridge but today is the anniversary of the siege at Waco, and not only that, but today is 'Patriot's day', the anniversary of the 'shot heard round the world', and I'm sure that the shot we are taking today will also be heard around the world.

Rufus can feel McVeigh smiling and thought "You bastard", as McVeigh's thoughts continues.

I remember Wayne Snell, a member of the Covenant, and a true leader in the white supremacist movement. He had planned to blow up the federal buildings in Oklahoma City using guided missiles, but his plan was abandoned when the missile, his team was going to use, blew up in the hands of his missile expert.

Today, April 19th, Wayne is scheduled to be executed in Arkansas for the killing of an Arkansas state trooper. I didn't know Wayne, but I hope he got the message I sent him; 'Armageddon is coming on the day of your death'. After today both of us will be considered heroes, and maybe martyrs.

For me and my team, this is a military mission and I know that in any combat mission, not all of the fighters return from the fight. But I, and I am sure the rest of this team, are ready to die for this cause. I have always known that someday I would die for a righteous cause.

'Shit!' This- could even be- the last day of my life.

'My life', I certainly went through a lot of shit in 'My life'.

Those bastards in grade school, back in New York thought they were so though, picking on me when I was so much smaller. I used to daydream about shooting those fuckers in the head or blowing them up, and then listen to them screaming in pain as they realized that I had made them pay.

Some people didn't think I was very smart, but I did hack into that government computer when I was still in high school, and even though I didn't get great grades, I was named Starpoint Central High School's most promising computer programmer.

My grandfather gave me a more important education. He's the one who taught me about guns, and with his help and studying on my own, I now really know a lot about guns. I also studied gun rights, gun laws and specifically the second amendment. I even thought that at one time I would open my own gun shop.

College sucked, all those smart asses, it just wasn't right for me, but at least I tried it for a while, but I spent most of my time reading Soldier of Fortune magazine. And in 1987 I joined the Army, best decision I ever made. I graduated from the U.S. Army Combat Engineering School in Fort Riley, KS. In 88', and in May of 91' Bush started the war to expel Iraq from Kuwait.

I remember that morning like it was yesterday, they told us they expected a 70% casualty rate. They told us that we would encounter mines, artillery, and antitank fire and that we should expect a deluge of ground forces with automatic weapons and possibly nerve gas.

Boy! That feeling is incredible, sitting in the gunner's seat of that Bradley Fighting Vehicle, ready to take out any enemy that fired on the task force. It was exciting, knowing that at any moment I could be hit by a bullet or a shell from a tank. One thing I knew for sure was that if I saw an Iraqi soldier, I wasn't going to wait for them to fire before I took 'em out.

I loved watching those M1 Abrams tanks, with their giant blades on the front, plowing up the desert, unearthing those Iraqis hiding in the sand, and then burying them alive. They were given sixty seconds to surrender or they would be wiped out, I wouldn't have given them any warning. But it didn't matter, the field was a massacre. They would come out of those holes with their hands up, and I would mow 'em down.

Most of the Iraqis were ready to give up from the very start, but the bastards were too afraid, or too stupid to come out, and as result, they were obliterated by the guns from the Bradley's or they were buried in shallow graves by the tanks. It went on for four days, and my slogan was 'If it's in front of us it dies.'

On the second day of the battle, I saw these Iraqis in a machine gun nest over a thousand yards ahead. I took out two of those bastards with one shot. I hit that first guy in the chest and obliterated his upper body and head, and with my scope. I could *see the bullet passing through the first man, leaving a vapor trail of blood, showing the path the bullet took on its way to the obliteration of the second man behind him.*

That shot made me a legend in the 16th Infantry and I received an Army Commendation Medal.

I was one brutal bastard back then. 'Desert Storm', they called it, and I received five medals, including a Bronze Star.

Rufus listened as McVeigh bragged about his accomplishments and seemed to be riding high on these drugged supported *emotions.* But then, all of a sudden, he changed, and his mood slumped.

But now I realize that the Iraqis were not evil but were just men following the lead of an evil government.

And now I realize that my own fucking government had manipulated me emotionally into fighting and killing that hapless army, they hyped us all up to kill everyone.

Logically the true enemy of America is an international cabal of money-grubbing liberals, multiculturalists and Jews bent on stripping Americans of their rights, including the right to bear arms. I remember reading the 'Turner Diaries' when I first joined the service and the more time I spent working for the government, the more I understood what that book was talking about.

The book was written by Luther Pierce, former leader of the white nationalist group the National Alliance, and it was about a revolution in the United States that eventually leads to the overthrow of the government, a nuclear war, and extermination of all 'impure' groups of people including Jews, gays, and all non-whites. The story started with the United States government confiscating all civilian firearms, this drives the organization that Turner belongs to underground, and they begin a campaign of terrorism, assassination, and sabotage against the Jewish controlled establishment. It all begins with acts such as, the revolutionist driving a truck full of ammonia nitrate-laced with fuel oil, into the basement of the FBI Headquarters and blowing it up. It continues with many other low-level acts against the United States government, all leading up to, taking over the state of

California and eventually to taking control of the entire planet. This resulted in extermination of all the Jews, blacks, Asians and liberal whites in the world who did not agree with their philosophies.

This book opened my eyes, I can now see that the government is constantly trying to exert total control over its citizens. But today I will fulfill a destiny, my destiny, as foretold by the Turner Diaries.

Rufus remembered how some of the white supremacist that Randy Weaver had associated with referred to the "Turner Diaries" as some kind of guide and now he can see how this book is having a huge influence on Tim as well. Rufus can also see how Tim is using the "Brady Bill" and what had happened at Ruby Ridge and Waco as some kind of *logical* justification for his actions. I's clear that McVeigh believed that this is all in alignment with the events in this book. The references to 'a truck full of ammonia nitrate-laced with fuel oil' makes Rufus wonder what is in the back of this truck McVeigh is driving, and where he is going, as he listens to McVeigh's continued ramblings.

The military brainwashed me, and I had to get out of there. I left the Army, but the Army gave me several things of importance. That's where I learned to become an expert marksman and learned some things about the use of explosives. But the most important acquisition from the army was my friendship with Terry Nichols.

Now Terry is a true explosives expert, but more importantly, he agrees with my philosophies on the problems in America and its failing government, and he docs whatever I tell him to do, like a good little soldier.

Rufus wonders if this 'Nichols' is one of the guys in the other vehicles, as McVeigh moves on to other thoughts.

I wish I could have afforded to keep up my memberships in the Ku Klux Klan and the National Rifle Association, those are two great American organizations. Fucking blacks in this country have no clue about what is going on in the government and around the world, and it's the Jews that are in control and their control in the US government needs to be taken care of.

When the US Marshals stormed Randy Weaver's cabin on Ruby Ridge, the mainstream media hardly covered the debacle, but the government ended up being humiliated by the event, and more importantly, it had a powerful impact on the countries militia movements, and it was widely publicized in the top Neo-Nazis and other anti-government publications.

I remember the words of Louis Beam in the speech he made at Estes Park Colorado, back in '92. Speaking of the despicable acts of the government at Ruby Ridge, Louis said 'Over the next ten years you will come to hate government more than anything else in your life.' And 'If you think that this generation of men will maintain its present freedoms without also having to fertilize the tree of liberty with the blood of both patriot and tyrant, then you are mistaken.'

I was inspired by that speech, and I tried to read everything he wrote. I especially liked the concept of a 'leaderless resistance'. He said, 'Let the coming night be filled with a thousand points of resistance.'

I am one of those points of resistance.

Rufus thought back to his encounter with McVeigh in October of 1992 and realized that the reason McVeigh had been in Colorado is to see this bigot Louis Beam speak in Estes Park.

I remember meeting Beam when I went to Waco to support the Branch Davidians. They had all of the roads blocked off so I couldn't get in, but that was a blessing in disguise for me, because that is where I met Louis. Louis was there to protest the government's obvious efforts to limit the Davidians constitutional right to bear arms. I told Beam, I was a soldier in the "leaderless resistance", and he told me he was proud of me.

But there's another reason I am headed down this highway this morning. On September 13, 1994, that fucker, Bill Clinton, approved a ten-year assault weapons ban. I knew this was a sign for me, because of how remarkably similar this was to the repressive gun law that set off the white supremacist resistance movement in the Turner Diaries.

I also knew that what I wanted to do would take some cash. The Federal Reserve, and all banks are just a bunch of criminals. 'Cash' as we know it, is counterfeit, and a dollar is just a worthless piece of paper, what's the harm in getting even…? It is a sort of Robin Hood thing and our government is the evil king. So, we extracted some of their ill-gotten gains. If you want true freedom, sometimes, you just have to take it, and I believe that the freedoms in this country, are those guaranteed by the jury box, the ballot box, and by the cartridge box.

After Waco, I decided to pursue my freedoms, associated with the third of these three and ordered a book called 'Homemade C-4', published by Paladin Press in Boulder Colorado. Homemade C-4 is Para-military slang for ammonium nitrate bombs. These bombs can provide a huge explosion and the ingredients are widely available.

It is becoming obvious to Rufus that Tim is intending to blow up some sort of Federal Building, and the back of this truck is filled with explosives.

Rufus is desperately struggling with how best to stop him. Maybe if he can somehow wake up and get out of this psychopath's mind, he can alert the authorities. But no matter what he did he could not get out, and is forced to continue down the road with this band of bigots and soon to be murderers. , "I need an assistant, someone to help me get out of this state of possession." Rufus thinks as McVeigh's thoughts continue.

Those robberies were necessary because I needed the cash to buy the ton of ammonium nitrate and nitro methane that's in the twelve, fifty-gallon drums in the back of this truck.

I could not have put this all together without Terry's help, but he's weak, and I was not sure I could count on him, or any of these guys, for that matter. That's why I had Terry drive me to Oklahoma City, so I could leave my Yellow Mercury Marquis just a short distance from the Federal Center, as a backup. I removed the license plate and put a note on the windshield, 'Not abandoned. Please do not tow, will move by April 25, and (Needs battery & cable.)' Pretty smart!

Rufus is now getting the impression that Terry is not with this band of executioners.

The convoy arrives in Oklahoma City just after 7:30 AM.

Rufus listens as Tim thinks about how he visited the city the previous year and thought he would be able to drive directly to the Federal Building in the center of the city. He thought he could drive to the parking lot in the basement, park the truck there, and set off the fuse and leave. The bomb, he thought, placed in the basement of the building, is large enough to take down the whole building and a large part of the surrounding complex.

But now, as they arrived in the city, Rufus can sense Tim's confusion. It seemed that the one-way streets in the city were making Tim unsure of his direction. Rufus watches as Tim stopped on several occasions to ask directions to the Murrah Building. Rufus hoped Tim will drive down a one-way street, the wrong way, and get stopped by the cops, but no such luck.

After a while, the Ryder Truck arrives at the Federal Center, and as they approach the entrance to the underground parking lot of the Murrah Building, Rufus senses more confusion.

"Oh! Shit!" Tim exclaimed.

"What the fuck" shouted the German! "You're such an idiot"

Tim gets out of the truck.

Rufus can see that the truck had a profile much too high to make it through the opening of the garage. Rufus hopes brightened; "Maybe this will make them put this off to another day, and then I can warn the authorities."

Tim gets back in the truck and drives around the city trying to find a place of higher ground where he can look over the situation and discuss with his team their next move.

The German is extremely upset. "How can you make such a stupid fucking mistake? You are a complete idiot. What are we going to do now? I think we should get out of here and regroup."

Rufus' hopes rose again, and he is yelling at Tim to abandon the project as the German has suggested.

Tim explained, "Look, when we added the additional explosives, I had to rent a larger truck and forgot about the height issue."

Tim, with a determined look, went on "I feel that I am on a stage and the audience demands a climax, and I must see this to its end. I am positive it is the right thing to do."

There are forces at work here that are driving me and must do this today.

Rufus is stunned "What is McVeigh saying? Am I his audience? Is he doing this because I am watching? Or is it possible that other people or other forces are observing this as well, giving him direction and encouragement, somehow expecting this, either consciously or unconsciously, to happen, and pushing him forward? Convincing him that he is the hero."

They park the Ryder truck a couple of blocks from the Murrah building. The German and Tim then walk to the yellow Mercury.

Now with the German driving the Mercury, they enter the basement garage of the Murrah building and assess their predicament. The German suggests that they take some of the explosives and primer cord and wrap it around the pillars in the basement. He says, "By taking out the pillars we will take down the whole building." Tim rejects this idea saying, "It's too risky trying to sneak that amount of explosive into the building and ultimately it might not work." But mostly Tim does not like it because the anger inside of him wanted the big explosion, he wanted to blow everything up.

The German is getting more and more, agitated. "If we can't get the explosives into the basement of the building, we will not be achieving our goal, and we will be blowing up a lot of innocent people instead of the judges and other government personnel that are in the back of the building. I really think we should leave the city and regroup."

But Tim insists "No! No! we must do this now. Too much time and effort has gone into getting us this far, and today is *April 19th*. It's the day this is supposed to happen."

The German reluctantly agrees to finish the job, but his last words to Tim were. "You fucked this up, not me. You're on your own now. I think it will be better if we part ways. You go your way and the rest of us will head back. I don't know what the repercussions of this will be, but it will not be good. Goodbye, Tim."

After all the arguing, accusing, cussing and blaming, they finally agreed on a plan. They backed the truck into the handicap parking spot that is right up against the building. Rufus, who is not scared easily, is now terrified, and so angry he could spit nails. As they backed the truck up, he felt Tim grab some earplugs and stuff them in his ears; the sounds of the city fading away.

Continuing to back up, Rufus saw the German light the fuse on his side of the truck and jump out. He feels Tim reach down, pull up the fuse on his side and light it. As the truck came to a stop, Tim jumped from the truck and began walking quickly towards a YMCA building nearby. He and the German ducked in behind the building.

Tim is looking at his wristwatch, and at 9:02 AM the ammonium nitrate barrels ignite.

Rufus knew from Tim's thoughts that the bomb must weigh about five thousand pounds. When it went off it literally stunned Rufus, the flimsy ear plugs provided no protection for Tim's ears, and Rufus can feel the force of the explosion compress every part of Tim's body as hurricane force winds, dust and debris pelt him. It had started with just the wind but then the debris increased exponentially in size, all of it flying through the air all around and past them. It became so ferocious it knocked Tim backwards, and the concussion was incredible. Rufus can feel that it hurt Tim's body and head as he lurched backward several feet from the force, and immediately Tim's head begins to throb.

There were two parts to the explosion. When the explosion first went off Rufus could feel the air moving past Tim's body away from the Murrah Building, Tim's pant legs flapped furiously, the air moved him backwards, and his baseball hat went flying. A second later the air changed direction and with a force even more violent than the initial blast of air, the air began to rush back towards the Murrah building sucking Tim with it taking him to the ground, and as the air moved in the other direction Rufus can hear a new round of destruction.

Rufus concluded that the initial blast had expanded outward forming a positive-pressure wave that had created a large vacuum at its core. As the initial pressure wave collapsed into the negative pressure hole it left behind, a second even more powerful implosion occurred. This second event brought all the air; gasses, concrete, steel and other debris back down to earth into the source of the explosion with such force that it surely caused additional damage to the Murrah Building, to the buildings in the surrounding area, and of course to all the occupants of those buildings. Now Rufus watches as the skies grew *dark* from the clouds of dust.

Rufus feels his *emotions* running wild as those *emotions* intermingle with those of Tim McVeigh. Tim casually stands up, retrieves his baseball cap and steps out from behind the YMCA building. As the dust cleared saw what looked like a war zone. From his new position, Tim and Rufus had a clear view of the Murrah Building. The area looked like it had been hit by an atomic bomb, and the whole area is smoldering. There were some fires, and the smell of ammonium nitrate is overwhelming. The whole area is littered with parts of buildings and cars. Cars and trucks were thrown, as giant projectiles, everywhere. The Murrah Building, still covered in swirling dust and debris, appeared to be still standing. The explosion ripped open the front of the building taking three floors of the building above the Ryder truck with it, and surely also lifting the building's occupants up high into the air. But the Murrah is not the only building affected, it appeared that every building in the area of the explosion was damaged to different degrees. Some had broken windows, many had large chunks of concrete missing and many of the buildings were impaled with parts of trucks and cars. The air is still full of smoke and dust, and though he can see no one, Rufus can hear screams coming from all directions. The human destruction must be incredible, Rufus imagens that people are crushed under large amounts of debris, limbs severed or blown off, many impaled by flying glass, concrete, and steel rebar.

A terrible *darkness* takes over Rufus' mind. Rufus can now feel all the *emotions* running through Tim's body. His heart is running a hundred miles an hour and he feels hot all over. Tim is frozen, looking at the scene in front of him.

I feel bad for those kids. But I know it needed to be done, and I will be recognized for my contribution when the world has changed.

"What kids?" Rufus thought. "You bastard, what did you do."

Rufus can see a vision in Tim's mind, it is the vision of a daycare center, obviously somewhere in the Murrah building. Rufus can now feel some sort of sorrow, a kind of empathy Tim is having for the victims.

"You fuck," Rufus thinkd.

Tim shakes his head.

This is all the fault of the US government, for the children they killed in Waco Texas and the atrocities at Ruby Ridge.

McVeigh looks around for the German, but he is nowhere to be seen. He then heads for his car walking through the rubble of concrete and mangled wires scattered on the street, now thinking about the German's last words, *'You fucked this all up.'*

As he walks, he makes small talk with some of the people he passes, commenting on how terrible it is and how close they were. When he reaches the Yellow Mercury parked in an alley on Eighth Street, he gets in. At first, it refuses to start, and Tim wonders if someone has stolen gas or tampered with it. But, after a bit, it starts, and Tim drives out of the city and heads north towards Kansas.

A few miles north of the tiny town of Perry, Tim looks in his rear-view mirror and sees a highway patrol car speeding up behind him; lights flashing. Tim thinks that he is driving the speed limit and does not panic. Rufus watches by way of the rearview mirror, as the cruiser pulls in behind Tim's Mercury. Tim is still not panicking; he is sure there is no way they could have tied him to the bombing that quickly. Tim pulls over and gets out of his car. Rufus knew that Tim had a loaded Glock and a knife under his windbreaker, and now feared for the trouper's life.

"Sir, can I see your license and registration. Are you aware that there are no license plates on this vehicle?"

Tim replied, "I just bought the car officer."

Rufus can see that the trooper isn't taking any chances as he stays a distance away.

"Sir, please get back in your car. I'll need to see your bill of sale."

Tim gets back in the car and says: "The dealer is still filling out the paperwork."

"Please sir, your driver's license."

Tim says, "I have a gun and I have a license for it."

At this point, the officer orders McVeigh to raise his hands and get back out of the car. He handcuffs McVeigh and puts him in the cruiser. McVeigh closes his eyes and for Rufus everything fades to *darkness*.

Rufus is now back in his room. He is covered with sweat and is experiencing an incredibly bad headache, but it feels as though his fever is gone, and he gets out of bed. He is still thinking about those children in the Murrah Building as he punches a hole in a nearby sheetrock wall.

"Is there any *Logic* to all of this?" He thinks, now overwhelmed with anger, and feeling the pain in his now bloody fist.

Then, just as with his experience with Randy Weaver, Rufus realizes, whether he likes it or not he has been changed by his close *connection* to another person. Once again, he is amazed at how a person's strong beliefs, either good or bad, can drive them to incredible actions.

Now, this *entanglement* is just another part of what will become Rufus Middleman.

Rufus turns on his TV. "Oh! My God."

CHAPTER 22 – NOT A PERFECT ALIBI

April 21st, 1995
Rufus Middleman, age 25

>   *With a body-blow greater than he ever felt from any MMA fighter, the air moves at hurricane force velocity, taking Tim and Rufus to the ground.   Smoke and flying debris rush past him leaving Rufus with hazy images of devastation.*

That is the last of Rufus' memory from his experience just two days ago in Oklahoma City, it is now a storm of confusion and anger for Rufus.

Rufus is horrified by what he had witnessed that day. It did not prepare him for the even higher elevation of anger that he feels, when he sees the crystal-clear imagery on television and in the papers.

"Over one-third of the Murrah building destroyed," The TV newsman was saying. "and hundreds of other buildings damaged over a 16-block area. Hundreds and hundreds of people killed or missing, and it has been confirmed that all of the children in the daycare center on the third floor have perished."

Rufus is alone in his tiny apartment. He fights his anger, waiting for the phone to ring, and tells himself he must stay in control.

He has been watching the news reports for the last two days. There is a tremendous amount of speculation and tons of false information being broadcast.   Much of the speculation is about the probability that the bombing is the work of a foreign terrorist. Rufus knows none of this is true, and Rufus had contacted the FBI office in Denver as soon as he could and has been waiting anxiously to hear back from them.

"No doubt they have received thousands of phone calls from people trying to help provide leads to the bombing. If only I could get through." Rufus thinks.

284 | P a g e

He had these two out of body experiences, but now they seem like a dream, and he is not even sure they really happened. He cannot sleep at night, constantly thinking about what he saw, and yet, Rufus must go on with his life.

Rufus is now in the Ph.D. program at the School of Mines in Golden Colorado, and as part of the program, he is required to teach undergraduates. These bright young people, full of life and full of themselves, have no idea what is happening in the world and Rufus hates it. He hated teaching, and he hated some of these snot nose bastards he was teaching.

All he really wants to do, is research, driven by a ravenous hunger to learn more about 'Light', 'Photons', 'Gravitons', 'Black Holes', and the 'substances' that connects it all together. He just wants to write papers, and in his spare time, kick the shit out of all these snot nose young bastards.

It is an understatement to say that Rufus is angry. "How could a 'just God' let the things I've witnessed happen? How could God let these snot nose college bastards get off so easy, with all their money and cars and girls, all with not a bit of hardship." It's all beyond Rufus' comprehension. It's times like this that he really missed fighting. Fighting made him feel alive when it was occurring, and it relaxed him when it was over.

The total release of *emotions* that he felt, even the pain somehow made him feel better about himself. Watching Timothy McVeigh blow up that Federal building and not being able to do anything to stop him, was more frustration than Rufus could stand. He wanted to grab that little bastard by the neck, just like he did at Kermit's that day, years ago. But this time he would not let go, and then he thinks to himself.

"But right now, I must remain calm."

The phone rings. Rufus grabs it. "Hello!!"

"Hello, I am Agent Phil Monroe from the FBI's office in Denver. I believe you called our office. How can I help?"

Rufus thought long and hard about what he would say to the FBI when got through. He believed he knew the person who committed the bombings and he wanted to give the FBI as much information as he could without divulging his source.

He is sure that if he revealed how he came about this information; they would think he is completely crazy or the bomber himself. So here he is, about to try to convince this federal agent he is not just some wacko off the street, when he is not absolutely sure, that he isn't just that.

He begins his conversation with the FBI agent by introducing himself. He informs the agent of his credentials, "I am pursuing a Ph.D. in Math and Physics, as well as teaching at the School of Mines, here in Colorado."

Rufus has a real problem; he knows too much. Not only did he know the bomber's name, he knows what kind of car McVeigh was driving when he left Oklahoma City, and he also knows other detailed background information on McVeigh. How could he transmit this information to this agent and not create a lot of problems for himself? Rufus had decided to make up an elaborate story.

"Besides my work and studies at the University, I am also very interested in acts associated with discrimination that receive national attention. You may not realize it, just talking to me on the phone, but I am Jewish, and I am also African American. I have done extensive studies in the area of White Supremacist in this country, and I am presently writing a novel on what happened to the Weaver family at Ruby Ridge, in Northern Idaho. By way of my research on white supremacist I came across the name of a man who was in the military and has fought in Iraq. He was a sharpshooter and has explosives training."

"This man, whose name is Timothy McVeigh, is also known to be associated with a White Supremacist group in eastern Oklahoma and wanted to make a name for himself with that group by doing something that would have a dramatic effect on the U.S. government. This could be the man who bombed that Murrah building in Oklahoma City."

The agent on the phone is silent for a few seconds and then replied. "Mr. Middleman, do you have any specific evidence that this person is the one who planted the bomb in Oklahoma?"

"Not specifically," Rufus replied, knowing he needed to be very careful here. "But I really think he is someone that you should check out. He could be your man."

The agent took down all the information and asks if he has any additional information. Rufus has tons of additional information, but he dared not say any more for fear they would suspect him of being in cahoots with McVeigh.

Rufus then says: "That's all I can really tell you" and then repeats. "But you really need to look into this guy."

They complete their conversation, the agent asked for some information about Rufus, including how to contact him if they needed to get in touch with him. The agent thanks Rufus and then hangs up.

After Agent Monroe hangs up, he enters his notes into the FBI computer database, along with the thousands of lines of information that he and other agents already had entered over the last two days since the bombing.

At that same time, in another part of the FBI office, Ron Chapman is on the phone with his contact, Phil Mendoza, in the Oklahoma field office.

Phil is saying "The day of the bombing we found a rear axle from a truck, it crashed through the front of a store an ended up covered with debris in the back of the store. The axel had a partial VIN number on it, and we traced it to a Ryder truck from Miami. We found out from the Ryder Truck Company, that it was last rented from a body shop in Junction City, Kansas, owned by a man named Eldon Elliott."

"Eldon rented trucks to soldiers who were moving in and out of Fort Riley, Kansas. Eldon told us that the truck, a twenty-foot van, was rented on April 14th and picked up on the 17th, by a man calling himself Robert Kling. The man is medium build and light brown hair that is cut short, and we developed some composite sketches."

"Our agents canvassed motels along I-40, which is on the east side of Junction City. When they checked out the Dreamland motel, the owner thought she recognized one of the men in the composite sketches. The motel owner said that this guy rented a room for four days over the Easter weekend and that he was driving a yellow Ryder rental truck. She said the guy had short light brown hair and stood about 6-foot-tall and registered under the name of Timothy McVeigh. She said she thought he seemed suspicious. When he originally drove in to rent the room, he was driving a beat-up Mercury Marquis, with a license plate that was barely hanging on to the front bumper. The license number did not match the number he put on the registration form. Also, when the agents followed up on the address that McVeigh put on the registration form, it led them to a guy named Terry Nichols."

Ron's contact went on to say "A criminal search of the name Timothy McVeigh had shown that he had been arrested by the Noble County Sheriff's department about an hour and a half after the bombing. He had been stopped on *April 19th* for driving with an improper license plate and he was hauled in for unlawful possession of a firearm. His bail bond hearing was delayed for two days because of the judge's caseload. When we called, they were just getting ready to release him on bail."

Phil went on to say that there is also some evidence that this guy Terry Nichols was involved and maybe some others as well. After some additional discussion Ron thanked Phil for the information and hung up.

Chapman had one of his agents do a search of their database to see if they had any leads associated with Timothy McVeigh or Terry Nichols. When his staff ran the search, Rufus Middleman showed up as having called, suggesting that Timothy McVeigh might be their man. Ron immediately sent out an agent to pick up this Rufus character.

Within a couple of hours, Rufus Middleman is sitting in the FBI interrogation room in downtown Denver. Rufus knew his alibi for *April 19th* was not perfect, in fact it was very weak. On that day he had not gone to any of his classes, no one had seen him, and he knew that not being in Oklahoma City that day would not clear him of involvement. But Rufus also knew he had to tell the FBI something. He could not remain silent and hoped that his credentials would help him appear less suspect. None the less, he had to be very careful about what he said.

Ron Chapman, as a Director, did not often get directly involved in the interrogation of suspects, but he knew this would be a very high-profile case, and he wanted to be on top of it. Ron had been very successful in the FBI and set up a network of very politically savvy contacts and supporters. Many of which had been encouraging him to run for Congress, and he was looking to do just that here in Colorado.

So, he sat in on and listened, as two of his agents, experienced in interrogation, ran this guy, Rufus Middleman, through the standard line of questioning. Ron could tell right away that Rufus Middleman was not some Joe off the street. This is a highly intelligent man and his story about having done research on the Ruby Ridge incident for a book seemed to be convincing, he certainly had considerable knowledge of the details of the days that lead up to Randy Weaver's arrest, details that Ron is certainly very familiar with, even though it was the ATF and US Marshals that were in charge of the arrest.

Ron remembers how happy he was that his men were not directly involved in the debacle at Ruby Ridge. He also remembers how he felt when they took over from the ATF in Waco, after they had screwed up the first assault on the Branch Davidians. He also remembered how everything went to shit from there. These two incidents turned into a huge mess and a huge black eye for the ATF, the FBI and for all law enforcement in the United States in general.

"But this guy seems to know what he is talking about." Ron was impressed. Often, in Ron's line of work, the people they interrogate are not so articulate.

After more than an hour of interrogation, Ron concludes that this guy is not involved with the bombing. It is still interesting how insistent he is that they check into Timothy McVeigh and Terry Nichols, their two main suspects. He also said that they should investigate Elohim City in northern Oklahoma for other people who might have been involved. Ron is already familiar with Elohim City, and the bad characters that resided there.

Ron knew that they would need to do further background checks on Mr. Middleman, but also believed that he is, at least for now, not providing any information that they did not already have. Ron, always interested in finding intelligent people to help him and his goals, wanted to get to know Rufus better.

Rufus had introduced himself as a Ph.D. candidate in math and physics, and Ron had a remedial understanding of physics and knew a little bit about Quantum Physics. So, he questioned Rufus in that area. It soon became apparent to Ron, that Mr. Middleman knew what he is talking about when it came to math and science. After about three hours, Ron tells Rufus the interview is complete and he is free to go, but he asks Rufus to not leave the metro area for a while, as they may have some follow up questions.

Rufus leaves the FBI offices relieved that he made it through the interrogation and had not let on that he knew any more than he initially told them. Then, on the radio, Rufus hears they made an arrest. Rufus hoped it was McVeigh.

Rufus believed he had built a pretty good relationship with Chapman, who seemed to be in charge, and they had a good discussion, well beyond the bombing case. Rufus thought that Chapman seemed to like him and might even contact him later on to continue some of those discussions on the Ruby Ridge case and possibly in other areas, like math and science.

Rufus is hoping that he can build a relationship with agent Chapman. He wanted to quiz him about not only the Oklahoma bombing but also about Randy Weaver. Chapman also seemed to be well versed in areas of math and science and Rufus hopes he can discuss some of his research with him.

Just like his visit to the mind of Randy Weaver, Rufus' visit to the mind of Timothy McVeigh left a lot of unanswered questions, and he is hoping that a relationship with Ron Chapman might help him answer some of these questions.

All Rufus knows at this point is: just because someone is labeled a White Supremacist doesn't mean that they are all the same. and Rufus wanted as much information as he could get about these men, Randy Weaver and Timothy McVeigh, two men who had the same label but who were so very different. Rufus now feels that his own *logic* and *emotions* are now completely *entangled* and entwined within the *logic* and *emotions* of these two now infamous men.

CHAPTER 23 – THE RIGHT TO BEAR ARMS

April 20th, 1999
Christine Basurto, age 31

Christine, recognizing the sick feeling in her stomach, and thinks to herself: "Oh No! I'm not going to let this happen again! I'll stay awake and fight it. Do not let this happen." She repeats to herself over and over. But she is getting sleepy and no *matter* how hard she fights it; sleep is coming, and now she knows she can no longer resist.

Immediately, Christine senses that it is a male body that she inhabits. She can sense the testosterone flowing through the body and the scale of the body and she is sure it is not feminine. Christine notices something else. Even though it has been years since her experience with weird John, she can remember it like it was yesterday.

At that time, she could feel the overwhelming sensations of uncertainty. John was very unsure of himself, and he would jump from one thought to another, think about doing one thing in one moment and then think about doing, or do something, completely different in the next. He was obsessive and compulsive. He obsessed over Jodie and yet yearned to be famous not just to imprcss Jodic but also to feed his own self-image. He would constantly run through short sessions of role plays, where he would be some heroic figure like the main character in "Taxi Driver", all in an effort to boost his own diminished ego. *Emotions* ruled, *logic* only played a role because he thought that he was being *logical* in what he was doing, while in reality, none of it made sense.

Just like with John, Christine can feel everything her host is doing and thinking. But this is different, this guy is very self-confident. He doesn't have that burning hunger in his belly or in his mind like John did. He is so confident it puts Christine at ease.

She can feel herself relax a bit and settle into observation of her host.

The next thing Christine knows, she is looking at a digital clock indicating it is 4:45 a.m., and the person she is inside of is talking into a tape recorder.

"Mom, Dad; this is Eric. It is Tuesday, April 20th, 1999. People will die because of me. It will be a day that will be remembered forever."

Christine forgot how strange it is to experience speech when you yourself are not actually doing the talking, and her host thoughts continue.

God, I've been up most of the night, I am hyped. Well at least I know I was awake at 2:00 AM, but now I'm not sleepy at all, and I'm ready to go.

Christine watched as Eric left a few more messages on the audio cassette that he apparently was leaving for his parents, and then Eric picks up, what looks like a journal. The title on the cover is: "The Book of God" and Eric reads from this journal.

I feel like God. I am higher than almost anyone in the world in terms of universal intelligence. Humans are pathetic fuck heads, to dense to perceive their lifeless existence as self-awareness. We fretted our lives away like automatons, following orders rather than realizing our potential. Ever wonder why we go to school? It's not too obvious to most of you stupid fucks, but for those who think a little more and deeper, you should realize, it is society's way of turning all the young people into good little robots, more of your human nature blown out your ass. Natural selection has failed; Man has had too much intervention. Medicines, vaccines, and special-ED programs had conspired to keep the rejects in the human herd.

Now Christine sees images. Large numbers of people being killed, and buildings being destroyed. Eric is imagining himself causing all of this mayhem. He is not only fascinated with, but also encouraged by the Oklahoma City bombings in 1995.

I was paying close attention to the shootings and other acts of violence around the country, but after Dylan and I were arrested in 98' for breaking into that van, things changed. Dad found that homemade bomb I made. After that, he was giving me hell all the time. That did it, I no longer just wanted to be an observer. I wanted to be an initiator, and I know, I can exceed the high bar set by McVeigh and all those other acts; they are just armatures.

I will rig up explosives all over town and detonate each one of them at will, after I mow down a whole fucking area full of your snotty ass rich mother fucking high strung godlike attitude having worthless pieces of shit whores, and I don't care if I live or die in the shootout.

Christine is at first frightened by these *emotional* ramblings, but somehow now that she is older, and having experienced this once before in her life, she seemed more at ease and analytical. She knew that this is important, and she hoped that she could avert her host intentions. Though, deep down she knew, that she probably would not be able to do anything but observe.

She also knew that it was important for her to pay attention to details, to stay *logical* and not let her own *emotions* get in the way. That way, she could hopefully turn this learning experience into something positive.

So, Christine observes as Eric thinks about how every day he indoctrinated his partner, Dylan Klebold, by expounded on his theories. Little by little Dylan was buying in and becoming more enthusiastic with Eric's master plan. Originally, Dylan did not want to kill anyone. What he really wanted was to have a meaningful relationship with a woman. But, after failing in that area, Dylan had told Eric what he really wanted, was to just die. He hated his life, and constantly had thoughts of suicide, and that the more he listened to Eric, the more he became convinced, that the way to die was in a blaze of glory, killing people and blowing things up, and Eric's thoughts continued.

After my arrest in 98', dad sent me to a psychiatrist. Boy, that was fun, I served up so much bullshit to that doctor, and he had no clue what I was about. I convinced him I was just having anxiety attacks and he prescribed Zoloft. I took that for a while and then he switched me to that antidepressant Luvox. It didn't matter, I'm the master of deception. I lie a lot, and almost constantly to everybody, just to keep my own ass out of water.

It wasn't just the doctor I had fooled. At my hearing in March of that year, I completely pulled the wool over the eyes of that Jefferson County judge, John DeVitta. These guys are such idiots. If you give them partial confessions, basically I would give them half the truth, only the parts I believed would get me off the hook, and they would buy it.

I told the judge how sorry Dylan and I were, and how I now understood the damage we caused to the owner of that van. The judge bought all that bullshit and put us in the Diversion program rather than giving us jail time.

At one point, I even pretended I was interested in joining the Marines. I even went down and talked to the Marines, but when they found out I was on Luvox they rejected me. I never intended to join the Marines; it was just another ruse to throw my parents off the scent of what I was really planning.

Christine could now since that her host's feelings of confidence, was partially derived from his ability to deceive others. Christine is now analyzing every thought that Eric is having. Then, Eric walks up to the mirror in his living room.

Christine's first thought is, "this kid looks familiar" and then it comes to her, it's the kid who held the door for her at the Burger King, only now a he's a bit taller at about 5'11' and maybe 140 lbs. Now she knew why she had such a strange feeling when she had touched his head. It is just like when she shook hands with weird John, back when she was just a kid.

As Eric continued to think about his upcoming day, he looked at his wristwatch. It is 6:00 AM.

I'm psyched for today. 'Judgment Day' we call it, and our code name is NBK for 'Natural Born Killers', and it is here at last. Damn! Though I am disappointed it did not happen yesterday, like we had originally planned. April 19th, the anniversary of the Oklahoma City bombings, that would have been great. But we only had seven hundred rounds of ammo for our four guns and I wanted more.

I have it all planned out. I will be carrying a sawed-off shotgun, I named "Arlene", after the heroine in the "Doom" books. I will also be carrying a Hi-Point 9mm carbine rifle. Dylan will carry a sawed-off shotgun and an Intratec TEC-DC9 9mm semiautomatic handgun.

I arranged for my friend to buy another hundred rounds of 9mm ammo, but he did not come through in time for our Monday execution. So, I went over there last night and picked up the ammo at his house. He said he is a member of an organization that wanted to help enterprising young men like myself.

I thought that was a strange thing for him to say, and I'm sure he had no idea what I was planning, but none the less, now we're ready to go. This is going to be spectacular. We not only have the guns, but we have assembled seven big bombs from a recipe I found in the Anarchist Handbook on the internet. One of the bombs consists of a twenty-pound propane tank, an aerosol can, and an old-fashioned alarm clock. Two other big bombs have the same propane tank, aerosol can and alarm clock, but also have nails, BBs and a can of gasoline, all stuffed into a duffle bag. The final two big bombs have the propane tanks, aerosol can and alarm clock, plus twenty gallons of gasoline. We will leave these two, one each, in Dylan and my cars, for Step3 of my plan. We will also, each carry forty small pipe and carbon dioxide bombs, called "Crickets" and several Molotov cocktails and some knives for hand to hand combat if necessary.

We will be dressed in military harnesses to help carry all the equipment. Dylan will wear a black t-shirt with the word "WRATH" printed on the front. He will also be wearing cargo pants, black combat boots and a Red Sox baseball cap. He likes to wear it turned backward.

I will wear the same black combat boots and cargo pants, but my t-shirt says "Natural Selection" on it. We will share a pair of black gloves. Dylan is left-handed, so he will wear the left glove, and I will wear the right glove.

When I'm wearing all the equipment covered with the black dusters, that we each will wear, I feel like a giant, I am completely invincible.

I know I'm ready, and I'm pretty sure Dylan is on board too. I've been working on this for a year and a half, and I need him to be with me, though he does seem to be a bit reluctant. I will have to push Dylan from time to time, but I think that if I give him baby steps, like setting the timers on the bombs, he will get into it, and be totally engaged for the rest of the plan, at least I hope so.

First, we will have one of the large bombs go off in the park near my house, miles from the school. This will be a diversion and draw the fire department and police to that location. We should already be at the school when that happens. In the next phase, we will stand about one hundred yards apart next to our cars outside the Commons area at the school. When the bell rings for the 'A' lunch period, there will be hundreds of students in that area. We will have already placed the two big bombs inside the school, near load-bearing pillars in the lunchroom. When those bombs explode, we will have taken down a good portion of the school, killing hundreds of students and teachers. As the students and teachers who survive the bombings, are rushing out of the school, we will catch them in a crossfire and kill hundreds more. We will then move into what was left of the school, and with our pipe bombs, Molotov cocktails and guns, we will continue killing until ---we too, are killed by the police.

The final act will occur when the police think they have everything under control, and the media is swarming the place. That is when the two remaining bombs, planted in our cars, will go off killing hundreds of cops, firemen and especially the media.

Christine, a bit overwhelmed, could feel Eric smile, and she thinks "This kid, thinks this is just a big video game or something.", as Eric's thoughts ramble on.

It seems a bit ironic, that we're blowing off our morning bowling class, just so we can meet up at the grocery store, buy more propane tanks to blow up the school.

Christine thinks to herself, "And I thought weird John was crazy. He can't hold a candle to this guy ---this guy is off the charts."

Christine attempted to disengage from Eric, if she could only get to the authorities before these two reached the school. But just as it had been with John, her attempts to escape were futile, and the best she could do was pay attention, so she could help the police afterward.

In no time Eric meets up with his accomplice, the one Eric had identified as Dylan Klebold.

As Eric approached Dylan in the grocery store parking lot, Dylan spoke first: "So Harris, are we ready for Judgment Day?" "Almost," Eric replied, "We just need a few more things and then we are good to go." Christine now remembers how strange it is to experience someone's speech and every movement as if it were her own, and Christine now knows that Eric's last name must be Harris. Another detail that she must remember.

At the grocery store the boys pick up four additional propane tanks, and then they go back to Eric's house and begin the bomb assembly, including setting up the bombs in the car. After about a half an hour, it is done, and they start practicing putting on all their gear and running through their master plan. After an hour of practice, Christine can feel that Eric is tired, but still very excited, and they start watching a videotape of themselves posturing with their guns, talking about all the planning they had done, and what they were going to do. It became obvious to Christine that, just as Eric had indicated, they had been working on this for a very long time. And, this is the second time that Christine can see what Eric looks like. He had the look of a midwestern farm boy, short brown hair, almost a kind of butch cut, but a little longer and little spikier looking. He is a very wholesome looking young man, and if it were not for all the military garb and guns, he would not look threatening at all. Eric then got out a video camera and pointed it at Dylan, and Dylan started talking.

"Hey Mom, I gotta go. It's about a half an hour to Judgment Day. I just wanted to apologize to you guys for any crap this might instigate. Just know, I am going to a better place. I didn't like life too much, and I know I'll be happy wherever the fuck I go. So, I'm gone. Goodbye. Reb…"

Eric handed the camera to Dylan as he thinks.

I wish I could explain to everyone how logical *all of this is to me. But they would never understand.*

All these thoughts are running through Eric's mind, and Christine is trying her best to digest and remember it all as Eric begins to speak:

"Yeah, Everyone I love, I am really sorry about all this. I know my mom and dad will be like just… Just shocked beyond belief. I am sorry. All right I can't help it."

"It's what we had to do," Dylan added from behind the camera.

"Susan, sorry." Eric continued. "Under different circumstances, it would've been a lot different. I want you to have that 'fly' CD."

Dylan started to become impatient and snapped his fingers. This pissed Eric off, and he shot an angry look at Dylan and that shut him down. Eric finished up.

"That's it. Sorry, Goodbye."

Eric said to Dylan "We need to chill out for a while. We don't want to get to the school too early. We want to be there right at lunchtime." For the next couple of hours, they relaxed and got something to eat.

Later, Eric looked at the clock; it read10:55 am.

"Oh my god! We need to get going."

They drove separately to a park that was not far from Eric's house, and there they planted one of the big bombs.

Eric told Dylan; "You set the timer on this bomb. Set it for 11:14 AM". Eric did as he was instructed and Christine watched as Dylan got back into his BMW, and Eric loaded himself in his Honda. Eric looks at his watch once more, it is 11:10 AM.

Shortly they arrive at school, Eric thinks to himself.
We are behind schedule.

As Eric enters the parking area, Christine can see a sign that says, "Columbine High School". Eric sees a couple of girls in a car, heading away from the school. They wave at Eric, and he waves back and smiles. Eric parks his car, and he can see Dylan parking his car in a lot off to his left.

Just like we planned.

Eric is now pulling one of the big duffel bags out of his car when he hears someone yelling,

"What's the matter with you? We had a test in Psychology."

Eric responded "It doesn't matter anymore, Brooks. I like you. Now get out of here. Go Home."

Brooks moved on, and Christine could see him shaking his head as he walked away.

Eric and Dylan proceeded towards the school carrying two of the big bombs.

I had this elaborate plan worked out to create a diversion, so we could sneak the bombs into the school.

But then he turned to Dylan and said, "Dylan, you know what, these idiots at school probably won't even notice, if we just carry these bombs right in, and set them down."

Christine is shocked and watched as they did exactly that. Throwing the straps of the duffel bags over their shoulders, and with their *dark* trench coats on, they marched right in past students and teachers, and just as Eric had thought nobody seemed to even notice. They placed the duffle bags in the cafeteria next to what looked like weight-bearing pillars.

Then they moved back out to the parking lot, to the positions near their cars, which were about one hundred yards apart. Eric set the timer on the big bomb in his car, and then put on his military harnesses loaded up his arsenals, put on his trench coat, and took up his position for the crossfire. The plan was for the crossfire to be initiated after the bombs went off in the school.

Eric could see Dylan across the parking lot, now dressed in his arsenal and trench coat as well.

We're running a bit behind schedule and that bomb in the park, by my house, should have gone off by now. But I didn't hear an explosion and I don't hear any sirens. It is several miles over to that park, and maybe it's just too far for me to hear.

Christine could hear the lunch bells going off at the school, but no explosion and she prayed the bomb didn't work.

The lunch bells went off several minutes ago, and still no explosion. Those bombs must have malfunctioned. Oh! Well, on with the plan.

Eric waived for Dylan to join him at his location. Dylan arrives and they proceed toward the steps that run up to the west exit of the school. Now at the top of the stairs, they open their duffel bags and strap them to their bodies. They loaded the semi-automatics and Eric yelled; "Go! Go!"

Christine had noticed that the skies were overcast before, but now it appeared to her that they were growing *darker*. Christine tried to compose herself, but actually, she is terrified. "Oh my God! It's started."

Eric began shooting at every student he could see, and Dylan followed along taking a couple of shots but did not appear to be actually shooting at anyone. But then, Eric hit two students and they went down. He kept firing, and then they both tossed pipe bombs down the stairs and on to the roof. Eric is wild with excitement, and he howled, and Dylan returned the howls encouraging Eric to "Rage on". Christine could feel Eric begin to perspire, as he rips off the duster he is wearing and throws it on the steps.

Christine can see three male students running across the grass towards their location, and Eric is thinking.

The stupid shits probably think this is some kind of a game.

Eric begins firing at them, and the first one is hit in the knee and goes down. Eric keeps firing and hits him two more times. His victim's buddy tries to catch him. Eric is firing round after round at them and she watches as the buddy gets hit in the foot, leg, knee, and chest. The third student, burst out laughing, not realizing that this is not a game. Eric shoots him twice, the student turns to run, and then collapses near his friends.

Eric then shoots at several students sitting under a tree on the lawn, they jump up and begin to run, and one goes down. Christine feels he chest clinch with the horror from what she is watching.

Eric and Dylan then move out to the lawn. As they are walking, Eric feels someone tugging at his pant leg. Eric looks down, it is one of the three boys that had been running towards him earlier. The boy begs. "Please help me."

Eric says, "Sure I'll help" and shoots the boy in the face with his 9 mm. Eric then watches as Dylan returns to the building, enters and then shortly re-emerges and joins Eric at the top of the stairs.

As they look out across the lawn, Christine can see students running in all directions. Eric fires at them but they are too far away. Christine can see that now Dylan is even taking a couple of shots.

Eric looks at his watch, it's 11:23.

As Eric turns to enter the school, he looks through the first set of doors, that separates the outside from the school hallway. Christine can see a teacher and a student coming towards him. She can tell by the look on the teacher's face that she is going to give him hell for making all this noise. The teacher and student are now just a few feet away on the other side of the doors. Eric smiles and shoots through the glass at the teacher, glass flies everywhere but he misses. He fires again and the teacher goes down, he fires again, and the student goes down as well.

Christine can see the teacher and the student scramble on their knees through the second set of doors and into the hallway, and now she can see them running away, but Eric does not take any additional shots.

Eric then turned toward the sound of a siren. It's an approaching police car. He immediately begins firing towards it and gets off ten rounds. Christine sees the cop jump out of his car to take up a position behind it. Eric fires again, but then his gun jams. The policeman at his car starts to return fire, and Eric spins back towards the school doors to avoid getting hit. Dylan is already inside, as Eric returns fire and then moves through the doors into the school.

Eric and Dylan move down the hallway. As they walk, they lob pipe bombs and fire their guns, shattering windows. Christine can see some students and teachers down the hallway and both of the boys start firing. Christine sees one of the teachers take a hit, crash into the lockers, and then go down. As they continue to fire, they hit the teacher once more. Christine sees the other students and teachers disappear into rooms, and out the end of the hallway.

Eric returns to the west end door they just entered, apparently to see what the cops are doing. As soon as he looks out, Christine hears gunfire and she can see the shots hitting the door frame near Eric's head. Eric returns fire, but when the shots come at him from another direction, he moves back into the school.

Eric and Dylan then move up the stairs to the second floor and walk through the hallway tossing pipe bombs here and there randomly, and shooting their guns again blowing out windows and just, in general, damaging the walls and ceiling.

Fire alarms are now screaming in the background. Eric yells to Dylan. "I Love this."

Dylan yells back "This is awesome, this is the most fantastic thing I have ever done."

They walk down the hall and as they pass the library, Eric looks through the glass in the doors. Christine can see that there are several students hiding under the tables, but Eric and Dylan walk on by.

After scouting out several other rooms, Eric says; "I think the library has our best opportunity". They return to the library and open the doors, Eric fires off a couple of rounds and yells. "Who wants to be killed next?"

Dylan takes off his trench coat, laughs and yells, "Yea who wants to die?"

Christine sees a boy to their left, jump trying to hide, but Eric shoots at him, and the boy goes down, but Eric doesn't take the time to see if he is acutely hit, and they move further into the room. As they walk around the room Christine can see that there are several students hiding in the room.

Eric yells: "Everyone is going to die" and Dylan follows with, "Who wants to die next?"

Eric walks up to a table that a student is hiding under, and pounds on the table.

I know this dipshit can see my legs and boots, I bet he is scared shitless. But I am in control here, and I decide who lives and dies.

Eric walks up to another table. Christine can see that there are two young girls hiding under the table, as Eric slams his hand on the table, and Christine sees the girls jump as they scream.

Christine is deplored by how much Eric is loving all of this, as she watches Eric go into a half squat position, down on the balls of his feet, right in front of the girls, and say, "Peek-a-boo".

Eric then, holding his shotgun in one hand, puts it up to the forehead of one of the girls, and fires. What Christine would have seen would have been horrific, but something unexpected happened. When Eric aimed the gun, he did not have it against his shoulder, as he had before. Instead, he put the butt of the gun in front of his face. When it goes off it recoils and hit Eric square in the face breaking his nose. When it hit Eric, his eyes shut, and he is knocked backward, this action along with the intense pain that followed prevented Christine from having to witness the death of the young girl under the table.

Now Christine is trying hard to keep her composure, but this last act of senseless murder is too much, and now along with feeling the pain of Eric's broken nose, she could feel the pain in her heart for these dying students. This is worse than any horror movie, it is the *darkest* of all *dark* places she could imagine. How could she keep it together? She thought she was going to lose her mind, and now she could tell that Eric's broken nose is not going to stop him, and she needed to try her best to pay attention despite the physical and mental pain.

With blood splattered over his face and on the floor mixing with the blood of others, Eric is unfazed. He ejected the spent cartridge, stood up and turned, and then took a couple of steps towards a different girl. She is lying on the floor, holding the hand of another student. Eric squatted again, laid the gun across his lap and yelled to Dylan laughing; "I hit myself in the face."

He is looking directly at this girl. Christine knew that the girl could see the blood pouring from his nose and the terrible grin on his face. Eric pointed the gun at several people on the floor and settled on this new girl. Christine could hear Dylan's gun firing in the background and he is laughing hysterically. But Eric paid little attention, instead, he said to this new girl; "Do you want to die?"

"No" she replied, pleading with him "No, no, no".

Christine could feel that Eric enjoyed the pleading; he had absolutely no empathy for these people. Christine thought, "He is a complete and utter psychopath."

"Are you sure you don't want to die?" Eric repeated.

The girl again begged "Don't shoot me, I don't want to die"

Eric laughed and said, "Everyone is going to die."

Dylan yelled, "Shoot her, Shoot her."

But Eric responded, "No, we are going to blow up the school anyway."

Christine is shocked, as Eric walked away from the new girl, and then began to shoot other students.

Until they had reached the library, Eric had done all the killings. It appeared to Christine that Dylan had not even been shooting very much. But now as Eric watched, Dylan pointed his shotgun at some students at a nearby table and fired several shots. Christine could see that Dylan had killed one girl and injured another. Christine then watched as Dylan started to walk away, but then he heard the second girl who had been injured and had fallen to her knees, crying; "OH my God, Oh my God. Don't let me die"

Dylan turned around and said "God, do you believe in God?"

"Yes, I believe in God."

Dylan asked, "Why?"

"Yes, because I believe, and my parents brought me up that way"

Dylan is reloading his gun to finish her off, but Eric said; "I'm getting bored, let's move on". So, Dylan and Eric left the Library and the injured girl is spared. Christine estimated that they killed at least ten people and injured many more. Eric looked at his watch, it is 11:36, they had only been in the library for seven and a half minutes.

Eric and Dylan moved back into the hallway and continued to throw pipe bombs and shoot at random. Christine could see that they were now entering another wing of the school. They pass classrooms, and as Eric looks in each one, Christine sees students; some looking back, and most are scared out of their minds.

I love the power of knowing that I am in complete control and can kill any of these students if I want too---- and that they know it.

They passed 'Science Room 3' and Christine could see some eagle scouts working on one of the injured students.

I remember shooting one of those guys, but I'm bored. I just want one more cataclysmic event to occur. I want the big bomb in the cafeteria to go off.

Eric headed down the stairs to the cafeteria, Dylan followed. It is 11:44. Halfway down the stairs, Eric stopped on the landing. Looking down on the cafeteria, he seemed to be searching the scattered backpacks and other debris below and then seemed to find what he is looking for. It's the duffel bag with his large bomb in it. Eric takes careful aim with his rifle.

I know we are in the blast area, but I really don't give a shit at this point.

Eric fired----and nothing, he fired again, still no results. The boys proceed down the stairs and walk up to the bomb. Christine can see students hiding under tables in the room, but Eric and Dylan were not interested. Eric stood by as Dylan tried to get the ignition system on the bomb to work but could not get it working.

Eric is becoming exhausted, Christine could tell that all the killings had given him such an adrenalin rush and it is all draining away and now he is very tired, especially after the disappointment of the big bomb failure.

Eric announces to the students left in the room: "Today the world is going to come to an end"

Dylan follows his lead with "Today's the day we die."

The boys headed out of the cafeteria. Dylan tosses a Molotov cocktail at the big bombs, hoping this would set them off. Christine watches as it burnt the duffle bags exposing the propane bottles and setting the gasoline on a fire, which sets off the sprinkler system in the room, but no explosion.

Christine could tell that Eric is getting very, very tired now and prayed that the killing had come to an end, as Christine felt exhausted from the stress.

Damn! I was hoping to go out in one big explosion, or at least, that a SWAT team would have charged the school and we could have gone down in a firefight, but it doesn't look like that is going to happen.

"Let's go back up the Library," Eric mumbled.

They move back upstairs and return to the library. The room smelled like blood, and the smell of death is everywhere. The carpet is soaked with blood and Christine cringes, as she can feel it squish beneath Eric's feet. The room is full of carnage, and splatters of blood and brains on the walls are now turning black. The bodies on the floor are white, purple and black with drying blood, and though there are some people still alive in the room, the two boys do not seem to take notice.

Eric said to Dylan "We should be able, to see our final blow to the world from here. The large bombs in our cars are set to go off any moment now, and that should kill all the cops and media in the parking lot. We should be able to see it all happen from here."

When they had left the library, it was full of the sounds of screaming, moaning and praying. Now Christine only hears the constant screams of the fire alarm and feels the cool breeze of air flowing in through the shattered windows.

Eric goes up to the windows. Christine can see paramedics below trying to get to some of the students back to safety, who were shot and lying in that area between the police line and the school.

Eric and Dylan open fire on the paramedics. The police return fire and Eric and Dylan move back from the windows.

I'm ready to die but I'm not going easy.

Then Eric says *"Fuck! No explosion"*.

Eric moves to the corner of the room and Dylan follows. Eric looks out the window towards the mountains and leans against a bookshelf.

"Thanks for being with me today, Dylan. I am absolutely sure that we were meant to do this." And then Eric thinks to himself.

You witnessed all of this and you cannot wash your hands of your involvement.

Christine thought "Who is he talking to? He is not speaking out loud, so he is not talking to Dylan. Is he talking to himself?" Christine tells herself; "I will not take any blame for what happened. It is not my fault." Christine then wonders about the powers of 'Observation'.

Christine then watches as Dylan lights the rag on a Molotov cocktail and sets it on a nearby table. But then she is shocked as she feels Eric put the barrel of his shotgun in his mouth and points it at his brain. At the same time, she is watching Dylan point his TEC-9 at his left temple. Christine is scared but glad it is all about to end. Eric closes his eyes, a sudden blast --- and then *darkness* devours Christine.

Christine awakes in her bed, covered in sweat, and exhausted. At first, she wants to grieve for all the young people that she believed had been killed, but she forces herself to push that aside for later. Right now, she needs to be analytical, she needs to be the psychologist and the scientist, and try to make sure she learned as much as she could before her memory faded. She goes to her desk and begins to write. She is convinced that Eric is a psychopath, but that did not seem important. It seemed, the more important part, had more to do with how it had affected her personally.

Here is a young man that is, except for maybe Dylan Klebold, *disconnected* with his friends, *disconnected* with his family, and certainly *disconnected* from his classmates and teachers, showing not even the least remorse for their brutal deaths. And yet Eric and Dylan did not kill some of the kids that were right in front of their weapons. Did those kids' belief in God or belief in themselves have some influence? Even though Eric was *disconnected* from any spiritual beliefs, or any kind of beliefs, other than an overwhelming belief in himself.

At the same time, Christine got the feeling that this all made sense to Eric. That somehow what he was doing, was the *logical* thing to do.

"How could anyone see this as *logical*?" she thinks.

"All of this darkness; what possible value could this have for me? I'm sure there is mountain of information for me to digest and learn from, but that will take time. I'm also sure that I did not cause this to happen. Why would he say that?" But then the *darkness* and depression overwhelm her, and she begins to cry.

After a while, Christine thinks, that she is beginning to feel better, but then she turns on the TV.

CHAPTER 24 – GET OUT OF DENVER BABY

April 19th, 2000
Jamaal Dell, age 15

Jamaal Dell is in his second year of High School, and he hates it. Honestly, he hates everything about his life. However, Jamaal is an expert at keeping his *emotions* hidden.

His mother is the main reason for his deep seeded hatred, but Jamaal hates his father as well. Not that Jamaal ever really knew his father, who divorced Jamaal's mother when Jamaal was just five. His mother said he was some kind of scientist, and so Jamal hated science. He sometimes pictured his father out there making some kind of scientific invention, that Jamaal hoped would be some kind Artificial Intelligence that would turn on him and kill him; or at least it would take over and destroy the whole fucking world.

Fucking-A, now that would be cool.

Jamaal's hate had to do with all aspects of his rotten life. His mother and father, his "could do no wrong" older brother, and even his fucking stupid teachers that always thought they knew what was best for him.

Teachers never really wanted to go out of their way to help me, and in general are not as smart as I am.

It doesn't help, that he is a black kid, attending a mostly white high school in Arvada Colorado, a suburb of mostly white Denver Colorado.

Then there were the girls in his life, which basically paid no attention to him, and on the rare occasion when Jamaal did have a real, not fantasized, relationship with a girl, she always ended up fucking him over.

At least Jamaal had one friend, Frank Waters. Frank was a screw-up, not very smart, and certainly not a popular guy, but he and Jamaal had a lot in common when it came to their opinions of the faculty and student body at the high school. Frank and Jamaal would sit around and fantasize about murdering everyone in the school, just like those guys at Columbine did a year ago tomorrow.

They also thought about blowing up the school or some other big building. Or they would talk about assassinating some asshole politician. They used to feed on each other's thoughts and would get so worked up that Jamaal often had to get away from Frank just to catch his breath and escape from their heady descent into *darkness*.

But Jamaal also knew that Frank was serious; In fact, he often seemed more fervent and intent on taking action than Jamaal. But Jamaal was smarter than Frank.

"Frank" Jamaal would say "Any of these plans for mayhem will require a considerable amount of planning, and we will need money to buy weapons, and weapons are not that easy to come by. Especially since Columbine."

But Jamaal is serious about wanting to do these things too, because they excited him, and made him feel alive. There is something at the core of it all that aligned with both his *logic* and his *emotions*. He fantasized about how superior he would feel once he had accomplished one of the many schemes he and Frank had worked on.

 He just knew that once his family, friends, and others, found out that he committed one of these incredible deeds, they would not only understand how smart and powerful he was, but they would also feel some of the pain that he feels.

But mostly there is the energy*, dark* as it may be, that came from the feeling that he is the only one that truly had the power, the power to change lives, the power to end lives. Jamaal wondered why these forces, that made him feel bad, could also provide him with the drive to become so powerful.

Jamaal's mother is a working mom, so she is gone most of the day, leaving at about 5:30 AM every day, before Jamaal got up for school, and she often worked late, sometimes not getting home until after midnight.

Jamaal's brother is always gone, why not; there is no one around to keep track of him. He is one year older than Jamaal, had lots of friends, and spent most his time with them. He is very popular because he is tall, athletic, good-looking, and a sports star at the high school. Jamaal's mother adored Jamaal's older brother, and in her eyes, he could do no wrong. So, Jamaal is alone all day long in the summertime, and even though there were other kids and teachers around when he was at school, he was still very much alone.

Jamaal felt that his mother did not care for him at all; he thought that his birth must have been a mistake and that his mother just wanted to forget that he was ever born. He had over the years attempted to extract some attention from her. He would try to get that attention by doing something good like cleaning the house, and sometimes by doing something bad like breaking something or stealing something small at school or at one of the local stores.

When he did something good often his mother never even noticed. She would come home, look around at the clean house and say "Have you seen your brother? I wonder when he's getting home." Or if she did notice she would say something like "Oh! You cleaned the house, that's nice." And go on about her business. If he did something bad like the time, he stole the action character from the hobby store. She would go to the store, pay for the stolen item and then get really angry with Jamaal. But there were never any consequences, very little or no punishment, and she would make some sort of excuse for Jamaal like it's probably because he doesn't have a father figure in his life. But Jamaal knew, it was because she did not care enough about Jamaal to actually expend the effort it would take to discipline him. She is much too wrapped up in her own life, and that of his older brother's, to care about Jamaal.

Jamaal was a good student in school, basically because he was so smart that the subject *matter* was easy for him, and he actually liked studying. It was something to do to keep his mind busy when he was alone. But sometimes he would purposely fail a subject to get his moms attention. And it did, but not in the way he wanted. His mom did not like the bother of having to go to school and talk to teachers. She is too busy at work, or whatever the hell she is doing. She is always working on something away from home.

Rather than talking to him to determine why he is acting the way he is, she would say "you're grounded for a week and no television." Like she was ever around to enforce such threats. Or she would say, "I want you to just study harder". He really hated this because she did not have a clue. She didn't even realize that he was staying home all the time anyway because he had no friends and no place to go, and he was already studying enough to easily pass all his courses, and he hated TV, he would rather play video games.

However, that was not what bothered Jamaal the most. What bothered him the most was when she was around his brother. All she could do was go on and on about how great he was, and how much she loved him, and how she saw his picture in the paper after they won the big game, and who is he dating now? Is she the captain of the cheerleading squad? Where does he want to go to college? Does he want to be a doctor or a lawyer or an engineer? She just knows he will be great at whatever he decides to do.

Jamaal would sometimes try to join in the conversation, but his mother would say "Jamaal, please do not interrupt, can't you see we're talking." Jamaal felt they treated him like he was not even in the room, and after a while, he wasn't. As soon as they got together, he would leave, either go up to his room, or go outside and walk around the block, thinking about how someday he would do something that would really get their attention, or maybe he would just kill both of them. Often when he thought of getting rid of them, he would sometimes think that it was not his brother's fault, it was really that bitches' fault, and if he eliminated her, maybe he and his brother could actually have some kind of relationship. But at that time, it was just a lot of thought that would constantly eat at Jamaal, with really no action.

Because Jamaal was a very intelligent person, *logically* he could understand a lot of the drivers in his life, but *emotionally* he could hardly deal with any of them.

So here he sits wishing he could get out of Denver, but not being able to budge.

Jamaal is aware that today's date was *April 19th*. He knew that the date was significant because it was the date when the government had killed the Branch Davidians in Waco Texas, and it was the date of the Oklahoma City bombing in 1995.

Maybe someday, I can add to this list.

But this was just a dream for Jamaal at this point in his life.

CHAPTER 25 – HIS ENTRANCE INTO PARADISE

September 11th, 2001
CyrIS Steel, Age 51

CyrIS wakes with a start. He is lying next to Ester in their luxurious home in the *Outer Richmond* district of San Francisco.

CyrIS loves being with Ester. They have been married now for almost five years. CyrIS and Ester do everything together, which is exactly the way he likes it, and CyrIS has vowed to never be far from Ester's side, fearing she would have another episode like those with the Reverend Jim Jones or David Koresh. It has been almost eight years, since the last event, and he is not sure if it would ever happen again, but he stayed close enough to be there if it did.

CyrIS, experiencing a bit of an upset stomach, and not wanting to wake Ester, got up and went to the bathroom. Afterward, he lays on the couch and tries to get back to sleep, it is about 2:30 am.

After just a few minutes, CyrIS dozes off, immediately he hears something he had never heard before, it is the sound of someone speaking in Arabic, but only a whisper.

"Be busy with the constant remembrance of God. God said 'Oh, ye faithful, when you find the enemy, be steadfast and remember God constantly, so that you may be successful.'"

"When the vehicle moves, even slightly toward the goal, say the supplication of travel. Because you are traveling to Almighty God, so be attentive on this trip."

CyrIS is confused, he can see nothing but darkness. He can feel his own lips, and tongue forming the Arabic words but, in his mind, he understands their meaning.

Then, eyes open. He is in line. Apparently in line to board an airplane. CyrIS reads the marquee above the airline reception desk and determined that he is currently in Portland Main, and the flight is to Boston Massachusetts, and it is departing a 6:00 AM.

CyrIS trying hard to orient himself, begins to realize, that what he is experiencing, is just like that described by Ester when she was trying to explain to CyrIS what she experienced in her journeys with Jim Jones and David Koresh.

CyrIS was shocked, he could not believe this was now happening to him. But here he was, he could feel his legs moving along with his host as he entered the plane, he could feel everything this person was doing and thinking as his host took his seat, just like Ester had described.

"What is going on here? Why am I here?" thought CyrIS.

Based on what had happened to Ester he was sure this was no simple journey, he had learned a lot from Ester's experiences, and he knew some of the things he needed to look for. He was sure there would be opportunities for learning, but that's not all. He and Ester had discussed her journeys at length and one thing they both agreed on was, that there were key points in her journeys when action could have been taken that would have averted an apparent disaster. And if at that point, she could have disengaged from her host, then 'that action' could have been taken external to her host.

However, they were never able to determine exactly how this disengagement could be accomplished, and because he had not awakened Ester, before he started this journey, he did not have her to help him, and had no way to get her help. The only thing he could do was to stay observant and see if he could detect those critical moments, and then see if he could, in any way, disengage.

As they had entered the plane, CyrIS' host had turned and looked at the fellow behind him. A very solemn Arabic looking fellow, to which he spoke to in Arabic, "God be with you." The fellow had replied the same, and they each continued to their seats in separate parts of the plane.

"Well, he has an accomplice." CyrIS thought.

CyrIS, now sitting in the coach section of the plane, was asking himself; "Are these guys planning on hijacking this plane?" CyrIS' host looked at his wristwatch, it was 5:55 AM, and then more prayers and some sort of inner thought.

Shehhi, Jarrah, and Hanjour should be arriving at their airports with their teams by now.

"Are there more?" CyrIS thought, now growing much more concerned. "Airports? Where are all these guys going, and what are they planning on doing? It wouldn't make sense for this to be a hijacking with people at different airports. They must be going someplace."

As the plane took off CyrIS waited, listening to the drone of the plane engines and the incessant internal repetition of prayers.

After an hour or so, CyrIS could hear that familiar feeling of reduction in acceleration, as the airplane began to descend, and then the deployment of the landing gear.

"Surely, if this guy was planning on hijacking this plane, he would have done it by now."

But nothing happened, the landing was normal and CyrIS' host and his accomplice departed the plane with no incident, they were now in Boston.

Upon leaving the plane CyrIS' host went directly to the men's room. After using one of the urinals, the man went to wash his hands, now approaching the mirror, CyrIS could see the man's face.

"I know this man. Where have I seen this guy before?" CyrIS searched his mind. "Airports? Airports? Oh, now I remember." CyrIS recalled a presentation that Ester and he had given at the 'Auburn Road Presbyterian Academy' in Venice Florida, in early July of this year.

When they arrived at the Venice airport, CyrIS had needed to use the restroom. While entering the restroom, he had literally run into a man that was leaving. The man looked shocked, and at first, did not say anything just stared into CyrIS' eyes. CyrIS was shocked as well, and not just because of the collision. Something else happened when they had touched each other, and they both knew it.

After a couple seconds of staring at the man, the man said with a deep Arabic accent, "Excuse me, sir." And went on his way. CyrIS said nothing at the time and watched, as the man walked away. CyrIS knew at that time, the incident was not insignificant, but did not say anything to Ester, knowing it would have only caused her to worry, and she worried about everything.

"But now, here he is, and so am I. Why? Why is he here? What does all of this mean?" CyrIS was growing frustrated with all the clues and very little answers. He hated it when things didn't make sense.

But then as the man finished washing his hands, he bent over and picked up the small carry-on bag, with the name tag; Mohamed Atta.

Atta then retrieved a boarding pass from the bag and left the restroom. Now CyrIS had a name, but he still had no clue as to what this man was planning.

As Atta approached the boarding area to his apparent connecting flight, CyrIS noticed two very large Arabic looking men turn and look towards Atta. The men nodded their heads and Atta returned the gesture, but no words were spoken.

"More accomplices. I am really concerned about where this is headed." CyrIS thought.

The marquee above the reception desk, indicated that they were about to board American Airlines, flight 11, to Los Angeles California, departing at 7:45 AM. And then the airline receptionist announced the boarding of first-class passengers, military personnel, and passengers with small children. Atta watched as the two large men disappeared into the tunnel leading to the plane. "These two guys are apparently flying first class." Thought CyrIS. "Maybe they are the bosses of this operation because it appears that this guy, Atta, is flying Business Class."

And now CyrIS heard Atta reviewing something besides prayers, it seemed to be some kind of instructions.

Do not seem confused or show signs of nervous tension. Be happy, optimistic, and calm.

CyrIS felt Atta force a smile.

You are heading for a deed that God loves and will accept. It will be the day, God willing, you will spend with the women of paradise.

"It's almost as if," CyrIS thought, "this guy is receiving directions from someone, are at least remembering these directions from someone, and he is using these directions to hype himself up for something big.".

CyrIS' thoughts continued, "'This day you will spend with women of paradise?' It sounds like this guy is planning on killing himself."

But then CyrIS realized something, he could feel that even though Atta was following some directions, and praying to himself, he needed neither, because he was absolutely convinced, that what he was doing, was the right thing to do, because he was doing it for God.

CyrIS was shocked by this man's *absolute belief* and invariable commitment. "No one could change this guy's mind, about what he is doing." CyrIS thought. "It's terrifying to think that there could be more out there, just like this one."

In no time Atta was in his seat on the plane and sitting next to him was the guy that had flown with him from Portland. After just a short amount of time, Atta looked at his watch again, and it was 7:45 AM, and the plane was beginning its departure. Atta said a short prayer and then began to review something else in his mind. "More directions?" CyrIS thought.

Remind your soul to listen and obey and remember that you will face decisive situations that may prevent you from one hundred percent obedience, so tame your soul, purify it, convince it, make it understand, and incite it. God said, "Obey God and His Messenger and do not fight among yourselves or you will fail. And be patient, for God is with the patient."

CyrIS agreed with Atta, "I have to be patient as well, I don't want to try to extract myself from this situation until I know what they are planning. ---That is, if I can extract myself."

About 15 minutes into the flight, one of the large Arabic men setting in a seat in the very front of 'first class', stood up and looked back at Atta. Atta nodded his head and the man sat back down, but Atta continued to concentrate his attention on the front of the plane.

"Something's happening." CyrIS thought.

As Atta watched, a stewardess approached the cockpit door and it opened. Immediately the two large men in the front of the plane jumped up, grabbed the stewardess and forced their way into the cockpit.

"It's happening. It's a hijacking" CyrIS thought, but Atta did not move. And then another man with a bright red scarf tied around his forehead, jumped up from a seat, right in front of Atta. He pulled, what looked like a bomb, out of his shirt, and raised something above his head for everyone to see, and it was a small trigger device of some sort, with a wire running back to and attached to, the bomb. He held the trigger device down with his thumb, indicating that if it was released it, the bomb would detonate.

Atta and his companion then stood up and looked around. CyrIS observed another hijacker with a red scarf and knife in hand, move up next to the man holding the bomb. Atta looked to the rear of the plane, where another man with a red scarf, had reached over the seat in front of him and was slashing the throat of the man who was sitting there.

"Oh! My God, this is complete chaos." CyrIS thinks.

Atta returned his vision to the front of the plane, and CyrIS could see one of the large men emerge from the cockpit. Atta and his companion immediately moved quickly in that direction. In no time he and his companion were in the cockpit. It was a horrifying scene, there was blood everywhere and the two pilots were behind the pilot seats on the floor, both with their throats slit.

Atta and his companion sat down in the pilot and co-pilot seats. The plane was apparently on autopilot. Atta immediately looked down at the control panel, and then at his watch, it was 8:25 AM. Atta then flicked a switch on the intercom, apparently to make an announcement to the passengers.

"We have some planes." CyrIS immediately recognized the heavily accented English, from the Venice airport. Remembering how strange Ester had said it was to feel someone else speak, he heard himself say…his host say, "Just stay quiet and you will be okay. We're returning to the airport." A few moments later, Atta followed with: "Nobody move. Everything will be okay. If you try to make any moves, you'll endanger yourself and the airplane. Just stay quiet."

Atta then moved the control on the 'Transponder' to another frequency, which was the maximum on the dial.

"He doesn't want them to know where the plane is," CyrIS concluded. "Well I've seen enough; I need to get myself out of this situation so I can do something about it." But no matter how much mental effort CyrIS poured into his attempts to escape, nothing changed.

Atta made some adjustments to the autopilot. He then just sat at the controls and did nothing for some time. After a while he once again looked at his watch, it was 8:44 AM. Atta reached to the control panels again and this time switched the autopilot to the 'Off' position.

The plane immediately went into a nosedive. CyrIS could hear screams from the back of the plane, as he felt Atta struggling to get the plane under control. Atta finally gained control of the plane, however at a much lower altitude.

"If he was planning on crashing the plane," CyrIS thought "why didn't he just let it crash? He must have something else in mind."

Atta looked up, and CyrIS could see downtown New York in the distance, and approaching very quickly. It looked like Atta was going to fly the plane right by the World Trade Center twin towers. But then he slowly moved the yoke of the plane, and it made a slight bank to the left. Now the plane was aimed directly at one of the towers. Atta said:

"God is great"

CyrIS felt Atta push the throttle forward for maximum thrust and watched in total disbelief. The plane hurtling toward this tower directly in front of them, the windows of the building growing in size, faster and faster. Atta released the yoke, spread his arms wide, bent his head slightly backward, apparently accepting his entrance into paradise ---- and then it hit. In a flash, CyrIS felt the yoke of the plane passing through Atta's body, glass, metal, and concrete ripping everything apart, and then nothing but *darkness*.

CyrIS was back in his home, disoriented but home.

"What the hell?" CyrIS is thinking, "Was that real? Where am I? Where's Ester? I've got to talk to her."

"What time is it?" The clock on the wall indicated it was 5:52 AM CyrIS is again confused.

"How could it be that early? Is it the next day, I swear Atta's watch last read 8:46 AM. Oh! No! Wait! The time difference, they were on the East Coast, three hours difference".

CyrIS jumped to his feet and rushed into the bedroom. "Ester wake up! Wake up!" he screamed.

Ester slightly lifting her head from the pillow; "What is it? Why did you wake me up, I was ….?" But CyrIS interrupted, "Just be quiet and listen. Are you awake? This is important."

Ester sat up in bed. "I'm awake. What's going on?"

"It happened! It happened to me! You know the journey."

Ester was trying to process what CyrIS was saying, and desperately trying to push the cobwebs from her brain. "You mean like my journeys with Jones and Koresh?"

"Yes exactly, it was incredible, and I just got out of it a few minutes ago. Oh! Shit! We need to turn on the TV." CyrIS grabbed the remote control off the stand next to their bed and aimed it at large flat screen on the wall. He pushed the 'on' button and the TV came to life.

Immediately they saw an image of the World Trade Center, one of the buildings was on fire, and the smoke was filling the clear blue skies of the New York skyline.

Ester said "Oh My Gosh! What has happened?"

The announcer was saying, "Apparently a plane has accidentally crashed into the North Tower of the World Trade Center. It occurred at 8:46 AM eastern time and emergency crews are on their way."

"Oh! My God! They think it was an accident." CyrIS exclaimed, "Ester, this was not an accident, I was on that plane and this is terrorism, and there are more planes, maybe three or more. I have got to get in touch with the authorities" But CyrIS now with a perplexed look on his face continued with, "Whoever that is?"

CyrIS looked at the clock on the vanity, it said it was 6:02 AM. CyrIS picked up the phone. "Who do I call? 911?"

Ester screamed, "Oh! My God! Oh! My God! CyrIS look!"

CyrIS turned his attention to the TV, only to see a second plane headed for the other Trade Center tower. In just seconds, they watched as this plane tore through the lower part of the South Tower, a huge ball of fire ejecting from the opposite side.

CyrIS stood up. "Oh! My God! We are under attack. What do I do? I am sure there are other planes?"

And then CyrIS dialed 911.

"Nine-one-one, what is your emergency." The operator answered.

CyrIS did not know where to begin. "Can you connect me with the FBI?"

"Sorry sir, we are only set up for contact with 'local' emergency response." The operator responded, speaking calmly not knowing the world was coming to an end, "Can you please tell me the nature of your emergency?"

CyrIS realized this approach was futile. "I'm sorry," he said, "I will call them directly." And then hung up.

"Ester, what about your guy at the FBI? What's his name? Chapman?"

CHAPTER 26 – THE DEVIL MAY CRY

December 12th, 2002
Jamaal Dell, age 17

Jamaal, all alone in the hallway of his high school, opened his locker. As usual, he was late for class, but he really didn't care.

They probably won't even notice that I am not there until I show up.

Pulling his math book from his locker, he noticed a small white piece of paper on the shelf in the back of his locker. It looked as if it had been pushed to the back of the locker when he had put his books in.

He reached in and retrieved the note and was startled by what he saw. He immediately looked around to see if anyone was watching him. *Was this a trap? Was someone about to spring something on him to embarrass and enrage him?* He felt the temperature in his body rising.

A quick look up and down the hallway, found no attackers. Jamaal's heart was beating so loud he could hear it in his ears. But there was nothing going on, and after a moment, Jamaal felt a bit embarrassed by his reaction.

"Where did that come from? Why am I so paranoid? He said softly to himself.

After he caught his breath and settled down, he read the note again, and again.

Jamaal

I know you are in my English class and sit in the back of the class. Do you have a girlfriend? Would you ever like to have a girlfriend? Where do you live? My friends say you moved here from the south someplace, but no one seems to know for sure.

I like you and would like to talk to you sometime. If you want, we can meet after school tonight, in the park on Maple Street, about 7:00 PM.
Cathy Schmidt

Jamaal had been startled by the note, because he did not know that Cathy even knew he existed. That was because she along with everyone else in the school mostly ignored him. Early on, some of the kids had tried to include him in their activities, but after a while, they got tired of his moody negative attitude and stopped asking him. That was, except for Frank, who also had a grudge against everyone.

Then Jamaal remembered something that happened in his English class on Tuesday. They were moving to their seats, when he had looked up at the front of the class, and that girl Cathy, who really had never even looked at him before, turned and smiled at him. He remembered thinking that the smile looked very genuine and he also remembered how it had made him feel warm inside. He was sure his face had flushed a bit at the time. All though it was virtually undetectable by any observer, because of the dark color of his skin. Besides he was a master at not giving any indication of what he was feeling inside, and he was sure that Cathy could see no reaction from her smile. He was suspicious, but allowed himself to fantasize a bit.

She might really want to meet with me, after all, what was all that smiling about?

Now his mind was bent toward a new problem.

When was this note put in my locker? There is no date on the note. If it was put in there by Cathy, maybe it was last week, and she wanted to meet last Thursday. If so, that meant I missed the meeting, and maybe she thought I snubbed her.

Does she really like me or is this an effort by some of the students who hate me, and who are way up on my "pick off list", just trying to set me up, like I've seen in some of those movies like "RED" or "Carry."

In any case, as always, Jamaal was very suspicious and decided he would not take any action yet, he was not going to fall into this trap. He would remain *logical* and in control. He was afraid, that if he opened up to anyone, they would find his vulnerabilities and that would put him at risk.

It was Thursday and that meant English class at 2:00. He was now looking forward to seeing Cathy and possibly another smile, especially given the note he received. He really hoped it was *not* some kind of setup.

He had a short break between classes, and this is when he usually met up with Frank. They would meet behind the school shops, on the south side of the campus, where they could have a smoke and discuss how the school assholes were treating them.

Jamaal wanted to discuss this note situation with Frank, but he also wanted to be careful to not give him all the details. He was concerned about Frank's reaction. If the meeting with Cathy was not an ambush and he had not blown the date of the meeting, then he did not want Frank to somehow mess it up. He just wanted to meet with Cathy, and he wanted it to not be 'fucked up' like everything else in his life.

At the usual time, behind the shops, Jamaal met with Frank, who was already there and smoking a cigarette. Frank looked like a gangster, in his leather jacket and leaning against the dumpster. He had once told Jamaal, that most of his relatives were mobsters, and he would often say:

"Hey! Don't fuck with me, I'm Sicilian."

Jamaal was not sure he could believe everything that Frank said, but he certainly looked the part.

Jamaal asked Frank "How's it going?" Frank shrugged his shoulders, not replying. He looked like he was down, probably something at home; his family life was not very good, but it might have been something that happened in school that day. Jamaal didn't usually pry, if Frank wanted to talk about it, he would. They sat there for a while and did not say anything. Then Jamaal decided to expose his problem to Frank.

"Frank, Cathy Schmidt said she wants to talk to me." Jamaal did not show Frank the note, that was too personal, so he gave Frank as little information as possible. He was not surprised by Frank's reaction. Frank went off like a sniper's machine gun.

"That fat pig, what does she want? She probably has some god damned plot that she, and those other fucking bitches, are working out, to fuck you over. I would tell her to get fucked! I think she's trying to fuck you and not in a good way. Everybody in this school is trying to fuck you and me, I think they sit around in those teachers lounges and just think up ways to screw us, and it's not just the teachers, I know those fucking classmates of ours are definitely plotting to get us. I can't wait for the day we can get our hands on some awesome firepower and go in there and blow every one of their fucking heads off.

So, What? --- Did she just come up to you and say she wanted to talk?"

Jamaal just shrugged his shoulders in reply.

Frank went on. "You know what? Maybe you can turn this around and somehow get in her pants and fuck her over and her friends too. Boy wouldn't that be great, we should think about how we can do that. I would love to watch you fuck her, and then watch you fuck her over. You know what I'd like to do. I'd like to shoot her in the head, and then fuck the hell out of her dead body."

Jamaal did not say anything he just sat and listened to Frank go on and on about fucking Cathy over and then the rest of the girls in the school, and then the boys, and then the teachers and parents and the whole rest of society.

Even though Jamaal agreed with most of what Frank was saying, especially the part about taking some heavy loads of ammunition into the school and really fucking the place up, he was not so sure this thing with Cathy was some kind of a setup, he had seen that smile from Cathy and it seemed so genuine, and right now, he could sure use some friendship or something that was not Frank. Whatever it was he was looking for, he certainly was not getting it at home, or anywhere else for that matter, and there seemed to be a *hole* inside of him that longed for something to fill it.

After they finished their smokes Frank headed off toward the school, he did not say anything else about the Cathy situation, he seemed to have his own problems to contend with and walked off with his head down and shoulders shrugged. Jamaal was happy that there was no more discussion and headed off for his own class.

When Jamaal arrived at his English class he went to his seat and looked up at the front of the room to see Cathy. She was there as usual, but she did not look back at Jamaal, no smile, no nothing. He was disappointed, but as usual, showed no emotions to his classmates. He was sure now that he must have missed the date and that she must be upset with him. He was also sure that any chances he might have had, were lost.

Then he thought:

Maybe I foiled the plot they had to embarrass me and since the plot had failed there was no longer any need for Cathy to come on to me.

He sat there and ran all these thoughts over and over in his mind until class was over. He got up to leave, looked up at Cathy, but still no smile. He was not sure what to think.

Most girls are bitches, I really have no time for this.

After school ended at about 3:30 PM Jamaal headed home to the house that was always empty. He actually liked it empty these days, because he hated being around his mother, who was always preoccupied with something that Jamaal could give a shit about. Besides, she never talked to him about anything anyway, so he would rather be alone.

As soon as he got home, he worked on his homework. He liked to get his homework done as soon as he could, so he wouldn't have to worry about it the rest of the evening, and he could play "Devil May Cry", his favorite '*hack and slash*' video game on the Play Station 2 that his dad had sent him. Or he could just watch TV or search the internet for whatever he was interested in at that time.

Jamaal always did his homework, not because he wanted to please the teachers and certainly not to please his mother, and not even to impress the other students. There was only one reason he did it, and that was to keep all of them off his back. He was actually smart enough to get all A's, but that would bring attention to him, and he just didn't want it. His purpose was to stay in the *middle* of the pack, do just enough so that his mom and teachers thought he was doing okay, and not so much that they would want to give him any praise or special attention. He wanted just to be left alone. However, there was one area that he really enjoyed, and that was writing, and he was good at it and had difficulty keeping his English grades below A's. So, as an outlet for this passion, he had recently started to write for an underground internet news blog. He was presently writing articles on "The excess of 'Hippocrates' in today's society" and he was attracting quite a following.

As he sat there doing his homework he could not stop thinking about Cathy. *Did I blow it?* Well, there was one way to find out, and that was to go to the park at 7:00 tonight, stay out of sight and see if she shows up.

Like everything in his life, he had to plan this out. He wanted to make sure that he did not get caught in some kind of a trap. He was always careful to think through all the details of how he would attack any situation that might be dangerous or might result in his embarrassment.

The park was small, so there would not be a lot of places for her to wait. He knew he would have to check out the area to make sure there were no other kids waiting to jump out at him for the big "Put Down". This would require him to leave the house a couple of hours early and circle the block several times to see if anyone was gathering that might be a threat. He would then need to find the right spot to stand and observe the park. This would require him to move around the neighborhood and check out several vantage points. The more he worked on the details, the more he liked it. It began to feel like preparation for an assassination. He was getting kind of excited as he planned each step. First he started planning his escape routes and then he thought about the types of weapons he might use if this was an assassination. But he also was thinking about something else, something really important. That was; what if she does show up, what if this is not a setup, then what; what was he going to do then?

This was almost like the kill shot; it was the most important part of the whole event and it was not something that he had rehearsed in his head like he had with assassinations so many times. This was a real dilemma. What would he say to her? He thought that his best approach would be to stay aloof. Tell her that he got her note and just ask her what she wanted. This would put the burden on her to hold up the conversation. But, what if during the conversation he realized that she really liked him. What then?

He hated this, how does one plan for the unknown, he did not like dealing with things beyond his control. In school and with his parents and with his classmates, all he had to do, was to just meet their simple expectations and keep a low profile, and then he could stay in control. But this was different, he wanted something from her, but he was not sure exactly what it was, or how to get it.

He finally determined, even though he hated it, that this might mean he would have to play it by ear. That is, he would have to have a conversation with her, not knowing what she would say or do, and then react, hopefully leading her to what he wanted. And yet, at the same time he would not be sure where he wanted it to go. All these thoughts had almost made him decide not to go to the park at all.

Eventually, he came to the conclusion that, *logically* there were more reasons to go than to not go. He liked the planning and scoping out of the area. He liked the idea of executing his escape plans if it turned out to be a trap. He liked finding the best place to observe the park and he liked the idea of observing her without her seeing him. He especially liked the idea of being able to pick her off with a high-powered weapon if he chose to do so. He told himself that if everything went exactly right and she was there, and it was not a trap, he could always just bail out. That way, he would not have to endure a very uncomfortable conversation that would be mostly out of his control.

Once Jamaal arrived at that park, he started by circling the park, just as he had planned. He had thought this through very carefully and made sure that if he ran into anyone who might ask him where he was going, he would have a reason for walking in that direction no matter which way he was going. After observing no suspicious activity in that circle, he then walked up one of the blocks that lead to the park and down one block along the park and then back one block to the original circle. He did this again and again until he had completely encircled the park and walked all the streets that led to the park.

This process had two purposes, one to see if there were any places that someone could hide and observe from. The second was to find the best place for he himself to observe the park.

It took him almost an hour to complete this process, and he did not see any signs of a trap being formed. He then picked a spot that he felt was a good observation point. It was on a side street behind some cars.

From this point, he could see the entire park and there was a fire hydrant for him to sit on. He also chose this street because it had the least traffic. If anyone asked him why he was there, he would tell them that he was supposed to meet a friend at that location and that it did not appear that his friend was going to show up, then he would just leave.

At about 6:50 PM he saw Cathy walking into the park. This made Jamaal's heart race. He then became keenly observant of all the side streets for any additional activity that might signal a trap and constantly looked behind him as well to make sure no one was sneaking up.

Cathy sat at a park bench and did not move, she was wearing the same dress that she had on at school, it was pink and pretty and she looked great in it. Jamaal was happy that he had not missed the day she would be there, and he was happy that, at least thus far, it did not appear to be a trap.

But now the dilemma. In some way he almost wished it had been a trap, he had plans all worked out on how he would deal with that. What he didn't have worked out was how he would deal with the thing he was hoping for most, which was, her being there just to meet up with him.

He sat on the fire hydrant and watched her, he had at least ten minutes until they were supposed to meet, and he thought he could probably count on a couple of minutes after 7:00 before she would give up and leave. So, he just sat and watched her. The longer he watched, the more he wanted to talk to her, she was very pretty, and he thought that if he blew this opportunity there may never be another, and he was sure he would never have the nerve to initiate another meeting. So, he sat there trying to build some confidence.

How could he do this, maybe he would just walk by and act like he had never seen the note, but just happen to be in the area? Or go back to the hard-nosed approach of "Got your note, what do you want?" Neither of these really appealed to him, he wanted to be smooth, he wanted to be cool. He finally decided what he would do and started walking towards her.

When he was about fifty feet away from her, she saw him, stood up and smiled. When he got to within ten feet of her, he said.

"I hope this is not some kind of a hoax. That you didn't just invite me here, to pull some kind of trick on me. Because if that is true, people could get hurt, don't mess with me."

Cathy, with a very shocked look on her face said, "No, no. This is not a trick; I just wanted to meet you and maybe get to know you better."

There was silence for a moment and then Jamaal said. "Well, I'm here."

Cathy seemed taken back a bit, by this abrupt approach, but then said.

"Do you like our English teacher?"

"I guess he's OK, he doesn't bother me as much as some of the other teachers."

Cathy looked perplexed.

Maybe I am coming across too strong. Jamaal thinks

Cathy then asked, "Do you like school?"

" I hate School" he replies.

By the look on Cathy's face, Jamaal could see that she was getting discouraged. Jamaal kept repeating in his mind.

Don't blow this, don't blow this.

Cathy seemed to take a deep breath and began again. "I saw that you got an 'A' on that last paper we had to write."

"Yea, I like to write."

Cathy smiled and replied, "I would love to read some of your writing's some time."

"Well, maybe some time." Jamaal replied with no smile.

"What do you do for fun?" Cathy was really smiling now, and Jamaal decided to make his best effort to be sociable and try to be more positive in his responses.

"Well I play video games and I like to do research and write on the internet."

"No sports?" she said.

This was a sore spot for Jamaal, given that his older brother was the 'Big Athlete' in the family.

"Not really". He said calmly.

The conversation went on like this for some time. She would ask him a question and he would respond trying to keep it positive.

Once, she asked about another one of his teachers, and Jamaal imitated the teacher's voice and said: "Come on Jamaal, you can do better than that".

Cathy laughed out loud at this and showed her perfect white teeth. Jamaal really liked that and tried a couple more times to make her laugh with less success but did manage to make her smile a few times.

Jamaal was really enjoying the conversation and he was proud of himself for mustering up the courage to make the long painful trip across the park to talk to her.

She had been carrying most of the conversation by asking him simple questions, with him responding with short succinct answers. But now he decided to ask her some questions. He started by trying to find out if she liked some of the things, he was interested in.

"Do you like video games?"

"I don't know much about video games, I like reading books, and there are some TV shows I like to watch. I also like talking on the phone with my girlfriends, and we like to talk about…..."

Jamaal's responses to her questions were short and to the point, but when he asked her a question, she would go on and on. Sometimes he was not even sure she answered the question, and she never really seemed to get to the point he was after, which was trying to determine where they might have some mutual interest.

He was certainly not interested in most of the things she was talking about, but he did like to hear her talk, she had a nice voice and she would often smile or sometimes frown to emphasize her point, and Jamaal loved to watch her face and see her smile.

At one-point Jamaal got really brave and said.

"You look nice in that dress"

Cathy suddenly stopped talking, smiled, blushed and said: "Thank you".

Then they just sat there in the silence for a while. Jamaal was wondering what she was thinking, and he was also feeling a little uncomfortable. It seemed as if she was waiting for him to say something else, but he wasn't sure what it was.

"I like to play the video game called "Devil May Cry.""

Cathy frowned "Is that the one, where they kill all of the people, all of the time?"

Jamaal could tell Cathy was not pleased with his choice in games.

"Well yes, but it is more than that, there is a lot of strategy and planning involved to become the master assassin."

She still had a look on her face like she just stepped in something very disgusting on the street. Jamaal tried to change the subject

"What teachers do you like at school?"

This made her light up and she was off and talking once again. Jamaal was pretty sure that they had nothing in common, except for their somewhat unlikely attraction for each other. He was determined to try to hang on to whatever relationship that they may be developing, at least for a while.

After an hour in the park, Cathy said:

"I have to go home now, but I could meet you here again sometime?"

Jamaal agreed and they set up a time for their next meeting. Jamaal said in parting "Cathy please do not let anyone else know that we're meeting. There are some people at school who would like to make me look stupid and they would take advantage of our meeting."

Cathy agreed that she would keep their meetings their secret, and they parted.

CHAPTER 27 – CAN I TRUST YOU?

March 15th, 2003
Jamaal Dell, age 18

KNOCK! KNOCK! KNOCK! Jamaal jumped hearing the loud knocking on the front door of his home. His mother, as usual, was gone, and only God knows where his brother could be. The knocking scared Jamaal a bit.

Could it be the police?

Over the past three months, with Cathy's encouragement, Jamaal had been developing a strong belief in Jesus Christ, and now realized that by strictly following the teachings of the bible one could survive life. At least this strict approach had seemed to be filling in some of the voids in Jamaal's life and made him realize, how others, including his screwed-up family, treated him, really didn't matter.

Christ gave up his life for all the sinners on earth, and now I am prepared to dedicate my life to protect the teachings of Christ, at all cost, even if it means giving up my own life.

I am a crusader for Christ, and now I realize that this is my purpose in life, to eradicate those that are a threat to all of Christ teachings.

It is obvious to me that almost everyone in this high school is either a hypocrite or some kind of techie elitist, ranting on about how evolution and how other scientific facts prove the fallacy of all religions.

They say they want to do 'good', or they say their intent is righteous, but on a daily basis they are lying and cheating and screwing someone like me, over and over.

This was now the focus of Jamaal's online blogs, and he was attracting a substantially large following. So, about a month ago when Jamaal and Frank first got together and discussed how they were going to massacre all of the fucking hypocrites and techies in their high school, Jamaal constantly reminded Frank that it would require planning, and it would require firepower and that was something that would not be easy to come by.

Frank had said "Let's just get online and buy some stuff. "

Jamaal had agreed that online was the place to do their shopping, but they had to be careful. You needed to be 21 and you had to have permits to own certain kinds of guns and ammo, especially the kind of semi-automatic weapons they were wanting. And there was a thing called the "Brady Law" which required a waiting period before you could buy guns. It would also take some money to buy this stuff, and even if they had money, they would need to figure out how to get it to the merchants, without leaving tracks leading back to themselves.

But Jamaal felt it could be done with the proper planning.

Jamaal had said to Frank; "Here is what we will do, we will start out small. I have an allowance, and I will start saving some money. I know you don't have much, but you can put in whatever you can."

"First, we will have to find an excuse to be doing these types of searches online. I have been hoping I will get an assignment at school to write a paper, which would give me an excuse to look into guns and ammo, false IDs, all the stuff we need. But I believe we can start by looking into false IDs. If anyone gets on to us, we can just say we were trying to get them, so we could buy some booze. That would not be too suspicious for teenage boys. Once we get the IDs we can start looking into ammo, which might not raise as much suspicion as buying the guns themselves. Hopefully, through our searches for the ammo, we can find leads to the weapons themselves."

Frank had said at that time: "The hell with all that, I know a guy, he's over 21, and he'll get whatever guns and ammo we want, it will just cost us." But Jamaal had responded, being ever so cautious "I'd rather not involve anyone else if we can avoid it. That's how people get caught. I'm not like those idiots at 'Columbine', I don't plan on getting killed or even caught when we're done with this."

"That's cool." Frank agreed.

So, they had started searching for false IDs online. At first, they ran into histories of false IDs and some warnings from the FBI that it was illegal to manufacture false IDs. But, on the internet, it seems like you never get directly to what you are looking for. One site leads to another and eventually, if you are persistent, you may find what you are looking for, and that is exactly what happened.

They found a site that professed its ability to develop any kind of false ID you might want, complete with photo and appropriate official seals. They advertised that they were especially proficient at American driver's licenses and showed copies of licenses they had produced in different states, including Colorado. They indicated that they could accept credit or debit cards, money orders, or even bank transfers, all they needed was a routing number and an account number. Once they received payment, they would send the IDs and they were only $150 each.

Jamaal had been very suspicious because of the many misspellings and grammatical errors on their web page, and he laughed at the idea of sending them routing and account numbers for a bank account. He assumed this must be from another country, maybe Mexico or maybe some offshore operation.

He told Frank "If we send them money, there is a very good chance that we will never see it again, and not get any IDs either. But I think, it's worth a $300 bet that we will get something."

The site asked for a digital photo and some of the personal information that was needed for the license. The site said they had the ability search state records to find a similar name and use that license number on a driver's license, which would make it a lot harder to detect as false when making purchases using the ID.

That had all sounded great to Jamaal and Frank. So, they filled out the form and clicked the button that indicated they would be following up with a money order mailed to the PO Box indicated by the site. Jamaal already had at least $300, in his savings account. His mother never checked on his account after she had set it up, and Jamaal deposited and withdrew money whenever he wanted.

So, Jamaal purchased a money order and mailed it off to a place in Barstow California, and almost a month later, somewhat to Jamaal's surprise, the false IDs had showed up in the mail. Two Colorado Drivers licenses with Jamaal and Frank's picture on them, indicating that they were both 21 years old.

As soon as Frank saw the license, he wanted to go buy some liquor, but Jamaal had said "Frank, listen, I am going to hang on to these licenses. I am afraid that we might get caught doing something like that and then we will not have the licenses available to buy weapons." Frank had reluctantly agreed.

This is all working out great. Jamaal had thought at that time. And just a week after the new IDs had shown up, Jamaal was sitting in his history class when the school presented him with the perfect cover for his searches for guns and ammo.

The teacher said: "I would like each of you to find an important event in history and write a 5000-word essay on that event. You will need to tie the historical event to some event or events in recent history and make comments on the similarities and differences between the historical event and the recent event. This essay will count for one-quarter of your grade and it is due one week prior to the end of the semester, any questions?" Jamaal only had one question.

This is perfect, and what part of your stupid brain do you want to be splattered on the blackboard?

There had been many assassinations, and assassination attempts throughout history, and there were always some recent events that this could be compared to. This would easily open the door for him, and Frank, to start their searches.

Jamaal's first thought was to look at John Hinckley's assassination attempt on President Reagan. John lived in Evergreen Colorado, near Denver and this seemed appropriate, maybe he could do a comparison to the Lincoln assassination, or better yet, to the Kennedy assassination. In any case, he was anxious to get started especially on the research.

So that day, after school, Jamaal had gone over to Frank's house. Even with this cover story Jamaal had wanted to do all of his research on Frank's computer and use Frank's fake I.D. to make all of the purchases. Frank didn't care, he liked being the one who would be buying all of this "Awesome Artillery", and over the last month or so this "Awesome Artillery" had been showing up.

And now this loud KNOCKING at the front door.
I hope it's not the police.
Jamaal opened the door and found Frank there, covered in blood, and frantic.

"Jamaal I am in big trouble," he said "My sister found the guns and said she was going to tell my parents. She was yelling at me, and I lost it."

"What did you do?" Jamaal yelled, concerned that someone would find out about the guns.

"Oh! Man. I beat that bitch bad. I'm not sure she is going to make it."

Now Jamaal was in a panic, not because he was worried about Frank's sister, but because he was sure this would throw a wrench into their plans to terrorize the school.

"What did you do, just leave her lying there?"

"Yeah, I hope she dies!"

"Frank, you idiot, this is going to fuck up everything we have been working for. You need to turn yourself in; maybe I can figure out how to still make this work."

"NO WAY AM I GOING TO JAIL." Frank screamed. "And if I do, I am taking everyone with me, including you."

He was out of control. Jamaal grabbed Frank and slapped him hard.

"You look at me; I am not fucking around now, so you look at me. They are going to catch you and when they do, if you expose our plans or even mention my name, you are going to be in deep shit. First of all, I know all of the shit, you have pulled off in the last few years, and I will spill my guts about that stuff. You mention me, and you are going to be in jail for a long, long time."

Jamaal now staring deep into Frank's eyes "And Frank that is not the worst of it, when you get out of jail, I will kill you. You understand what I am saying, *I WILL KILL YOU.*"

Frank truly had a freighted look on his face, as he agreed to not squeal on Jamaal, and then he left.

Jamaal sat on the couch in his living room and thought about his predicament. He decided he would have to call off the attack; at least for now.

That fucking idiot, I should have known not to trust him. There is no way that dipshit can keep his mouth shut. I just know it.

Jamaal was downtrodden. Here he thought he had a true friend, but it turned out he was just like everyone else in his life. All a bunch of fucking hypocrites.

That bastard is going to sell me out just like Judas.

Jamaal ranted on for a while and then he thought.

There is one person who does seem to care for me, --- Cathy.

Jamaal had met with Cathy off and on in the park since they first met there. They had even tried to have sex a couple of times, but Jamaal always struggled in that department, so after the second time they never tried again. Jamaal, as always, was very careful about everything he did. He did not want anyone to know about anything he was doing, and he especially, did not want anyone to know about his relationship with Cathy. He just hated being vulnerable, and for that reason, he never wanted to have loose ends. So, as he did every time, he went down to one of the few pay phones that were left in town, and he called Cathy on her cell phone.

"Cathy I really need to see you. Can you meet me at the park in about thirty minutes?" Cathy said she would.

In no time they were together in the park. When Cathy arrived, Jamaal asked the usual question.

"Did you tell anyone you were coming?" She responded, just as she promised, "No one knows that we are seeing each other," and she said that she did not let anyone know she was going to the park.

Jamaal was agitated and she immediately sensed it. "Jamaal, what is the matter?"

He wanted to tell her everything but was not sure if he could trust her.

"Can I trust you?"

"Jamaal, you can tell me anything, I can keep a secret."

Jamaal was suspicious, but right now he needed to talk to someone. He was so pissed off. So, he broke one of his cardinal rules, and began to open up a little. He said:

"Cathy, I am so pissed off, that I just want to punch somebody. You know my friend Frank; ---- well he and I had been working on something for a long time, and I have put in a tremendous amount of planning and effort in collecting the equipment needed. But today, Frank beat up his sister and has totally screwed up all my plans. ---Frank is probably going to jail."

Cathy gasped "Is she okay?"

"Who?" Jamaal asked.

"Frank's sister."

Jamaal could see the concern on Cathy's face, Jamaal could give a shit about Frank's sister.

"Oh, Frank said she was probably going to be all right, but did you hear what I said? This is going to totally mess up my plans."

"What were your plans?"

"You know. Those assholes at school are out to get me. They're constantly thinking of ways to screw up my life. --- You know it, and Frank knew it too. And Frank and I were planning to make them pay and pay big." Jamaal looked at Cathy and he could see the fear forming on her face.

Jamaal tried to calm her down. "Look Cathy. That's not why I wanted to meet with you. --- you see, that's all behind me now, that's all over."

Now with the calmest voice Jamaal could muster, and looking directly into Cathy's eyes, he said.

"Cathy look, I really care for you and I think you care for me. I think my life is destroyed here. I have to leave this place, and I want you to go with me."

Cathy took a step backward and said "Jamaal, you're scaring me. I think we should tell the authorities about Frank hurting his sister."

There was a hesitation and then Jamaal said: "But if we leave, we don't have to worry about any of that."

Cathy, looking extremely frightened now, said: "Jamaal, I can't go with you, and I think I better go home now."

Jamaal was trying to think as clearly as he could. It had all been very *logical* to him. He would ask Cathy to go with him, she would agree, and they would leave all his problems behind him. They just needed to get out of there. But now he could feel all his *emotions* and her *emotions* getting wrapped around each other and interfering with his *logic*.

"Cathy, wait a second. I'm sorry, I didn't mean any of that. I love you; can you stay here with me for a while."

Cathy's face softened, "Jamaal, I love you too, but I'm scared. I guess I can stay a little longer."

Jamaal looking intently at Cathy said. "Cathy, I think I know how to fix this, but first, I need to make a call, like you suggested."

Jamaal pulled his cell phone out of his back pocket, opened it up, and dialed.

CHAPTER 28
"THE NRA"

March 23rd, 2003

Congressman Ron Chapman sits at his kitchen table eating breakfast before heading to church. Susan, his wife, reads the morning newspaper, and then says: "Ron did you see this article about the boy and girl who were found dead in a park near the High School in Arvada?"

"The girl's name was Cathy Schmidt. It says here, she had been shot with a .38 special revolver. The boy had apparently shot the girl, and then turned the gun on himself."

"The boy's name was Frank Waters, he had beaten up his sister earlier in the day, and she is in a coma at St. Anthony's hospital in critical condition. They speculate that Frank's sister was threatening to reveal something about Frank's relationship with Cathy; apparently, nobody was even aware that Frank and Cathy even knew each other. Anyway, they speculate that the *emotional* pressure was too much for the boy and he slipped. He apparently, beat up his sister, met up with Cathy in the park, killed her and then killed himself."

"When they searched Frank's home, they found an arsenal of guns and ammunition. They also found a journal that described plans for an assault on his high school. Apparently, he and some other person, possibly this Cathy, were planning on going to the school and killing hundreds of teachers and students, just like those two boys did at Columbine."

Susan, with a very distressed look on her face continues. "But, where did this kid Frank get all of those guns and ammunition? I'll bet he got it through the internet somehow. I'm telling you, Ron, this is going to be just one more thing that the anti-gun fanatics will use to attack the 2nd amendment. You better get with your NRA buddies today at church and think of a response, you know the media will be attacking you on this. I just don't understand, why God lets things like this happen, but I'm going to pray hard for their families today."

Ron listens as his wife went on about how she is glad that this sinner, Frank, killed himself. Ron agreed that there was no use in wasting taxpayer money on a trial, and then housing and feeding this "piece of trash" for years to come.

"Sue, I am positive that God allows these things to happen to rid the world of trash, like this Frank. If you look closely, you'll probably find out, that this Cathy, was a worthless whore as well."

Then, Ron thinks to himself.

Well God; just know that I am here to help.

CHAPTER 29 – A SLIVER OF SUNSHINE

November 10th, 2004
Rufus Middleman, age 34

Rufus Middleman wakes up in total darkness; something or someone had jolted him awake. He does not know where he is or why he is there.

"This must be another journey?" Rufus thinks, now in a bit of a panic and unsure of what to do. Then there is a flash off to his left, and a window lights up with a bright white light for just an instant. A second later he hears a large explosion that shakes the floor he is sitting on and the wall he is leaning against. Dust descends upon him from a ceiling he cannot see. Another flash and Rufus can now see the dust, it is everywhere, and then another thundering explosion, and then another, then silence, followed by only the sound of men coughing from the dust.

"Wake up Middleman, get your shit together, we're moving out in five minutes"

It was Captain Garney, Rufus' unit leader, and now it all came back to him in a flash. He was in Iraq, specifically in the city of Fallujah, in the middle of the battle for the city, against thousands of Iraqi insurgents. He was terrified at first, but then when he remembers that his unit was guarding this building and it had been his turn to catch some shut eye, his nerves steadies. He thinks how strange it is: the range of *emotions* that he has gone through since joining the army, and especially since starting on this mission. Sometimes he felt invincible and charged ahead fearlessly. Sometimes it was uncontrollable anger, and sometimes like right now, he was terrified. He looked at his watch; it was 3:00 AM, and as he sat there in the *darkness* he began to think about how, and why, he was here:

After his disastrous attempt, to be a Mixed Martial Arts fighter, he decided he would knuckle down and concentrate on getting his Ph.D. in Mathematics and Physics, and in the spring of 1998, he did just that. But then he was once again frustrated. The University had hired him as a professor, to teach mathematics, and in his spare time he was doing research in physics and math. He had published a paper, which included a mathematical model supporting the existence of gravitons, which, if proven to exist, would be the 'particle' form of gravitational waves. But his paper, not only supported the existence of gravitons, it also tied them closely, through the concepts of *entanglement*, to photons, which are the particle form of light waves.

It had already been proven that photons, from the same source, can become *entangled*, and Rufus hypothesized that not only could gravitons become entangled with each other, but that photons and gravitons could become entangled as well.

His theory was; that there were scalar particles in the universe, similar to that of the proposed Higg's boson, which would prove the existence of a new 'field', a field which made this entanglement possible. And he speculated that these scalar particles could be observed by way of experimentation at the Large Hadron Collider in CERN, Switzerland.

Rufus' believed his paper proved by way of the power of mathematics, that if these scalar particles could be detected, they would, in turn, prove the existence of this new field, which Rufus called the 'lightlessness' field, or the (L^2N) field, this is not a gray area between *light* and *darkness*, but rather, a field which extracts energy from this close relationship between *light* and *darkness*, between photons and gravitons, and would form the basis for a connection between all things in the universe, and it would take the field of science, one step closer to a unified theory of everything. But Rufus was not a well-recognized physicist, and as such, it would have to remain an unrecognized hypothesis.

Rufus loved research but hated teaching. He could tolerate most of the undergraduate students that were just getting started. However, there were several of the smart-ass graduate students, which he could not stand at all. All he really wanted to do was knock their fucking teeth out, and then see how smart they were, but then one day, he did just that. One of the physically larger master's degrees student's got in his face about some inane point on physics or math or something, it didn't matter, Rufus had enough, and he lost it. He broke the student's jaw and knocked out a couple of his teeth.

The school had asked Rufus to resign, and the judge had told Rufus he would have to spend time in jail. But Rufus had his lawyer work out a deal with the District Attorney. Rufus would agree to join the Army and if he stayed in the Army and out of trouble for a year, it would be considered time served.

So, on July 10th, 1999, Rufus started training at the Basic Combat Training (BCT) School in Fort Benning, Georgia, as part of the Officer Candidate School of the United States Army, a 12-week program. When he completed his BCT he was commissioned as a 2nd Lieutenant, followed by the rest of his Basic Officer Leadership courses.

All the time he was at Fort Benning, he made it very clear that he wanted to join the 1st Infantry, because Rufus knew that was where the action was, and where he was most likely to see actual battle. And after several official applications and some political maneuvering, it was on January 8th Lieutenant Rufus Middleman arrived at Fort Riley Kansas and became officially a member of 'The Fighting First'. Rufus thought it was ironic that he would end up training at the Combative school at Fort Riley, because Tim McVeigh had graduated from the Combat Engineering School right there in 1988.

Oh well, I guess my entanglement with McVeigh continues.

At Fort Riley, just as it was at Fort Benning, Rufus' superiors and his peers recognized his exceptional abilities in hand to hand combat. But, in The Big Red One, you may have an area of expertise, but you are always a soldier first, and Rufus always made it clear that if there was any chance that he could be assigned to a combat unit in Iraq, he wanted to go.

In March 2004 he got his wish, Task Force 2-2 was formed from the 2nd Battalion 2nd Infantry of the 1st Division and deployed to Iraq. Before Rufus could pronounce Diyala, he was in Diyala, Iraq. It took him a while to get adjusted to the new surroundings lots of sand and a lot of heat. Rufus was a big guy and he was black and staying cool was always difficult for him, and it was especially tough in Iraq because along with the heat, you had the bugs and biting flies.

Over the summer they had lost 27 men in firefights and skirmishes. By the end of the summer Rufus clearly understood the reality of war, these were his friends dying, this was not a video game.

On Nov 3 of 2004, Rufus' squad leader had come to them and laid out the plan for the mission in Fallujah. His squad leader reaffirmed most of what Rufus comrades were telling him about Fallujah, including an expectation of a 30% attrition, in the first assault on the city.

Rufus' mind snaps back to the present as he hears his team leader yell. "Middleman lets go, let's hit the street" in a matter of seconds the whole squad is on the street and the team leader is giving them a briefing on their objectives. They would be moving down the block, going building to building clearing each house of insurgents and working their way to a very tall building at end of the block. At that point, they would clear that building to secure it and set up an outpost using the roof of the building to cover the courtyard and plaza just beyond the end of the block.

Rufus is well practiced in the process of clearing buildings; he had done this with his team many times over the summer in towns like Muqdadiyah. But this is not Muqdadiyah, this is Fallujah and all the things that his buddies had told him about it were true, and more. One thing they didn't tell him about, was seeing body parts along the street all chewed up, probably from 'Ferrell' dogs, which were constantly roaming the streets.

Rufus concentrates hard on the job at hand not only does it help keep him from getting killed, but it also keeps him from getting sick to his stomach from the sights on the street. They had now reached the tall building at the end of the block and his team is moving into position to enter and clear the building. Rufus tells himself that he needs to keep a clear head here.

First, his team puts charges on the front door and blows it open. Immediately two members of his team enter the front hallway of the building and take up positions. It is now Rufus' turn, he runs into the building keeping his eyes wide open, the transition from the bright outside *light* to the *darkness* of the hallway is very disconcerting, as he needs to be vigilant to any movement in the building.

He takes up his position at the end of a hallway as his eyes adjust to the *dark* interior. Thankfully, there is no movement in the house while his eyes were adjusting. A second later another two members of his team come running past him to take up the next positions. There appears to be a stairway going up at the end of the hall, but once again it had been brick-and-mortared shut. Rufus thinks about the purpose of these tactics by the insurgents.

What are we walking into?

They set up charges on the brick wall blocking the stairwell and clear the hallway. "Fire in the hole". They let it rip. Shit is flying everywhere. Once the smoke has cleared Rufus can see that the walls of the hallway were riddled with holes from the blast. *God, I hope this building doesn't fall down.* Rufus thinks, as he inspects the wall blocking the stairwell. They had blasted a hole about two feet into the wall, and still, there was brick and mortar.

After two more tries and at least five feet into the brick wall they still found more brick and mortar, it was as though they had filled the entire stairwell. With this and their legitimate concern about the remaining structural integrity of the building, they decided to move on and see if they could find another path to the roof.

They are now moving room to room, clearing each and finding nothing of importance, and thankfully no insurgents. At this point, they find themselves at a back door which led to a large open courtyard. There were no brick walls blocking the way into the courtyard.

This certainly smells of ambush.

The courtyard was very quiet and except for some large potted plants and a few chairs, it was empty. They stayed in the house for what seemed like a very long time, scouring the windows of the courtyard for any movement or signs of an impending ambush, but there was nothing.

The squad begins moving again, very slowly, with the intention of going door to door within the courtyard. As Private Johnson takes the first step out into the open part of the courtyard area, all hell breaks loose. An IED went off under him, taking off a part of his foot. Immediately there was a barrage of fire coming at them from the opposite side of the courtyard and from above. Rufus spots an insurgent only a few yards away duck into one of the branching hallways, and Rufus follows him. Rufus wanted to get out of the line of fire in the courtyard and to maybe kill his first insurgent.

The hallway was extremely dark, but then Rufus catches a glimpse of the insurgent, he is climbing a ladder in one of the alcoves. Rufus, with the butt of his AK-47 already on his shoulder and up next to his chin, ripped off a rapid succession of shots at the ascending legs of the insurgent.

Even in the darkness Rufus can see the insurgent's rifle drop from above, immediately followed by the insurgent himself. As soon as the enemy hit the floor, the insurgent grabs his rifle and turns it toward Rufus. Rufus does not hesitate and pumps fifteen quick shots into the insurgent's chest. Slumping to the floor, eyes wide open, the insurgent is no longer moving. Rufus could now see the insurgents face, not the face of a man, but the face of a boy, not more than twelve or thirteen years old.

Shit, my first kill and it's a fucking kid.

Then Rufus begins to panic.

Why would they send a kid out here, only to lead me into this hallway? Oh! Shit!

Rufus' answer was immediate, as the wall to his right became a mass of flying bricks and concrete. Rufus slammed into a wall to his left, his head hitting the wall so hard that the chin strap on his helmet snapped and the helmet went flying, and then the whole house came down on top of him.

A moment later, a sliver of sunshine, from a crack in the roof above, pierced through the clouds of dust filling the air. Rufus is in a daze, his body trapped in a pile of brick and mortar, now directs his attention back to the insurgent. It was still *dark* in the hallway, only the light that filtered in from above offered any relief and Rufus' eyes were now just beginning to adjust to that new *light*.

But as the air clears, he can clearly see his adversary. The color of everything in the desert, and in these buildings, is muted, a dull pastel of light brown, yellow and green. The dust does not allow any color to be vibrant or bright. However, Rufus senses are now assaulted by the stark scarlet color of the blood, now pouring from the insurgent's chest. It is, in stark contrast to its surroundings, as the insurgent now sits motionless against the wall, bleeding profusely. Rufus can see that his eyes are still wide open, a look of pure shock on his face, and he is staring directly at Rufus.

The boy suddenly lifts his arm, reaching towards Rufus' face, as if to say, '*Help me.*' Rufus becomes dizzy and confused, he is lightheaded and thinks he is about to pass out.

Then Rufus sees it. It is a *light*, and it is coming, not from above, but instead from the center of the boy's chest, directly from the center of all that scarlet, and it is a perfectly white *light*.

The *light* grows brighter and brighter and begins to move slowly upward. Rufus can feel the *light* wash over him, like stepping in front of a window on a bright sunny day and feeling the heat of the sun penetrate your clothes. But it is more than just warmth it is something else, he can feel the boy's *spirit*, he can feel the energy of the whole universe. He feels a connection with many other people both living and dead. He feels that all of this is touching his very soul, he feels that his *emotions* are becoming *entangled* with that of the boy's and then the *light* becomes even brighter and totally engulfs him.

"Middleman! Middleman!"

CHAPTER 30 – IS THIS A POISON PILL?

April 19th[th], 2006
Jamaal Dell, age 21

Jamaal's eyes fight to adjust to the blinding light, as the silk bag covering his face is removed. His hands, tied behind his back, are now smashed between his butt and the hard-wooden chair he had been pushed so roughly into. Just thirty minutes ago, at about 8:00pm, a black Mercedes van had pulled up next to his car in the Walmart parking lot near his apartment. Two men jumped out, dragged Jamaal from his car, threw the black bag over his head, pushed him into the truck, and sped away.

"Free his hands!" a voice, as silky as the petals of roses, commanded. As Jamaal's eyes continue to adjust, he could see three figures seated at a table just a few feet away, all in hooded robes. The single figure seated in the center of the three was dressed in a solid white robe. An intense white light is shining directly down on him from above. This *light* which focused on the figure in the center, did not shine on the other two figures seated on either side. The figures outside of the *light* were dressed in black hooded robes and were very difficult to see because of the cloak of *darkness* just outside of the intense *light*. But one thing was prominent on each of the hooded figures, and that was what appeared to be an ornamental pendant. The pendent was strung around the neck of each figure, on the outside of their cloaks. The gold pendant appeared to be a series of three 'Xs', or maybe three-hour glasses.

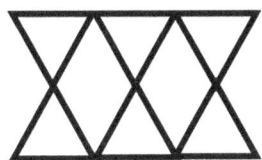

What kind of bullshit is this? Jamaal thinks.

Jamaal strains to see the faces of the men at the table hidden deep within the thick material of their hoods, while at the same time he feels the ropes binding his hands being released. He turns to see the man releasing the ropes.

"Jamaal, please stay seated and face forward, we are not here to hurt you." the silky voice at the table, now sounding even calmer and reassuring.

"Who are you?" Jamaal shouted as he turned to face forward once again. "How do you know me? What do you want?"

The calm voice began again: "Well, actually Jamaal, as much as you have strived to be anonymous, we know a lot about you. Some of it from your internet blogs, but our due diligence goes much, much further. We know about your parents and brother, and how you feel about them. We know a lot about, what you have been doing for the last few years since high school. We know about Cathy and Frank, and the others that you have disposed of because of your beliefs, and that is why you are here."

Jamaal sat in silence.

"Our organization is known as 'The King's Crusaders', and our symbol can be seen in the pendant of three Xs, that each of us wears."

"Let me explain because we do want you to know all about us."

"As you probably are aware 'XXX' is the Roman numeral for 30, and we, here at this table, are three of the 30 members of the higher archival portion of the King's Crusaders. We are known as the 'Keepers', and I am the Grand Master Keeper."

"You may also be aware that when you put numbers next to each other in math, that implies multiplication. So, X times X times X, or 10 times 10 time 10 equals 1000. And there are 1000 members of the King's Crusaders, 'a thousand points of resistance', and the Keepers are responsible for making sure that that number of crusaders is maintained."

"You see, we have recently lost a member, and that is why you are here. We would like you to join our organization, as we believe your philosophies and goals line up well with our own."

Jamaal sat patiently and continued to listen.

"But of course, before you decide to join, you need to know more about our organization." And then the calm voice rose in volume, to a voice of authority.

"The organization has existed for hundreds of years, with very little publicity, and THAT IS BECAUSE WE KEEP IT THAT WAY!"

This sounded like a threat to Jamaal, but after a short pause, the calming voice returned.

"We know from your blogs that you believe in Christianity in its purest form, and so do we. In fact, we believe that most religions in their purest form are worthy of devoted followers."

"For many, many years now we have had a secret communiqué with various religious leaders both organized and evangelical, which we call 'our benefactors'. We have promoted ourselves as an organization that secretly fights the evils that push people away from religion. Our benefactors are aware that we also provide 'incentives' by which people can see the need to return to God as their source of redemption and thus once again join a religious community."

"There are two primary reasons why people lose their belief and thus discontinue support of the various religions. The first of these is the loss of faith due to hypocrisy in the churches: Hypocrisy such as priest-pedophiles, or evangelical leaders and cult leaders that are raping their followers both financially and literally."

"The second reason is embedded in the advancement of science. The government cannot be trusted, just look at what happened at Ruby Ridge and at Mount Carmel near Waco. They are not here to help people, instead, governments are stealing what people have. They are taxing the poor to fund scientific advancement that is providing alternatives to religious beliefs, and as science advances toward a 'unified theory of everything', more and more souls are drifting away from their belief in God and their belief in the scriptures. Governments and the scientist who are developing these godless theories must be stopped."

"TKC has developed methods for reducing and or eliminating these two evils that push people away from religion."

"As I have mentioned we have one thousand members and everyday our members pray for things to happen that will emphasize the dangers people are subject to in today's world. Things that will emphasize the apocalyptic nature of events in the world, and thus incent people to return to God. Our members also pray for the elimination of those who would create false theories which draw people from their belief in God."

"Our members believe in the power of prayer, but also believe in the power of action. So, we provide the financial, as well as other means of support, which helps our member's prayers to become realized."

"We have demonstrated to our benefactors that many of the techniques we use, are beyond the limits accepted by those in society, but have proven to be most effective."

"Over the many years, that this organization has been in existence, we have received overwhelmingly positive responses from these high levels of religious communities. Many indicated they were happy to supply financial support, and most did not need to be made aware of any details. And though our response to those who have requested details have been vague at best, we let them know that we are not limited in our prayers and other tools that we use to make a difference."

"These tools can be used to punish or eliminate hypocrisy or distract or remove the scientist from their pursuit of scientific theories that provide alternatives to religion."

"Our member's prayers are strong, and those prayers along with the resources our members take advantage of, discourage or eliminate that which would drive people away from their religion."

"But our members do more than just pray to eliminate that which would push people away from their religion. They also pray for forces which would push them back to their religion."

"You see sometimes terrorist and terrorism are seen as a bad thing. However, when something that seems bad pushes people back to their religion, then it is a good thing."

"The Twin Towers, Oklahoma City, and even Columbine High School are all examples of the types of apocalyptic and demonic events that drive people back to religion, and our members pray for, and support, these events to drive even more needed souls back to God. You know that Armageddon, the Rapture and so on, are very effective incentives to find God."

"Our organization was formed in 1870, to meet the needs of our benefactors by combating the threats to the purest forms of religious belief."

"We believe that early scientific theories, along with more recent theories in physics, and the efforts to prove these theories are a threat to our benefactors. Key individuals in these scientific efforts, have been identified by those who support us, and have been eliminated over the last century. Today even more of these enemies of God have been identified and must be dealt with."

Jamaal liked what he was hearing, this was very much in line with his developing philosophy of life, and they were right, he hated hypocrites and he especially hated science and scientist.

"So, Jamaal, are you interested?"

Jamaal did not speak for a moment and then said. "I am interested, but what's in it for me."

The man in the hood responds. "Greed? I see! Well before we get to that let me describe the multitude of resources that can be at your disposal."

"In many cases, we take advantage of radical religious sects. We just convince them that, what we want to be done, is in support of their own goals. For example, we may provide them with instructions in the form of prayers, such as;"

"'Oh, ye faithful, when you find the enemy, be steadfast and remember God constantly, so that you may be successful.'"

"Or 'Obey God and His Messenger, and do not fight among yourselves or you will fail. And be patient, for God is with the patient.'"

"Always making sure that they believe these instructions are coming from their own religious leadership or scriptures."

"We also have members in just the right places that can support our Crusaders in their quest, by getting them into the right areas, with the right tools. And maybe even more importantly we have other resources to get them out without detection."

"We are confident that our designated targets are well in line with your own agenda. We provide the tools and the training you will need to be highly successful in answering the prayers of our membership, and by way of our benefactors, we provide monetary compensation to make your off time very, very comfortable."

"So, what do I have to do?" Asked Jamaal.

"Under your chair is a small box. Reach down, pick it up, and open it."

Jamaal did as he was directed. The box contained a map, a bottle of pills, and a name. 'Dr. Rufus Middleman and Dr. Stephen Weber.'

"So??" Jamaal said looking puzzled.

"Dr. Middleman is a physicist. A few years back Dr. Middleman published a paper. The paper expounded a theory, which not only included the mathematical proof of the existence of a particle form of gravitational waves, known as 'gravitons', but also theoretical proof that a field exists in the universe, that allows for the entanglement of these gravitons with photons, thus furthering a universal theory of everything."

"Recently Dr. Weber working at the Large Hadron Collider, in Switzerland, has found evidence that Dr. Middleman's theories may be correct. Dr. Middleman's theories are a great threat to our benefactor's religious convictions, and our membership is praying that they will be deterred from their pursuits."

"So, what do you want me to do?"

"We want you to take action such that our membership's prayers will be answered, and thus prove yourself worthy of induction to the 'King's Crusaders'."

"You can use any method you see fit, as long as TKC is not implicated. But we suggest just getting one of these pills inside of your intended target. God will take care of the rest."

"Is this a poison pill?" Jamaal, not clear on the reference to getting the pill 'Inside of your intended target.'

"No not at all, the ancient ingredients in this pill, once inside a person's body, assist God in the development of a variety of illnesses, including cancer. There are always cells associated with these diseases, though they maybe dormant, somewhere in the body. Once the ingredients find these cells, they can assist God in stimulating growth of the disease."

"God will determine if and when our enemy will be punished, sometimes it is six months to a year, and because it is natural causes there is no suspicion of foul play. When you get a chance, you might want to look up how some famous physicists have died."

"Do you understand, that if you prove yourself capable, you will be considered for induction as one of The King's Crusaders? So, do you accept?"

Jamaal thought about the stern warning given by the hooded man: "the organization was not very well known, and THAT IS BECAUSE WE KEEP IT THAT WAY!"

It may be, that if I do not accept, I will not get out of this place alive. Besides the whole offer is very appealing, it's like becoming a secret agent or something, and it's all in line with my own goals. Armageddon, Science, and Hypocrisy, ... ASH. I will answer their prayers and help them turn everything into ASH, I like it.

"I accept."

CHAPTER 31 – WE ARE ALL HERE FOR A REASON

April 17th, 2012

Christine Basurto, Age 44

Rufus Middleman, Age 42

Ester Suni Nate, Age 60

CyrIS Steel, Age 62

"CyrIS, this is my friend Christine that I was telling you about." Ester politely making the introduction, as they stood just inside of Ron Chapman's hotel suite. Christine offered her hand to CyrIS, saying, "It's nice to meet you. I've heard a lot about you, and not only from Ester. I have done some research on my own, and you certainly have a different approach as a preacher, I'm very interested, and hope to hear more about it."

"Well, it's nice to meet you as well," CyrIS responded, "Ester has spoken highly of you and your work."

As CyrIS was speaking, Ron came through the door and walked up to the group, a very large black man at his side.

"Hello everyone," Chapman began, "I am so happy that you could all make it. I don't believe you have met my chauffeur and bodyguard, Rufus Middleman. Rufus this is Christine Basurto, Ester Suni Nati, and CyrIS Steel. I will be giving a formal introduction for each of you once we begin the meeting." Rufus shook each of their hands.

CyrIS responded; "Thanks Ron, your billing for this conference, made it almost impossible to resist. And by the way, congratulation on your recent re-election to Congress."

"Thanks, CyrIS, I hoped my invitation would entice each of you to attend, and I hope you will find that I did not oversell it."

Each added their congratulations, and Ron responded, "Thanks to all of you for your help in my re-election, and I would especially like to thank Christine. Hiring Christine as my media consultant has been one of the best decisions I have ever made. I'm certain that I would not have been successful in my bid for re-election without her advice and guidance in the area of social media." Ron was looking at Christine the whole time and smiling.

CyrIS then asked, "Ron where is the conference meeting, and how many people will be attending?"

"Oh! --- It will only be the five of us, and this is the room we are meeting in. I will explain soon if you would please take a seat?"

The suite was very comfortable, with a view of downtown Denver and the mountains. In the living room portion of the suit was a couple of couches and easy chairs. Each participant found a seat, Ester, and CyrIS sitting next to each other on one of the couches, Rufus and Christine finding individual chairs. Ron continued to stand as the group settled in.

Ron Chapman had been re-elected congressman of the 1st congressional district of Colorado. He had worked hard to get there and even harder to stay there. That work had included a lot of time working with the FBI and developing his network of political and private contacts that helped get him re-elected, and Ron knew that you do not stay a congressman because you are smart or because you're necessarily the best person for the job. You stay there by being a good speaker and, by knowing the right people. That is, being *connected*, --- *connected* to the right people that can get you the votes, and Ron had developed a strong base, in a variety of areas that could bring in those votes.

Ron realized that there was one additional thing that a person needed to be successful in politics, or in any endeavor as far as that goes, and that was information. The more information you had about everything was important, but the information you had about people, in general, was the most important, and the more data you had about individuals, both friend and foe was really important. Because information of this nature is the source of power, and Ron wanted power.

Ron begins, "Again I want to thank you for agreeing to be here. I am sure that it was difficult to fit these three days into your busy schedules. However, I believe you will find it worthwhile, and I hope you will come to appreciate the task in front of us."

"I am the sponsor of the congressional Quantum Computing task force, and I will be eventually sponsoring a bill to provide a very large sum of money to support the development of a Quantum Computer."

"What exactly are you trying to do Congressman?" asked Ester.

"Well Ester, a Quantum Computer is a computer that takes advantage of the nature of Quantum Physics to accomplish massive amounts of calculations by using the atomic particles to establish the binary codes necessary to do those calculations. This could allow for the creation of a computer with almost unlimited capacity for calculations, information storage, and analysis."

Ron knew that this project was an exceptional opportunity for not only him, but for his ability to impress his supporters as well. Ron liked playing all sides of the board. Computers and their growing ability to collect and process large amounts of data was just what Ron had been looking for, and this was his inside track on getting into the latest and greatest method for knowing as much as one could know about the interest of specific segments of the nation's population. Maybe even to know specifics about his competition and where the money is moving and how to get more of it.

Ron was sure that he could use his involvement in Homeland Security as a reason to tap into some of the nation's largest corporately owned data bases, like the phone companies, the power companies and large retailers like Target, Amazon, and Google. With the superpower of this new Quantum computer, it would be easy to digest and capitalize on all these data sources. All under the guise of improving national security, improving the space program, and improving general intelligence for all the intelligence agencies.

Ron made it a point, to always stay abreast of all the latest advancements in math and modern physics, and he did this by watching all the TV shows on the subjects like those shown in "Through the Worm Hole: with Morgan Freeman" or "Futurescape, with James Woods" or "Nova".

He also had been reading a lot of the latest articles on these subjects, in magazines like "Scientific American" and in books on the subject of Quantum Physics. He had to admit, that he did not understand a great deal of what he read, but during his research, he ran upon a book called the "Quantum Mind: the edge between physics and psychology" by Arnold Mendell, Ph.D.

This book explained how there could be a connection between the science of Quantum Physics and Psychology and Religion and Shamanism or Psychic abilities. In other words, the book explained that if you wanted to truly understand the *flow* of information between the cosmos and people and between people and other people, and other things in general, that one needed to have an understanding of all of these disciplines.

Over the years Ron had established connections with people who were considered leaders in all these areas, and today he was bringing some of these thought leaders together in one room, to see what, if anything, they had in common and to see if the information they might share could have any value in the advancement of Quantum Computing.

Ron continued his introduction, "This is an effort that is supported by the scientist at NASA, the National Renewable Energy Laboratories, and the National Center for Atmospheric Research. As part of this conference, we will be taking tours or NREL, in Golden, and NCAR, in Boulder, tomorrow, and talking to some of the scientists there as well."

"But this effort is also being sponsored by the U.S. military, as well as other government agencies such as the NSA, CIA, and FBI. So, you can see that this is not an effort that should be taken lightly, and your participation is important."

"The world is becoming a very dangerous and confusing place. Just look at some of the major events over the last couple of decades. There was the bombing of the Federal Center in Oklahoma City in 1995. There was the school shooting at Columbine High School right here in Colorado in 1999. There was the destruction of the World Trade Center buildings in New York in 2001. Just to name a few. I am sure you are aware, there have been many other tragic events and wars occurring all around the world."

The group was more than just a little aware of these events, as Ron continued. "It is our hope that through the development of a super powerful Quantum Computing system we can begin to understand the sources of these types of terrible events, predict these events before they occur, track down potential perpetrators and therefore avoid them while still preserving our constitutional freedoms, including our second amendment right to bear arms."

'But that is not all that such a computing system could be used for, it could also be used to help crack some of the greatest scientific questions presently facing the world today, especially in the area of Quantum Physics."

"I have already spent a considerable amount of time in various conferences with the scientist that have been working on Quantum computing and other relevant areas, receiving and documenting their inputs on this effort. And if relevant information comes out of these conference discussions, then I will need to share that information with those scientists as the need arises."

"I picked the four of you for these discussions specifically for your individual expertise and I wanted this group to be small so that you would each feel open to share your true feelings and insights as they might relate to our discussions. So, let me start with some formal introductions."

"First, we have my own favorite media consultant: Christine Basurto, Ph.D. in psychology, with expertise in the area of psychopaths and schizophrenia. Christine." Christine forced a smile.

"Next, we have, Ester Suni Nati, Ph.D. in Extra Sensory Perception, Shamanism and Psychic Phenomenon. Ester." Ron slightly moved his hand in Ester's direction as he spoke her name.

"And next, we have Ester's assistant. --- Just kidding CyrIS. CyrIS Steel, Ester's husband has an advanced degree in Divinity from the 'Graduate Theological Union' at the University of Berkley. But he also has a degree in Mathematics, and a master's degree in physics, from the University of Berkley as well. But CyrIS is more widely known as an evangelical leader and biblical expert and is now well celebrated for his sermons, which tie science closely to the scriptures and to other philosophical theories."

Ron then introduced Rufus Middleman. "This morning I informally introduced you to Rufus Middleman, as my personal chauffeur and bodyguard. But Rufus has a Ph.D. in Math and Physics and has written many papers on these subjects. Some of you may have read some of his work. They have been published in many major Physics Journals and in magazines. And not long ago, Rufus published a paper on the relationship between photons and gravitons, which hopefully he will tell us more about today. I believe that Rufus can help us to understand some of the issues presently facing the scientist all over the world."

The light went on for CyrIS.

Oh! Crap, I've heard of this guy, Dr. Middleman. He is looking for a scaler particle to prove the existence of a field that connects photons and the hypothetical gravitons.

Ron went on, "I know that this seems like a very diverse group, to be discussing Quantum Computing, and some would question the need to combine the *logic* of math and science with the more *emotional* disciplines of religion, psychology, and shamanism. But I would point out, that Albert Einstein once said:

'What is the meaning of human life, or of organic life altogether? To answer that question at all implies religion. Science without religion is lame: religion without science is blind.'"

As Ron let this sink in, he continued, "Our mission is very important, but I would like to keep the discussions informal. Please dispense with all titles such as doctor or congressman. Please, just first names."

"I have asked Rufus to give us a bit of a scientific primer to start our day. Rufus, would you like to begin?"

Rufus stood up. "Thank you, Congressman Chapman, Oh! I'm sorry, I mean Ron."

"I know that our basic purpose here today is to see how this group can contribute to the advancement of Quantum Computing, and I am anxious to hear what each of you has to offer."

"But first, I want to thank Ron for giving me this job as his bodyguard and chauffeur; it has afforded me the time, which I feel I require, to do extensive research into the latest advancements in math and science and specifically in the field of physics. It also allows me the time to write my own research papers, which I do hope, some of you have had the chance to read."

"I also want to give thanks to the *Light* of God for my presence here today. You see I grew up, a very angry young man, pissed off at everything and everybody. All I wanted to do was study and fight, and I mean that literally, I had fist fights with other kids when I was young, and I really liked arguing and physically fighting with adults most of my life. And after I broke a graduate student's jaw in college, and got arrested for assault, I joined the army. It just seemed like a good place for a guy who wanted to fight everyone. Anyway, I was eventually sent to fight in Iraqi, and there I had an epiphany, which changed my outlook on life and made me a true believer in the *Light* of the scriptures. But when I left the army, I tried to find a job in teaching, but because of my history no university would have me. However, Ron was kind enough to give me this job."

"So, with all of that said, I would first like to talk about some of the interesting discoveries, which are a result of scientific research over the years. I believe you will find that these discoveries are relevant to today's discussions."

Rufus first told the story of the double slit experiment, just as he had done with his friend Steve, and too many others, over the years. He explained how photons act as a wave if they are not observed and how they can change to the characteristics of a particle when they are observed. Rufus explained how photons from the same source can be *entangled*, and what happens to one of the photons can affect the other photon no matter how far apart the two photons are, even *light* years apart. He then explained the theory of *non-locality*, that is, how one can observe the speed or the location of an atomic particle but not both at the same time.

Rufus said, "It is, as if, all things in the universe, including people, are *connected* together with a field that we are unable to see, which is a critical element of my published papers on this subject."

Ester thought about her father's comments on the *fabric* of life, as Rufus went on.

"Now I would like to talk for a bit about "*Dark Matter*" and "*Dark Energy*".

Ron interrupted "Is '*Dark Matter*' the same as 'Anti-Matter'?"

Rufus replied "Anti-*matter* is different than *Dark matter*. Anti-*Matter* is the polar opposite of *matter* and when the two come in contact they destroy each other and release a tremendous amount of energy. A half a gram of anti-matter would cause a 13 kilo-ton blast, an explosion as big as the Hiroshima bomb. Fortunately, most anti-mater dissipated during the Big Bang and there is very little of it left."

"*Dark Matter* is completely different, and I would like to point out that *Dark Matter* is called '*Dark*' only because it cannot be seen. In fact, *Dark Matter* is a very positive thing. Though it was proposed 40 years ago, recently Richard Massey, of the Royal Observatory in Edinburg, used a process called "Gravitational lensing" to determine how much *dark matter* existed, and his process has shown that there is more *dark matter* than visible *matter* in the universe."

"Some scientists have been running computer models to determine how the galaxies in our universe were formed. They discovered through these models that to form galaxies, there needed to be even more of a 'gravitational effect' than that which can be provided by the existing known visible *matter*. They also found that if they added the additional gravitational force, which would be provided by the *dark matter*, as observed by Richard Massey, their computer models were able to form galaxies."

"So, without *Dark Matter*, there would be no galaxies, without galaxies, there would be no stars, without stars there would be no planets, without planets there would be no life. So, you can see that *Dark Matter* is very important to us all."

"*Dark Matter* particles are called Weakly Interacting Massive Particles (WIMPs). They are weakly interacting with regular particles, and only interact by the weak force of gravity, and therefore they are extremely difficult to detect."

"So now let's talk about the universe for a second. Let's imagine an explosion, one caused by a stick of dynamite. You can probably understand, that right after the initial explosion, that is, after all the explosive material has extinguished, the material in the blast is moving away from the center of the explosion. You can also probably understand that from that moment on, all of the material moving away from the center is slowing down because there is no longer anything to accelerate it."

"Well most scientists believed that because billions of years had passed since the initial blast of the Big Bang, that most of the material was moving away from the center of that explosion, and that it was slowing down, mostly due to the gravitational effect of all of the planets and stars that were out there. And additionally, that it had slowed down to the point, that now all of the galaxies should be moving towards each other."

"Now let's talk about '*Dark Energy*'. The distinguished astronomer Edwin Hubble discovered in the 1920s that the galaxies were not moving towards each other but in fact, we're moving away from each other. The scientific world was amazed but assumed that even though the galaxies were moving away from each other, that the rate at which they were moving away from each other, was slowing down, again due to the forces of gravity caused by the mass of all of the stars and planets…it was only *logical."*

"However, a cosmologist, named Saul Pearlmutter, a nice Jewish boy, was observing the explosions of white dwarf stars, and by way of these observations was able to determine the rate at which the expansion of the universe is slowing. What he found, to the utter amazement of the scientific world, was that the universe was not slowing down in its expansion; instead, it was speeding up in its expansion. It was determined that there must be some unknown energy that was causing the universe to accelerate, to literally blow up. They called this energy '*Dark Energy*.'"

"And then in 2001, The Wilkinson Microwave Anisotropy Probe was launched into outer space from Cape Canaveral, Florida. This probe used echo analysis of the waves formed by the big bang, to map the universe. By way of this process, they came up with measurements of what makes up the universe. They determined that atoms, i.e. *matter*, make up about 5% of the Universe, *Dark Matter* makes up 23%, and *Dark Energy* makes up 72%."

"You see, we are fairly insignificant in universal terms, wouldn't you say?"

"But that's not all. It has been determined that eventually *Dark Energy*, because of its constant acceleration of all *matter*, will eventually rip apart and then destroy the entire universe as we know it. Bringing all things to an end."

Ron interrupted asking "So what is holding everything together right now?"

"Well Ron, thanks for asking." Rufus continued "Because that brings us back to *matter*."

"The nucleus of an atom is 100,000 times smaller than its radius; that is to say, the nucleus of an atom, relative to the electron flying around its radius, is equivalent to a head of a pin in a football stadium. So, atoms are basically hollow, and if we are all made up of pinpoint bits of material, that are made mostly of nothing, which are atoms, and between those atoms is more space, it becomes easy to see that everything is mostly made of nothing. So then, what is holding the atoms together? What holds everything together? What makes things solid? What are these forces?"

"There are four known forces in the universe: Gravity is what holds us to earth. The Electromagnetic Force is the force within photons, i.e. *light.* An example of this force can be seen in magnetism. The Weak Force can be seen in radioactive decay. And finally, the Strong Force is what holds protons and neutrons together. And without the precise balance, which presently exists between these four forces, we would not exist."

"Scientists have proven that even the slightest variation in the balance between these four forces would bring an end to our entire universe. Some people say it is proof of the existence of God, and I am one of those people."

Rufus paused for a moment.

Ester thought to herself: *It seems that everything must be the way it is, just to maintain this balance. Maybe, we are all part of that cosmic balance. Maybe, each and every one of us must exist exactly as we are.*

Rufus continued "At high temperatures, that is at millions of degrees, the electromagnetic force, and the weak force combine. This is called Electro Weak Unification. This led to the Standard Model of Particle Physics, which stated that all forces are related."

"But the Electro Week Unification was the only relation between forces that could be proven, and the Standard Model could not explain the variation in the mass of particles. Then a scientist named Peter Higgs proposed a solution. He proposed a theory, that there is a large 'field' that runs through *everything* in the universe. Scientist gave this field the name the 'Higgs Field', and if this field exist, the interaction of particles with this field is what would give particles mass, it is what would make mass stick together, it is what would make things solid."

Ester's eyes lit up, and she felt as if a *Light* had just been turned on inside of her as well.

Oh, my God, it's the fabric of life, just as her father had said. This may also explain my psychic abilities. Maybe this is the medium by which clairvoyance can occur.

Rufus continued, "Peter Higgs also said that when mass is created through its interaction with this field, a matching particle is created called the *Higgs Boson*. And guess what scientists are calling this particle? They are calling it the 'God' particle because this particle would be proof of the existence of the *Higgs Field*, and the *Higgs Field*, just like God, is what holds *everything* together and creates everything, it is literally the 'Creator'."

Each person in the room was, in their own way, a bit overwhelmed with what they were hearing.

Rufus continued, "However, the existence of the Higgs Boson has not yet been proven, but proving its existence is one of the main purposes of the CERN Large Hadron Collider, in Switzerland, and proof of its existence would further support the standard model."

"But the collider has been working on other experiments as well. Many years ago, I produced a theory which would not only prove the existence of a particle form of gravitational waves, called the graviton; it would also prove the existence of a field that would allow for the *entanglement* of photons and gravitons. Proof of the existence of this field would bring us even closer to a unified 'Theory of everything.'"

"My theory proposes that a scalar particle exist, that I call the 'lightlessness' particle. And since 2005 I have been working closely with Dr. Stephen Weber, who is an experimental physicist at the CERN Collider. This particle would prove the existence of a field that unites photons and gravitons, and until Dr. Weber's death from cancer just three years ago, he was very close to experimentally proving the existence of this particle. The only good thing that has come out of this, is that now, after several years of red tape, I have been invited to take Dr. Weber's place at the CERN collider."

The group offered their condolences and congratulations, as Rufus continued his presentation.

"I would also like to add, that there is significant work, which is already being performed at major universities around the country, in the area of Quantum Computing. And because Quantum Computing uses atomic particles and the laws of Quantum Mechanics as the basis for computing, some people, like Seth Loyd at MIT, are pointing out that the universe, which is made up of atomic particles and forces that are all following the laws of Quantum Mechanics, may therefore be a giant computer itself. And still, other scientist conjecture that the universe is a 'living being', that has a brain and has been calculating and thinking, since the beginning of time, and is constantly developing new ideas from its calculations such as 'Life' itself. And still others, such as Dr. Robert Lansler, in his book 'Biocentrism', have put forth the notion that the universe is a 'living thing', but it exists only as a figment of the imagination of all that observe it. I suggest that when you get a chance, that you get on the internet and research some of these concepts for yourself."

"I believe that all of this is just more proof, of the existence of a supreme being."

Rufus stopped speaking. His audience was obviously in deep thought. The implications that these theories could support the possibility of a supreme being certainly had them all thinking.

Ron then thanked Rufus and turned to Ester. "Ester, would you like to go next?"

Ester tried to clear her thoughts as she said: "It is becoming obvious to me that we have all been drawn here for a reason. "

Ester began by explaining that her Catholic mother was from Nigeria and her shaman father was from Southern Colorado, an Native American, and that her father had once said; "That for the Native American's, religion is just part of the *fabric* of your life. Everything you do is immersed in your beliefs, and to call it a 'religion' is misleading. Everything is a part of Mother Earth, and one should live their lives as though you are a part of that *fabric* which makes up all things, and you should allow yourself to be immersed within the *flow* of life."

Then Ester went on to say, "I am sure you can see how this all relates to some of the scientific principles that Rufus has talked to us about this morning. Over the course of my life, I have had several psychic experiences. I believe strongly in a 'Sixth Sense', some of you may know this as Extrasensory Perception or Telepathy."

"I would like to relay to you, one of my favorite verses from the bible. Let me first recite the 'King James Version'."

"The spirit of man is the candle of the LORD, searching all the inward parts of the belly."

"However, I much prefer the 'New International Version'. 'The human spirit is the lamp of the Lord that sheds light on one's inmost being.' Proverbs 20:27'"

"I have also relied heavily on the concepts from a book by New York city pastor named Norman Vincent Peale, it's called the 'Power of Positive Thinking" and this power has provided me with the magical and mystical strength to survive some very emotional experiences in my life, which I will be explaining to you here shortly."

"Just a few years ago I also discovered a new version of the 'Power of Positive Thinking', it is called "The Secret" or "The Secret of Attraction" developed by Rhonda Byrne in 2006. Byrne re-introduces a notion originally popularized by Madame Blavatsky and Norman Peale, which suggests that thinking about certain things will make them appear in one's life. Byrne provides examples of historical persons who have achieved this, and cites a three-step process: ask, believe, and receive, and this is based on a quotation from the Bible; Matthew 21:22: 'And all things, whatsoever ye shall ask in prayer, believing, ye shall receive.'"

"I have incorporated these principles into my everyday life, and I can testify that they work for me. But more than that, Science is beginning to prove that such 'senses' and 'powers' exist. A scientist named Rodger Nelson who had been searching for a global consciousness found that in the 1980s other researchers had noticed that 'Random number generators' could be affected by someone standing near them and concentrating on them. They were affected very slightly, but significantly. Mr. Nelson decided that if one person could affect a number generator, then the thought patterns of entire cities may also have an effect. Nelson and his team set up random number generators in cities around the world. It was called the 'Global Consciousness Project', you can look it up. I believe the instruments are still there today."

"The information is collected 24 hours a day, seven days a week and sent back to Rodger's server at Princeton. The scientists record the largest deviations, from what are expected to happen, from around the world. Some of the largest deviations happened at the time of the 2008 presidential election when Barack Obama was elected president of the United States. Rodger's team has determined that the chances of these deviations happening at that precise time are in the range of 1000 to 1. They have also found that all the deviations that they have seen over time when all added up are in the range of a billion to one."

"And, there is one date that stands out in this experiment, and as you might guess, that date is Sept 11th, 2001, the date of the attack on the World Trade Center in New York City. It was the largest deviation from expected that the project had seen."

CyrIS' mind recalled his experience and started to say something, but then decided he would wait for another time.

"But that is not, what was most amazing, --- what really shocked the researchers, were that significant deviations in the data started hours before the actual attacks occurred, and they believe that this is proof of a global consciousness. I believe that this research along with many other scientific researches are proof that we all have a sixth sense."

"This 'sense' is just more prominent in some, than others. I have always had a 'sixth sense', and my abilities have shown up in a variety of ways, some were small things, like seeing where things were hidden or what a person was thinking, and some were huge, like the two times I had actually inhabited someone else's body."

"It is the belief of Shamans that one can take a journey to other dimensions of existence. This journey is taken by inducing an altered state of consciousness, similar to a state of self-hypnosis called 'a state of *flow*', and in a state of *flow*, the shaman actually becomes one with the person they are focused on."

Ester was used to people thinking she was just another wacko psychic, and so, other than the *emotional* impact to her personally, she was never afraid to tell people about her experiences. She figured, --- they either accepted them, --- or they didn't. So, without hesitation, she spent the next hour giving an overview of her visits to the mind of Jim Jones and her two visits to the mind of David Koresh.

"In those visits, I learned a lot about the dramatic difference between remote observation and actually living the experiences of the person being observed. I learned that one cannot 'judge a book by its cover' or even by the book's reviews. Read the book, live within the *emotions*, understand the drivers, and understand the experiences that create the filters which, for each individual, make the *illogical*, ---*logical*."

"For me personally, having found myself drowning in the *emotions* of these events, I realized that I needed a lifeboat or someone on firm ground to help balance out my *emotional*-centric personality. And luckily, I have found that, in the rock-solid *logical* person of, CyrIS Steel. He helps to complete me, and I believe, we are all incomplete, and we all need others to help complete us."

"I have always had a feeling that something was missing, an emptiness of sorts, an emptiness, that not even CyrIS has been able to completely fill. Part of that emptiness was a result of having psychic powers, which I could not explain. I have been searching continuously for an explanation for those powers. I have studied the Bible, and I have always been especially interested in the concept of the *Holy Spirit*. I have spent a considerable amount of time studying Spiritualism and of course Shamanism. All of these areas seemed to brush up against an answer but never gave me complete satisfaction."

"But, I have to admit, hearing Rufus' explanation of the 'Higgs field', a field that creates mass, a field that connects all things together, --- for me, it's as if a *light* has been turned on, my heart nearly jumped out of my chest, thinking that this may be what I have been looking for, and I am anxious to hear more."

Ester then said, "It seems to me that we may be suggesting here that there is a relationship between what we consider our finite material world and that of the infinite beyond. I would like to point out that there is an ancient study called the Kabbalah."

"The Kabbalah is a set of teachings meant to explain the relationship between the eternal mysterious infinite (no end) and the finite mortal universe. The Kabbalah is not a religion, but it forms the foundation of mystical religious interpretations. It seeks to define the nature of the universe and the human being. It also presents methods for understanding this relationship between humans and the universe. You see, I am not the only one searching."

"I am extremely excited that Congressman... I mean Ron, has invited CyrIS and myself, to attend this conference. I am anxious to hear from the other attendees, and I will surely add additional information to the meeting if necessary. But for now, I would like to hear from some of the others."

Ron looked at the attendees sitting around the room; all had been locked into what Ester was saying. Ron was not sure if it was because they couldn't believe that he would invite a psychic to their scientific conference, or if they were just amazed by her detailed descriptions of her visits to Jim Jones and David Koresh.

Ron turned to Christine who seemed the most enthralled with Ester's speech and asked her if she would like to address the group next. But CyrIS interrupts and ask if they would mind if he followed Ester. Christine seemed to accept the interruption and Ron nodded to CyrIS.

"First of all, I want to say how proud I am of my wife Ester. Ester, I love you very much."

Smiling at Ester and then directing his attention to the group.

"As you all know my background is in interpretation of the scriptures. However, these days, I am finding more answers to my questions in the realm of science than religion. The questions are great, and the puzzles are difficult, but the clues are everywhere, they are in the Bible, the Quran, the Tora, the Dead Sea scrolls and other religious documents such as those included in the Kabbalah."

"There are also clues in the study of mysticism, spiritualism, and shamanism, as well as in the study of Psychology and Philosophy."

"For many, many years now there has been an apparent gap between these studies, and that of science. But now, science is not only validating some of the concepts from these areas of study, --- now science, specifically physics, is getting to the very root of understanding these vital questions. Science is helping to solve the puzzles. But it will take more than just observation; it will take imagination."

"Albert Einstein said: '*Logic* will get you from A to Z; imagination will get you *everywhere*.'"

"And William S. Burroughs once said: 'Nothing exists until, or unless, it is *observed*. An artist is making something exist by *observing* it, and his hope for other people; is that they will also make it exist by *observing it.*'"

"And just like Ester, I was very moved by Rufus' speech, I think that Imagination is like *Dark Matter*. In other words, nothing can exist without being imagined first. Imagination, just like *Dark Matter*, is the creator, it is what makes things come into existence. On the other hand, *Observation* is like the Higgs Field, it is what makes things solid, it is what holds things together; nothing can continue to exist without being *observed*. I believe that we are all products of imagination i.e. *Dark Matter*, and figments of *observation* i.e. the Higgs field."

"I believe that the Bible, as well as science, as shown by Rufus, indicates that the *Holy Spirit* is the *fabric* of the universe and that our lives, just as Ester has indicated, are *flowing* within that *fabric*. I would like to point out that there have been references to the *Holy Spirit* from the very beginning of the Bible."

"'And the earth was without form and void, and *darkness* was upon the face of the deep. And the *Spirit* of God moved upon the face of the waters.' Genesis 1:2"

"Now I would like to tell you about an ancient scroll I found one day in the wall of a very old church. This scroll has had a very dramatic impact on me, and I believe Ester as well. It has dramatically shaped our search for answers. Answers to the puzzles all around us, and the answers to the cause of voids within us all."

CyrIS reached into his briefcase and pulled out a document and began to read from it. He then explained how he developed his name and the name of his church based on information from the scroll and how the scroll had pointed him to the connections between science and religion, and in general to the mysteries that can be uncovered by both.

"I believe that many theologians have long believed that there was a great mystery hidden in the Bible, and that the solutions to that puzzle were also hidden within the pages of the Bible. Many have dedicated their lives to the interpretation of the Bible in an effort to uncover that mystery and to solve that puzzle."

"I also believe that the Bible eludes to a great mystery, a master puzzle so to speak. However, it is clear to me that the answers to this master riddle do not reside solely within the Bible. I believe that the Bible only has portions of the solution. The pieces of the master puzzle reside within many boxes. They reside within religion, psychology, mysticism and science. And it is my hope that this group, just as Rufus has, will provide more clues to the solution of this master riddle."

And then CyrIS recited one more section from the scroll: "My son as the science of man is born of the *logic* of man, and as the religion of man is born of the *emotion* of man. Then you should know that *logic* and *emotion* are threads in the fabric of the mystery. Search within that fabric."

CyrIS then explained to the group how he and Ester had looked at the words "*Logic and Emotion*" and how they had developed what they called the "God's *Fabric*", and then he pulled a small poster board of the God's *Fabric, from* his briefcase.

"This may appear to make no sense," CyrIS says while pointing to the poster board. "But just like the scriptures and much of the other things we are discussing today. It requires closer examination." Then CyrIS showed them how the words '*Logic*' and '*Emotion*' made up the fabric of the matrix on the poster board, and how it was like a giant crossword puzzle that extended infinitely in all directions. Then CyrIS explained how he and Ester had looked at the matrix for hours and then determined that there must be a hidden field that *connects* the letters and thus the words together.

CyrIS pointed out that this is what they believed the scroll intended for them to find, and now they believe that much of what Rufus was talking about is the source of that hidden *connection*.

CyrIS then turned to Rufus and said, "Does this not also sound a lot like your descriptions of the Big Bang, and of Matter, *Dark Matter, Light, Energy and Dark Energy*. It is all the parts that make up the whole. All *connected*. "

Rufus trying to digest what CyrIS had just said, slowly responded. "I always believed that at the beginning of the universe there was nothing". Rufus then quoting the bible said. "'And the earth was without form and void, and darkness was upon the face of the deep. And the Spirit of God moved upon the face of the waters.' Genesis 1:2"

"But now I understand that before the Big Bang there was something and it was God and the *Holy Spirit* as one. I now believe that God is all *Energy*, and God is revealed in the form of *Light*. As Einstein once said about *Light*; 'it is the one constant in the universe.' I also believe that the *Holy Spirit* is a combination of the *Higgs Field* and *Dark Matter*. That is, the *Holy Spirit, as Dark Matter,* is what created *matter* from *energy,* in the form of *light,* in the early development of the universe, and continues to do that today."

"Do you see that we are all made up of the substance of God, that is, *energy* and *light*? And I believe, as you have just stated, that the *Holy Spirit* as the *Higgs Field* is what continues to hold all matter together, and it is what keeps us *connected* to each other and to *all things* in the universe. And yes, I agree that a combination of information from a variety of disciplines will be necessary to explain the connections between all things."

Rufus hesitated for a moment, but CyrIS did not interrupt. It was obvious Rufus had more to contribute.

Rufus began again, "If you don't mind, I would like to make a few comments on Ester's references to the Kabala?""

CyrIS responded immediately, "No, please."

Rufus continued "I know that my primary purpose, at these meetings, is to provide a scientific perspective."

"You all can see that I am black, but I am also Jewish, and I am a student of Jewish historical beliefs."

"Earlier, Ester mentioned the 'Kabbalah', and I think you will find the concepts in 'the books of the Kabbalah' very pertinent to the nature of our discussions."

"The relationship, that Ester mentioned, between human beings and the universe was of special interest to many followers of the early scriptures. The Kabbalah was an effort by these followers to explain that relationship, and the concepts of the Kabbalah are considered to unfold in three stages."

"You see, prior to the first stage, it was believed that people were as one, in unity with each other and the universe, and there was only one force governing the world, and that was the Creator."

"Kabbalist believe that this is what the Bible means by, 'And the whole earth was of one language and of one speech' in

Genesis 11:1, and 'The Lord said, 'Behold, they are one people, and they all have the same language. …and now nothing which they purpose to do will be impossible for them' Genesis 11:6."

"Everyone knew about the Creator, the force of love and giving, and all were united with it. However, there was a prolonged spiritual decline, and the people forgot this unity. Instead, people began to believe that there were many forces in the world, and egoism and selfishness prevailed."

"But thousands of years ago, Abraham noticed that all these forces obeyed the same rules of birth and death, budding and withering. Abraham developed a teaching method that would help him to once again reveal this concept to the people, and this was a prototype of the teaching method we now call the 'Kabbalah', and stage one of the Kabbalah, was Moses' Torah, or the Old Testament."

Rufus looked at Ester. "Ester, you are probably familiar with the Native American tradition of the Council Circle, where the members sit in a circle, each member expressing a different aspect of the same issue."

Ester nodded in agreement.

"You see," Rufus continued. "Abraham didn't want to see things only from his perspective. He wanted to see through everyone's eyes, and thus discover the one force that made different people see different things. Certainly, this was something that Ester was able to do with Jim Jones and David Koresh."

Ester was familiar with the Kabbalah but had never thought about it from this perspective.

Rufus continued. "So, while Moses' Torah was a big step forward since it helped a whole nation *connect* with the Creator, it was not the end of the road. The end of the road, being that point when all of humanity reclaims what it once had, and then lost. That being, to once again be as one."

"The second stage was primarily described in the 'The Book of Zohar' written by Rabbi Shimon Bar Yochai (Rashbi)."

"Rashbi's 'Book of Zohar' is a commentary on Moses' Torah. It is an interpretation of the Torah, intended to help teach people the importance of unity and *connection* with each other, and that this is a force that opposes individual egoism and selfishness."

"In the third and final stage, the Messiah will come, and every single member of humankind will personally experience the Creator in the deepest sense of the word. The bible says, 'they shall all know me, from the least of them unto the greatest of them' Jeremiah 31:33."

"I believe that this, in a sense, is a description of the fabric of the universe. And that if the Kabbalah was pointing toward a point in time when 'all of humanity reclaims what it once had, and then lost', it could be pointing to a point in time when 'man' discovers a 'Unified theory of everything.' Just as Abraham had envisioned, this may be the time when we begin looking at this master puzzle from a variety of perspectives, religious, psychiatric, mystic, and scientific.

Christine then ask, "Is the Kabbalah a book?"

"It is not one book" Rufus responded, "but several, including 'The Bible', 'The Book of Zohar', 'The Tree of Life', and 'The Study of the Ten Sefirot'. These books are considered to be authentic Kabbalistic sources and were intended to promote the Kabbalistic principles of the *spiritual* realms. There are other Kabbalistic books as well, all of which, form the Kabbalah."

Ron, thinking this would allow for a good transition to Christine, jumped in.

"Thanks, Rufus, this has all been very enlightening. However, we have not heard Christine's perspective on all of this, and it is starting to get late in the day." And then turning to Christine, and with a voice much silkier and softer than he had used with the others, he said. "Christine?"

It was easy for everyone in the group, including Christine, to see that Ron had feelings for her. But, Christine, pretended not to notice, as she began.

"I have never been a believer in the mystics, I consider myself to be, too much of a scientist, to believe in such hocus-pocus. However, in the last several years, since Ester and I have been friends, I have learned a lot from her, and I have since been fascinated by the parallels between Shamanism and Psychology, and specifically with the concepts of 'flow' that Ester has previously described."

"Most of my adult life has been dedicated to the study of the subconscious mind. I have studied the dreams, the consciousness, and the morals, formed by the human brain, and I have specifically studied the minds of psychopaths. And I would like to point out that there are many areas of psychology that deal with 'flow'. Areas, such as process-oriented psychology, which studies the process of stepping out of time but remaining aware of time while experiencing the *flow* of it, Soto Zen calls this 'stream entering. 'And there are other areas of psychology such as Dr. Carl Jung's 'active imagination' and 'Gestalt Psychology' which are also about *flow*. Furthermore, Jung's concept of 'Synchronicity' which is all about an interconnection between humans, is all very similar to Rufus' description of '*Entanglement*'."

Christine looked at Rufus as she said this, and thought to herself, that even though Rufus was very rugged looking, he was still very attractive. But as she looked at him, following her comment on "*entanglement*", she was careful not to show any of those feelings, as Ron shown towards her.

Christine went on "And the more I studied, the more I realized that there was a lot more to the subconscious than just 'a voice in my head' or just 'dreams.'"

"Maybe the subconscious provided the path to a larger connection, a connection to other people. But now I see that it may provide an even larger connection, and that is to the entire universe."

"But that is not all" Christine went on to say, "now I am about to tell you something that I have never told anyone else. I too have had the experience of inhabiting someone else's body." Christine looked at the faces of each person in the group, looking for skepticism. But all she could see were looks of expectation, so she continued.

Christine explained how when she was just 13 years old, she visited the mind of John Hinckley on the day of his attempt to assassinate President Reagan. Christine told the story of that day's events, in graphic detail. She then went on to describe the events of April 20th, 1999 at Columbine High School and her visit with Eric Harris, again in graphic detail. Christine explained that both of these young men were, what she considered to be, psychopaths, but they were very different in their basic natures.

The group was fascinated by Christine's description of the mind of a psychopath, their lack of empathy, their needs, and driving forces. It was obvious to all in attendance that Christine had spent a lot of time thinking about and analyzing the mind of a psychopath and other aspects of the subconscious. And she spent a considerable amount of time describing the scientific research that she had completed in this area, and the amount of time that she had spent trying to get those two events and the reasons for her visitations worked out in her mind.

"You see," she continued, "I have to admit that, as a young girl, I was a very fragile, very naïve, very innocent and very weak. I was so shy and helpless and so scared of everything, that I had a lot of trouble navigating life. I depended heavily on my parents to get by, and on several occasions considered suicide as a remedy, but here again, I was too weak to actually follow through."

"But then this incredible event happened where I witnessed the attempt on President Reagan's life from inside of the mind of the actual assailant. It changed me, and at least at first, not for the better. I was horrified by the event. I was scared to death that John would come looking for me, just like he had been looking for Jodie. I went to a very, very dark place and became extremely depressed, and this time I didn't just consider suicide, I attempted it."

"I took a bunch of pills from my mother's medicine cabinet, but my mother found me and rushed me to the hospital. When I woke up that day, still held deep within the grasp of *darkness* and depression, I felt something. I had this thought about how much my mother must love me to have saved me, and then I thought about how weak I was, but not dead. I thought to myself, why should I let this *darkness* take my life. Why should I let this *darkness* be in control? And I felt a glimmer of strength. I thought, I only have one life, one chance at living, why should I have to give it up to *darkness*."

"That's when I began my fight against *darkness*. For years I worked hard to get stronger and stronger, and then it happened again, at Columbine High School. Only this time it was much worse. It was not adults being shot and killed, it was children, --- and some were the same age as my own son's. Once again, the *darkness* tried to take me, but I fought back and now I am stronger than ever. Now I can take on anything, I can take on the world. Now, I am a true believer in the power of *darkness*. Because *what does not kill you makes you stronger.*"

"Rufus, you said that *Light* saved you, I think that your strength came from your years in darkness, and that *light* you saw was just a sign for you to begin the process of gaining strength from your struggle with *darkness*."

"You're wrong about that" Rufus responded quickly. "I think you were mired in *darkness* and your strength came from the *light* that you moved toward."

"Don't tell me I'm wrong, I know what I am talking about." Christine, a bit of anger in her tone.

Rufus then responded, now definitely raising his voice "Look, I don't think you know 'shit from shine-olla' much less anything about the difference between *light and darkness*. Bitch." Rufus stood up and was now towering over Christine.

"Hey! FUCK YOU! You, black bastard, and sit down, you don't scare me." Christine, almost screaming.

"Whoa! Whoa! Whoa!" Ron jumped in, as Ester and CyrIS sat in shock. "Settle down. Where did all that come from? Let's be civilized, I realize that these are all very personal subjects for each of us, but we are not going to accomplish anything if we can't be civilized. Please, just calm down." Ron was now glaring at Rufus for getting sharp with Christine.

After a moment or two, Christine spoke again, as Rufus returned to his seat. "I apologize. It has taken me years to wrestle with these demons and my strength is very much based on these beliefs in the power of *darkness*."

Christine paused for a second to see if Rufus was ready to apologize, but he was still fuming, so she continued. "It took a lot for me to tell you the stories of my journeys into the minds of those two young men. I frankly couldn't have done it without witnessing the strength and fortitude that Ester exhibited in exposing her own journeys. Thank you, Ester. But even though it felt good to finally tell someone about these events, it was still very stressful for me and I am afraid I let that stress get to me. "

Rufus, could not believe how this lily-white princess, had somehow resurrected some of the anger and fire from his previous life, and she did it in just a few simple words. And then he spoke.

"I also want to apologize for my outburst. I'm not sure what happened there. But I am also very steadfast in my convictions of right and wrong, and I am afraid I let some of that fighting nature of mine, creep in from my past in defense of my positions."

It was obvious to everyone that neither of them had apologized to the other but had only apologized to the group in general for their actions.

Christine, then said, "Ron if it is alright with you, I would like to elaborate on some of the points I was making before our slight diversion."

Ron smiles at Christine. "Certainly, please continue."

"It is apparent that we are talking about a *connection* between people that is beyond accepted reality. And I believe that the portal to that connection is most likely through the subconscious."

"What I have learned from my experience is that these young men had tremendous voids within them that they were trying to fill. And I also experienced something else, and that was that even though these boys obviously both had a subconscious, they were both missing a key ingredient of the subconscious, and that was 'empathy', they just did not care what anyone else felt. That lack of empathy is hard to imagine for anyone that can feel empathy. But being inside of them, I could understand their perspective, they not only, could not feel anything for anyone else, they could not understand why anyone would care about anyone other than themselves. They were completely narcissistic."

"I have concluded that all of us may have this emptiness inside that we are longing to fill. And most of us have the ability, though we may not be aware of it, to tap into this mystical *connection* to other people by way of our subconscious minds. But for the psychopath, these *connections* are much harder, if not impossible to make. And thus, there is no relief for the emptiness they feel, resulting in an exacerbation of the feelings within them, and manifesting in much more outlandish efforts to resolve those feelings."

"I am not sure what the events, that Ester and I have experienced, have to do with our purpose here today, but somehow I feel exposing my stories to this group were not only appropriate but required. I'm starting to feel, that it is only *logical*, that everyone in this room, is here for a reason."

Once again, the room was silent. Ron could not believe what he had just heard. He had not been totally shocked by the stories from Ester, after all, she was a known psychic and one would expect to hear such stories from her. But Christine was someone that Ron had strong feelings for, and she was a renowned psychologist, highly regarded in her field, and he certainly did not expect to hear such a story from her. Ron was also starting to think that this group was headed towards something significant, and he was excited to be a part of it and hoped that he would be able to capitalize on it as well.

Ron thought this might be a good stopping point and said "It's almost 4:00 and we have been working for nearly 8 hours. I suggest we quit for today and start again at 8:00 in the morning."

Everyone agreed, and all retired for the day.

CHAPTER 32 –
TAKING IT TO THE LIMIT

April 18ᵗʰ, 2012

Rufus Middleman age 42

Christine Basurto, age 44

CyrIS Steel, age 62

Ester Suni Nate, age 60

The group once again gathers in Ron's hotel suite. Ron begins: "I know that Rufus has a lot more to contribute and I am going to ask him to once again kick off our meeting."

Rufus begins: "Good morning everyone."

"I am not sure how familiar you are with Calculus. But Calculus was invented by Sir Isaac Newton. He did this by way of what Einstein called a 'thought experiment'. It went something like this: He thought about taking a one-second walk and traveling the distance it took him in one second. He then thought about a half second walk and that distance, and he kept repeating this reduction in the time and distance of the walk. In fact, he took this process to infinity. He then thought about what happens when the time and distance was infinitesimally small. He called this: *taking it to the Limit*. As he thought about this, he realized that at the limit there is no longer any measurement of time or distance, there is only the *flow* to the next instant in time. He called this point a 'fluxion' which means '*flow*'. Later other mathematician changed this to the term 'differential'. Some of you may be familiar with the term 'Differential Calculus'. Differential Calculus is about the mathematical world of, continuous change or *flow*. I would point out, that this is where we may be seeing the beginning of the relationship between math or science, and the world of religion and psychology."

Rufus then says: "I have been a fighter my whole life, and I am not speaking figuratively I am talking literally. When I was a young boy, I used to get into fist fights almost daily. I loved fighting and now listening to all of this talk, I realize that it was a way for me to feel alive, to be a part of the *flow* of life."

Rufus, standing before the group is now silent. He stares down at the floor and looks extremely anxious, it was obvious that he had something else to say and was either trying to determine exactly how to say it, or whether he should say it all. He stood for a very long time, to the point where the group became a bit uncomfortable, but no one said a word and waited patiently for Rufus to gather his thoughts.

Then suddenly, Rufus turned to Ron and asked him if the group could make a pact. Ron was surprised, hesitated and then asked him exactly what he was talking about.

Rufus went on to explain "I too, feel that there is something very important happening in this conference. Ester and Christine have opened up and exposed some very personal events in their lives, and if we all want to continue to speak freely along these lines, maybe the group should make an agreement about disclosure."

Ron then pointed out, "Rufus this meeting has been sanctioned by the federal government and as such the meeting's contents are classified 'Top Secret'. And for this reason, you have each had background checks prior to the meeting. And you have all signed non-disclosure agreements, what else could you want."

Rufus responded "Ron, I am aware of all of that, but we are all professionals and it is apparent that we will not only be discussing, what could be considered, highly sensitive scientific information, but we will also be discussing highly personal information, which if not handled with extreme sensitivity, could be damaging to our personal careers. I may be just a chauffeur and bodyguard, but I still want to protect my reputation as a scientist. I may have an opportunity to work with the CERN supercollider in Switzerland, and I don't want to blow that opportunity."

Rufus then suggested that they make a pact among the group that nothing would leave the room or be published without the unanimous consent of all the parties involved. The group readily agreed, and for the next half an hour they argued over the wording of the pact but eventually came to an agreement. They made copies for everyone and they all signed each copy.

Ron then directing his next question to Rufus, said, "Rufus, I don't think you asked for this special agreement just for the hell of it. Do you have something else you want to share with the group?"

"Ron, that is correct. You see, I am a scientist, and scientists are supposed to base their findings on facts that are repeatable through experimental observation. I have a reputation to maintain, but I have had two experiences, which I am unable to replicate in a laboratory. But just as I believe they did for Ester and Christine; these events did happen to me."

He went on to explain that he too had spent a day in the minds of some infamous characters, at very critical moments in their lives. Rufus then described in great detail his internal journeys with Randy Weaver and Timothy McVeigh. He described not only what he observed and the feelings and thoughts of these individuals, but he also described his own feelings and thoughts as he observed them.

Rufus went on to explain that when he had visited the minds of these two people, he had been subjected not only to what they could see, hear and touch, but he was also subjected to their thoughts, feelings and their *logic and emotions,* just as Ester and Christine had described. And that is what made the experience so profound.

"You can obviously see that I am black, and I believe that you also know that I am Jewish. Well, I am also human, with all of the weaknesses that any human being might be susceptible too."

"Both of these men were prejudiced against blacks and they were especially prejudiced against Jews. And I was extremely angry with both of them. There were points in those visits that if I could have, I would have kicked the shit out of both them, and at other points, maybe even killed them. I didn't understand why I was there, and why I was being subjected to this, without having any power to do anything about it."

"Afterwards, my anger and hatred continued to grow, and that anger got me deeper and deeper into trouble. And as I mentioned yesterday, those troubles eventually forced me to join the army."

"I also mentioned to you that, in Iraq, I had an epiphany that completely changed my life. You see, while I was there, I only killed one insurgent, and it turned out, that this insurgent, this horrible demon that I was eradicating to save our country from the evils of Islam, turned out to be just a boy. A boy about thirteen years old, and killing this boy is what changed me. I don't know if it was caused by the concussion, I suffered in the blast that occurred just seconds after I shot this young man, or if it was something more. But a bright *light* emerged from this young boy's chest, and that '*Light*' totally enveloped me, body and soul."

"When I woke up in a medivac hospital, I was a different person. The '*Light*' had completely changed me. No, what it really did was save me. I was floundering in the *darkness* of anger and hatred, and this "*Light*" drew me up and gave me the strength and courage to face the world from a whole new perspective. I was no longer angry at the world and no longer angry at everyone in it. To me, it was the power of the '*Light* of God', and I have since dedicated myself, to use this new-found strength and courage to use the scriptures and scientific research to prove God's existence."

"This event not only changed my outlook for the future, but it made me reevaluate my past, including everything that happened to me during the times I spent with Weaver and McVeigh. That was when I realized, why I was sent on those journeys, not to stop them from happening, but to learn from those experiences."

"You see, observing prejudice from a distance, is much different than living and breathing it. And as I said, I am human, and I have my own prejudices. That is to say, I have always thought that I understood prejudice of other people. 'I am better than you.' 'I am more important than you.' 'The group I am a member of is entitled to more', and all of the other reasons they believe are *logical*."

"But after having experienced visits to these two very prejudice individuals, my attitude and understanding of prejudice have now completely changed. Let me explain."

"Timothy McVeigh had been brought up in a prejudiced environment, and he had this raging emptiness in his life. McVeigh believed that he could fill that *void* by becoming famous, especially in the eyes of his fellow white supremacist. I would point out here, that many in the white supremacist community think, that he irreparably damaged their movement by killing innocent children when he bombed the Murrah building in Oklahoma City. But McVeigh was so driven by his need to satisfy this emptiness in his life, that he pressed on, thinking only that 'The end justifies the means'. It was his intent, to have the bombing result in a revolution against the United States government, which would result in a white-dominated and controlled United States."

"Now let's take a look at my experience with Randy Weaver. I found this experience to be in many ways the same, but also completely different. Randy Weaver had been brought up in a southern religious environment certainly prejudice against blacks and Jews, but that was not truly the basis for his prejudice. He had a *void* in his soul as well, I could feel it. It was something missing in his life that he desperately needed. He, and especially his wife Vickie, found what they were looking for in the Old Testament of the Bible. It's ironic, that most of the Old Testaments of the bible were written by Jews, and it was those very scriptures that Randy and his wife, and many other people as far as that goes, used as a basis for their prejudice against Jews, and blacks or whoever they thought were not chosen."

"Randy and Vickie actually thought that Jews were the instruments of Satan. But it was clear to me that Randy had an overwhelming feeling, that his point of view was absolutely correct, and that only in total dedication to this belief in the bible, would his soul be saved. It gave Randy a sense of satisfaction that he was doing the right thing, and his beliefs, along with his love for his wife Vickie and his family, helped fill most of the voids in his life. These connections to the Old Testament, to Yahweh, and to his family, were essential to his life."

"The fact that there are people out there, who are extremely prejudiced, is not news to anyone, and that they base their prejudice on the Bible or the Koran or the Constitution of the United States or any other source is not news either. However, What I learned, through my experience with these two, was something I could not see by observing their behaviors from the outside, but rather what I felt while observing their behavior from the inside. And what I felt was that the *voids* in their lives were so overwhelming, that at least for these people, there could be no stopping them in their quest to relieve the pain associated with that emptiness."

"My connection to Randy Weaver and to Timothy McVeigh taught me similar lessons to those described by Ester and Christine. I too learned a lot from their *connections* and *disconnections* from other people and from God. But also, and possibly even more important, I learned a huge lesson regarding prejudice. And that lesson was that; the misunderstandings between people, that are caused by the lack of a positive *connection*, may push a person away from and *disconnect* them from the very people, that can fill those *voids* in their lives that they are so desperately seeking to fill."

"This is very hard for me to say, but I can now empathize with these two desperate men. There is no way, for anyone to understand how they were driven unless one can take the trip that I, and several others in this room, have taken. One must do more than 'Walk in their shoes', you must live with the understanding of what drives them. You must live behind the filters for their *logic*."

"It is interesting that Christine earlier used the word '*Logical*' when referring to the formation of this group. I would like to talk about "*logic*" for a bit. I am obviously a man of science, and to me, *logic* always implied something that was fact-based. That is, if something has facts to back it up, then the conclusion is *logical*. But I have learned over time, to the contrary. Let me give you some examples: To Aristotle, because the sun and the stars moved around the earth, it was *logical* that the earth was the center of the universe. Guess what? Copernicus and Galileo looked at that same sun and those same stars and came up with a completely different *logical* conclusion. And when I entered the mind of Randy Weaver it soon became clear to me that from his perspective the bible was the source of all knowledge and it was only *logical* that whatever the Bible decreed had to be the total and only truth. And if the bible said, referring to the 'Hittites', which were black: 'Thou shalt smite them, and utterly destroy them; thou shalt make no covenant with them, nor show mercy unto them: Neither shalt thou make marriages with them; thy daughter thou shalt not give unto his son, nor his daughter shalt thou take unto thy son.' Deuteronomy 7:2-3. Then *logically,* to Randy, it must be the truth."

Then Rufus quotes a question from the Old Testament:

"'Have we not all one father? Hath not one God created us? Why do we deal treacherously every man against his brother, by profaning the covenant of our fathers?' Malachi 2:10"

And then Rufus said: "And to me, it is only *logical* that all men should be treated equally because they are all decedents of the same parents."

"My point here is that what is perfectly *logical* to one person, or group of people, can be diametrically opposed to the *logic* of another. It all depends on how the information, which is the basis for the *logic* of each individual, is filtered. And I believe that the intersection of these *logical* conclusions can create an *emotional entanglement* of disagreement, which can result in damage to both parties."

"This, however, in no way means that I now condone any kind of prejudice. To the contrary, it has just made me that much more determined to work towards the elimination of it. I have looked at the conventional methods of eliminating prejudice, which has been mostly through education. And I do admit that there has been some success. But now I believe that the source of many of the problems in the world is often a result of these *voids,* and the resultant drivers to fill these *voids* in people's lives. If there was only some way for these people to experience the *logic* of those they discriminate against, maybe things would be different."

"I must point out that these *voids* in people's lives are not all bad. Those needs to fill voids have driven people too, --- explore the unknown, --- construct the impossible, --- Create the magnificent, --- and solve the mysteries. I think that is why we are all here."

"These experiences of *logical* and *emotional* possession, of another person, have created a very large *void*, for me personally. That *void* has driven me, for several years, to seek understanding of the sources of the more destructive of these *voids*, not completely by way of mysticism, or religion, or psychology, but primarily by way of my work in science, especially in the area of physics. I do agree with Christine, --- at least on one thing, and that is that we have all been drawn together here for a reason. "

"From my experiences and after listening to you describe your experiences; It is apparent that these close, extremely personal, *connections* to another human has helped fill in the *voids* in each of our lives. It made each of us a more complete person, it helped us to understand, that we do not stand alone, that we are part of a much larger existence and that only through these *connections* to others, can we feel complete."

Rufus paused for a moment and then went on.

"I am not sure how these *connections* can occur. Maybe by way of meditation, our prayers or the prayers of others, and it might be related to our subconscious. But I believe that the medium for these *connections* is formed by the *fabric* of the universe."

"It could be, in the form of a *logical* and *emotional fabric,* or the *fabric* formed by the *Higgs Field, Dark Matter or Dark Energy*. And it does not *matter* whether it is called the *spirit* world, or the *Holy Spirit* or even God; it does exist and needs to be taken advantage of to *connect* all of us together to resolve these differences in filtered *Logic*, which is a kind of *Dark Energy* driving the people of this world apart."

"I also believe that the journeys we have each taken were meant to teach us a very important lesson and serve to motivate us to work together. I also now agree with CyrIS. The answers to our search may reside in some combination of religion, psychology, psychic phenomena, and science, and I believe each of us, in this room, now contains a portion of the solution to a much larger puzzle, a mystery to be solved, and it is my responsibility to support the scientific portion of that solution."

Rufus hesitates for a second and then says, "Two monks are crossing a bridge over a stream. The one monk asks the other, 'How deep is the stream?' The other monk throws the first monk off the bridge into the stream."

"The point here is that one can tell you how deep the stream is, or you can be thrown into the stream and you can experience its depth for yourself. I believe that some of us have been thrown into the stream."

The group was silent for several minutes, a bit weary with all of the information they were trying to digest. They had started at 8:00 AM and had been working for four hours.

Ron then stood up and said, "As I had previously mentioned, I have an important meeting this evening and I must prepare. So, I suggest that we break at this time and get together again tomorrow."

Ron, then with a large smile on his face, apparently to lighten the mood, says,

"I would like all of you, to come down to the Capitol building in the morning. I will take you on a short tour of the building and then we will proceed to the National Renewable Energy Laboratories in Golden and then to the National Center for Atmospheric Research in Boulder. There we will meet with some of the scientist interested in the Quantum Computing project. After that, we will come back here and see if we can bring all of this together into some concise conclusions and determine if there is some relevance to the advancement of Quantum Computing."

The group agrees and once again depart from the meeting room.

After the meeting, Ron asks Christine if she would join him for lunch. Christine knew that Ron was supposed to have an important meeting with high-level Republican leaders that evening, and she hoped that if she went to lunch with him, he would invite her to that meeting. She admired Ron's position in government and in the Republican Party. She truly felt that, even though he had been in government, and in the party, for quite some time, he had only recently seemed to become more popular with the public and with the party. She admired him for that, but sometimes she detected a shifty side to the Congressman that concerned her. None the less, she agreed to have lunch with Ron, and she went to her room to get ready.

Ron had arranged for Christine and himself to have suites on the top floor and he arranged for Rufus to have a room on a lower floor, which was not a suite but was very nice just the same, and Ester and CyrIS had arranged for their own accommodations.

Christine meets Ron for lunch in the main dining room of the hotel, she is a bit concerned that it will be just the two of them as the others were left to manage on their own. But Ron was very polite and casual during their lunch, which relaxed Christine, and she enjoyed their short visit.

After lunch, Ron told Christine that he had to go to his room and prepare for the meeting which was scheduled at 6:00 p.m. He then asked Christine if she would like to attend the meeting. Christine quickly agrees, but then Ron also suggests that Christine and he get together and go to one of the exclusive stores in downtown and do a little shopping before the meeting. Christine reluctantly agrees to this seemingly inappropriate addition to their evening. But as she leaves for her room, Christine is thrilled with the possibility of meeting some of the big wigs in the Republican Party and being involved in such an important strategy session.

At 3:00 Ron meets with Christine in front of the hotel. As they get into the limousine Christine is a bit shocked to have Rufus holding the door for her. She thinks to herself, "I shouldn't be shocked; after all, he is the congressman's chauffeur. But it does seem strange after hearing Rufus deliver such eloquent speeches on such highly technical subjects."

"Rufus speaks with such confidence, and exposes such personal experiences with passion, that it almost made me cry. Now to see him here, in such a different role, the contrast is a bit overwhelming."

Rufus did not say or do anything; he just stayed in his role as chauffeur perfectly, exhibiting a whole new level of poise and confidence. But Christine could not help but notice how attractive he looked in his uniform, and once again felt a flush of *emotion*, but at the same time, hoping that her new feelings for Rufus would not be exposed to the congressman.

Rufus closed the door after they were in. He then went around to the front of the car and got into the driver's seat. The window was closed between the front and back seat and the small curtain between the seats was also closed, which makes Christine a little nervous. However, during the trip to the store, Ron is a perfect gentleman. He even has Christine laughing at several points along their way.

When they had first met to go on this excursion, Christine could tell that Ron was surprised at how she was dressed. She was gorgeous, she was in a dress that was fairly tight fitting and with a hem about 6 inches above her knees, it was also low cut and showed some cleavage, the dress had a bit of sparkle to it and really accentuated her large breast. Her makeup was perfect, and she looked like she was going to a ball. Ron's only comment was "Christine you look very lovely" apparently not trying to gush over her, though Christine could see that he was a bit excited.

Christine had dressed this way for two reasons, first Ron had told her the name of the store they were going to visit and she knew it was very exclusive and she wanted to look like she was worthy of shopping there. Her second reason was the real reason, and that was that she hoped she would be meeting with some of the Republican bigwigs and she was very anxious to make a good impression.

Rufus dropped them off at the store and waited in the car while they shopped.

Christine really liked the store but found that most items were out of her price range. The congressman made several offers to buy her some expensive things, but she said she would not be comfortable with that. She was not that interested in developing a personal relationship with Ron, after all, he was married. He finally talked her into letting him buy her a small locket that cost $100.00. Christine liked nice things, like those in the store and told herself that accepting something as small as the locket would not make her feel any obligations to the congressman. But Christine could tell that Ron was very happy that he was able to break this barrier with her, even in this small way.

When they got back to the hotel, Rufus dropped them off in front and then drove away, and Christine wondered where Rufus would go.

Ron asked Christine to wait in the lobby while he found out where the other meeting attendees were. In a few minutes, he returns with Reince Priebus, Chairman of the Republican National Committee and Sharon Day, Co-Chair of the Republican National Committee. Christine was very excited; these were very high-level members of the Republican Party. Ron introduced Christine. She was very formal and expressed her concern over the recent mass shootings at Oikos University in Oakland, California, and in Tulsa Oklahoma.

Christine then used these shootings as an opportunity to express her belief in the rights of all Americans to bear arms. "I hope that eventually laws can be enacted that would protect the public from those who would be irresponsible with guns and yet protect constitutional rights of all Americans at the same time".

They seemed to like what she had said, and Christine felt good that she had made an impression. The senator and congressman told Christine that it was nice to meet her, and they excused themselves and left for the meeting room. Christine thought this was strange as they left her and the congressman standing in the lobby.

Ron then turned to Christine and said. "Christine, I apologize, I thought you would be able to attend the meeting with me. They informed me that the meeting is of such a delicate nature, that they would not be comfortable with any attendees other than me. I am very sorry."

Christine said she understood but was extremely disappointed. Ron then told Christine to get some dinner and just charge it to her room and he would take care of the cost. Ron said goodbye, and off he went, leaving Christine dressed to the nines, standing in the lobby with no date.

It was almost 5:45p.m. Christine was feeling great about the fact that she had impressed the bigwigs, but now she was hungry, and she hated eating alone and wondered where Rufus was. She went up to the concierge and asked,

"Where do the limousines drivers go when they are waiting to be called?"

The Concierge asked, "Do you need a limo?"

"No, I just need to talk to our limousine driver."

The Concierge pointed to the front of the hotel and said "In front of the hotel, talk to the captain. He can direct you to the limousine parking area."

Christine talked to the valet captain and he pointed to a parking lot, which was full of Limousines.

Rufus is leaning against the congressman's limo smoking a cigarette, thinking about the discussions from that morning's meeting, when he looks up and sees Christine walking across the parking lot towards him. He is startled when he sees Christine.

First, because he did not expect to see her in the parking lot, and secondly because she walked right up to him, and even though he had seen her earlier in this dress, he had not seen her so, --- up close and personal.

Christine spoke right up saying: "The congressman is off to his big meeting. That meeting will run until after midnight. I am all alone, hungry, and I hate eating alone. I know you haven't eaten yet and I was hoping you would go down to the restaurant and have some dinner and drinks with me. I'll buy, I feel bad about our argument earlier."

Rufus responds with a forced grin, "I'm not sure, that this is a good idea."

Rufus stands there looking down into Christine's beautiful eyes. She is dressed to the hilt, and it is incredibly inviting. Rufus knows from experience that what she is saying is true. When the congressman goes into these kinds of meetings, he would be there for four or five hours.

Christine does not smile and says, "That is not a response to my invitation."

OK, one drink and something to eat. That should be OK. Rufus thinks, and then says: "I would like to have dinner with you, but after dinner, I really need to get back to my room and get some good sleep. I want to be fresh in the morning."

Christine smiles.

The dining room was full and there was a bit of a waiting line, so they decided instead to go into the bar. They agreed that they would just have some appetizers and drinks and be on their way.

They sat down in a horseshoe-shaped booth but kept on opposite sides of the booth. They ordered some Calamari and Ahi Tuna appetizers for starters. Christine ordered a Tanqueray and Tonic and Rufus ordered a "Fat Tire" on tap.

Christine began, "You know Rufus we have a lot in common". Rufus looked at Christine with a questioning eye, and with a bit of sarcasm, said "Oh yeah, how's that? I kind of thought we were exact opposites."

Christine continued, she seemed to by trying to lighten the mood after their earlier Tift. "Well you study *dark matter*, and I study *gray matter*." Christine giggled. Rufus smiled, and that seemed to break the ice a bit.

"Rufus, how did you end up as a bodyguard and chauffeur for the congressman. With your Ph.D. in Math and Physics, I would think you would be working for some big corporation or be a professor at some university."

Rufus replied, "Yea, I can see how one might think that." Then Rufus, with only one beer inside of him, told his life story, finishing with:

"I had worked with Ron Chapman when he was working in the FBI. After being released from the service, I contacted Ron and explained that because of my history, I could not get a job at any university. The congressman suggested this job as bodyguard and chauffeur, and I jumped at it. It was perfect. The job took advantage of my training in firearms and fighting, and the congressman also liked to use my expertise in math and physics from time to time, as you have seen. But that was not what was most attractive about the job. I love doing research and writing papers in the areas of math and physics, and this job offered me the time to do those things."

Rufus then said, "By the way, why are you working for Chapman? It seems to me, that with your education, you could be doing a lot better as well."

Christine explained how she grew up with a father that was a staunch Republican, and that she not only believed in the Republican principles, but she also thought, that by getting involved in politics she could do research in the psychological impact that politics could have on society. "And frankly, I thought that if I could link up with the right politician, I could change the world."

Rufus stared at Christine, "Do you think that Congressman Chapman is that man?"

"No, maybe not." She responded hesitantly.

"By the way" Rufus said "You mentioned that you had a son. Are you married?"

"I was married a long time ago, and we were very physically attracted to each other, but philosophically we were not a match and eventually that eroded our relationship and we decided to part? How about you? Do you have a significant other?"

"No, not me. Just never seemed to find the right person."

They kept talking and kept ordering drinks until almost 9:00 PM. Rufus had about 5 beers and Christine had three gin and tonics. They appeared to be feeling no pain and also seemed to be very much enjoying their conversation.

Rufus had Christine laughing most of the evening and some of the humorous stories he told were a bit on the crude side, which Christine seemed to thoroughly enjoy, and which appeared to give her an excuse to slide closer to him in the horseshoe booth so she could hear the jokes without offending the other patrons of the bar.

But then Christine, maybe because she had too much to drink, said, "Rufus you are obviously a very intelligent man. I don't understand how you can be so religious, so righteous. All this talk about the '*Light*' saving you, and then giving you strength. You have to know, that is all a bunch of bullshit. The only true source of strength is from *darkness*, you yourself said you were in a *dark* place and then recovered. That *darkness* is what gave you strength, not the '*Light*'."

Rufus looked stunned, and with a 'I thought we were passed this' look on his face said, "You don't have a clue, do you? Don't you realize that '*Darkness*' is the problem; *darkness* is a state of being that devours you. Strength does not come from the '*Darkness*', the strength you received, came from the '*Light*' that drew you from the *darkness*, not the other way around. And by the way, you are a 'bitch' aren't you?"

Christine glared at Rufus but did not move away, appearing ready to launch her next salvo. They had been facing each other in the booth, Rufus had his coat off, his sleeves rolled up, and his

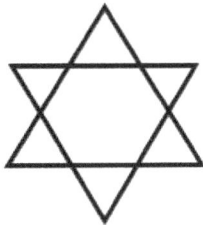

right arm was resting on the table. It was apparent that Christine was about to let him have it when she looked down at his arm on the table and stopped cold.

On the inner surface of Rufus' left forearm, there was a tattoo. The tattoo was perfectly white and stood out dramatically against his very dark skin.

'Wow, now that's *very* interesting'," Christine remarked, pointing to the tattoo.

Rufus responded, looking a bit pissed, "Yea, it's the 'Star of David' and it is very important to me. It symbolizes the most perfect '*Light*' of Yahweh, the ultimate expression of my beliefs in the teachings of the scriptures.' Why do you find it so interesting?" He says while trying to calm himself after her earlier insults.

Christine did not say anything; she just rolled up the sleeve of her dress on her left arm, which exposed her inner forearm. Rufus can now see Christine's tattoo. It is the same symbol, only in solid black. It too stood out dramatically on her very white skin.

"It's a 'Hexagon'" she said, "and it is also very important to me. It symbolizes the power of perfect 'Darkness'."

So, there they sat mirror images, or maybe negative images, of each other with so many obvious differences, and one glaring similarity. They did not say anything, but obviously, everything had changed. It was about 11:00 PM and Christine excused herself to go to the restroom.

When she returned, she sat down in the booth next to him, she said nothing about the tattoos, but instead said.

"Going to the restroom reminded me of a poem I wrote when I was younger." And she moved closer to Rufus.

"I called the poem 'P' and it goes like this:"

Two old ladies sitting in a tree
Drinking tea from nine to three
One old lady "No more for me!"
Dropped her cup and jumped from the tree
On the way down, catastrophe
She didn't pass her cup, but she passed her tea."

Rufus laughed, Christine smiled, and then without warning, she said,

"We better go to bed," She pauses and lowers her eyes. "I mean, I better go to bed" and she laughs. Rufus smiles and agrees, the situation was awkward, and he appeared to be relieved that she would suggest that they retire for the evening.

When they arrived at her room, Christine opened the door, and then softly said: "Come in for a second there is something I want to tell you." Rufus quickly looks, up and down the hallway, and then steps inside.

Christine says: "Oh! What's this?" leaning to pick up a note on the floor just beyond the door. Christine, seeing who the note was from, read it aloud to Rufus.

> *Christine,*
> *Ester and I would like to meet with you and Rufus tomorrow, separate from the congressman. We have more to share than what was said today.*

We will leave a similar note at Rufus' room.

CyrIS

Christine just said, "I wonder what that's about?" Rufus said nothing, it seemed that he wanted to get the door closed before anyone saw them.

The room was very nice; Chapman always took very good care of Christine. As they entered the room, they walked down a small hallway that led to a combination living area and bedroom. Off to the right was an entrance to a kitchen area and a bar. The curtains on the window in the room were open wide, and there was an incredible view of the city lights below.

Christine walked to the side of the bed and turned on a small lamp. She then walked to the window where Rufus was looking out over the scene, which not only included the city below but also had an open view towards the mountains in the west.

"Look," Ester exclaimed, "There's a thunderstorm in the mountains." With each flash of lighting, a silhouette of the mountains blending with the clouds above them, could be seen. They stood silently and watched for several moments.

"You see the power of *light*" Rufus begins, "It is the *light* that makes this scene possible."

"Yes," Christine replies, "But it is the power of *darkness* that makes it beautiful! It makes it romantic."

Rufus looks down at Christine as she turns and looks up at him. She was right next to him, so close he could smell the liquor on her breath. Even in his slightly inebriated state, he can tell she is intoxicated. Intoxicated and intoxicating, she always looks gorgeous, but standing there with the city in the background and the *light* from that small lamp on her face she was irresistible. It was obvious that she wanted to be kissed, and Rufus realized at that moment that they had never physically touched each other before.

Rufus reaches up and touches Christine's face, with a touch as light as his shadow on her cheek. Rufus hesitates for a moment, and then pushes all thoughts of Chapman out of his mind and pulls her to him and kisses her hard. Christine wraps her arms around him and melts. The moment Rufus touches her, he feels it, that familiar feeling from the past, that connection to another person that is not ordinary, but extraordinary. They each backed their faces away enough to stare into each other's eyes. Christine says, "I know this feeling, this feeling of *connection*." Rufus is sure that nothing else is needed to be said. He reaches down with both hands and starts pulling her skirt upwards. Christine adjust her position to help accommodate his efforts and soon her dress was up above her waist. Christine tugs at Rufus' tie. In no time, they are both *emotionally* and physically naked, Christine pulls Rufus towards the bed.

As he lowers her to the bed, she spread her legs slightly apart and looks up at him and smiles. She looks so sexy, Rufus is on fire, he could not even think about stopping, there was no turning back, his body was in control and no amount of *logic* his brain could conjure up would be able to hold him back now.

They were melting together, he inside of her, she wrapped around him. She could not only feel him inside of her, she could feel him, feeling himself, inside of her. Rufus could feel the same. They were both experiencing this moment from their own, and the other's perception, each inside of the other.

He and She, melt to They
Black and White, now as *Gray*
"He in me", "She in me"
Black and White, *Dark* and *Light*.
Entanglement and *Energy*.
Who set the scene, who wrote the script?
Who set the sail on this ship?
We're not the ship, we are the sea.
You and me. You and me.

It felt like it could last forever, now together and in love, they embrace, *entangle;* their hearts beat, and they breathe as one. It was not enough to say, that neither had ever felt like this before, both had experienced the *'Darkness' and the 'Light'*, but this, this was both at the same time, they had 'taken it to the Limit', they could feel the 'flow' of each other. And though they *wanted* it to last forever, it did not. And even though they would now be forever *connected*, --- they separated, and lie on the bed overwhelmed, and deep in contemplation of what they had just experienced.

Now, each knowing, why they were brought together, and slowly returning to reality, Rufus kissed Christine and said. "I love you Christine, but I'm sorry, I have to go. The congressman could be back at any moment." Christine said. "I understand".

They pushed the flood of *emotions* aside trying to give *logic* a chance. They both knew that Rufus needed this job and that the congressman would not be just a little bit unhappy with Rufus if he knew what had just happened.

Christine and Rufus stood up. Rufus got dressed and Christine put on a robe and they walked together to the door. Then in unison, they said, "We have to do this again." Christine's lily-white skin turned crimson, they kissed, and Rufus left the room.

Christine went to the edge of the bed and sat down; she was still a little tipsy from the alcohol and the vortex of *emotions*. She knew she could not lie down on that spinning bed again, and after a bit, she got up and went into the bathroom, she needed to clean up a bit.

Afterwards she went into the little bar area and got a bottle of Fuji water and filled a glass. She drank it down, she was really thirsty, and the water tasted great. She was also hoping that the water would help her sober up so she could shower and go to bed. She walked over to the side of the bed and set a fresh glass of water and the bottle on the nightstand. Then she walked around the room for a while hoping that would help in the sobering process, and then she heard the very faint sound of someone tapping at the door.

Ron's meeting had gone great. He had been approached about the possibility of running for president of the United States, and Ron was thrilled. They spent most of the time in the meeting comparing notes on who Ron could get to support and help fund his campaign. The meeting ended with an agreement that it would all be kept confidential, as there was no final decision at this point, and a lot more work needed to be done before any announcements could even be thought about. Ron agreed and the meeting was adjourned.

After his meeting, which had run for several hours, Ron was feeling great, he had just been asked if he was interested in running for president of the United States in 2012, and, at least at this point, he had the support of some of the top Republicans in the country. He realized it was late, but he wanted to share the news with someone, and of course, the first person that came to mind was Christine. He would go to her room and see if she was still up.

It was about 11:30 PM when he approached Christine's hotel room door. His plan was to tap lightly on her door and see if she responded. However, when he got up to the door and reached up to knock, he thought he could hear some noises inside, so he hesitated before knocking and listened closely. Yes, he could hear something. Was that the TV? No, it sounded like moaning, was she alright? Ron checked the hallway, no one was around. He put his ear up to the door and then he could hear what it was. Someone was having sex. Could it be Christine, did she meet someone in the bar, which certainly was not like her? Did a boyfriend come down from Boulder to spend the night? Ron was not even sure if she had a boyfriend.

The longer he listened the more he was sure that she was having sex with someone. As he stood there his *emotions* running wild, he was both angry with her for having sex with anybody that was not himself, and at the same time he was a bit turned on by the sounds coming from her room. He remembered how she was dressed earlier, and he fantasized about making love to her while she was wearing that dress.

After a few minutes, the noises stopped and he could hear nothing at all, then after a while, he could hear them talking, but could not make out what they were saying, nor did he recognize the voices. He was not even sure it was Christine's voice. Was this the right room, he checked the number, he was pretty sure it was right.

Then he felt a little panic, he thought they might be coming out of the room, how would it look if they opened the door and he was standing there? So, he headed down the corridor away from the elevator and ducked down a side corridor that led to the stairwell. He stopped there and waited for a while. Then he heard the door open, some more muffled talk, and then the door shut. He could only hope that they would go towards the elevator and not in his direction. He listened very closely to see if he could hear the footsteps. But it was very difficult given the carpeted hallway. He could always go down the stairwell if he thought they were coming his way. But soft as it was, he could hear footsteps and they were going away from him. He could not stand it any longer, he had to look and see if he recognized the person, so he peeked around the corner, and to his amazement and disgust, he did know who it was, it was Rufus.

How could she. Rufus? How could she prefer that black bastard over me, a white man, a congressman and possibly the next president of the United States.

He was burning with jealousy and rage. He told himself, that he needed to settle down. He wanted to see her badly, would she see his face and know he knew, would she break down and confess her sins to him? So, he could console her and become her soul mate and more. A thousand thoughts and feelings shot through his head. But he knew one thing, he was angry, and he wanted to see her now.

So, after about 10 minutes of waiting in the hallway, he went up and tapped every so lightly on the door.

Christine thinking that Rufus had forgotten something immediately opened the door.

"Congressman?" Christine was shocked; there was no way she expected him to be standing at her door.

"I need to talk to you; I have something very important to tell you." He said.

He immediately started to walk towards her as if he had already been invited in. She stepped aside and as he passed, she said. "I was just getting ready for bed I am extremely tired."

Ron replied, "This won't take long, but it is very important."

Hesitantly she said "Okay, have a seat, I will be with you in a second" and she headed toward the bathroom.

Christine wanted to look herself over, what did she look like, a ravished drunken whore or worse? She looked in the mirror and was pleasantly surprised. She did not look that bad, her eyes were a little red from the drinking, but all in all her looks had survived the ordeal with Rufus rather well. Her hair was a little messy, but it was late in the day and that can happen. She reached into her vanity case and pulled out a bottle of Extra Strength Excedrin tablets, she was already starting to get a headache and she knew it would be worse in the morning. Then she brushed her hair and took a deep breath, popped the pills into her mouth, and got herself ready to go back into the room with Ron.

When the congressman had entered the room and Christine had excused herself, he walked directly to the window and looked out at the city. He was furious with her and was trying to control the rage. He then turned around and looked at the room. The bed looked like it had been laid on and then someone had attempted to straighten it out. He saw the bottle of Fuji water and the glass next to it.

In 2007 Ron had been on a House Subcommittee on Crime, Terrorism, and Homeland Security, which had been investigating a rape case of a U.S. contractor in Iraq, involving the use of

Rohypnol, the date rape drug, also known as 'Rophies'. The committee was trying to determine who was responsible for enforcing federal law to protect Americans working for U.S. contractors in Iraq. During the investigation sample packets of Rohypnol were shown to the congressman. When the hearings were completed, and when no one was looking Ron had picked up two packets of the drug and had been carrying them around in his wallet for the last several years.

Without any elaborate thought, he reached in his pocket, pulled out his wallet, pulled out one of the packets, and walked over to Christine's glass of water on the table, and poured in the contents. He was amazed as he watched himself stir the water with his finger; he was on autopilot, no thinking, no *logic*, just doing it. But there was one immediate result; his anger was subsiding a bit. He had taken some action to get back at her, now he would wait to see where it went.

When Christine came back into the room, she did something that shocked Ron; she did not say a word but walked directly to the nightstand picked up the glass of water and drank it down. At first, he did not know what to think, but then she said: "I had to take some aspirin, I have a headache and I really need to get some sleep."

"I am sorry you have a headache, so I will not stay long, but I have very big news and I did not want to wait until tomorrow to share it with you. As you know I met with some high-ranking members of the Republican Party this evening. And well, they have asked me to run for president of the United States. They say I have a very good chance and they will all endorse me and support my effort. They say that I may be Republicans best chance of beating Obama"

"Congressman that is great" Christine moved toward him and gave him a quick hug and then just as quickly moved away looking a bit embarrassed by her actions. Christine then became dizzy and stumbled a bit before sitting on the bed. "I am so happy for you." She mumbled.

After sitting down, she seemed to regain her composure "Congressman what does this mean, when do you start, how can I help".

He responded "Christine you will certainly have a key role in my campaign, but it will be a while before we can make the announcement. We need to get some more people on board including some of my key contributors; it will take money and lots of it."

As Christine sat there, she began to look progressively sleepier. "Congressman, that is wonderful news and I am so happy for you and I certainly look forward to working on the campaign with you, but right now I am just exhausted, and you are going to have to excuse me, so I can retire."

"Of course, I will get out of your hair, and I am looking forward to working with you on this as well"

The congressman started to walk for the door, and as he did Christine laid back on the bed. He stood there for a while to see if she would move. She did not, so he walked over to her and spoke her name. She mumbled something but did not move. Ron was not sure exactly what he was going to do; he certainly did not plan for things to happen this way. If he could change things, he would not have invited Christine to the conference, and she would not have been able to link up with Rufus, and so on and so forth, all leading up to this moment.

He then walked up to the bed and looked at Christine, she looked gorgeous as usual, but much more sexy than usual, her robe had parted at the bottom, exposing her beautiful legs, and Ron was getting turned on again, this time without quite so much rage mixed in. Her eyes were open, but she did not appear to be conscious. He then reached down and pulled her robe open, she did not move, and he was surprised to find her completely naked underneath. He started to think about her and Rufus, together but then blocked it from his mind; he did not want to get angry again. But the site of her was overwhelming.

Christine lying on the bed, though a bit hazy could see and hear what was happening, but she could not move. Christine thought that he must have put something in her glass of water. And now, it was just like her visits to the bodies of John Hinckley and Eric Harris, but this time she was in her own body, but had absolutely no control over what was happening to her.

CHAPTER 33 – A QUEEN OF DARKNESS

April 19th, 2012

Christine Basurto, Age 44

Rufus Middleman, Age 42

Ester Suni Nate, Age 60

CyrIS Steel, Age 62

Christine walks from the hotel, to the capitol building in Denver. It's a nice day and it is only about two blocks from the parking lot on 15th street.

Christine has a lot on her mind and is intent on telling the congressman that she will no longer work for him. She does not want to let him know what she knows about the previous night. She just wants to tell him that she is not interested in working on a presidential campaign, because she is going to pursue some recent opportunities in the area of psychology.

She now just wants to complete the sessions on Quantum Computing, even though she is not sure that she will be able to spend any more time around the congressman, given the circumstances. She mostly wants to say goodbye to Rufus and give him her contact information. She also wants to get some of her things out of her office in the capitol building.

When she arrives at her office, she immediately feels very melancholy. She did love this office and her job working for a prominent republican politician. It would have been even greater to work for a presidential candidate, maybe someday even a president. However, that is all history now and it makes her very sad.

Her intention, when she talks to the congressman, is to come right out with it, and as she walks toward the congressman's office, she practices the speech in her head.

"Congressman Chapman, I am sorry to have to tell you this, but I have decided to leave the position as your media secretary. I have some plans for my life that I am afraid would conflict with the effort necessary to support you during a presidential bid. I feel that in such a support role, I would need to concentrate all my attention and make every effort to make sure you would have the best chance to be the next president. I am afraid I cannot make that commitment at this time, and I am resigning today."

As Christine approaches the congressman's office, she notices that Jane, the congressman's secretary, is not at her usual position at her desk.

Usually, when the congressman is in, she is always there - ever vigilant - making sure that the congressman is well prepared before anyone is allowed entrance.

With no guard at the door, and with a purposeful task at hand, Christine marches up to the closed door. The blinds are closed, and Christine could hear him on the phone practically screaming.

"No, we can't wait that long. It must be done today! I don't give a shit; you know who. Just do it!" He slams the phone hard against the receiver.

Christine looks around to see if anyone is watching. It is her intention to wait a minute or two and then knock on the door, but she hears Ron's voice on the phone again. He has calmed down some but continues with a very gruff voice.

"Rufus, come up to my office now, I need to talk to you." Once again, he hangs up the phone.

Christine looks around, but this time she sees CyrIS and Ester walking towards her. Christine mutters internally: *'I guess my speech will have to wait.'*

Ester begins speaking as they approach, "Are you ready for the tour."

Christine had completely forgotten about the tour. Christine responds: "I have already seen everything there is to see. I think the congressman is just planning on taking the two of you." Trying not to let on, just how much had changed since the previous day.

"Are you okay?" Ester, with a concerned look on her face, says, just as the door to Ron's office flies open. Ron almost running directly into Christine, exclaims. "Oh! Christine!" Ron looks surprised to see her, and immediately looks down at the floor.

"I didn't know you would be here." Then, looks up and says "Fuck!"

Christine looks in the same direction that Ron is looking and sees Rufus walking towards them. As Rufus draws closer, Ron says, "Rufus, would you please wait in my office, we will be back shortly."

Not wanting to leave Christine alone with Rufus, Ron says to her. "Christine, I know you have seen the building, but would you please join us for the short tour?"

"Okay." Christine agrees, not wanting to cause a scene.

When they return from the tour, Ron grabs his suit coat from his office. Rufus seated in Ron's office now stands up and says, "You wanted to talk to me?"

The congressman looks perturbed, then looks at his watch and says "That will have to wait. We need to go. They are expecting us at the national labs." Ron is now looking extremely rushed.

It had been previously agreed that they would ride together in Ron's limousine to the laboratories. But now, Christine is saying. "I will need to drive separately. I have an appointment immediately after the tour. So, I will follow you up there." Ron turns to her and say's "Christine?", but Christine is not looking at him, he then turns again and starts walking towards the front doors of the capitol building.

Christine is thinking about the previous night when she and the others approach the bottom of the steps in front of the Capitol. A man, wearing a dark hoodie, is walking along the sidewalk in front of them, and they are about five steps from the bottom, when the man is directly in front of them. Suddenly, he pulls the hood back from his head and moves directly toward them. Christine is shocked by the face she is looking at. It is her ex-husband, Rod. The features are unmistakable, those dark eyes, that incredibly handsome face and very dark skin. Then it hits her, she is not looking at her husband, Rodney Dell, she instead, looking at the face of her youngest son, Jamaal.

Jamaal feels the monster, that his mother had created, rise up inside him. He is on fire. All the anger, all the frustrations and pain, are at the tips of every nerve in his body.

Why did she do this to me? Why had she created this monster? I hate her! She is so evil. This queen of darkness deserves to die.

Rufus sees the young man reach inside his pocket, and now the gun in his hand. Rufus' sight moves up to, and is now locked in on, the young man's eyes. He has seen this look before, and in an instant, he is back in Iraq, to that moment when the gaze of another young man changed his life. Frozen for just an instant as the gun is raised and aimed. Rufus now reaches his right hand toward the gun inside his coat, at the same time he is moving his whole body to his left to get in front of the congressman, but the congressman grabs Christine and pulls her in front of him and points at Rufus.

Rufus has his gun out now but hesitates. '*Oh! My God what is wrong with me,*' trying to shake the images from Iraq.

Christine is locked on Jamaal's face.

'*What is he doing here, where had he been all these years?*'

Then she hears the explosion, and even though she is still locked on Jamaal's face, she sees the small flash from the gun in his hand, and immediately feels something hit her chest. She is pushed backward, as her head jerks down towards her chest, she can see the small hole in her blouse. She feels no pain as the *light* fades to *darkness.*

A half a second after the first shot, a second shot is fired. The Congressman is still using Christine as a shield. This shot misses everyone, as the shooter now takes careful aim. The armor-piercing bullet from the third shot hits Rufus in the right shoulder, just as he continues to move to protect Christine and the congressman. The bullet passes directly through the fleshy part of Rufus' shoulder and hits the congressman in the upper part of his skull. The congressman's head is jerked to his left. The bullet now glances off the inner part of Ron's skull and blasts brains and bone into Ron's left shoulder.

In less than ten seconds, it's all over, and the sound of Ester's screams now fills the air, as the shooter turns and runs away, pulling the hoody over his head as he runs.

CyrIS turns his attention from the shooter, to the three bodies to his left, as Ester collapses to the stairs in tears: her screams descending into uncontrolled sobbing, and then into a sea of silence.

CHAPTER 34 – ARE YOU NOT TELLING US SOMETHING

April 22nd, 2012

Christine Basurto, Age 44

Rufus Middleman, Age 42

Ester Suni Nate, Age 60

CyrIS Steel, Age 62

Speaking very softly, CyrIS address his congregation, "Do you have a chunk missing? I think we all do in some way or another. You know that void in your soul that makes you feel incomplete?"

"What is it that we are trying to find?" CyrIS seems to be asking himself these questions, as much as he is his audience. "We are all seeking answers to the questions of life. Often, we are not sure what the questions are, or even what they mean. "

"Is there a God?"

"Why am I here?"

"What happens to me when I die?"

CyrIS pauses ---- then a very sad expression settles on his expression, as his shoulder slump.

"I am sure that you are all aware of the recent assassination of Congressman Ron Chapman. Well, my wife Ester and I were with the congressman when it happened. It is a terrible thing, and two of our very close friends, Christine Basurto, and Rufus Middleman, were severely injured in that shooting. They are presently both in the hospital, and I ask for your prayers for them, but especially for Christine who is in critical condition."

"Events like this really make you think about your life. It makes you question, even more than ever, those voids in your life. I am speaking to your soul now. Your soul shouts out: 'I want something. I need something. I may think I know what that something is, but surprisingly, when I get what I think I want, I am still not satisfied.' It is as if you are not a whole person; like there is a chunk missing."

CyrIS expression lifts and his shoulders lift, as he begins the next portion of his sermon.

"So, let us look at this problem from a scientific perspective."

"In the world of science, there is a proven concept. It is the concept of the *Entanglement of photons*. You should look it up. *Entanglement* is the process by which two photons have a relationship in which the spin of one photon is connected to the spin off its sister photon, and no matter how far apart these two photons are, they have this relationship. If the direction of spin of one of the photons is changed, the direction of the other photon is changed as well. This change in direction happens immediately, and again, independent of how far apart the two photons are. Even if they are *light*-years apart, it does not *matter*. The change still happens immediately. Again, I say, this has been proven scientifically many times."

CyrIS looks at his audience, searching for understanding but seeing only puzzled faces, forges on.

"It has been shown that all photons which come from the same source are *entangled*, and thus an individual photon is not an entity unto itself. It is, in fact, part of a group of photons that are all *connected*, *entangled* in a large *fabric*, and at least so far, science has not been able to determine the mechanics behind this *connection*."

"So, when one observes an individual photon, it may appear to be complete, but then, for no apparent reason, the spin of that photon may change. However, if the observer could see all the *entangled* photons as a group, it would become obvious that the changes in the individual photons are dependent on changes to the group, and thus the group of photons would make sense as a whole."

CyrIS pauses again. He can see the looks of doubt on some of the faces in front of him, and some are looking around to see if anyone else is following. Hoping that they will get it eventually, CyrIS continues.

"The point is, that you may think of yourself as an individual, but in fact, you are a part of a larger body or system. You are in some way *connected* to other human beings, and *connected* to much, much more throughout the universe. That *void,* that you feel, may be filled if you could make the *connection* to the rest of your being; a *connection* to the whole that you are a part of."

"I certainly know that I have this connection with my wife, and with my friends, and with each and every one of you as well. I am sure that you also feel these connections with those who are close in your life."

"So why is this *connection* to others so important, beyond completing you as a human being?"

"Let's say two people or two countries, have a disagreement. From each of their perspectives, they are each right. 'I must protect my position. There is no room for compromise.' From their perspectives, they are both right. They are following their own ideology, their own interpretations of their scriptures or whatever might be their motivation. The *logic* that each is using is processed through their own *emotionally* filtered goggles. There is no way for each to actually experience the *logic* and *emotion* contained in the heart and soul of the other side."

"Here is a simple example: when the US was involved in the Korean War, the US government believed that North Korea was fighting for the advancement of communism at the direction of the communist government in China. That is why they were fighting to take over South Korea. The US government also believed that if South Korea fell, the Chinese would just move forward to take over other third world nations in the region in an effort to convert the whole world to communism. This was known as the 'Domino Effect', and it was a highly *emotional* issue for the U.S. during that period."

"As such, the US believed that the North Korean's would give up the fight, once they realized that the odds against them being able to defeat the 'Great War Machine' of the United States of America, were so high. After all, why would they keep fighting just to promote China's aggression to advance communism?"

"When the war was over, a representative of the U.S. went to meet with the leaders in North Korea. He found out, that if the US had studied the history of Korea more thoroughly; they would have known, that Korea fought the Chinese for centuries, and that they hated the Chinese."

"The reason they were fighting for South Korea was to preserve the existence of their country, much like the US did in its civil war, and as it did in its war for independence. The North Koreans saw the war with South Korea as a war for their very existence. It was a highly *emotional* issue in Korea at that time, and as such, they would never give up. They would fight to the death. To them it was only *logical*."

CyrIS now shaking his head with a look of exasperation. "Thousands of lives could have been saved, if only there had been a better line of communication between the two sides."

"Communication is part of the solution to any problem and it is no different in the message I am trying to convey to you here today. The facilitation of clear communications is always a major element in solving any problem; in solving any puzzle. For there to be communication, there needs to be a *connection,* and a medium for that *connection.*"

CyrIS eyes light up and his voice rises, "If there was a 'field' that could provide that *connection* because it was *everywhere* in the universe, it would then be able to facilitate that communication between all things in many, many ways. It could facilitate the transfer of many forms of knowledge both *emotional* and *logical.*"

"So, if you are like me, and you had a religious upbringing, you probably remember being told things by your parents, teachers or ministers, such as "God created all things', 'God is all knowing', 'God is the source of all knowledge', 'God is everywhere', 'God is inside each of you', 'You have a Guardian

Angel', 'Pray to God, he will meet your needs'. Just to mention a few."

"And just like me, you have probably also heard stories of clairvoyance, you know, the girl who knew her twin sister had just been in a car accident, or the mother who knew her son was in danger even though he was miles away. And, just like me, you probably have had your own brief moments of clairvoyance. You know 'I Just had a feeling' or 'I dreamed that would happen". And finally, you have heard that your sub-conscious makes up a large part of 'who you are' and can have significant impacts on your day to day life."

"All these things; religion, clairvoyance, and your own psyche, suggests that there is a *connection* between you and what is 'not you', and that you can use that *connection* to acquire knowledge and accomplish what is needed."

"So, if there was a field out there, that created all things, all matter and all energy, and that field was everywhere, even inside of you, and that field connected you to all things and to all knowledge. What would you call that field? Would you call that field God?"

"And what if there was a final resting place for all matter and energy, and for all knowledge, including the mater, energy, and knowledge, which is you? What would you call that place? Would you call that place 'Heaven'?"

"And what if all matter and energy in the universe is perfectly balanced. That is to say; that the amount and configuration of the energy and matter in the universe is perfect and can be no different than it is, given the evolution of the entire universe to this point. Would that mean that YOU" CyrIS is now pointing to his audience, "are here because you are an essential element in the balance of the universe?"

"I believe that science is providing proof that the 'Fields' that we are talking about truly exist. 'Fields' that create matter and energy. 'Fields that ultimately retain all matter, energy and knowledge. And proof that the universe is in perfect balance."

CyrIS pauses and takes a deep breath.

"I know that this is a lot to absorb, and I can tell that you are tired. This is a new way of looking at the existence of a supreme entity, and I am sure that you need to take some time to integrate these concepts. However, in future sessions we will explore, in details, the specific scientific discoveries that support each of these areas, to help us answer the questions."

"Is there a God?"

"What happens to me when I die?"

"Why am I here?"

"Because, you see, the answers to these questions lie in the *middle* of this *Fabric* that *connects* all things...."

CyrIS closes his service as usual and greets his church members at the rear of the church, and today CyrIS is barraged with questions from his followers. He attempts to answer their questions but, in most cases, tells them, "We will be exploring that area further in our future sessions. Please be patient."

Later that day, CyrIS and Ester, enter the hospital to visit their friends, Christine, and Rufus.

Ester asks the receptionist: "We're here to see Rufus Middleman and Christine Basurto. Can you tell us how they are doing?"

The nurse looks at the computer in front of her and says: "Mr. Middleman is fine, he was released this morning. I believe he is in the room with Ms. Basurto now. Ms. Basurto's operation on Thursday evening went very well. They were able to remove the bullet from her chest, and she is recovering nicely. It is visiting hours, and she is doing well enough now to take visitors, you can see her if you want. She is in room 302."

Upon entering room 302, they see Rufus sitting next to Christine's bed, holding her hand.

Ester whispers to CyrIS as they enter the room: "We may never be able to get these two apart again." Ester starts speaking very softly at first. "Christine, how are you doing dear?"

Christine smiles indicating she is doing okay. Ester knows that the pain Christine is enduring is well beyond the physical wound she was recovering from. The psychological wound associated with knowing that her own son had killed the congressman and tried to kill her as well, would never heal. Ester had discussed this at length with CyrIS prior to their arrival and they agreed that today was not the time to discuss such personal issues with Christine.

"Rufus, how's that shoulder?" CyrIS asks and Ester follows with: "Yes dear and how are you doing?"

"I'm fine," Rufus responds. "I survived Iraq and cancer; this is nothing."

Ester now turns her attention back too Christine, "How are you feeling, is there anything I can get for you?"

Christine smiles again, "Actually, I am doing very well, they say I should be able to leave early next week. I am really happy that you are all here, especially Rufus. I can't tell you what he means to me now."

"Lying here the last couple of days have given me time to reflect on what has happened to me. Actually, to reflect on what has happened to all of us. I thought about the stories that Ester and Rufus told about their journeys, as well as my own story. Though, I know that CyrIS has not had such a journey, I believe that these events have brought us all together."

Ester looks at CyrIS expectantly. Christine noticing the look says: "What? What's going on? Are you not telling us something?"

"Well!" CyrIS begins, "Actually, on September 11th, I had a journey as well."

Christine gasps, "Nine Eleven - the World Trade Center - Yes! I knew it. It was meant for the four of us to be together."

Rufus puts his hand on CyrIS shoulder. "Why didn't you tell us at the conference?"

"Well," CyrIS replies, "Ester, of course already knew, and I didn't want to diminish the impact of your stories. Frankly, I didn't trust the motives of Congressman Chapman, and therefore I just couldn't tell my story then. But, I'm willing to tell it to you now."

The others remain silent as CyrIS tells his story and all its details as best he can remember them. He also explains how he tried to contact the authorities that day but could not get through to anyone before the whole incident was complete.

"I decided, I would not tell anyone else about my experience. That is; until today."

"Incredible," Christine mutters, slowly shaking her head, then turning her attention to Ester.

"Ester, you once told me that you and CyrIS have been able to communicate while on your journeys by squeezing his hand. But he was unable to bring you out of your condition even after he had received the signal."

"Well," Christine continues, "I believe that we have been sent on these journeys for a reason. I don't believe that CyrIS' journey is the last one that the four of us will experience, and I have an idea how we might revive the one that is on that next journey."

"I have access to a very strong drug; it is called *Epinephrine* and it would create a very strong rush of *Adrenaline* in the body. I hope it's strong enough to pull one of us from our journey in time so we can take action and possibly avoid a pending disaster. I truly believe this is our purpose."

Rufus then chimes in: "Well I'm not sure who wants to go next on one of these journeys. They're not exactly vacations."

"Oh! Speaking of Journeys," CyrIS exclaims, "On some of our journeys we have seen a symbol. It is the symbol of the three Xs or three-hour glasses. You remember? Well, that seemed to be a significant tie between our journeys, so I did some research on that symbol. I did a lot of digging on the internet and eventually, I found some references to the symbol. Apparently, it is associated with an organization known as *The King's Crusaders*."

"Interesting," Rufus says: "I saw a reference to *The King's Crusaders* on the back of a biker gang's bike. It might have belonged to some white supremacist."

"Well," CyrIS continues, "Apparently, the cops arrested some guy who was supposedly a member of this group. He was carrying this piece of paper with a symbol on it. Here I have a copy." CyrIS pulls a piece of folded paper from his back pocket and places it on Christine's bed for all to see.

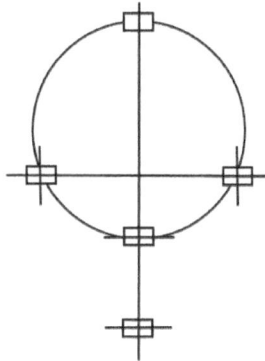

Christine asks, "Ester you know a lot about symbols, do you recognize this? Is it some kind of Shaman thing?"

Ester responds, "No. I'm afraid I don't recognize this, and I am sure it is not of shaman origin."

CyrIS adds, "It looks to me like it could be the crosshairs of a rifle scope or something."

"Shit!" Rufus exclaims, "You know what it could be? It could be the Hadron Collider. You see, there are the four experiments at the collider." He says while pointing to each of their relative positions on the diagram. "Atlas, Alice, LHCb, and CMS. They are not exactly in the right positions but close enough."

"I'm not sure about this additional box on the bottom."

Rufus has his laptop PC with him, and he opens it and pulls up a picture of the collider layout.

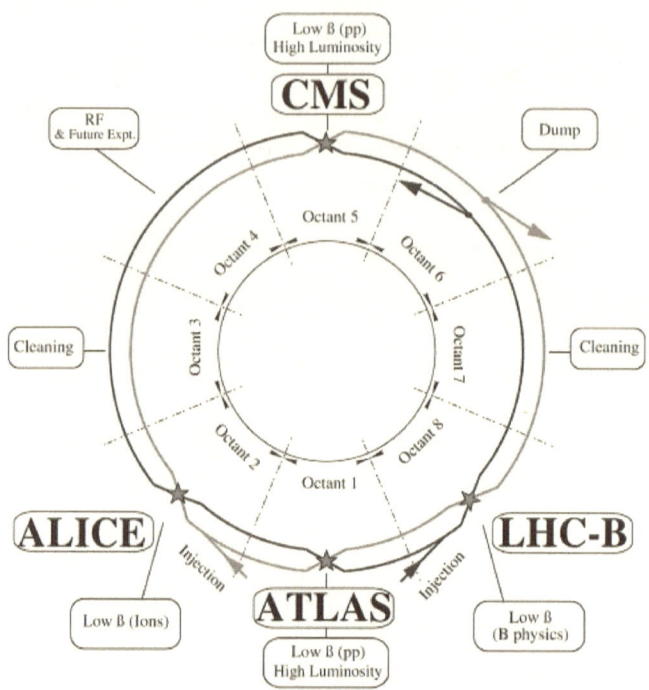

"Look here, see what I mean?"

"Do you think the Collider is some kind of target?" CyrIS asks.

"I don't know." Rufus responds, "But we will all be there in July when I present my paper and start my experiments. Maybe we will know more by then."

CHAPTER 35 – PROMISE EVERYTHING

June 27th[th]*, 2012*

"Order, Order, Order!" The meeting leader demands, "This emergency meeting of the King's Crusaders is now in session!"

"First of all, I want to offer my condolences on the recent passing of our Grand Master. His assassination was certainly the work of conspirators against our crusade. His leadership will be missed."

"But now, I proudly introduce our new Grand Master, confirmed at a secret meeting of the Keepers just days ago."

"As always, we will keep his true identity a secret, but from this day forward he is the Grand Master. Sir, I pass to you, the gilded *three-hourglass* pendant to adorn your new white robe; the symbol of your new position and leadership."

In his new white robe, with the hood concealing his face, Jamaal takes a step forward from the darkness, into the spotlight, and accepts the pendant and the position. Elected to the Keepers just three years prior, he has been a shooting star within The King's Crusaders, and now he is the new Grand Master of the Keepers. He addresses his audience around the world; some on the phone, some on Skype, and some in the room.

"As you know, Hypocrisy is the enemy of our benefactors, because it causes believers to lose faith in the leadership of their various religions. But, an even greater threat to our benefactors is the pursuit of science to undermine all religious beliefs. They expose secrets of the universe which are meant to remain secret."

"Our organization has always felt that one way we could stifle the progress of the scientific threat to our benefactors would be to get a person elected to the US Presidency. We need someone that would side with our position on these matters. Our organization believed we had the right person in position to become president. None other, then our former Grand Master, Congressman Ron Chapman. His untimely and unexpected death has set us back but has not deterred us."

"In the early part of this year, scientists at the Large Hadron Collider in Cern Switzerland, have discovered what they think is the Higg's boson. This might confirm the existence of the long-speculated *Higgs Field*, and bring them one step closer to a "Unified Theory" and thus one step closer to the destruction of traditional religions. This certainly opposes the intentions of our benefactors."

"On June 24th, just a few days ago, these same scientists may have confirmed the existence of the Higg's boson. On July 4th, they have planned an announcement at a media event at the Collider in CERN. It is now obvious, that we must take action. You see, there will be hundreds and hundreds of scientists from all over the world at this event. This will be a great opportunity for us to meet at least two of the goals of our benefactors. That is, to inhibit the movement of science towards a unified theory and secondly, to exhibit dramatic examples of the coming apocalypse. Believe me, my brothers and sisters, we will be creating fireworks at CERN, on the 4th of July."

CHAPTER 36 – THIS PLACE COULD GO UP ANY SECOND

July 4th, 2012

Christine Basurto, Age 44

Rufus Middleman, Age 42

Ester Suni Nate, Age 60

CyrIS Steel, Age 62

"I can't sleep." CyrIS thinks, as he lies in bed in the darkened hotel room, with Ester at his side. On the nightstand sits a small digital clock. The numbers illuminated by a small backlight indicating it is 6:00 AM.

They had arrived in Geneva just three days ago for the presentation of Rufus's paper, and Rufus and Christine are now asleep in the adjacent hotel room.

CyrIS is excited to be here for Rufus' presentation. But actually, he is even more excited to be present for the historic announcement of the possible discovery of the, *Higgs' Boson*. And all of this excitement is the reason he cannot sleep, but then, with a sudden jerk, he sits up in bed. "Ester! Wake up! It's happening!" CyrIS has the old but familiar feeling in his stomach, and he is pretty sure he knows what is about to happen.

"Go wake up Rufus and Christine, we must be prepared! I don't have much time."

When Ester returns with Rufus and Christine at her side, CyrIS is already in a state of trance lying on the bed.

Ester, a bit frightened knowing what they were planning on doing, says: "What should we do now? I'm really scared."

Christine consolingly says: "It will be okay. Just sit next to him and take his hand. All we can do now, is wait for him to give us the signal."

CyrIS once again finds himself in darkness, listening to prayers in Arabic. *"Not this again,"* The memories of his previous journey flood his thoughts.

"I have to stay calm. Come on! Open your eyes and give me something to go on." CyrIS thinks. Soon, the eyes begin to open and CyrIS looks to the ceiling. A ceiling that looked familiar. "I think this guy might be in a hotel room."

CyrIS' host then sits up in bed and looks into a mirror on the chest of drawers directly in front of him, and CyrIS decides that he is in a hotel room and from the looks of it; it could be the same hotel that CyrIS and Ester are staying in.

CyrIS waits for the man's eyes to focus, anxious to determine the identity of his host. "Just as I suspected: it's Joseph, that Muslim guy Ester and I met just a week ago right here in Switzerland." CyrIS knew as soon as he shook the man's hand that they were then *connected*.

The man gets out of bed, showers, trims his beard and puts on a pair of glasses, which he obviously does not need, as the glasses are non-prescription. He then puts on a lab coat with a chest-pocket protector full of ink pens. All of this makes him look very much like a scientist. After picking up a small travel pack and a clipboard, which appears to have some floor plans on it, he heads out.

'None of this stuff looks dangerous,' CyrIS thinks.

In the hotel lobby, Joseph meets up with three other Arabic looking fellows also wearing lab coats. Each looks very scientific in their own way, and none of them seem to be carrying anything that looked lethal.

Nothing is said as they proceed to the parking area directly in front of the hotel. Joseph looks around, spots an expensive looking black Mercedes. He points it out to the other three men, and the four of them proceed in its direction. The three other men get into the back of the car while Joseph gets into the front passenger seat.

"Are you ready?" the driver says.

Joseph turns to the driver and says: "Yes, we are prepared to meet our God."

It is still dark out, so the interior lights of the car stay on for just a moment after the car doors shut. CyrIS immediately recognizes the driver. It is Jamaal, Christine's son.

Joseph faces forward as the car pulls away from the hotel. Joseph concentrates on his prayers. He occasionally tells himself that he and his team know exactly what they need to do, and he appears confident that they are doing what *God* wants.

The Mercedes, after making several turns, heads west along Route De Meyrin. The previous day CyrIS, with Ester, Rufus, and Christine, had all toured the visitors' centers and museums that were intended to explain the purpose and capabilities of the Large Hadron Collider. These facilities were all located in the CERN complex area, just south of the collider. However, CyrIS knew that tourists were not allowed to tour the actual experiments or the collider facility itself. And now he also notices that the Mercedes does not turn into the CERN complex, but continues past its entrance to the west.

The Mercedes makes a couple more turns and approaches a guarded gate, which looks like a material receiving dock. The sign at the gate reads: "LHC-P1.8". Jamaal opens his window, shows the guard some kind of credentials, and proceeds to a parking area in the rear of the building.

Once parked, all the men exit the vehicle and move to the now open trunk, at the rear of the car. As Joseph looks into the trunk, CyrIS can see four, very large, duffle bags. Three of the Arabs, including Joseph, take a duffle bag. Jamaal closes the trunk leaving one of the duffle bags remaining in the trunk.

Joseph and the other two men, still not saying a word, then follow Jamaal to a darkened door again on the building's backside. One of the Arabic men remains in the car.

Jamaal pulls a very standard looking key from his pocket and inserts it into the door lock opening the door.

CyrIS thinks to himself. *'I remember reading somewhere that the LHC did not use software locking systems for fear of being hacked and relied instead upon standard key systems and switches.'*

CyrIS is a bit surprised upon entering the facility. There is no one in sight. He realizes it is early in the morning, but still thought there should be at least a few people around. After walking down several halls and making several turns, they arrive at another sentry station. This one looks like it had a metal detection entryway, and has a uniformed guard sitting at a control station.

When Jamaal sees the guard, he stops. The guard clearly sees the four men, but turns his back, and does something with the control panel. Jamaal, Joseph, and the other two men then proceed to the station and through the metal detectors.

'No alarm!' CyrIS thinks.

The men do not look back and proceed to an elevator directly in front of them. Jamaal pushes the only button next to the doors, and they open. Joseph and the other two men board the elevator, sit the very heavy duffle bags on the floor and turn to Jamaal, still outside of the elevator. Jamaal, with no expression at all, watches as the elevator doors close. The elevator begins to descend, and CyrIS thinks, "One hundred and ten meters down to the LHC tunnels."

When the doors once again open, they are at an entrance to the collider tunnels. The men pick up the duffle bags and proceed. CyrIS can see that this area is bustling with people in lab coats or technician uniforms, and all on the move. No one pays any attention to the three men as they enter the tunnels, and soon, they approach a very large and complex set of machinery. CyrIS sees a relatively small sign indicating the 'Atlas Experiment'.

"Wow! This is incredible." CyrIS thinks, "This would be really cool if I were here under different circumstances."

Joseph talks in Arabic, looking at the other two men: "God be your guide". They respond in Arabic and then turn in opposite directions down the tunnels, past the clearly marked, black and yellow, radiation warning signs.

CyrIS, remembering the layout of the collider, thought about the other two experiments 'Alice' and 'LHC-B', which would be just over one mile in each of those directions.

Joseph looks around, sees that no one is looking at him, and slips behind some of the large machinery. It is clear to CyrIS that no one would be able to see Joseph in this location. Joseph then sits the duffle bag on its end and opens it.

Not to CyrIS' surprise, inside is what appears to be a large bomb, with a small detonation device attached at the opening of the bag. Joseph pushes a small button on the device, and CyrIS mentally braces himself for the explosion. Instead, a set of red digital lights illuminates the front of the device. Joseph then sets the reading on the display to 9:00. Joseph looks at his wristwatch it reads, 7:32. He then sits on the floor next to the bag and says in Arabic. "And now we make the enemy pay, and I will defend this station with my life, on this road to paradise."

Joseph begins to repeat prayers that CyrIS had heard many times before. CyrIS thinks to himself: "Nine o'clock, that is about the time they are planning on making the announcement at the Main Auditorium. I know what they are planning now! I must get out of here! It is time to send a signal to Ester."

CyrIS's three comrades had been sitting by his side now for about 2 hours. And then it happens...

"Oh God!" Ester yells out. "I just felt it!" Ester stands up. "Just now, he squeezed my hand three times."

Christine already had the syringes with large doses of epinephrine and the adrenaline antidotes laid out on a small nightstand next to the bed.

"Are you ready Rufus? Here we go!" She says.

Rufus stands over CyrIS, still lying motionless on the bed. "I'm ready!"

Christine, a bit hesitant says: "I'm not sure what is going to happen when I put this in him. It will create a very large dose of adrenaline in his body. I hope it wakes him up, and if it does, he may be hard to control. You will have to try to hold him still so I can then inject the antidote. Are you sure you're ready?"

"Yes! Just do it! We're wasting time!"

Christine injects the epinephrine into CyrIS' leg just below his boxer shorts and waits. Nothing happens.

A moment later, CyrIS begins to tremble and his whole body begins to quake. He swings his arms violently and then jumps straight up. He is now standing in the bed screaming at the top of his voice: "It's a bomb, it's a bomb!"

Rufus tackles CyrIS at the knees, bringing him back to the bed. He wrestles hard to get to CyrIS' backside, so he can wrap himself around CyrIS' arms and legs to hold him down. CyrIS is not going down easy. He fights back hard, and almost knocks Rufus out while putting a large gash in his elbow. As they struggle, neither gets the advantage. They drop to the floor, knocking over the lamp, the nightstand, and the syringes, causing them to fly across the room.

Ester is screaming and crying as Christine tries desperately to retrieve the syringes and get into position, she knows she must get the antidote into CyrIS before he and Rufus do serious damage to each other.

They are now in the corner of the room next to the window, punching, clawing and scratching each other like alley cats fighting over a last morsel of food. Finally, Rufus gets the advantage and wraps his arms and legs around those of CyrIS'. Though CyrIS continues to struggle, Rufus has him down.

"Christine, hurry up! I don't know how much longer I can hold him."

Christine has the antidote ready. She dives on top of CyrIS and jams the needle deep into his leg. CyrIS struggles for a minute or so, but eventually settles down, and they all slump to the floor exhausted.

Ester is immediately next to CyrIS, looking into his face. "Oh! My God! Are you alright?" She yells.

CyrIS opens his eyes, "Oh God, I'm so thirsty!"

No one moves to get him water.

"CyrIS! CyrIS!" Christine yells. "What happened? What do we need to do?"

CyrIS says exhausted: "Help me get dressed, we must hurry, there is not much time. It's just like we thought: four experiments and four bombs!"

Once CyrIS is dressed, they load into their rental car and get on the move.

CyrIS explains: "Joseph, the man I had possessed, planted his bomb at the 'Atlas Experiment'. The two men he was with were headed to set their bombs at the 'Alice' and 'LHC-B' experiments, about a mile in each direction away from the 'Atlas' location. There was what looked like a fourth bomb left in the trunk of the car that delivered us to the collider. I believe the fourth terrorist and that fourth bomb were intended for the 'CMS' experiment at the far north end of the collider, about 12 miles away. I believe that Jamaal is planning on driving him up there, getting the terrorist into the facility and then leaving."

This is the first time CyrIS mentions that Jamaal was driving the car. He planned not to mention it, but it slipped.

Cyrus now with a distressed look on his face, looks at Christine and says, "Sorry, Christine; he seems to be the leader behind this whole plot."

Christine's expression drops, as CyrIS continues: "In any case, the terrorist I was with, set his bomb to go off at 9:00. It is my guess that all of the bombs are set to go off at that time. We have less than an hour."

As they race down Route De Meyrin to the building that holds the collider, CyrIS says: "Rufus, do you think we can get local police to respond?"

Rufus responds: "I don't think we have time to deal with the authorities, we could call in the bomb threat, and I think I can get us into the collider."

Christine opens her cell phone and begins to dial.

"Wait! No! Stop!" Rufus demands. "If we call the police, they will shut down all the entrances to the collider, and we'll never get in. I'm not sure they will know what to do, or if they can even get there in time. I'm just not sure."

"Fuck!" CyrIS exclaims unsure of their fate. "I don't think the dramatic events in our lives, all of this learning, all of this preparation, were meant for us to just turn it over to the police and hope it gets solved. We were all drawn here for a reason, and I think this is OUR job. I say we don't call the police and just go for it. What do you say, team?"

"Fuck! You're right." Rufus responds, "I'm all in!"

With no hesitation, everyone agrees.

When they arrive at one of the outer gates surrounding the collider, Rufus' heart is pounding as he shows his new credentials to the guard at the gate.

"Let me check on that." The guard says, as he goes back into his shack.

"What time is it?" CyrIS says, looking at his wristwatch while sitting next to Ester in the back seat. "Shit! We are never going to make it at this rate. Tell this idiot to hurry up!"

Rufus calmly replies. "Just settle down, we've got enough time. We don't want to blow it right here."

"Well, Dr. Middleman, you're not on the list of people who have access." The attendant says.

"Damn," Rufus says softly, gritting his teeth to remain calm. "Are you sure? I was just added recently."

"Fuck! I'm going to have to kill this guy". Rufus thinks to himself.

"Come on! Come on!" CyrIS whispers.

Ester appears to be on the verge of a panic attack, just as Christine says sweetly while smiling at the young man. "Can you call someone and check on Dr. Middleman's credentials? We really need to get in and check on some critical items, right away."

The guard smiles and says, "Dr. Middleman, I need the names of your guests so I can call it in."

Rufus, on the verge of losing it, once again forces himself to remain calm, but then almost shouting he says,

"This is: Dr. Christine Basurto"

"How do you spell that last name?"

"B-A-S-U-R-T-O." Rufus spells the name though almost gritted teeth but continues the introductions.

"In the back seat we have: Dr. Ester Suni Nate."

"How do you spell that name?"

Rufus slowly spells Ester's last name, trying hard to conceal the growing rage inside him.

"Finally, we have: Dr. CyrIS Steel."

"Oh!" the guard exclaims. "Are you the evangelistic preacher that ties science to religion?"

CyrIS leans forward: "Yes I am."

"Wow! It's really nice to meet you! I love your sermons."

"Well thanks, is there anything you can do to hurry this along. We are in a very big hurry. We need to get back to the auditorium for the big announcement."

"Oh! You bet. Yes, sir! I'll be right back."

After an agonizing minute he returns. "You guys are cleared to go. They just hadn't added your name to the list yet."

Rufus smiles and 'floors' it, accelerating towards the collider and pushing CyrIS back in his seat.

Rufus is not sure how they will get to the fourth bomb in time, which he understood will be planted at the 'CMS' experiment at the far north end of the collider. As they drive to the facility, Rufus convinces Christine that she should drive back to the auditorium, contact the authorities and let them know about the location of the fourth bomb.

'Even if she does not get there in time, at least she will be out of danger.' Rufus thinks. Christine hesitates, but finally agrees to her assignment.

When the car arrives at the building and everyone gets out, Christine kisses Rufus, and then she drives away. Rufus watches as she drives away, not knowing if he would ever see her again.

Once the three of them are inside the building, CyrIS looks around confused: "Rufus, can you get us to the 'Atlas' experiment? I'll know where to go from there."

"I think so," He says unconfidently. "Let's find an elevator. I know we have to go down."

"God, I hope we're in the right building", Rufus thinks.

They all start searching the hallways for an elevator. Not finding one, Rufus starts to panic. "Oh! God! This place could go up any second".

"Over here," Ester yells. They run to the elevator. There is less than twenty minutes before it is nine o'clock.

Once descended to the collider floor, Rufus leads them to the 'Atlas Experiment', and CyrIS points out where the terrorist Joseph is hiding.

CyrIS whispers "Ester stay here! Rufus and I will run to the other two experiments. We will try to eliminate those terrorists and then get back here as quickly as we can to help you. But Ester you may have to take this one out yourself. Can you do that?"

Ester says: "I think so." Not looking confident in the least bit.

Christine arrives at the auditorium and uses her good looks and media credentials to easily navigate security. She has the small earbud radio in her ear. Rufus not only equipped each of them with radios to communicate, he had also built plastic 3D single-shot pistols that he said would easily clear the metal detectors.

"Be prepared for anything," she hears the voice of one of her comrades' whisper. "And be prepared to do anything." A second voice emphasizes. The hall is packed.

"What should I do?" She thinks. "I can't just yell out that there is a bomb in the collider. People could get killed just in the panic."

Christine starts looking for someone with authority. But then she sees something shocking. There he was, her son, Jamaal, off in the distance walking through the crowd of scientist and reporters. He emerged from one of the adjacent hallways and looks like he is leaving the building. It all seems so surreal. Her emotions ramp up again as she pictures him at the bottom of the capitol steps.

"Don't let these emotions rule. What is the logical thing to do?"

"Why is he here? That trip to the CMS experiment and back would have taken at least a half hour. I don't think he could have made it back here that quick. Besides, why would he come back here? Why wouldn't he just leave?"

Christine tries hard to fight the emotions associated with seeing him again, and suddenly. "Oh! Shit!" Christine visualizes the diagram that CyrIS had shown them before.

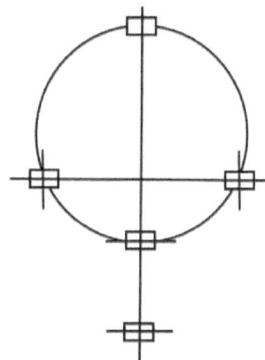

"The crosshairs are not on all four experiments. They are only on the three experiments at the bottom of the circle. The fourth crosshair is on the box below the circle.' She quickly remembers the auditorium she is in is just south of the collider."

'Oh! Shit! He did not plant that fourth bomb at the CMS experiment, he planted it HERE. He plans on killing all these scientists. Where did he go? I must find that bomb. What time is it?"

"Holy Fuck, less than fifteen minutes."

Christine immediately tries to contact her team on the radio, but there is nothing but static in response, as she pushes her way through the crowd yelling: "Excuse me! Excuse me!" to the angry people as she pushes past them.

"I don't think he saw me. Where did he go? It looked like he was leaving. I should follow him. No! Wait. CyrIS said he was with an Arabic looking man and he had a large duffle bag. I should find that guy! That's where the bomb will be! But what do I do, if I find him?"

Everyone in the hall, except Christine, is moving towards the main auditorium. It is difficult for Christine to make her way in the opposite direction, but eventually she is alone. Christine looks around to see if anyone is looking at her, but most of the attention is concentrated toward the main hall, so she lifts her skirt and grabs the 3D pistol form between her legs.

"Sure, the gun had made its way through the metal detectors, but will it work? And more importantly will I have the nerve to use it?" she thinks as she is now walking down the hallway that she had seen her son emerge from.

"Where would I put a bomb?" Then noticing the Men's Room, she thinks, "It would have a wall adjacent to the auditorium. Maybe in there; no time for being shy."

Christine marches into to the restroom. It appears empty at first, but then Christine sees a pair of shoes with trousers and boxer shorts draped over them under one of the stalls. Above that, is a pair of very hairy legs.

"Shit! - Shit, Shit, SHIT!" She thinks.

Christine thinks about the shyness she endured in her life; and all that fear. She was afraid of everything.

Not now, NOT NOW!' She screams internally.

The *darkness* made her stronger, and now this new combination of the power of *'Light'* AND *'Darkness'* that she had received from Rufus, made her a 'Wonder Woman'.

She grabs the top of the stall door and rips it open.

There he is. In his lap is the large duffle-bag. It is leaning against the cinderblock wall. He is totally shocked to see this gorgeous, blonde, lily-white woman staring right at him with her teeth clenched, and this tiny plastic gun aimed at his forehead.

"Gotcha! Mother Fucker" Christine says calmly.

Rufus ran the entire mile to the 'Alice Experiment' and breathing heavily, was now slowly creeping up on it. The area appears to be vacant, but he could hear a radio or TV off in the distance. The commentator is talking about the impending announcement.

Rufus begins looking around some of the machinery in the area, straining his eyes to see into some of the dark areas. Finally, he sees, what looks like the bottom edge of a duffle bag and part of a shoe. Rufus, not wanting to chance the one shot of the plastic gun, decides to charge the terrorist's hiding place.

In less than a second, he is on the guy, wrestling him to the ground. He easily takes away the small knife he was brandishing. He grabs the man's head and twists hard. Snap; it's done. Rufus reaches inside of the duffle bag and pulls out the timer. It's just as CyrIS had described it. Rufus immediately rips the two wires away from the bomb it is connected too. No explosion. The red numbers on the timer continued towards 9:00. Rufus panics.

"Shit! I hope this is not some kind of remote ignition device."

Rufus turns the device over. He can see two small double-A batteries. He removes one of the batteries and the device goes dead.

Rufus whispers into his radio, "I got mine. I'll be there shortly." Hearing no response, Rufus begins running back in the direction of his two comrades.

Ester looks at her watch. It has been well over ten minutes since the two men left, and time was running out.

'*Just two minutes until Nine O'clock*'. Ester thinks.

Ester decides that she must do this by herself, and slowly takes the gun out of her pocket and creeps towards the location that

CyrIS indicated the terrorist would be, but arriving at the spot, she finds no one.

Suddenly, a hand grabs her mouth, and she feels a knife blade against her throat.

He had her.

Ester tries to scream, but his hand muffles the sound. Ester kicks the man in the lower part of his shins and struggles to get away, but the man is too strong.

"He's going to kill me. He's going to kill me!" Ester screams internally, and then. "Why hasn't he killed me?"

Ester looks up and there is her answer, standing just a few feet away -breathing like a freight train - plastic gun in his hand, stood the enormous mountain that was Rufus Middleman.

"Let her go!" Rufus demands, while staring directly into the eyes of the terrorist.

The terrorist lifts Ester up so that her head was directly in front of his face, obviously with no intention of letting her go. He just waits for time to pass; waits for everything to pass.

But he makes a huge mistake though. Ester was short and because he had raised her up so high, she could now kick backwards and upwards, which she did, kicking him squarely in the balls. At the same time, Ester jerks her head to the left, exposing a bit of the man's face.

"Sorry Ester," Rufus says as he squeezes the trigger on the plastic gun.

CyrIS had also located the terrorist guarding his bomb at the 'LHC-B' experiment. He heard the whisper in his earbud earlier when Rufus eliminated the threat at the 'Alice' experiment. CyrIS could not reply because at the time he was just a few feet behind his own target.

CyrIS now pulls out his plastic gun, points it at his man and says: "Hey!"

The terrorist spins around, not paying any attention to the small plastic gun, and immediately charges CyrIS. CyrIS fires the small weapon but it has no effect. The terrorist takes CyrIS to the floor, it's a brawl, and the terrorist has a knife. CyrIS sees the knife and grabs the man's wrist. They begin punching, scratching and pushing each other against the wall, then back to the center of the hall, and they fall to the floor. The terrorist winds up on top of CyrIS, trying to force the knife towards his face. CyrIS can see blood on the knife, then on his own hand, and he feels it dripping on to his face.

"Have I been stabbed? I've got to get this knife away." CyrIS thinks.

The battle goes on for several minutes, CyrIS, now concerned about the bomb, head-butts the man several times and the man slumps on top of him. At first, CyrIS thought he knocked the man out but then he saw it. Blood is flowing from a small hole in the side of the man's head. His plastic gun had worked.

"Thanks, Rufus," CyrIS thought, and with the man still on top of him, looks at his watch, there are only seconds left. CyrIS pushes the man aside and rushes towards the bomb.

Back in the main auditorium, a man in a gray suit enters the stage at the front, and after a moment begins to speak. "This is a very, very preliminary result, but we think it is very strong, very valid; otherwise we wouldn't present it."

On the screen above the speaker's head was a slide with an image of many lines of refracted light. In the center of the slide are the words: "Status of CMS, SM Higgs Search". As the next slide comes up with a very complicated looking chart and table, the speaker continues.

"Slowly as we have gathered data, we discovered the standard model for more and more rare processes. Basically, we are more confident now that we can go after the rarest molecule, which is the Higgs". The screen brings a new slide, a graph with several horizontal lines on it and a large dip in the center of the lines.

The speaker goes on: "If we combine the ZZ and the Gama, Gama, this is what we get. They line up extremely well. In the region of 125 GeV, they combine to give us a combined significance of 5 standard deviations."

The room explodes with thunderous applause. All the cameras in the room turn to Peter Higgs, now wiping a tear from his eye.

EPILOGUE

"The underlying, primary psychic reality is so inconceivably complex that it can be grasped only at the farthest reach of intuition, and even then, very dimly. That is why it needs symbols."

– Carl Jung

July 4th, 2016

Ester Suni Nati, age 65

CyrIS Steel, 66

Rufus Middleman, 47

Christine Basurto, 49

"Happy 4th of July!" CyrIS addresses his three comrades. Everyone is sitting comfortably in CyrIS and Ester's living room, each with a glass of wine in hand. The only item out of place in this warm, inviting atmosphere is the large white board standing just off to the side of a large fire burning in the fireplace.

"Over my entire life", CyrIS continued, "I have believed that all of the pieces of the *puzzle* were there for me to solve. I now realize that it was never there for me to solve alone. I needed each of you to even have a chance!"

"So, I raise my glass in salute to the four of us!" Everyone raises their glass as CyrIS continues.

"To Rufus, to Christine, to Ester, and to myself."

"Here, here!" the group responds.

"Well, this is the fourth year we have celebrated the anniversary of our escapades in Switzerland, and not a peep from the media about what happened there. I can only assume that the

Swiss authorities cleaned up the whole mess and kept it a secret to protect the fact that their security was so lax."

"Oh, Well! That probably means they are not looking very hard to find us."

"But this year's anniversary is special because we have great news which further supports our search for the pieces needed to solve the puzzle, and which brings our search, and that of all science, closer to a 'Universal Theory of Everything'."

"The news I am referring to, is the discovery of proof of the existence of 'Gravitational Waves' earlier this year, and which is further support for Rufus' theories in this area. This event has also been the impetus for me to put together a summary of what we have all pulled together over the years, and we will be delving deeper into each aspect of what we have gathered, including 'Gravitational Waves'."

"But, before we get started here, I just want to say that I am still pissed at Rufus for shooting that terrorist's eye out, right next to my wife's face!"

Ester interrupts, looking a little perturbed with CyrIS, "Yes, thank you Rufus, for saving me from getting my throat cut by that terrorist! And, thank you for eliminating not one, but two terrorists while dismantling two bombs. But, most of all, thank you for not shooting me in the face."

CyrIS adds, with a bit of sarcasm. "Oh! Ester said I'm supposed to say: 'Thank you for saving my wife's life'. And yea, that's a great story, but the one I like the most is Christine's. Can you tell us again, Christine?"

"Sure" Christine begins, "I'd love too."

"When I entered the auditorium and saw my son, Jamaal. I immediately figured that the bomb must be planted there in the auditorium and not at the CMS experiment as we had originally thought. I then determined that I should not follow my son but rather find the terrorist and the bomb first."

"I concluded that the bomb was probably in the men's room because it shared a common wall with the auditorium. When I got in the restroom, I found that there was someone in one of the stalls. I immediately ripped open the door to the stall, and there he was, with the duffle bag on his lap. When he saw me, he pushed the bag aside, jumped up, and charged me. But he had his trousers and boxer shorts down around his ankles, probably so that people would think he was taking a crap. Or maybe he was actually taking a crap. Or, maybe he was just getting ready for all those virgins in paradise."

"Anyway, when he charged me, he tripped over his pants, and fell flat on his face in front of me. He had a knife, but it went flying when he fell. I backed up a bit to avoid his fall, but he grabbed me by my ankles. And then, I simply leaned down, put the plastic gun to the back of his head and, POW! 'That's for you!' Or, something like that; it's a little fuzzy now."

"Anyway, I disengaged from his grip on my ankles, stepped into the stall, and straddled his naked hairy ass. Very gross. I then disconnected the timer from the bomb, just like CyrIS had instructed us. But the timer kept running, so I just stuck it in my pocket turned and left the restroom."

"As I passed the open doors to the main auditorium, I heard a thunderous uproar of applause. Assuming it was for me, I just kept walking, raised my hand and waved, saying: 'Thank You, Thank you very much! It was nothing; All in a day's work!' And, as I left the hall, I added: 'Christine has left the building; there will be NO encore performances today. '"

The group laughed and then applauded.

"I swear Christine that story gets better every time you tell it," CyrIS adds.

Now, with a look of intensity on his face, CyrIS begins again. "One, Two, Three, Four. *"*

With puzzled looks on all their faces, CyrIS's audience did not respond.

"And, though I believe the four of us are important; we are not as important as the summation of your inputs that I, with your help, am about to present."

"So; One, Two, Three, Four!"

"Let's start with *One*. We are all a bit narcissistic to some degree, that is to say, we are all about 'One' person: ourselves."

"But, is that true? Is it only 'to some degree'? Some would argue that everything we say and do is about ourselves and our own beliefs. Mother Theresa may be one of the most giving people we have ever heard of. She dedicated her entire life to giving to others, at all cost to her personally. But, is that true? Why did she do all those acts of kindness? One could argue that it gave her great deal of personal gratification to give as she did, and, it is possible, that the driving force, pushing her to sacrifice as she did, may have been all about her? Was it all about her own internal feelings and beliefs; her own personal driving *emotions* and *logic*?"

"So, how can we say that anything we do is not ultimately to satisfy ourselves?"

"As such, the word 'I' may be the most important word in the English language. We will be coming back to 'One' and 'I' a bit later."

"Now, let's talk about 'Two'; '*Logic* and *Emotion*', the 'Two' most important things dominating each of our lives."

"Ester and I have shared with you the '*Logic* and *Emotion*' matrix that we discovered many years ago."

CyrIS places a small, hard backed, example of the '*Logic* and *Emotion*' matrix in front of the white board.

O	G	I	C	N	E	M	O	T
T	I	O	N	E	*L*	O	G	I
I	C	N	E	M	*O*	T	I	O
O	N	E	L	O	*G*	I	C	N
N	*E*	*M*	*O*	*T*	*I*	*O*	*N*	E
E	L	O	G	I	*C*	N	E	M
M	O	T	I	O	N	E	L	O
O	G	I	C	N	E	M	O	T

"This is a '*Two*' dimensional representation. We call it: the fabric of '*Logic* and *Emotion*', or the fabric of life, and we believe this fabric is very important. So, we look very closely at this fabric for clues to its significance."

"The first thing I did when analyzing this matrix, was a kind of statistical evaluation of its components. I found that about 30% of the letters in this fabric are associated only with the word '*Logic*'. Another 50% of the letters, including one third of the letter 'O's, are only associated with the word '*Emotion*'. There are *Two* letters that make up the remaining 20%, and they are associated with both words."

"Maybe the most interesting statistic is that there is only One letter that is associated with all words in all cases: The One letter, is the letter 'I'."

CyrIS pauses for a second to let this sink in before continuing.

"Ester and I also found that no matter how small you make each letter in the matrix, or how far apart you spread them, they still were part of a word, thus still part of the fabric. It seemed to us that there is an unseen field connecting them to each other."

"Christine, when I first showed you the '*Logic* and *Emotion*' matrix, you shared some interesting statistics with me about these '*Two*' words. Can you share that with the group?"

"Sure," Christine begins, "Studies show that people often think that they are using '*Logic*' to make decisions. In reality they are using their '*Emotions*'. These studies indicate that most decisions are made with '*Emotions*' 75 to 80 percent of the time."

"We only use '*Logic*' 20 to 25 percent of the time. And I further point out that people, who think they are using '*Logic*', are actually using a form of their own filtered '*Logic*'. Filtered logic that conforms to their needs and is really based on '*Emotion*' and not true '*Logic*': i.e. it seems *logical* to them but may not seem that way to others."

"Thank you, Christine," CyrIS says, "I just wanted you to see the correlation in the weight of the words and in the fabric to that of the real world."

CyrIS continues, "And, you are all aware of the importance of a *'Trinity'* in most religious beliefs. The *'Three'* major components are generally fashioned after the *'Three'* concepts of *'Mind'*, *'Body'* and *'Spirit'*, usually represented by the upright triangle."

"In most Christian religions, it is the *'Father'*, the *'Son'* and the *'Holy Spirit'*. There are similar references to a trinity in other non-Christian religions as well. And, there are also references to a trinity, in many of the *dark* religions, usually represented by the inverted triangle."

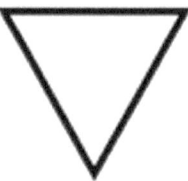

"But that is not all that these symbols of 'Three', represent."

"Over the past three weeks, each of you has shared intimate information with me to compile this summary of our learning. I appreciate that you have agreed to share those intimate details today."

"Ester, what is your middle name?"

"My father gave me the middle name, Aira." Ester responds unsurprised. She was expecting the question from CyrIS as she had helped him formulate some, but not all, the presentation.

"And, what does the name 'Aira' mean?" CyrIS asks.

"It means: '*Air*' or '*Wind*', and it is tied closely to the emotional aspects of the '*Spirit*'."

CyrIS turns to the white board and begins drawing on its right side. "And, here is the alchemist's symbol for '*Air*', an upright triangle with a horizontal line passing through it."

"I love Ester," CyrIS continues, "I truly believe she is the embodiment of the wind, a true free '*Spirit*'. She has, on many occasions, demonstrated what can be accomplished through '*The Power of Positive Thinking*' and '*The Secrets of Attraction*.' She has accomplished things that often seemed beyond comprehension and sometimes in the realm of mysticism."

CyrIS, now pointing to himself; "My middle name is not quite so romantic, and when I gave myself this name, I thought it was just something I made up. Now, I believe it was not as random as I originally thought. Sometimes, as we all know, we are led by hidden forces."

"After reading the scroll I found in Billy's old church, I gave myself the name CyrIS Steel. I also gave myself the middle name of '*Kaj-El*'. As all of you know, I am a fan of Superman. So, along with the last name '*Steel*', I wanted to give myself a middle name that represented: 'Down to Earth', being 'logical'. I also wanted my name to be somewhat like that of Superman's real name; 'Kal-El', meaning the '*Voice of God*'. So, I gave myself the middle name '*Kaj-El*'. '*Kaj*' is Greek for 'Earth' and just as in Superman's name '*El*' means 'Of God', and thus the 'Earth of God'.

"How was I to know that this name held so much significance? Much later, I found out that the alchemist symbol for 'Earth' is the inverted triangle with a horizontal line through it.

The exact inverse of Ester's alchemist symbol." CyrIS draws the symbol on the left side of the whiteboard, while, at the same time, showing the group the bracelet Ester had given him.

CyrIS now looks at Rufus, "Rufus, what is your middle name?"

"Esh-Ban", Rufus responds knowingly, and adds. "It is of Israeli origin and means '*Fire of the Sun*'".

CyrIS adds, "Indicating the '*Light*' of the '*Sun*' and the '*Flame*' of a '*Fire*'. Certainly, you have exhibited that you are a '*Hot blooded*' male over the course of your life."

"But you have also demonstrated your strong beliefs in the teachings of the scriptures, and in righteousness they represent. You are truly a '*Light of God*'."

Once again, CyrIS begins drawing on the whiteboard, but this time at the top of the board.

CyrIS then says, "The alchemist symbol for '*Fire*' is a representation of a '*Flame*', an upright triangle."

"And finally; Christine, what is your middle name?"

"It's 'Nixie", meaning '*Water Spirit*'", she responds.

CyrIS continues. "And, though we all now know, you are a believer in the power of absolute *darkness*. It has been your deeply feminine perspective and enlightened philosophical approach that has helped us so much in our quest."

CyrIS once again turns to the white board and begins drawing again, now at its bottom. "The alchemist symbol for *'Water'* is the symbol for the *'Cup'*, an inverted triangle. The exact opposite of that of Rufus."

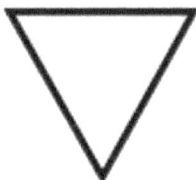

"And, I would add, that the upright triangle is also the symbol of the *'Blade'*, which symbolizes the 'Male', and the inverted triangle, the symbol of the *'Chalice'*, symbolizes the 'Female'."

The whiteboard now holds all four symbols.

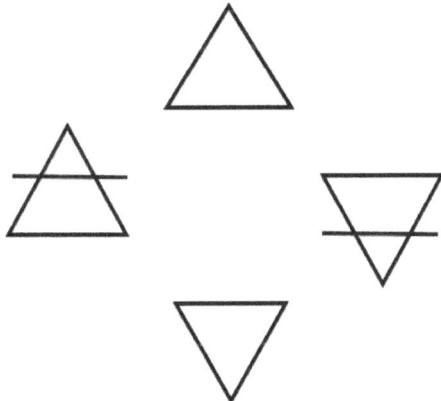

"And, when you combine these four symbols," CyrIS now indicates, with his hand, the direction that each symbol must move.

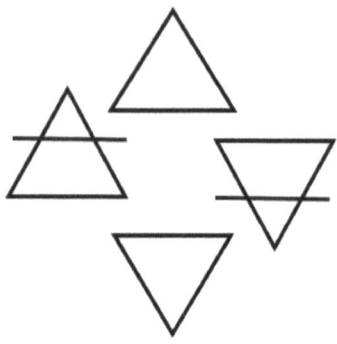

"And once they have completely overlapped each other," CyrIS erases the four symbols on the board. Then, in the middle of the board, he draws a composite of the four overlapped symbols. "What do you have?"

"You see it is the overlapping triangles which is Rufus' 'Star of David' and Christine's 'Hexagram', one and the same."

"It is the symbol of the combination of the '*Trinity*' of '*Light*' and the '*Trinity*' of '*Darkness*'. They combine to form 'One' entity, which we will discuss in more detail a little latter."

"Once again, I must thank you all for your willingness to share very intimate details of your lives with us today."

"Christine? Rufus? May I ask you to now share with us, what you learned from thar very intimate encounter that you had with each other?"

There was silence for a moment and then Christine begins to speak.

"Of course, CyrIS. We have already explained this to you, but we would be glad to repeat it for Ester's sake."

"I would not normally share a description of such an intimate encounter, however, both Rufus and I believe that what we learned is very important and necds to be shared. Rufus, do you agree?"

"Yes, and you are doing fine. Please continue." Rufus replied.

"Well, I believe that you are aware of the rocky start that Rufus and I had when we first met. I have to admit I was immediately physically attracted to him, however, it appeared that politically, religiously, theoretically, and morally, we did not agree on anything."

"However, that night when we got together after the conference, I noticed that on the inner surface of Rufus' left forearm, there is a tattoo. The tattoo was perfectly white and stood out dramatically against his very dark skin."

"We were facing each other at the time, and I said 'Wow, that's very interesting', as I was pointing at his tattoo."

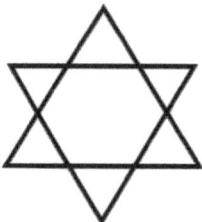

"Rufus responded, saying to me: 'Yea, it's the 'Star of David' and it is very important to me. It symbolizes the most perfect 'Light' of Yahweh, the ultimate expression of my beliefs in the teachings of the scriptures.' Why do you find it so interesting?"

"I did not say anything; I just rolled up the sleeve on my left arm and exposed my inner forearm. There for Rufus to see, was my own tattoo, the same symbol in black, highlighted by my very white skin."

"It's a Hexagon, I said, and it is also very important to me. It symbolizes the power of perfect 'Darkness'."

"So, there we sat, and was thinking, 'how we can be so different and yet the same'."

"It changed everything. After that, we did not fight. We had a new, almost inquisitive respect for one another. Wouldn't you agree, Rufus?"

Rufus, anxious to jump in says: "Yes, it was like being tempted by a huge mystery. We knew this could not be coincidence, and, despite our differences, we were somehow now *connected*. We were even more attracted to each other, well beyond the physical attractions that we each obviously had. Right Christine?"

"Absolutely, all of our differences seemed to be of no consequence, and, without getting into great detail, it was not long before we consummated this new relationship."

"It was magnificent." Rufus could not contain himself. He turns to look at Christine. Christine, looks back at Rufus, turns a bit red but shakes her head in agreement.

"But that is not why we are sharing this with you." Rufus continues.

"During that sexual encounter, we discovered something extremely incredible. We had thought that our beliefs were the extreme opposites of the spectrum, black and white, '*Light*' and '*Darkness*'."

"What we found in that encounter, was that the two symbols of our beliefs, the 'Star of David' and the 'Hexagon' were exactly the same for a reason. We found that all our beliefs were actually, exactly the same. We found that there is no difference between '*Light*' and '*Darkness*'. They are one and the same. One cannot exist without the other. I can't exactly explain this, but even though they are separate, the power derived from one, is dependent on the other. '*Light*' has no power without '*Darkness*', and '*Darkness*' has no power without '*Light*'.

Rufus and Christine looked a bit exhausted, just recalling this experience seemed to wear them down, and CyrIS felt this was a good time to jump back in.

"Thank you for sharing that with us. I know that was extremely personal. I believe that once we have all presented our learning, what you have observed will make a lot more sense."

"So, are we ready to move on to 'Four'?"

"One of the basic representations of 'Four' is the cross. Possibly the most well-known 'Four' is the four compass directions: North, South, East, and West.

CyrIS erases the overlapping triangles on the whiteboard, and in the center of the board, he draws a cross with the four compass directions on it.

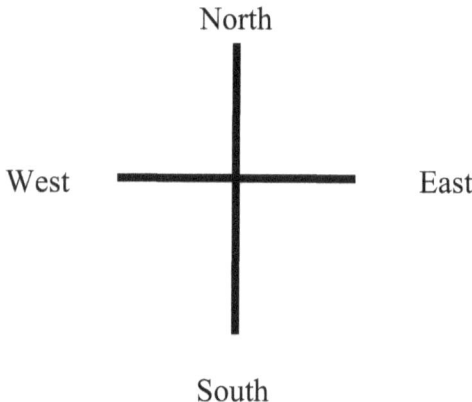

"We will be using this representation to illustrate some of our conclusions from our life experiences. And, as you know, I have asked each of you, if you would, to use this basic format to explain your perspective on your learnings."

"Starting with a small pun: 'We all have our crosses to bear'. Christine, what is yours?

As CyrIS takes a seat, Christine stands up, walks to the whiteboard, and begins addressing the group. She erases CyrIS's four compass directions, but not the cross itself.

"The Swiss Psychologist and Psychoanalyst Carl Jung, once said: *'If a union is to take place between opposites like spirit and matter, conscious and unconscious, bright and dark, and so on, it will happen in a third thing, which represents not a compromise but something new'.*"

Christine continues, "In Western culture, there has always been an implied separation between the *'Objective'* physical realm, and that of the *'Subjective'* psychic realm. Some would say it is the difference between what is thought and what is real. In fact, this material view considers thought as just a product of the material composition of the brain. It considers this *'Objective'* view almost to the complete exclusion of the *'Subjective'* view. Therefore, mental phenomena are just products of a brain made of matter and governed by the known physical laws."

" However, in the last 100 years or so, with the advent of *'Relativity'* and *'Quantum'* theories, things have changed. These more recent theories in physics have radically undermined the base of this longstanding materialistic view. For example: the special and general theories of relativity have pushed physicist to drastically change their understanding and perception of space, time, matter, and energy. On the other hand, quantum theory has forced revisions in the concepts of determinism, causality and locality. And now, these theories have even proposed the possibility that the properties of matter have no existence independent of observation."

"You know about the puzzling results of experiments showing that electrons, once considered to be only particles, were exhibiting properties of waves, and vice-a-versa. And it was Werner Heisenberg and Erwin Schrodinger, who independently, created the basic theories of quantum physics."

"I will come back to all of that shortly. But, for now, let's move on to the world of psychology. Carl Jung studied with Sigmund Freud and expanded on Freud's theories of the unconscious. In his *'Psychology of the Unconscious'*, published in 1912, and his *'Archetypes of the Collective Unconscious'*, published in 1934. Let me read some of what Jung wrote:"

"*'We must distinguish between a personal unconscious and an impersonal or transpersonal unconscious. We speak of the latter also as the collective unconscious, because it is detached from anything personal and is common to all men, since its contents can be found everywhere, which is naturally not the case with the personal consciousness.'*"

"What Jung is implying here is: beyond our *'Personal'* unconscious, which is made up of things that we have personally experienced but forgotten, there is also a *'Collective'* unconscious. The *'Collective'* unconscious is deep within our unconscious and is an innate function of our being and is universal to everyone."

"Jung also expressed a theory that a person's psyche allows for the integration of the *'Conscious'* and *'Unconscious'* minds, including this *'Collective Unconscious'*, in order to make sense of the observed world. Jung referred to this process as *'Synchronicity'* and it involves a connection between inner psychological experience and outer experiences of the world."

"Synchronicity requires coordination between the inner, *'Conscious'* and *'Unconscious'* worlds, with that of the outer physical world. Thus, it is not just psychological or just physical but instead *'psychoid'*; meaning it involves both the psyche and matter. Jung hypothesized that our view of the world is a combination of the physical and the psychological aspect of our being. He called this the *'Unus Mundus'*, Latin for *'One World'*. Let me read to you what Jung wrote about this:"

"*'Conscious and unconscious have no clear demarcations, the one beginning where the other leaves off...The psyche is a conscious-unconscious whole.'*"

"And referring to the relationship between psyche and matter he wrote:"

"*'Since psyche and matter are contained in one and the same world, and moreover are in continuous contact with one another and ultimately rest on irrepresentable, transcendental factors, it is not only possible but fairly probable, even, that psyche and matter are two different aspects of one and the same thing.'*"

"He also wrote:"

"*'Psyche and matter exist in one and the same world, and each partakes of the other, otherwise any reciprocal action would be impossible. If research could only advance far enough, therefore, we would arrive at an ultimate agreement between physical and psychological concepts.'*"

"So, let's compare '*Psyche*' and '*Matter*', '*Psychology*' and '*Physics*'."

"Let's begin with quantum physics. The nature of quantum particles was realized by accepting the principle of *Complementarity*; A principle which states that mutually exclusive concepts must be utilized to completely understand quantum events. And this principle of *Complementarity* applies to the field of psychology just as well. Let me read a quote from the noted psychologist, Marie-Louise von Fran:"

"*'Bohr's idea of complementarity is especially interesting to Jungian psychologists, for Jung saw that the relationship between the conscious and unconscious mind also forms a complementary pair of opposites.'*"

"This suggests that the *wave-particle* complementarity in quantum physics can parallel the *unconscious-conscious* complementarity in psychology. And so, just as waves are unbounded, and particles are discrete; the unconscious is unbounded, and the conscious is discrete. Waves are continuous throughout space, and particles have a limited location, and Jung states:"

"*'The area of the unconscious is enormous and always continuous, while the area of consciousness is a restricted field of momentary vision.'*"

"I am sure you can see the parallels"

"I would like to make one final point here, and let me start with another quote from Marie-Louise von Fran:"

"*The deepest and most clearly distinguishable archetypal factor, which forms the basis of psycho-physical equivalence is, the archetypal patterns of natural numbers.*"

Christine continues, "Numbers are aspects of both the psychological and physical domains, they are of the mind, but obviously very effective in representing the physical world. And this order of '*One World*' can then help explain the mystery of how mathematics, a product of the mind, is so well suited to explain the physical world."

"And, with all of this in mind, here is my representative cross."

Christine turns to the white board and begins writing in the spots previously held by the four compass directions. In the 'North' location, she writes the 'Conscious'. In the 'South' location she writes the 'Unconscious'. In the 'West' location she puts 'Psyche', and finally in the 'East' location she puts 'Matter'.

Christine turns, to the group, pauses for a moment and then says: "CyrIS?"

CyrIS, caught off guard, jumps to his feet and says: "Thanks Christine, that was amazing."

Addressing the group, he says: "When we have heard each of your presentations, I am sure that you will see how this will, not only, help us in understanding the mysteries we have been pursuing, but will also hopefully, help us plot a course for our future."

CyrIS pauses for a moment and then looks to Ester, "Would you like to go next?"

"Thank you dear." Ester begins.

"I have had many discussions with Christine on the points she has made here this morning. It has become obvious to me, by way of my studies and these discussions, that there are very strong connections between this vast *Subconscious* region of our existence, and that of *Mysticism* and *Shamanism*."

"It does appear, as CyrIS has often pointed out, that his roots are in *Logic* while my roots lay primarily in *Emotion*. It would also seem that the conscious portion of our being relies on *Logic*, while at the same time, is driven primarily by the *Emotions* of the subconscious portion of our being. So, even though we think we use *logic* to make most of our decisions, as Christine earlier pointed out, actually about eighty percent of our decisions are made based on *emotion*, or some sort of *emotionally* filtered *logic*. "

"It seems to me, that we appear to be riding on an island in a vast ocean. The island appears to be stable and is composed of our conscious, *logical* being. We feel we have control of where we are going and what we are doing. But, the island, as it turns out, is just the tip of a mountain, floating free in an ocean. Most of this mountain exists in the form of a mass of sub-consciousness below the surface of the ocean waves. The ocean, which this mountain is floating in, is an ocean of *emotion*. The effect of this ocean of *emotion* on our subconscious is what truly determines our course."

"Let me repeat a quote from Carl Jung that Christine gave you earlier.

" *'We must distinguish between a personal unconscious and an impersonal or transpersonal unconscious. We speak of the latter also as the collective unconscious, because it is detached from anything personal and is common to all men, since its contents can be found everywhere, which is naturally not the case with the personal consciousness.'"*

"Here, we have an indication that our subconscious is connected to others well beyond our own personal sub-consciousness. And, I believe, this is the basis for what has been called 'Psychic Phenomena'. It is a tie to the *Mystic*; it is the path for *Shamans* to connect to beyond our own personal existence. It is the path to the *Lower*, *Middle*, and *Upper* worlds. It may be our connection to the *Fabric* of the universe, the very fabric of *logic* and *emotion*."

"I believe that is why, *The Secret of Attraction*, actually works. We are what we believe we are, and what we truly believe is ours, comes to us."

"Now let me also quote the Jungian psychologist Marie-Louise von Franz."

"*'The unexpected parallelisms of ideas in psychology and physics suggest, as Jung pointed out, a possible ultimate oneness of both fields of reality that physics and psychology study. . .. The concept of a Unitarian idea of reality was called by Jung the unus mundus.'"*

Ester continues: "In this *Unus Mundus*, *one world* view, matter and psyche are not discriminated or separately actualized. Reality and the mystic world are also one and the same."

"All of these, tied together in a fabric of *Conscious*, *Collective Unconscious*, *Reality* and *Mysticism*, are all a part of the Unus Mundus, or *One World*."

Ester turns to the whiteboard and begins to erase the four poles of the cross that Christine had entered.

In the 'North' location she enters the word 'Conscious', in the 'South' location she enters the word 'Collective Unconscious'. In the 'East' location she enters the word 'Reality' and lastly in the 'West' location she enters the word 'Mysticism'.

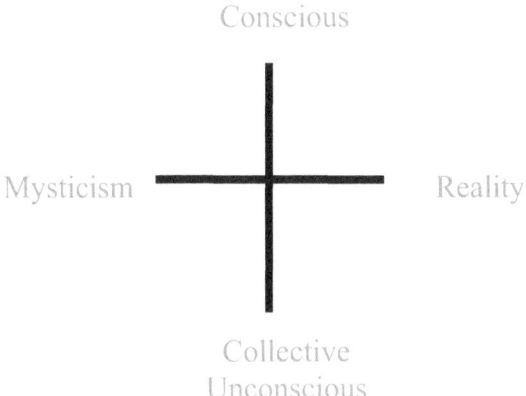

Ester turns to the group, saying: "Once again, these seem separate, but they are all one and the same; each affecting the other."

"But that is not all," Ester hesitates for a moment and then continues. "As a child growing up in Colorado, I attended a catholic grade school and high school. We, of course, learned about Reading, Writing and Arithmetic. But we also received intensive religious studies, including emphasis on the power of praying to God."

"Looking back on that now, I realize that the emphasis appeared to be on the negative, not the positive. What I am saying is: it was acceptable to pray for such things as forgiveness for some sin we had committed. We could pray that we would be a good person and do good things. We could pray for others to do good things. We could pray for the unfortunate. We even were encouraged to pray for the souls of the departed, because Catholics believe that when people pass away their souls can get stuck in a place called *Purgatory*. This is the place you must go as a kind of holding area for those who have committed sins. The sins are not so bad that you must go to hell, but bad enough to keep you out of heaven for a while. That is, until those still living have said enough prayers to free your soul so that it can proceed into heaven."

"It seemed that there were plenty of praying for those kinds of things, but it was not acceptable for you to pray for things that you personally wanted. You see, it was not acceptable to pray for a new bicycle or a new dress, or God forbid you prayed for something that someone else had. That would all be considered the sin of *Envy*. You could also not pray to have sex with Johnny down the street, which would be the sin of *Lustfulness*, and it goes on and on."

"However, CyrIS and I have discovered that none of this is true and it can explain why the, *Secrets of Attraction*, methods are so powerful. It would appear that God or the Universe does not care what you pray for and attempts to meet all the needs of those who truly believe."

"CyrIS?"

CyrIS stands up and walks to the whiteboard as Ester hands him the dry erase marker.

"Thanks Ester. We are getting closer to putting this all together. Now let's talk about *drama* and *order* for a moment."

"Everyone has a need for varying levels of *Drama* in their lives. Everyone also has a need for varying levels of *Order* in their lives."

"Additionally, everyone has their own filters for *emotion* and *logic*. They make sense of the world through these *logical* filters and experience the world through *emotional* filters. These filters and the nature of this need for *drama* and *order* may be driven by both the personal subconscious and the collective subconscious: *Drama* effects *Order* and vice-versa."

"I sometimes like to say: I love the *emotion* of drama and the *logic* of order. But, it's not carrots - or- peas; its carrot and pea soup."

CyrIS turns to the whiteboard and begins to erase the four poles of the cross Ester had entered. In the 'North' location he enters the words: 'Filtered Logic'. In the 'South' location he enters the words: 'Filtered Emotion'. In the 'East' location he enters the word: 'Order' and in the 'West' location he enters the word 'Drama'.

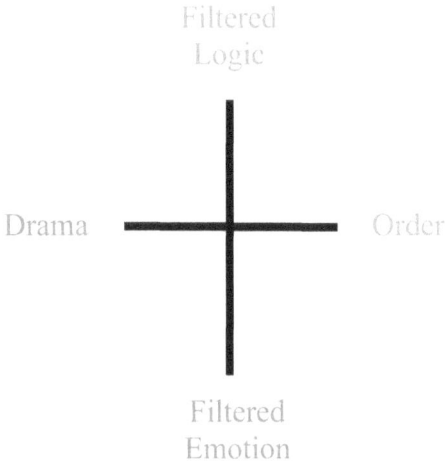

CyrIS turns back to the group, "Rufus it's your turn." Rufus moves to the whiteboard.

"So, let's talk some more about polar opposites, north and south, *light* and *darkness*. What are the extremes of *light* and *darkness*? What are the brightest *lights* in the universe? Well one of the brightest *lights* in the universe is a *Super Nova*."

"You may already know that a Super Nova is formed when a very massive star collapse in upon itself. When that happens, a *Stellar Black Hole* is formed. A *Black Hole...* is the *Darkest* object in the universe."

"Do you see where I'm heading here? One of the *brightest* objects in the universe creates one of the *darkest* objects in the universe."

"In January, an international team reported the most luminous supernova yet. It was a cosmic explosion 3.8 billion *light*-years away that flashed 200 times brighter than a normal supernova, or 20 times more brilliant than the 100 billion stars in the Milky Way galaxy combined. ... So, is that the brightest object in the universe?"

"The answer is no! There are objects much brighter, and they are called quasars. Scientists now believe that a quasar is formed by a super massive black hole sucking in extraordinary amounts of matter in an acceleration disk. It is estimated that some quasars emit more *light,* than 100 galaxies."

"So, let's talk specifically about *Light*."

"How is *light* created? *Light* is created by consuming matter. For example: stars consume their own mass, through the process of fusion."

"How fast does *light* travel? Of course, it travels at *the speed of light*, or 186,000 miles per second. Einstein used the letter C to represent this speed and called it the universal constant. You know: $E=mc^2$."

"What is *light*? *Light,* as we now know, is a wave and a particle."

"So now, let's talk specifically about *Darkness*."

"How does all of what we just talked about compare to *Darkness*? The extremes of *darkness* are that produced by Super Massive Black holes. Now we know that black holes are a source of gravitational waves."

"In 1916, gravitational waves were predicted by Albert Einstein's, *Theory of Relativity*, but the first actual observation of gravitational waves was not made until September 14th, 2015. Yes, not that long ago. It was announced by the LIGO and Virgo collaborations at Caltech and MIT, on February 11th 2016, that's right, just this year."

"Previously, gravitational waves had only been inferred indirectly, via their effect on the timing of pulsars in binary star systems. But now, scientists working with the Laser Interferometer Gravitational Wave Observatory, LIGO, have proven their existence. It is just one step closer to the discovery of Einstein's elusive *Unified Theory*."

"So, what is a *Gravitational wave*? Gravitational waves are ripples in the curvature of space-time that travel outward from the source that created them. Thus far, these sources have been black holes, or at least the collisions of black holes."

"That's right; they are created by sources of *darkness*."

"How are black holes formed? They are formed by the consumption of *matter*."

"How fast does a gravitational wave travel? Well, just as you might expect, they travel at 186,000 miles per second. They travel at the same speed as *light*, and again, represented by the letter *C*, the universal constant."

"What is a gravitational wave made of? Well, it is a wave of course. And, though this has not yet been proven, it is believed by scientists that it is also a particle called a *Graviton*. You know, just like *light*, it is also a *wave-particle*."

"We may discover someday that *gravitational waves* are everywhere and are produced by more sources of *darkness* than just *Black Holes*. We may also find that we are just as dependent upon gravitational wave particles as we are on light wave particles for our very existence.

You know that my work at CERN is committed to my theory that not only *photons* can be *entangled* and thus affect each other. *Gravitons* can also be *entangled* and can affect one another. And as you know, I am searching for that scalar particle that proves that *photons* and *gravitons* can be *entangled* as well. This moves us all one step closer to proving that all things are *entangled* and *connected*."

"So, the point I am trying to make here is: that what Christine and I discovered has some basis in science. That there is

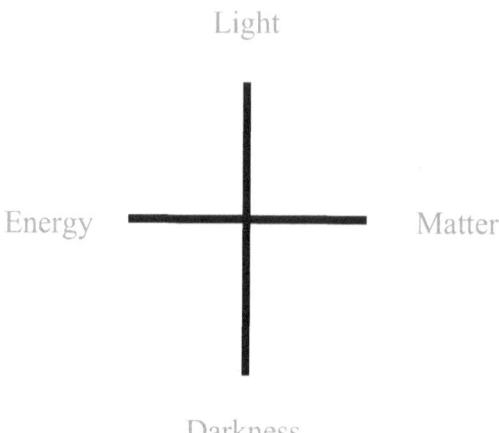

Light

Energy   Matter

Darkness

no difference between *Light and Darkness*; they are the source of each other's existence, and one cannot exist without the other."

"So, *Light and Darkness* are two of the *four* components. The other two components are *Matter* and *Energy*. And, you know that *Matter* is *Energy* and *Energy* is *Matter*. You know: E=mc^2." Rufus turns to the whiteboard, erases Ester's entries on the four poles of the cross. He then writes '*Light*' in the 'North' location, '*Darkness*' in the 'South' location, 'Matter' in the 'East' location and 'Energy' in the 'West' location.

"They are each separate, but at the same time, all a part of one thing..."

"CyrIS?"

CyrIS walks to the white board, turns to the group and says.

"Scientists have thus far determined that roughly 68% of the universe is dark energy. Dark matter makes up about 27%. The rest - everything on Earth - everything ever observed with all of our instruments, all normal matter - ads up to less than 5% of the universe."

"It is obvious that *Matter* and *Dark Matter* are the vehicles of our experience and that *Dark Energy* is our motivating spirit. It is the fuel for our vehicle, but at the same time, accelerating all things to an eventual end."

"By studying *sub-atomic levels*, scientists are discovering answers to questions at the *cosmic level* and finding that it all ties together."

CyrIS, once again, turns to the whiteboard; He writes, on the 'East' pole he writes 'Dark Matter' and on the 'West' pole he writes 'Dark Energy'. Adding 'Light' in the 'North' and 'Darkness' in the 'South'.

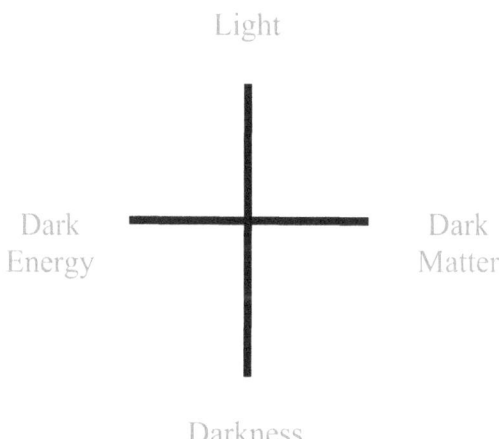

CyrIS continues: "Every day, despite the distractions and resistance in the world today, scientists are learning more and more about these special substances. And they are striving to make ties not only between these cosmic properties, but also to, and between, properties at the sub-atomic levels."

"Each day modern science is putting together the pieces of the puzzle. The pieces consisting not only of *Dark Energy, Dark Matter, Matter, Darkness* and *Light*, but also of: *Logic, Emotion, Consciousness* and *Sub-consciousness*. They are striving for a *unified theory* of everything. A theory that may well show that all of these components are a function of non-locality; that is, they are like waves and particles, they are desperate and distinct at the same time."

"There is more! As you heard from Christine and Ester, there is evidence now that these components are tied to more than just each other. They are also tied to our Psyche, and to the Spiritual nature of our existence. Everything is tied together, and someday a *Grand Unified Theory* will be discovered. Bringing us ever closer to solving this grand puzzle and answering such questions as:"

"Is there a God?"

"Why are we here?"

"Where do we go when we die?"

"As we have seen, when those pieces of the puzzle come together; there will be more and more distractions, more mass shootings, more bombings, and possibly even greater forms of varied destruction."

"Each day that we get closer to a solution, the forces of resistance will also become greater. Those forces of resistance will show themselves in many forms, including both political and extremist religious movements. We do not need to look far to see evidence of these things; they are everywhere and growing."

"It is now obvious to me that the four of us play a very important role in the grand scheme of solving these puzzles and diminishing this resistance."

CyrIS takes a deep breath, hesitates for a moment and then continues.

"So now, let's talk about the *Four* of us."

"You heard Rufus and Christine describe how even though they are polar opposites; they found that they are somehow the same. Well, Ester and I have found that we have a similar relationship. I consider myself grounded in, and all about, *logic*, whereas Ester is primarily of *spirit* and *emotion*."

"However, earlier this morning, when talking about '*Two*' you heard me describe the close relationship of *Logic* and *Emotion* as shown in the *Logic* and *Emotion* matrix. Well, Ester and I feel that close relationship in ourselves as well. Of course, there is our

Earth and *Wind* relationship, and their integral relationships to the overlapping triangles forming the *Star of David* and the *Hexagon*. This also gives us the special relationship we have with the two of you." CyrIS, causally points towards Rufus and Christine. "And there is the *Power of Light, and Darkness* that you two have, as well."

"So, look around you. What do you see? You see four individuals: right? That is what we observe."

"Now, I ask you to close your eyes;" everyone complies.

"Think about the four of us, and what we have learned here today. When you think about the four of us in that way, we are not individuals. No, we are a blend of *logic* and *emotion, light* and *darkness*.

It is the theory of non-locality, when observed we are individuals but when not, we are combination of all of these things. There is energy in the separation of these things and there is energy in the combination of these things."

CyrIS then turns to the white board and replaces the four points of the compass crosses. He replaces 'North' with 'Rufus, 'The Power of Light', and the word 'Fire'. He then replaces 'South' with 'Christine, 'The Power of Darkness', and the word 'Water'. He goes on to replace 'West' with 'Ester, *Emotion* and Wind' and finally replacing 'East' with 'CyrIS, *Logic* and Earth'.

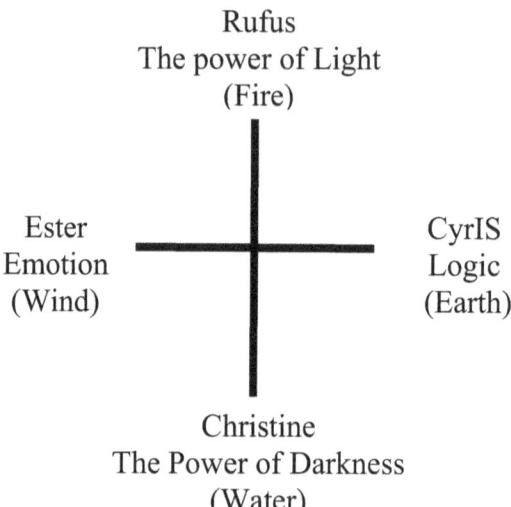

Rufus
The power of Light
(Fire)

Ester
Emotion
(Wind)

CyrIS
Logic
(Earth)

Christine
The Power of Darkness
(Water)

"The relationship we have with each other gives us power and we are all champions in a war. A war against those who would oppose all progress towards a *Grand Unified Theory*."

CyrIS pauses for a moment and then begins again.

"Now, please think about the symbol for *The King's Crusaders*; those three *Xs*, or three-Hour *Glasses*, which ever you prefer."

CyrIS erases everything on the white board, and in the center of the board draws '*The King's Crusaders*' symbol.

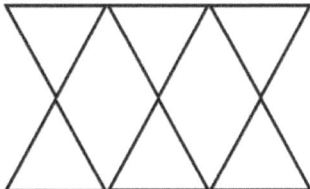

CyrIS now turns back to his audience, "Well, I prefer to look at it as six triangles; do you see them?" The group nods their heads.

"And, if you separate the two central triangles," CyrIS erases the two central triangles and re-draws them, one above the symbol and one below the symbol.

"Now, if you move the top triangle, to the bottom of the symbol, and you move the bottom triangle, to the top of the symbol, what do you get?'

CyrIS erases the triangles at the top and bottom of the drawing and redraws the six triangles as he had described.

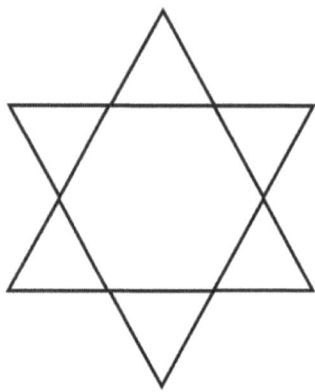

Once again, in the center of the white board appears the 'Two' overlapping triangles.

CyrIS turns back to the group: "It's a symbol, which we are all familiar with, and one that by now, should be extremely meaningful to us all."

"You see, we are all connected, even to those who oppose us."

"Do you remember that at the end of the book, *The Da Vinci Code*? The main character Robert Langdon illustrates that the triangle, a symbol for the blade representing the male, and the inverted triangle, a symbol for the chalice representing the female. When combined, the symbols form the overlapping triangles I have drawn here on the board."

"But Langdon was just looking at the tip of the iceberg. We have shown here today that the combination of our alchemist symbols for *Fire, Water, Air and Earth* also form these overlapping triangles, and thus are all one and the same. We have seen that *Energy* and *Matter* are the same, i.e. $E=mc^2$. That *Psyche* and *Matter* are one and the same. That the *Conscious* and

Unconscious minds are connected and one and the same. We have seen that *Logic* and *Emotions* are separate but at the same time a blend that makes up the fabric of life."

"Finally, we have seen that the symbol of *Light*, the *Star of David* and the symbol of *Darkness*, the *Hexagon,* are all one and the same. In fact, *Light* and *Darkness* itself are one and the same."

"Now, think about Jim Jones and David Koresh: very different yet the same. Randy Weaver and Timothy McVeigh: different and yet the same. Finally, John Hinckley and Eric Harris: different and yet the same. However, each of them driven by their own immoveable beliefs."

"Now, think about the four men we killed at CERN. We felt very justified in killing those men. Not only because we were protecting the lives of those scientist and technicians, but probably even more so, because we believed we were protecting our belief in the righteousness of science and its pursuit of a *Unified Theory*, a theory that would prove that everything is *connected*."

"What about those four men we killed in support of our beliefs? Those men were willing to die in support of their own beliefs. We seem so much different than them, and yet we are the same."

"So, what have we learned?"

"From the beginning of the human race, we have been chasing a dream. In 1952 Dr. Norman Vincent Peale wrote the book: *The power of positive thinking*. His book pushed the principle: if you think positively you will reap positive rewards. A psychologist might say that is because you are creating positive images for your subconscious to follow that encourages you to do positive things. Still, there was more to this book than just internal speech. The book also espouses concepts that would indicate *positive thinking* could have effects external to your own being."

"Now, let's look at the more modern version of these concepts. The book: *The Secret*, also known as: *The Secret of Attraction*, proposed by Rhonda Byrne."

"In her video and the following books, she proposes that one can get their desires just by asking the *universe* for it. She indicates that the universe is like a *Genie in a bottle*; '*Ask and you shall receive*'. As you have seen, this works both ways. It can work for good or bad, positive or negative, righteousness or evil."

"You can look at *Shamanism, Psychic Phenomena*, and other forms of Mysticism. Or you can look at the *dark* side of these concepts, *Black Magic*, *Witchcraft*, *Wicca*, *Devil Worship* and *Voodoo*. They all have strong beliefs as well. They believe that there are powers available to them to make things happen through some form of prayer or other mental or physical exercise and belief."

"Finally, let's look at religion and the power of prayer. Religions have been around since the earliest existence of mankind. All religions have a belief in a higher power; a divine, *Supreme Being*. There has always been a belief that praying, and or other mental and physical activity in worship of that Supreme Being will provide what they need. This supreme being, be it Yahweh, Allah, God or any other, has been the center of this belief."

"What do all of these beliefs have in common; no matter if it is a belief in a religion, or the power positive thinking, or a belief in the supernatural? It is simply: other than testimonials, they have no factual basis for their beliefs."

"Dr. Peale and Ms. Byrne, have no proof, other than the testimonials of people who have said that these techniques of positive thinking work. And there is not a single believer in the Supernatural that can prove how the Supernatural works - or that it even works at all."

"This is just as true for every religion as well. They have no proof of the existence of any *Supreme Being*; or that there is any medium by which any type of prayer is received or acted upon."

"Finally, there is no proof of the existence of an afterlife, heaven or hell."

"This is the nature of the cosmic puzzles that have faced mankind from the very beginning."

"That is what is so amazing about what we have discovered. We have found growing proof in the area of physics and modern science, that there is a fabric in the universe that connects all things."

"I call this fabric, *the Infinite Sprit,* and it consists of the *Higgs Field, Dark Matter, Dark Energy* and the combination of Light and Darkness."

"All of these things have been proven to exist by modern science. And even though we are all still on an incomplete path to a complete *Unified Theory of Everything*, scientist have at least proven that the fabric of the universe does exist. This could very well be the missing piece to every cosmic puzzle confronting mankind!"

"It's just like when a small bug lands in a spider web and struggles to get free. The spider feels the vibrations of the web and takes action."

"It appears that each of us; our thoughts - both consciously and subconsciously - are causing the fabric of the universe - the web - to be stimulated. There is no spider, I hope. But, the universe, or the web, tries to respond to all of these stimulations. It tries to create harmony or balance by trying to comply with our wishes, no matter if they are good or bad. All of this is consistent with: *The Power of Positive Thinking, The Secret of Attraction, and The Power of Prayer.*"

"However, some wishes are in conflict with other wishes; some wishes are weak, and some are strong. No matter what, the universe still tries to create harmony between wishes and prayers. That is why absolute *belief* is so important and so impactful."

"And most importantly we are all in this together. You see just as individual photons are entangled with other photons, to form waves of light, individual people are entangled with other people to form waves of life. And together we have learned from our *dark* experiences and have been en*light*ened by those experiences, which in turn has helped fill some of the voids in our lives, and helped to provide solutions to some of the complex puzzles we face."

"Isaiah 45: *And I will give thee the treasures of darkness and the hidden riches of secret places.*"

"We have uncovered a Fact-Faith approach which ties science to non-science. And I believe that scientists, philosophers, theologians, mystics and the four of us, will eventually find all of the answers; *in the light of dark matters.*"

Dedication Continued

As you may remember, I dedicated this book to Stephen Weber. As I mentioned in the 'Dedication' Stephen died in 2007. Well, I didn't start writing this novel until 2011, and I had been working on it, on and off, over the years. In 2020 I decided to re-work the novel again.

I wanted to include Steve's name in the book, and I had given his name to a very minor character, which was Rufus' colleague who was working on Rufus' theories in CERN Switzerland before his mysterious death. So I had decided to change the Prologue of the book, to include the portion of the novel surrounding that character's death and how it led Rufus to discover that many physicist had died mysteriously, and that is when I found something astonishing.

On April 30th of 2020 I wrote the first two words of the new Prologue; "Steve died". I thought to myself "When did Steve die?" You see, I am also good friends with Steve's brother Mike, and so, I sent a text to Mike, see the following thread.

Me: "I was recently thinking about Steve. When did Steve die?"
Mike: "In 2007 April, 54 years old. Sounds young doesn't it."
Me: "Oh thanks. Yes, much too young."
Mike: "We are heading back to Colorado on Saturday;"
Me: "Do you know exactly when?"
Mike: "Yes this Saturday, in two days."
Me: "I was actually asking if you knew the exact date of Steve's death?"
Mike: "The exact date was like April 19th."

Mike knew nothing about the novel. I was astonished, because this is such an important date in this novel.

Please visit the Fact-Faith.com website for more information.

Reference Material:

"Raven" The story of the Reverend Jim Jones and the events at Jonestown, by Tim Reiterman/with John Jacobs.

"Ruby Ridge" The story of Randy Weaver and the events at Ruby Ridge, by Jess Walter.

"A place called Waco" The story of David Koresh at Waco Texas by one of Koresh's followers, Mr. Thibodeau, written by David Thibodeau and Leon Whiteson.

"Inside the Cult" The story of David Koresh at Waco Texas by one of Koresh's followers Mr. Breault, Written by Marc Breault/ with Martin King

"Oklahoma City" The story of Timothy McVeigh and the Oklahoma City bombing, by Andrew Gumbel and Roger G. Charles

"Columbine" The story of the Columbine High School massacre, by Dave Cullen.

"No Easy Day" a story about the war in Iraq, by Mark Owen/ with Kevin Maurer

"House to House: An Epic Memoir of War" 2008 by Sgt. David Bellavia (Author), John Bruning.

"Quantum Mind, the edge between physics and psychology" by Arnold Mindell, Ph.D.

"Surprise, the Union of Quantum Physics, Relativity, and THE BIBLE" by Mark Hicks

"The Insanity Defense and the Trial of John W. Hinckley, Jr." by Lincoln Caplan.

A lot of the math and physics in this novel, is based on researching hypothesis proposed by the TV series "Through the Wormhole" with Morgan Freeman, and "Futurescape" with James Woods.

"Quantum Physics, Depth Psychology, and Beyond" by Thomas J. McFarlane, www.integrlscience.org, February 26, 2000, revised June 21, 2000.

"The Turner Diaries" 1978 by William Luther Pierce

"The Science Behind Psychic Phenomena" by M.J. Stephey, 2008

"The ESP Enigma: The Scientific Case for Psychic Phenomena", by Harvard professor Diane Hennacy Powell

"The Reality of ESP" A Physicist's Proof of Psychic Abilities, by Russell Targ. Targ presents evidence from the $20 million investigatory program he co-founded at Stanford Research Institute (SRI) in the 1970s